Anthology of the Damned

Twisted Yuletide

Christopher D. Schmitz, T R Nickel
Jeri Shepherd, Evan Clouse, Joe
Prosit, Ivy Ru, E.H. Drake, Jared
Bartemeyer, Megan Mackie
Justin Rose, Joshua Pruett, John
Helfers, Kevin J Anderson, M.R.
James, William Douglas O'Connor

TreeShaker Books

CONTENTS

SANTY CLAUS VS. THE KRAMPUS, OR HOW MIKEY T. JR. AND I SAVED CHRISTMAS, JOISEY STYLE

BY JOHN HELFERS

'Twas da night befaw Christmas,
and all trew da house,
Not a guido was stirrin',
not even no friggin' mouse!

"AWRIGHT, AWRIGHT, ENUFFA' DAT Christmas crap. I'm gonna tell ya a *real* story—the night Mikey T. Jr. and me saved Santy Claus.

No, I ain't friggin' kiddin', this really happened...you wanna go? Do ya? Come at me, bro! I'll take ya outside and beat yer ass like you owe me money, jagoff! Awright den, jus' shaddup and listen.

Where was I? Oh yeah, so, it was Christmas Eve, and Mikey and I was hangin' at my place, just kickin' back with a bottle a'Goose and annudah a'Jager, but we wasn't stayin' up hopin' ta see Santy Claus squeeze his fat ass down no friggin' chimney.

Nah, we was waitin' on another uninvited guest...

Whadaminute—befaw I get ta dat, I gotta fill you in wit what led up to this sitcheation. See, Mikey T. Jr. and me are almost friggin' twins, despite bein' born two years apart, and ta different mom's. But dat don't mean shit, 'cause our blood's thicker'n friggin' water, knowwhatI'msayin'?

Anyways, Mikey's always been a little bit of a hothead. He's always goin' out and mixin' it up, ya know what I mean? Like even in sixth grade, when he noticed Tommy Terletti was gettin' a little...pudgy. No. No...Terletti. Yeah, his dad was in construction, least till he tooka pinta Jim Beam up twenty stories and turned left when he shoulda turned right and took the express elevator down—SPLAT!! Yeah, and he's gotta little sister—well, not *dat* little, bazooms outta here—yeah, dat's the one.

Damn it, I forgot what I was sayin'—oh yeah, Tommy Terletti's porkin' out. I mean, he was gettin' so fat when he had ta haul ass, he made two trips, knowwhatI'msayin'? Anyway, now he's sproutin' man-boobs, so what does Mikey do?

Yeah, you got it, bro—he was da first guy calling him 'Tommy Two-Titties.' And as you prob'ly remember, Tommy didn't take too kindly ta dat. One day he got tree'a his brudders, and was gonna teach Mikey a lesson, right? And *you know* I got my bro's back, so I stand wit him after school, and we beat the everlovin' crap outa all dem Terletti brudders. Dey *never* came after us again, and peoples still callin' him 'Tommy Two-Titties,' to dis day."

Our Jets caps wuz hangin' by the chimney wit care,
In hopes dat St. Nicholas soon would be dere.

"Like I said, Mikey never had ta look too fah for trouble—it always seemed ta find him. One night last December, when he was comin' home from Seaside Heights in da Beemah, when he hits somethin' inna middle of da road, messed up his ride real good. Yeah, dat cherry '09 coupe his dad got him—I swear, his old man practically stole it, he got such a friggin' deal—yeah, dat one.

Anyway, he was droppin' the hammer when sumpin' comes outta nowhere right at him. Even standin' on the brakes Mikey can't stop in time, and plows over whatever it was—yeah, dat's why you ain't seen his car around, jagoff! Now shut yer' big friggin' mouth', 'fore I shut it for ya!

So Mikey almost totals his cah, but when he gets out to see what the hell he hit, the road's empty—not a sign a nuttin', no blood, *nuttin'!* He called me up, and I take da cruisah out ta get 'im, right?

Only, when we came back, we knew he was in big friggin' trouble. Written on da wall of da house in foot-tall letters, drippin' red, was a message:

I'm coming for you Mikey
Christmas Eve
See you soon
K.

Well, it don't take no genius to know what's gonna happen on Christmas Eve—the Krampus is comin' for my bro's ass.

Hey, it's *not* freakin' *funny*! You dumbass townies don't know yer ass from a hole inna ground—what, you wanna go? Let's go, right here, right now! Alright then, *shaddup* and listen!

See, what you people who ain't from Joisey don't know is dat the friggin' Krampus lives in our state. Tourists and nobs call him da Joisey Devil, but dat ain't it—accordin' to my granfaddah, it's the Krampus, awright. He saw him once, back in the day, but dat's anuddah story—

Yeah, yeah, dat half-man, half-goat thing they say hangs out in the Barre ns...look, who's friggin' tellin' this story, you or me, huh? Jesus *H.* Kee-rist. Anyways, me and Mikey know what's comin' our way, and he ain't gonna just leave a lump of coal in my bro's fedora, neiddah. But we wasn't gonna take it lyin' down—hell, we ain't never backed down from a fight before, we sure as hell wasn't gonna start now.

My Ma was lyin' passed out in her bed,
while visions of slot machines danced in ha' head.

"'Course, we hadda take carea few things before we could get downna business. First, dere was my Moms. Things was gonna get a little hairy—and not just 'cuz *yer* muddah was gonna drop by later—OH!

Anyways, I spiked her eggnog—more like topped it off, that stuff was so fulla Crown Royal it coulda stripped paint offa cah door. I set her up in her bedroom wit the Bruce Springsteen Christmas Special on da fuckin' flatscreen dat she just hadda have in her fuckin' bedroom. An hour later, she'd drained the whole friggin' bottle and was snorin' like a goddamn freight train. Swearda God, she was shakin' the whole second floor.

Anyways, wit her outta da way, Mikey and I sets up in the livin' room to wait for our uninvited guest. I had my Louisville Slugger warmed up and ready to bust some head. Mikey brung his bruddah's Army knife—Mikey T. Sr. brought it back from Iraq or Afghanistan or some such pilea shit sand. He was ready to slice n' dice any friggin' goat-boy who came trew da door.

So we're sitting and sippin' on Goose and Jager, when his celly goes off. Mikey whips out his phone and gets dis big friggin' shit-eatin' grin on his face.

'Yo, it's Wine Box.'

Now, noneayas can argue that Jennifer, "Wine Box" DiMazzo is *the friggin' hottest* guidette on the Shore, *right?* What? Shuddah fuck up...yer's sister's like a birthday cake—everybody's had a piece. *Yeah?* Let's step outside right now and settle dis once and for all—alright then. Not only is she smokin' hot, but I heard she can suck a golf ball through a garden hose, knowwhatI'm sayin'?

Whaddaya mean, 'why's she called Wine Box?' You don't know? *Seriously?* You wasn't at the Figueroa sisters' house when their 'rents were outta town, and we ripped the place *up*? Hell, everybody was there—Stone Sammy, Big Chop, Mart-Ray, Tricky-T, the whole friggin' gang. Anyhow, Jenny takes a bet she can down an entire boxa Franzia, which she grabs and chugs 'til it's empty. But get this—she don't stop. Just grabbed another one and pounded it down—bro, I have *no* idea where da hell she put it all. Didn't puke or nuttin'—sickest shit I ever saw.

Anyway, Wine Box had the hots bad for Mikey, and was sendin' him selfies a'her all tricked out. The one she sent dat night was unbelievable—she was 'Dressed ta Kill,' wit her skirt leavin' *nothin'* to the imagination, and her thong peekin' out on both sides of those hips that could shake all night long both on the dance floor *and off.* Her crop top was shoving dose bazooms of hers so far up I thought they might fly out and hit her in da face. She had her pouf going on, and was made up real nice, with a killer tan, long nails, and those falsie eyelashes so long dey could blind a man from two feet away. I nearly popped a stiffie in my guido tuxedo right dere.

Bitch sent a message to Mikey, too: 'Going out with the girls tonight...wish I was going down on you tonight instead.' I know, right?

'*Damn...*' Mikey said as I whistled. 'We gotta take care'a dis, den I'm gonna head to da' city and see if I can hook up wit her, knowhutI'msayin'?'

I saluted him with da' Goose, then took a slug. 'Hells, yeah.' I was amped, ready to come all outta my face at that friggin' Krampus. I knew Mikey felt the same way. All that goat-boy hadda do was stick his nose in *my* house, and he was gonna get a nice, warm welcome—Joisey style."

When out on the lawn I heard such a friggin' clatter,
I grabbed my ball bat and went to see what da hell was da matter.

"Right about den we hear footsteps comin' up the driveway—some kinda weird *step-clomp, step-clomp, step-clomp* sorta shit—If you'd *shaddup* for a goddamn second, I'll tell ya what was makin' it!

Mikey went to da window and peeped out, but couldn't see nothin'. I got up too, and was about to brace the door when the whole damn thing smashed down onna floor—and in the doorway stood the Krampus.

What'd he look like? Well, if you'd stop flapping ya lips', I'll tell ya. Thin-ka' the ugliest relative you got—drunk dad, pervy uncle, soft-in-da'-head sistah, whatever—and times dat by a hundred. The Krampus—no wait, I got it! Imagine Tommy Two-Titties's mom screwed a goat. Da kid—that'd be a little baby Krampus!

He's big—'bouta head taller'n me—and ugly as sin, with huge, staring, red eyes and wrinkled, leathery skin. Oh, and he's got horns—big, curly ones comin' outta each sidea his head. He's mostly covered in goat fur, all shaggy and dirty and shit, and here's the really weird part—he's got one goat foot, and one human foot! SweardaGod! Come look at the tracks inna carpet—we still can't get that shit out.

What? No, he wasn't wearin' any clothes. No, not even pants, *why*—Whaddaya mean did I see his—*getdafuckouttahere!* I sure as hell didn't check to see what was doin', *fer Christ's sake*! First of all, like I said, he was all hairy and shit down there anyway—you know, like your sistah—OH! Second, I was lookin' to put the hurt on the guy, not mess around wit him. If I *had* looked anywheres south of the border—*which I didn't*—it woulda been to find a place to cram my baseball bat, knowwhatI'msayin'?

Anyways, the friggin' Krampus's standin' there like he owns the place, then he points a gnarly, clawed finger at my bro, and says, "Yer comin' wit me, Mikey T."

"Aw, *hell, no*!" Mikey don't stand for nonna dat crap, and thumps his chest. "You want me, bro? *Come on*—come at me, let's trow down."

The Krampus don't need no invite. He steps inside and comes straight at Mikey. I'm off to the side, and charge at him wit my bat ready to clobber his ass straight into da bleachers at Yankee Stadium. When—hold da fuckin' phone, I'm gettin' to it!

S'anyhow, without even lookin' at me, Krampus sticks his big, disgusting hand out and palms my friggin' head! I know—*my blowout*, right?! He shoves me back, and I go flyin' into mom's curio cabinet, break about a dozen of those damn Hummah figures—no, it's Hummah, you ignorant asshole, I'm sure of it—I'm tellin' you—You wanna *go*?

I hit the ground, and the bottle of Jager spills all over my frickin' favorite Ed Hardy t-shirt. Not only did this asshat break my door, but he friggin' fucked up my hair *and* my shirt, ya know?

Now I'm pissed.

I come up offa da floor and go at him again, leadin' with my bat this time. He's tryin' ta play punch the head offa Mikey—who somehow lost his knife—near the couch, and don't even notice me comin' up behind him. I haul off and lay my bat over da top of his baldy.

What happened? I'll tell ya what happened—my oak broke, that's what happened! Naw, it' wasn't hickory—*shaddup*, I'm talkin' here! Anyway, who cares what kinda wood it was? The point is I broke the damn thing over the Krampus's head!

Dat got his attention, lemme tell *you*! He let Mikey go—well, not quite, he was still holdin' onta him by his gold chains—and turned ta me. That's when I saw Mikey's knife—the damn thing was sticking outta the Krampus' ribs! SweardaGod!"

As I cocked my Jets cap, and was turnin' around,
Down da chimney came St. Nicholas wit' a bound.

"About this time, I'm thinkin' we might be inna bita trouble, when all us hear dis *THUMP!* on the roof, right? I mean, we *all*—Mikey, the Krampus, and me—turned to look like, *Who da hell's up there?*

Den come dese slow, heavy footsteps. We're all jus' standin' there, listenin' as someone walks across da roof and then outa the chimney comes a big cloud of ashes and soot from the damn fireplace I was supposed to clean last Easta'.

All us just stand there wit' our mouths open—dere, in fronta da fireplace, was *Santy-friggin'-Claus* himself!

Yeah, yeah, I'm gettin' to it, I'm gettin' to it. So, the first thing youse all gotta understand is the real Santy don't look nothin' like those red-and-white pussies at the mall. I mean, yeah, he's old, but he's a *tough* old, knowwhatImean? He's got the red suit and the belly and everythin', but I'm tellin' ya, Santy looked like he could kick some serious ass if he had to.

'*Krampus!* What you doin' here?' Santy asked in a voice so deep it shook da room.

'My job, old man!' the hornhead replies. 'This fuckin' guy ran me down wit his fuckin' cah! He's comin' wit me!'

'What da hell?' Mikey said. 'Ya jumped out in da middleada road right in fronta me, ya furry freak!'

'Is that true?' Santy asked.

'No, it ain't!' the Krampus screeched. '*He* hit *me*!'

Santy *tsk-tsk-tsked*. 'Oh, *Krampus*—you know I can always tell when someone's lyin' t'me...and you know what happens ta dose who lie to me?'

Krampus opens his mouth to answer, but was cut off by Santy Claus. 'I kick their *fuckin'* asses, that's what!'

He said a few choice woids, and got straight ta woik,
Beatin' the friggin' Krampus's head in widda smoik!

"Well, ol' furry Krampus wasn't gonna have nonadat. He lets Mikey go and comes at Santy Claus with his fists ready ta deliver the beat down of all beat downs. Santy meets him in the middle of the room, and dem two go at it like a coupla guidettes fightin' ovah the last cab outta the city at midnight.

They was staggerin' around the place like me on my 21st b-day, only no one's throwin' up—yeah, that *was* a killer party, bro! First the Krampus is on top, poundin' Santy's head, then the big guy is tearing the Krampus a new asshole, just beatin' the shit outta him.

This goes on for a few minutes—trashin' my livin' room in da process, which I'm *still* catching shit from Moms for. I mean, these two were goin' at it like wrestlers at Madison Square Garden. Dey knocked over our Christmas tree, sending ornaments flyin' every which way. Da Krampus even tried ta strangle Santy Claus wit a garland of tinsel, but it broke as soon as he started pullin' on it. At one point Santy hoisted the Krampus over his head and trew him across the livin' room. That furry fuck slammed inta my mom's cabinet, breakin' the resta her Hummah crap—don't even say it—they're *Hummahs*!

But then the Krampus gets the upper hand and jumps on toppa Santy again, just whalin' away on him wit a huge fist. Santy's takin' it, but he's not lookin' so good...

Mikey and I know we gotta do somethin', but *what? Yeah*, I'm about ta tell ya what, dumbass!

I look around and see Mikey's phone lyin' onna floor, wit the picture of Wine Box in all her glory on it. I grab it, go up to the Krampus, and stick it in his face, sayin', "Hey fuckface, check *dis* shit out!"

I dunno why he looked, but look he did, and that was all she wrote, 'specially when you gotta guidette as fine as DiMazzio starin' back atcha. One look at her, and I thought his eyes were gonna pop outta his head. His tongue fell out, and if I hadn't known any better, I'da thought he was gonna trip over it.

That was the break Santy was lookin' for, and he plants his size 16 boot right between the Krampus's legs. Whatever he had down there, it was damn near busted off after *that* shot to the nutsack, lemme tell ya. He just froze up and keeled over, cuppin' his junk wit both hands. Santy gets up and plants another boot upside the Krampus's head, knockin' 'im right the fuck out!"

Layin' his finger aside his big nose,
And givin' a nod, up da chimney he goes!

"Santa took a sec to catch his breath, and Mikey has da brains to offer him da Goose, which he grabs and drains da whole friggin' bottle. Then he picks up the Krampus and slings him over his shoulder.

'Well, boys, dis was fun, but I gotta gets back ta woik—I'm late finishin' up the East Coast as it is. I wanna thank ya both for yer help tonight—couldna done this witout youse.'

'Hey, no problem, Mr. Santy Claus,' I says. 'Whatcha gonna do with—' I pointed to da out-cold Krampus.

The fat man laughed, and damn if his belly didn't shake like a bowl fulla Jell-o shots. 'Why, take him home, of course. He's been lost a long time, but youse guys helped me find him. We're bruddahs, inna way, him n' me. Next year he'll be comin' 'round wit me, visiting naughty kids like he should.'

Then Santy Clause walks over the chimney and don't ask me how, but he squeezes himself *and* the Krampus inside da fireplace. 'And Mikey,' he says, 'watch yerself on dose back roads.' He waggled his bushy, white eyebrows. 'Take it from someone who knows a ting or two about goin' fast.'

'*Wait,* Santa...' Mikey, ever the wiseass, says, 'What, *no presents?*'

St. Nick's face turned from jolly to pissed off in a second flat. "Yer both still alive, *ain'tcha?* I think dat's pretty good for dis year." And wit dat, he was sucked up the chimney in a sec.

Mikey an' I just stared at each other, den da empty bottle a' Goose, and shouted, *"NO WAY!"*

And as he flew away, we heard his warning real clear,
'Keep your noses clean, ya little shits, and you won't see no
Krampus next year!'

"My Moms? Hell, she slept trough da whole ting, like.... Hell, we coulda had a dance party right outside her bedroom door, and she'd sleep right trew it.

Anyways, me an' Mikey starts cleanin' up the mess dose two made bustin' around my livin' room. I had *no idea* what I was gonna tell my moms the next mornin'.

'Hey, Johnny,' Mikey asks as we're getting' everything togeddah in da middla da room. 'Did alla dat shit *really* just happen?'

I stared at him. 'You kiddin'? Whaddya tink, *I'd* evah bust up my own friggin' livin' room for no reason?! Fuggedahbout dat shit!'

'Ain't no one evah gonna believe us,' he says.

'Might be a couple dat do,' I replied, tinkin'a my granfadder. 'All I know is I'm gonna be a *very* good boy next year.'

Mikey nodded. 'You got *dat* right, bro. By da way, how'd you know the Krampus'd be distracted by dat selfie'a Wine Box?'

'Ah hell, I knew it da second he opened his mouth, Mikey." I grinned. "I mean, come on—the friggin' guy's from Joisey!'"

About the Author

John Helfers is a full-time freelance writer and editor, and is the president of Stonehenge Editorial, an editorial/literary management company. He has published almost fifty short stories in anthologies such as *Schemers* (Stone Skin Press) and *Shattered Shields* (Baen Books). His media tie-in fiction has appeared in anthologies, game books, and novels for the *Dragonlance®*, *Transformers®*, *BattleTech®*, *Shadowrun®* and *Warlock II®* universes. He's also written fiction and nonfiction, including a novel based on *The Twilight Zone*™ television series, the young adult novel *Tom Clancy's Net Force Explorers*™: *Cloak and Dagger*, the original fantasy novel *Siege of Night and Fire*, and a history of the United States Navy.

Currently he's the Executive Editor at Catalyst Game Labs, where he oversees the fiction lines for *BattleTech*, *Shadowrun*, and *Leviathans*, publishing more than one million words of original fiction among these IPs each year. He lives and works in Green Bay, Wisconsin.

GINGER

BY CHRISTOPHER D. SCHMITZ

"GET YOUR ASSES DOWN here, 'ya little twerps!" bellowed Grandpa's voice from the main level of the old farmhouse.

The sounds of knees clomping on flooring as children scrambled to comply. It was, after all, Christmas Eve and not a time for activities that might be interpreted by magical gift-giving beings as naughty... or even reluctant obedience.

Several of the larger children bumped their heads on the too-low roof as they rounded the knee-high wall meant to prevent tumbling down the stairwell from the attic bedrooms. Those two pass-through bedrooms had raised five children and temporarily re-homed a few grandchildren during their mothers' first or second divorces. A third was likely underway.

Slack-jawed and with mouth hanging agape, Ginger watched as Veronica followed the rest of her cousins down the stairs. Veronica's eyes never turned up from her mobile device as her thumbs worked the digital keypad furiously. Ginger didn't know who Veronica was communicating with. It didn't matter. She could have been texting Krampus himself, and Ginger still would have worshiped her.

Ginger's oldest cousin was almost 16 and about 6 years her senior; to her delight, Veronica's birthday was only 1 day different from hers... plus a few years, of course. If Ginger could have had anything she wanted for Christmas, it would have been to crawl inside of Veronica's skin and *be* her. The 9-year-old was short for her age and pudgier than the other girls in her class. Her freckles were so thick that it was practically her default skin tone and her tightly wound red pigtails stuck out at odd angles. By contrast, Veronica had recently won their local beauty pageant. She had blond hair and had blossomed earlier than expected into the same amount of Ds as there were on her report card. Ginger heard Grandma once say Veronica had *dough for brains,* but Ginger thought her cousin was the coolest, smartest girl she knew.

Grandpa growled at the rest of the kids, "All of you settle down or Santa won't come."

That put the fear of Christmas into the children who ranged from 5 years old to Veronica. Some gasped. Ginger's idol looked up only long enough to roll her eyes and scowl with disapproval, as if she knew something that the younger children did not.

The red-haired girl copied her cousin's expression, although she crossed her arms instead of resuming her typing. Ginger did not have a smartphone.

An old mantle clock in the living room chimed seven times, making Grandpa turn his head.

"You all know the drill. Evening chores first, and then you can all get back to whatever you were doing upstairs," Grandpa said. "And then, if you're lucky, Santa will come tonight and we'll do presents in the morning when your parents are all back."

Veronica rolled her eyes again, making them flash white against the charcoal black that rimmed them. Ginger wondered how to put mascara on.

"Now y'all tell me who's coming outside to finish chores at the barn and who's going to stay here with Grandma?" Most of the kids clamored to go with Grandpa. He was a rail thin man who had no reason to be. He kept a secret stash of bulk candy he picked up during regular visits to the local hardware store. Of course, all the sugared-up little urchins wanted to go with him.

By contrast, Grandma was a plump woman who was rarely seen to eat a thing. Mainly because she hid it well. She had her own stash secreted somewhere away. The woman simply didn't have the labor of barnyard chores or the necessary metabolism to combat the extra calories. But Ginger knew Grandma loved the sweets. She'd seen Grandma sneak a cookie or six, or more, and Ginger's mother had once given her two rules about staying with her grandparents: never mention Grandma's weight or eating habits, and never drink from Grandpa's teeth cup.

In the other room, Veronica plopped down onto the couch with her eyes still glued to the glow of the electronic screen. It flickered even more brightly than the lights of the nearby tree. Backlit by the iPhone's glow, Ginger thought she looked every bit like an angel.

With the clear indication that Veronica was not going outside, Ginger offered, "I'll stay inside with Grandma." Her sibilants whistled through teeth that hadn't come in correctly.

Grandpa nodded and headed out into the cold. The other children hurried after him. It didn't matter that two of the boys didn't have gloves on their hands. The barn's milk-room was always kept warm.

One of the younger boys laughed and commented, "Ew, gross. It smells like cow poop out here." And then the door clicked shut.

Grandma tilted her head and put her hands on her expansive hips. "Well, Ginger, we've got some chores of our own. I don't know who keeps eating all of these cookies, but we're going to need to make some more. Veronica? Please come in here."

With a heavy sigh, the teenager emerged from the living room and darkened the kitchen doorway. "What?"

"We're going to do what we do every year, dear. We're going to make some more cookies." Grandma's voice dripped enthusiastically at the suggestion of more cookies.

Ginger lit up at the idea, too. "Can we? Can we make some Veronica? That will be so much fun."

"You'll get to decorate them and everything," Grandma said as she rummaged through the cabinets in search of tubes of frosting.

"No thanks. I'm out," Veronica grumbled.

"Out of what?" Ginger asked. She understood that her super-awesome cousin might be too cool to hang out with a fourth grader, but *too cool for cookies? Even Grandma loves cookies... like, a lot. And she's practically a mummy without all that toilet paper.*

"Out of *here,*" Veronica groused. "I didn't sign up for this. And I don't think a woman's place is in the home. I want to be a strong independent woman like the ones I see on TV, not some Betty Crocker housewife."

"Oh, you can't be serious," Grandma said. "Besides, it's fun. And you can't back out of chores this late in the game. That might put you on the naughty list."

Ginger gasped that her favorite cousin might so flagrantly defy Santa. Or his elves. Or whoever it was who kept track of the actual lists so close to the delivery deadline.

"I'm just not much for societal norms, Grandma," Veronica said.

Ginger noticed how her grandmother's eyes kept looking from Ginger and then insistently back at Veronica. Ginger didn't know what that was all about. But it didn't matter. All she really wanted to do now was make gingerbread cookies with her cousin. Her amazing, awesome, probably going to be a supermodel cousin.

"Remember that time we played paper dolls, and we made our own dolls and we made our own clothes and we got to dress them up together? Do you remember Veronica? Do you? That was so much fun. We could do that, but with gingerbread men. We could dress them up and make them look just like whoever you're texting on your phone," Ginger begged.

"Gaaaawwwwd, you little snoop. No. I'm not texting anyone, even. We're using a photo messaging app. It's completely different."

"Oh, can I see?" Ginger asked, very excited to see what kind of fancy outfits her beautiful cousin might be wearing in those pictures.

When Ginger reached for the iPhone, Veronica recoiled, practically snarling. "No," she snapped. "It's private. Besides, Grandma. I can't touch the dough. I'm allergic to gluten."

"What's gluten?" Ginger wondered aloud.

"I'm pretty sure that's not true," Grandma said. "I think gluten is just something all you kids like to complain about. If a gluten allergy ran in our family, I would probably know."

"Just ask my mom," Veronica challenged. "She knows about it."

"You know I can't do that," Grandma said. "Your parents and all your aunts and uncles are out caroling."

Veronica nearly burst into laughter. "If that's what you want to call it."

Grandma tilted her head with a disapproving look.

"We all know where they are, Grandma. They're getting trucked on eggnog at Smitty's Bar."

Grandma was about to say something, and her eyes had narrowed for some reason that Ginger wasn't quite sure of. She wasn't sure of a lot of things. *What's trucked mean?*

With a red-face and Veronica barely holding in her amusement, Grandma put the tubes of frosting into Ginger's hands and told her to place them on the table where they were prepping dough. "Fine."

Ginger wasn't an expert in tones of voice. She was only nine, but she hoped that the obvious lie Grandma had just told would not result in her losing a present in the morning. Santa would never bring her coal if she was misbehaving—even that was useful out in the rural corners of the state; Ginger knew the furnace in the old farm house's basement burned coal. Grandpa once told her that's why it smelled funny down there, even though Ginger had been sure at the time that Grandpa had farted.

As Veronica abandoned the kitchen and returned to the dull glow of light from both the tree and her iPhone, Ginger and her grandma began mixing ingredients at the table.

The little red-haired girl looked mournfully back at her beautiful, stunning cousin. Ginger had not seen many people outwit her grandpa. Grandma had even gotten the better of Grandpa on most occasions whenever sharp words came into play. She stared out the kitchen window.

I wonder if I'll be as pretty and as sharp witted as Veronica when I'm her age?

"What are you thinking about?" Grandma asked her. "You look like you're lost far and away in the sky."

Ginger shook herself back to reality. She was supposed to be kneading dough while Grandma rolled the stuff flat and readied the cookie cutters.

"Oh nothing. Just my nickname," Ginger said.

"You have a nickname?"

"Just something the other kids at school call me," Ginger said. "They call me Dump Truck."

"Dump Truck?" Grandma's voice filled with concern. "Who says that."

"Jimmy... and *other* kids, too."

"Whatever for?"

"They say it's because I'm short and squat and kind of slow."

More mortified glances from Grandma. "I don't think that's true of dump trucks. I think they're pretty big and fairly fast. And they're strong, too. Like you."

"I don't know," Ginger said. "We only know about the ones made by Tonka. There's one in the sandbox by the school, but Jimmy lit it on fire after school. He lives close to the school so he can play on the playground whenever he wants... Jimmy likes fire."

"Well, what does Jimmy know, anyhow?" Grandma frowned, and both she and Ginger fell silent for several long moments. The little girl stared out and into the sky again; a trio of shooting stars blazed through the night air.

"Oh look," Grandma pointed. "It's a Christmas star. Make a wish. If you're the first one to make a wish on the Christmas Star when it appears your wish will come true. Everyone knows that."

"Oh," gasped Ginger. She squeezed her eyes tight and summoned all of her inner magic reserves that she knew must have been there. She'd heard about it on an animated Christmas special once, so it had to be true. If she knew anything, it was that you can't lie on TV; that doomed someone directly to the naughty list.

Squeezing two fistfuls of gingerbread dough, Ginger weighed her odds of who else out there might be making a wish. She had to pick *one wish* and do it fast.

Ginger wanted only two things in the world. She wanted to not be a dump truck. And she wanted more than anything else to make gingerbread cookies with Veronica.

With a gasp, Ginger released the dough and opened her eyes.

"Did you make a wish?" Grandmother asked.

"I did," Ginger said. "Do you think it will come true?"

Grandma's eyes sparkled. "There's something magical about Christmas. I'm sure it will come true... Even if magic has a funny way of putting its own special spin on things, sometimes."

VERONICA'S EYES FIXED ON the steady light of her screen. *Stupid grandma and stupid Ginger... I can't wait to get out of this po-dunk town and do something. To really make my mark.*

Her phone buzzed again and her eyes refocused on the chat. She'd been flirting with a college-aged boy for a while now. Things had been getting pretty serious between her and Harry… the photos they'd sent each other would *definitely* put them on the naughty list.

Harry? Hah–more like man-scaped. It barely registered in her mind that Harry and Hairy were not the same thing.

Veronica smirked as she thought about what places she might stick Christmas bows for her next round of selfies. She was gonna give him a gift that would make Santa blush and baby Jesus cry… but she felt certain it would be enough to make her beau invite her out for spring break. That would make all the other girls in her grade jealous.

Jessica can suck it. My photo stream is gonna be so much more popular than hers.

Her ears perked up at the sounds of her obnoxious little cousin laughing with Grandma. "Annoying little dump truck," she grumbled. And then Veronica turned her eyes back to the screen and the sender's inappropriate Christmas photo he'd snapped for her with the caption, "What are Christmas trees made of?"

Veronica grinned. Not because she was particularly horned up, but because she knew she'd gained power over this man. She liked him, sure… but she *really* liked that he was an appealing bet, and a potential ticket out of the small backwoods town that had a hold on her. Not many people ever escaped these towns of five thousand without some kind of drastic measures, and Veronica knew a college scholarship wasn't in the cards. She could always wear a low-cut blouse, lean forward, and bump her scores by at least a letter grade with the male teachers, but that wouldn't work on a college entrance exam. Instead, Veronica got her hooks into a promising civic engineering major who would graduate college just as she got her diploma.

What's better than being a six-point-o student, or whatever? Being a trophy wife. "I think everything is going to be just fine," Veronica mumbled in defiance of the universe. "I have a plan that's going to give me the perfect life."

And then, as she stared at the highly inappropriate photo, her vision began to blur. *Wait, is this what they talked about in church… am–am I going blind? No, that can't be. Joey's older brother works at the porno store on route nine and he's got perfect vision.*

She pinched the bridge of her nose and squinted, wondering if she was getting a migraine. Veronica turned off her screen and stood up. That action only made everything so much blurrier, but she headed for the kitchen, hoping to beg some ibuprofen off of Grandma.

And then her vision crowded with shadows and went fully dark.

A strange calm fell over her as she blacked out. *Strange... I thought migraines were supposed to hurt. But I don't feel much at all...*

VERONICA CAME BACK TO consciousness to a fuzzy image of Ginger leaning over her. The edges of her sight were frayed, blurry, like some of the special effects filters she'd used to accent different images she'd edited on her phone. The glamor girl blinked and tried to make her vision clear. It didn't.

No... blinked isn't right–what's wrong with my eyes?

A sense of whelming dread washed over Veronica as she tried to push Ginger away and rub her eyes. Her hands refused to move. Veronica concentrated on them and realized she couldn't even feel them. She couldn't even turn her head.

Grandma's face joined Ginger's, and they both stared down at her.

Veronica tried to scream for help. She could not–she couldn't make her mouth work. *Why can't I feel my mouth?* She could only feel the whelming sense of panic, and the only thing that grounded her was the fact that Grandma was there.

She'll know what to do. Grandma was a nurse before she was, well, Grandma... this must be a seizure or something? Maybe a severe allergic reaction?

"Now what?" Ginger asked.

That little twerp better not go into my phone while Grandma takes me to the hospital.

Grandma tilted her head slightly and grinned.

"And now for the beating," Grandma said with a dark glimmer in her eye. She punched Veronica. "And now it's your turn."

Ginger's mouth upturned wickedly, and she pounded Veronica over and over.

Ouch. ow! Dammit! Ouch–I'll kill you, you little dump truck!

Try as she could, Veronica could neither move nor complain–and she had no idea why her grandmother was letting Ginger do this. *Was it because I was a bitch to her earlier?*

"Why are we doing this?" Ginger asked as Grandmother pulled out a rolling pin.

Dread fell into the pit of Veronica's gut–or whatever passed for it, now. She'd seen the old battle-axe shake it at her grandfather before and never doubted that Grandma had whacked him with it a time or two.

"You have to knead it to make it mix up good. It develops the gluten, and that helps it all stick together."

"The stuff that Veronica's allergic to?"

Grandma scowled. "Veronica's just being difficult and told a lie. She's not allergic." Grandma sighed the girl's name. "Oh, Veronica."

"Ron-uh-cuh?" called a voice.

Grandma and Ginger turned their faces. Veronica could not do likewise. But terror rippled through her when she recognized the sound of the voice—*her* voice.

"Ron-uh-cuh?" the voice repeated as Veronica's face came into view from an unflattering lower angle.

That's not me! Oh Lord, somebody help me! Something is in my body or is impersonating me!

Ronuhcuh stared down at the frozen Veronica; the impostor practically drooled from the edge of her mouth. Pointing directly at the frozen diva, and said, "Ron-uh-cuh?"

Ginger laughed. "That's a funny nickname. Is that some kind of Internet thing? Can I be Injer? You know, like Ginger, but shortened too?"

"Injer," Ronuhcuh said with a stupid, hollow chuckle. The idiot in the teen girl's body still stared down at the real Veronica. "Switched?"

"The dough?" Ginger asked. "You want to switch and knead the dough?"

Veronica tried to scream again as dread realization washed over her as Grandma gave Ronuhcuh the rolling pin. Ronuhcuh laughed dumbly while she went to work.

The pain of the rolling pin was excruciating, like being stretched and pulled, squeezed and pinched. Then came the slicing pain of a cookie cutter. Veronica felt loopy as Ginger picked her up, dangled her for a moment, and then laid her down again.

After a momentary respite, Grandma picked up whatever Veronica now rested on. The old woman nudged Ronuhcuh and winked. "I'm so glad you came to your senses and helped us. I think you made Ginger's wish come true. I think she needed a friend tonight."

No–that's not me! Put me back. Dear Lord, put me back!

"Injer friend," Ronuhcuh slurred.

"Cousins are often some of our best friends when we are young."

Ronuhcuh said, "Injer best friend."

No–no, help! Veronica wanted to cry, but she couldn't even do that. She could only watch as the little red-haired twerp clamped a big hug onto that dough-brained impersonation, and then the real Veronica heard the sound of metal on metal as her grandmother slid the baking sheet she lay upon into the pre-heated oven.

The door banged shut with a hellish sound of finality and the scorching heat burned the disembodied gingerbread Veronica with Promethean torment. The oven did its work and burned her alive.

VERONICA CAME BACK TO consciousness, but slowly. *What the hell was that terrible dream I had? It must've been something like that Muppet movie with the old British man and the frog on crutches.*

She hadn't felt this wasted since the time Jessica stole a handful of Fireball samplers at the grocery store, and they'd skipped gym class to get wasted. Oddly, that smell of cinnamon seemed to cling in the air as she thought about it.

Veronica heard a door bang shut, followed by the sound of someone puking in the kitchen wastebasket: a clear indication that her parents, aunts, and uncles must have returned from a night of heavy caroling. *I think Smitty's closes early on the holidays?*

"Oh, you're back," Grandma called to them. "We've been having a great time here. And you should have seen it–Ronuhcuh did something so nice for Ginger. They're such good friends."

Wait–what?

Veronica tried to stand up but could not. She felt brittle, and stiff–*and that damned cinnamon is so strong!*

Panic. Dread. Terror... and whatever else the thesaurus had to say on the matter enveloped her again. *It wasn't a dream!*

Veronica watched her parents stumble past. A moment later, her uncle picked up a cinnamon dusted shortbread cookie lying directly next to her.

I–I'm on the freaking cookie tray in the living room!

A few moments later, the rest of the late-night carolers headed for their rooms and Grandma watched them, beaming with pride.

Veronica tried to keep calm. *It's gotta be almost midnight, right? If I know anything about curses and holiday magic, this sort of thing's got to end at midnight. Right? Right! I think that's how Scrooge survived.*

Grandma flipped off the lights throughout the rest of the house while Veronica did her best to remain calm. The mantle clock in the living room began its chime as the older woman flipped the last switch. Only the lights of the tree and its star-shaped topper lit the home now.

By the fifth chime Veronica felt funny, almost tingly, like a limb that had been sat upon too long and gone to sleep. The white static noise of pins and needles flooded through her.

Oh, thank God–I learned my lesson. I'll be nicer to Grandma and my cousin. I swear!

The eighth chime on the way to midnight encouraged her all the more.

This spell, or whatever it is, is lifting. I'm finally cured!

"What a wonderful Christmas it's going to be," Grandma said to nobody in particular.

On the tenth chime, Veronica felt suddenly lifted in the darkness. The only thing she saw was her plump grandma's open mouth, and then she felt the teeth.

RONUHCUH GRINNED DUMBLY WHERE she stood over the sink in her elderly grandmother's home. The old woman had clung on for fifteen years after her husband's passing and had still insisted that they do Christmas at her house.

None dared cross the old woman–she had an almost supernatural power over the rest of the family. Ronuhcuh's husband had once confided in her that he wondered if she might secretly be a witch. It might have been true, even, but none would ever bring it up for fear of the rolling pin. Plus, witches were known to put their mysterious powers to ill-intent when it came to baking and today was not the day for such thoughts. Today was Christmas eve.

Besides... Ronuhcuh didn't have many thoughts. She rarely had much going on upstairs.

Grandma smiled as she watched the gaggle of Ronuhcuh and Harry's children play in the snow outside the window. Ronuhcuh watched the old woman. *Maybe she* is *a witch. I don't know anyone else who bakes cookies like her.*

Ronuhcuh only ever seemed capable of baking well at her grandmother's home.

Ginger opened the door and entered. "Sorry I'm late," said the red-haired twenty-something as she came in. "I didn't miss it, did I?"

Harry winked at his wife and then playfully tapped the simple girl on the rump. "I'll leave you two to your annual tradition."

"Tradition," Ronuhcuh repeated.

"I've got to take a few calls, anyway," Harry said as Ginger hung her coat near the table where the baking supplies were.

"On Christmas Eve?" Ginger asked, screwing up her face. The result was almost an improvement.

"The senate never rests," Harry said, slipping away to the sixth chime of the old mantle clock.

Ginger shrugged and began kneading dough as Ronuhcuh joined her. "Speaking of tradition," the freckled cousin laughed as she scanned Ronuhcuh. "You look pretty good for having popped out five children... I mean, I'm not keen on being a tradwife or anything, but it's working for *you,* I see. You somehow got the perfect life. How'd you do it?"

Ronuhcuh tilted her head. There were no thoughts inside it, but she'd learned it helped make others *think* she was thinking. And besides, Pilates and a boob job was clearly the answer to Ginger's question, but Pilates was hard to say.

"Got the perfect life," Ronuhcuh repeated with a shrug.

Ginger smiled broadly at her cousin. At some point, the girl had no longer desired to be the exact copy of her perfect cousin. Ginger had gone a different way.

She'd gotten married straight out of high school—to Jimmy the Tonka Torcher, of all people—and quickly divorced. Ginger came into her own unique identity and had done her own thing, and she didn't give two flying figgy puddings what others thought.

She still cared what her beloved Ronuhcuh thought, of course. But the blond bombshell rarely did. Both still loved making cookies with their favorite cousin.

But Ginger was still, however, a dump truck.

About the Author

Christopher D. Schmitz is an indie author from the fly-over states who dabbles in game design. He has published award winning science fiction, fantasy, and humor. He's written and freelanced for a variety of outlets, including a blog that has helped countless writers on their publishing journey. On any given weekend, he can be found at pop culture and comic conventions across the USA or playing his bagpipes for people. You can look him up at:

www.authorchristopherdschmitz.com.

THE OAK KING

BY JUSTIN ROSE

"The holly and the ivy, when they are both full grown, of all the trees that are in the wood, the holly bears the crown."
– The Holly and the Ivy

THE YULE HAD COME to Cadwallings, and Beorn could feel the might of Holly's grasp withering. Even now, in the cold heart of winter, amidst icy, prickling air, the scent of warm blood and sizzling fat filled the streets with life. The herds were being slaughtered, sparing the dwindling granaries from further months of feeding.

In the daylight, the houses of Cadwallings lay draped in boughs of holly gathered by Beorn and the other village children. Waxen green and brightest red, they shone along the ridges of slanted roofs, bringing summer color to the drab of winter death, adorning Cadwallings with more life than it had known in months. At night, though the shadows dimmed and darkened the details of these lively decorations, still, extra candles and lanterns burned at every window, casting defiant light out into the year's darkest nights.

Yule was a time for defiance. The defiance of light. The defiance of life. The defiance of feasting in the cold and the dark. The defiance of a people crying out, "No ice can freeze us, no cold can drive us hence, and summer *will* come again."

Beorn scurried down the whitened street, kicking up puffs of soft powder from the morning's fresh snow. He carried a bundle of tools slung across his shoulder, clanking cold iron against cold iron. Little awls and punches, thick needles made to puncture strong leather.

He arrived at his father's shop and ducked quickly inside, pausing momentarily to stamp his feet and breathe into his tingling fingers. A hundred strange scents intensified as his frozen nasal passages loosened, and he sniffed in frustration as the mucus started to run. Lime and urine and dung were strongest of the scents, but behind them he could smell the underlying rot of fatty scraps and stains as old as he was. It was strange to smell rot in winter, but in the warm tanner's shop, the fires kept up a fine pretense of summer, and the constant presence of animal hides put through their various stages of tanning gave off their varied fumes.

"Boy!" his father called, beckoning him closer with a gnarled hand stained a permanent blue by the woad dyes favored in his tribe. He lifted the heavy sack from Beorn's shoulder with careless ease, tossing it onto a nearby table. "Good lad. Help your sister with the fleshing. We've got a whole cartload of new hides to get through."

Beorn nodded quickly. "Yes, Father!" Then he darted toward the far end of the shop where his sister Eadgyth stood with her hips pinning a fresh cowhide to the end of a slanted fleshing beam. Her sleeves were rolled up, and her strong arms moved in a stubborn, grinding rhythm, driving the dull, double-handled fleshing knife down along the gory flesh of her hide, peeling away clinging strings of fat and bits of incidental muscle.

Ulf sat beside her patiently, eyes fixed on every knife stroke, tail wagging against the packed earth floor. A strand of flesh dropped from the handle of the knife, and Ulf snapped it greedily from the air, letting out a contented snuff.

Beorn grinned at the old hound and lifted his own hide from a stinking pile, a pile Ulf knew far better than to mess with. Carefully, Beorn spread the massive hide across the end of a lower fleshing beam, struggling with its wet, flopping weight. But once he had it in position, head side closest to him, he lifted a second fleshing knife and began to make his opening cuts. Grinding hard against the moist flesh, he pushed aside layers of fat and gristle until he had opened a patch of bare skin and could work outward from there, using that opening to keep his blade flush with the skin on each new stroke. Every so often, he shifted the hide and started on a new patch, hurrying in an eager bid to match Eadgyth's pace.

After a few minutes, he felt the first hints of tiredness creeping into his arms and the first stiffness in his back as he leaned hard against the slippery hide, pinning it to the fleshing board so it wouldn't shift underneath his knife.

He glanced eagerly at the door, wishing he could be back outside among the sounds of a village buzzing with the knowledge of coming celebration, so he could watch the festival pyres being built, see the tables being set in the festival field. In that moment of distraction, he felt one handle of his fleshing knife turn slightly, biting into the skin and cutting through.

Beorn cursed quietly and glanced swiftly to his sister, hoping his mistake had been missed.

He saw her raise an eyebrow and shake her head. "Idiot," she said, but it was perfunctory, barely meant.

He grimaced. "Father will have my hide for that..."

She chuckled. "He won't even want your hide if you keep putting holes in it." Then she winked, lifted her own well-fleshed hide, and carried it over to the wooden lime vats to let it soak. "Ready for the festival?" she asked when she'd returned and draped another hide on her beam.

Beorn nodded eagerly. "Father says I will play my whistle for the dance!"

Eadgyth smiled kindly. "What an honor. I'm sure your music will lift the dancers' heels."

Beorn nodded proudly. "They won't be able to help themselves. The song will give them flight!" He held his fleshing knife handle against his lips, fingering its dull blade like a flute, then burst into laughter.

Eadgyth smirked. "Such surety!"

"What about you?" Beorn asked. "What are you excited for tonight?"

Eadgyth stilled her face and assumed an air of mystery. "Oh, you'll see. Just don't miss Old Offa's stories."

Beorn snorted. "You're not doing anything."

Eadgyth stuck her tongue out. "You'll see."

"Come on," Beorn urged her. "Are you a dancer? Are you telling the stories? Are you joining the horse races? Are you..."

His sister glared at him. "You'll see."

"Less chatting, more scraping!" their father called out, and Beorn hurriedly resumed the rhythm of his knife, grinding away the stubborn gristle of his hide. He felt Ulf rubbing up against his leg, and he grinned at the old hound. "Fine," he murmured, then picked a blob of fat off his blade and tossed it to the hound. "There you go, old boy."

The day dragged as days before celebration are wont to, each hour stretching till it felt like evening would never come, the work seeming unending. And every hide that Beorn dropped into the lime vat felt like it should be the last. But there were always more. After all, it was Yule, the time of slaughter, when hides were all too plentiful. And though it was the shortest day in all the year, somehow, it still felt very, very long.

Finally, he heard the familiar, decisive thunk of his father thrusting his favorite knife into a ruined corner of his work bench, a signal that the knife was done for the day and would have its rest.

Beorn looked up eagerly. "Father?" he asked.

And his father's face, as leathery as the materials he worked with, broke into a smile. "Aye, you're free to go, lad. Good work. Enjoy your Yule. And don't forget your flute!"

Beorn darted out the door and promptly shivered as a cold blast of air met him. The town was darkening, and already the houses were turning to shapes, the holly boughs losing their waxy sheen, the red berries blending into the green and brown. He saw Osred and Waldere darting past and ran to join them, shouting out for them to wait. They slowed and let him join them, the three instantly becoming a single pack, with that instinct shared by predators like wolves and orcas and young boys with time to kill. They shot off down the street, planning what mischiefs they could with the powdery, unpackable snow.

Behind them, Beorn's father stood before the door of his shop and smiled, glancing about at the holly and watching the fading light of sunset. It was a good day for Yule, cold enough that you could not forget that it was winter, cold enough to tell you why you yearned for summer. The bonfires would feel all the warmer, the roasted meat all the heartier, the songs all the livelier—all intended to spite this cold. He fondly remembered when he had the energy and the wonder to dart rather than stride down these streets, when he had roved in his own little pack, when he had burned with youth's fire, casting his own spite against winter.

An hour later, Beorn nestled behind a hastily formed bulwark of snow and clutched the handle of his wooden spear, his pack-mates Osred and Waldere beside him clutching theirs. Firelight played across their faces, lighting features set in grim determination.

The whole of the village now blazed with scattered blooms of light. Scores of bonfires, countless lanterns, a lavish, extravagant number of candles—all of them burned against the night, marking Cadwallings with civilization's fingerprint, marking it as man's, claimed and conquered, fiercely wrested from nature's grasp.

Laughter and singing rose from the nearby square where hundreds danced around the fires, where tables laden with steaming meat and warm mulled mead offered themselves freely. But Beorn had no time for singing, no time for dance, no time for feasting. There were Northmen about. Prowling monsters waiting to strike.

Beorn thrust his head up over the edge of the bulwark, and a missile of packed, icy snow struck his face. He snarled and wiped a drop of blood from his nose with his sleeve. "They've wet the snow so they can pack it!" he reported to Osred and Waldere.

"Savages!" Waldere replied.

Osred hefted his spear. "We'll just have to charge."

And over the bulwark they went, leather boots pelting through the powder, weapons lifted, casting flickering shadows large as giants. And before them, the Northmen quailed and hesitated and died. Laughter and shouts lifted as they threw down their opponents in the snow, as weapons were gradually discarded in favor of unarmed wrestling. And the boys of Beorn's street fought their cousins from one street over.

As Beorn wrestled with his cousin in the snow, a heavy hand fell upon his shoulder and hoisted him to his feet. "Well fought, lad, but you can slay Northmen later. It's time for the stories."

Beorn looked up and glared at his father. "I was winning!"

His father grinned. "That you were! Now, come. Old Offa is gathering us in the festival field."

Beorn sighed and recovered his spear from the powder, his numb fingers stinging slightly as they slipped into the snow. Then he trotted after his father, back toward the festival field in the village center. The night brightened as they grew closer, bonfires burning along the streets and lanterns swaying from eves.

Entering the field, he felt the temperature begin to subtly rise, increasing as he moved deeper among the packed gathering of people surrounded in a ring of fires.

Old Offa stood upon a table, his withered frame draped in layers upon layers of fur and leather and cloth, his white beard and hair adorned with clacking beads, his face painted with lines of woad.

"And so, they cast him down!" the old man thundered, and from another table, three men hurled down a fourth into a waiting pile of snow.

"And they slew him, using the first patricide to pave a way for life! From his form, they carved what they would, his blood to form the oceans, his flesh to mark the land, his skull to contain it all as a dome of sky!"

Beorn stared in rapt fascination as the actors lifted trophies from the snow around the body, pretending as though they tore it all from the body itself. One poured a stream of red blood from a pitcher, another hoisted high a pale cow skull and set it upon a pole, and the third laid out bloody steaks upon the snow as continents.

"The children of Ymir thus made the world. And for this we should thank them! For the sacrifice of their father that gave us the framework of all!"

And the four actors rose and chorused, "All thanks to the children of Ymir!"

And Beorn joined the chorus along with many others in the crowd. He grinned at his father. "This is so much better than last year."

His father ruffled his hair. "That's why I fetched you."Then the three patricidal gods began to stride in company, gesticulating as if in conversation, until they came upon two pine boughs thrust into the snow.

"And the godly brothers walked upon a shore in their new world," continued Offa, "till they came upon two shapely trees and plucked them forth."

Two of the gods lifted the boughs and raised them in triumph.

"And from these boughs," called Offa, "they made man and woman!"

And two actors leapt from the table to land behind the boughs as the gods swept them aside. Beorn pointed and laughed. "Father, it's Eadgyth!"

His father nodded, smiling. "It is."

Then the actors portrayed the first coming of man and woman and the guidance of the gods.

"And the world was dark and full of strange things that threatened. The wolf, the bear, the demon, the cold. All tried and try now still to snuff out human life." Offa gazed out at his audience. "For the world has always threatened, always hounded, always hunted. And winter comes each year and strives again to drive us hence, and the darkness shelters our predators and robs our warmth. But Woden took these new souls and gave them gifts, taught them of fire to ward against the dark and the cold, of iron to cut and shape the world to our needs. And Woden's favorite children of those first became our fathers! And from that proud lineage, we now stand secure against the dark! Our homes filled with warmth! Our streets lit this darkest of all nights by fire! We have defeated winter and night!"

Just then, a howl rose in the distance, and Beorn shivered. Another answered. Howls in the distant dark. Wolves.

Offa shook his fist at the forest and laughed. "Hear nature howl in the cold! Hear her threaten! But this night is the last night of Holly, the last night of cold. Now, the Oak rises, the warmth starts its slow return! And nature swaps out the mask of predator for the mask of nurturer! The time of planting shall come again!"

And then the cattle in their pens at the village edge began to low. Beorn looked nervously at his father. The wolves redoubled their howling, and it all came from the north, fearsome cries that echoed in the dark and reverberated with that strange shudder so natural to their voices. "Father?" Beorn asked.

His father squeezed his shoulder reassuringly. "They won't come near the village, especially not tonight with the fires and the shouting."

But already the howls sounded closer than they had, and a strange cold that was not only the cold of winter crept into Beorn's heart. Something felt... wrong. Looking at the others around him in the crowd, he saw that all felt it. They looked puzzled. Uneasy. Something old and strange moved within them, a fear of the unknown dark that had no place in this settled village, in this settled time, a fear that belonged in the stories of Old Offa.

Beorn shifted his feet in the snow and wished he were warmer so that he could tell if his shivers were from fear or cold.

Old Offa's voice had weakened, but gamely the old man resumed. "Each winter, Woden taught his children how to shelter, how to fight off the longer dark and the cold snow, how to gather in the summer and save after the harvest, how to slaughter the herds in the cold and replenish them in the spring."

Just then a thunderous rattle and beating of hooves echoed overhead, and a booming voice called out too loud to come from the lungs of any man, as cold and empty as a sepulcher, a voice fitted only to winter's cold and night time's dark. "Brother! Come forth!"

Beorn dropped to the ground, clasping his hands over his ears and cowering. He saw something flash by overhead, vast and dark and drawn by shadowy, four-legged figures whose tossing heads bore great, spreading antlers. Like a chariot borne upon the air, the shape raced past. His eyes went wide, and he looked to his father for comfort, only to see his father's eyes widening as well, filled with the same terror. Terror of the unknown. Of the sacred. Of the inhuman and strange and forgotten. Of cold and winter and night.

And then the cattle went mad in their pens and children screamed, and Beorn realized that he was one of them. He heard cracking wood and the stamp of hooves and the thuds of heavy bodies jostling in a mass.

The cattle. They were free. They had shattered their enclosures and entered the streets. Beorn's father dragged Beorn to his feet and leaned down close. Bodies struck against both of them as all their friends and family and neighbors began to run, shouting questions and objections and disbelief.

The chariot swung by overhead once more. And Beorn thought he saw a tall figure within, immeasurably larger than a man, wielding a fearsome, twisted mace, waving it overhead in raucous delight. And the booming, godly voice echoed again. "Each year, you come! Each year, you challenge! Come forth! Show your mettle!"

Beorn realized only then that he was crying, that the warm nipping sensation on his cheeks was the dripping touch of his own tears.

His father was shaking him, shouting, "Go! Get inside! I'm going... your sister!"

Beorn nodded dumbly and broke into a staggering run toward the nearest buildings. He saw the first of the stampeding cattle enter the festival field, and he saw smaller, dark shadows running among them, somehow shaggy and lithe at the same time. Wolves. But they did not snap or bite at the cattle, did not slink at the sight of the village people. No, they ran. Ran with the same madness as the cattle. Ran with fear.

Beorn saw a large bull stumble its way directly into a bonfire, scattering burning brands and logs and embers, igniting its own fur, turning itself into a charging, bludgeoning, thousand-pound torch.

Beorn saw Uhtred and Inga fall beneath trampling hooves, saw another burning cow smash straight through the door of the inn, charging inside to ignite whatever would burn in its madness.

And the Yule went from a night of joy to a night of darkest horror. And the world suddenly felt like a darker place to Beorn, a place with things he neither knew nor understood, a place of danger and death.

He sheltered against the wall of his father's shop, praying to Woden that none of the cattle or wolves would turn down this alley. From there, he watched as everything comprising the world he had known… shattered. He had never imagined that so much could change so swiftly, that the eternal buildings that upheld the framework of his reality… could simply burn. He saw people who, all throughout his brief life, had been as immutable as ground or sky or the cycles of night and day… broken.

Then he saw his father, striding through the chaos, a limp form slung over his broad shoulders, his woad-stained hands now dripping red as well, the blue and the red shining in the growing firelight. His eyes blazed, and his lips dripped more red droplets. His grimace showed new gaps from missing teeth. If it had been any other man, Beorn would have considered this the most terrifying sight he had ever seen. The rage and the power and the blood and the animal intensity. But this was not anyone else. This was his father. And Beorn only felt admiration, awe, and relief.

Beorn crept out from the shadow of the building, from the alley where no beasts rampaged and no fires burned. Seeing a lull in the chaos, he darted forward and grasped his father's massive hand, trying to lead him to safety. "Please, come!" he shouted.

They made it a dozen steps before a mass of mad cattle rounded the next corner and bore down on them. Beorn's father slid Eadgyth from his shoulders and thrust her into Beorn's frail arms. Then he waved his arms and bellowed out in wordless rage, making himself as large as possible, trying to divert the charging cattle.

Beorn staggered back toward the shelter of the building, his sister's form, which had seemed so small on their father's shoulder, now heavy and cumbersome to him. His fingers dug in beneath her arms, and her head lolled against his chest, and he hauled with all his strength. It was not until he finally reached the safety of the building's shadow that he looked up and realized his father was no longer shouting, that he no longer loomed in the street, that he was—gone.

He sat for several moments, Eadgyth lying unconscious in his lap, until he felt the icy chill of the snow melting through his trousers, until the sounds of rampage and lowing quieted, until the dark shadows of the wolves were gone.

And then he heard the tramp of heavy boots upon the earth, unnaturally loud, each step like the thud of falling trees.

A darkness blotted the skyline over the burning homes of his village, the vague outline of... a man. But no natural man. The being stood taller than the Eōten of Old Offa's stories, a vastness too large to properly characterize, to capture, to understand.

A voice rolled forth from that darkness, as terrible as the voice from the sky, but as warm as that voice was cold, as rich as that was empty. "Brother... I come."

The flames over the village seemed to intensify at that voice and to turn toward it in answer, and all the straw upon the roofs, whether whole or burning, came suddenly into a kind of life, greening and growing toward that voice. By the light of the growing flames, Beorn suddenly saw the features of this strange giant.

He was green all over, from the crown of his head to the lowest point of his chest that Beorn could see. And not just green, but growing. For he had no hair, only tumbling bunches of grass and boughs of leafy summer trees that clustered around his head and blotted out the details of his face. And when his mouth opened, limbs of oak and ash sprouted forth from between his lips beside his words. Antlers crowned his head like spreading limbs.

The Oak King.

Beorn knew him in a moment. A myth outside his people, a myth that never fit with Woden and Frige and the rest. A strange story. A whispered story. A story of the seasons and the way of the world. The two brothers who waged endless war to revolve the earth in its seasons and give all life a time of warmth and a time of cold, a time of light and a time of darkness.

Beorn whimpered softly and shook his sister, striving to wake her. "Eadgyth! Eadgyth..." He did not want to be anywhere near when these titanic figures met in their yearly combat.

Eadgyth stirred softly and opened bleary eyes. Beorn saw for the first time the gash across her forehead that must have laid her out. She whispered, "Where's Father?"

Then a slam and trundle of wooden wheels as large as mill wheels and the stamp of reindeer larger still drowned out her voice. Beorn clutched her to his frail chest, as much for his comfort as for hers, and he wished that she weren't hurt, that she could stand and take his hand and be the stronger of them as she always was, that she could tell him in her bossiest voice that he needed to pull himself together, that she could take his hand and lead him to safety and take him to a place where their father was waiting.

But her eyes were soft and wide with terror and confusion, and she seemed ready to slip back out of consciousness, and she was too heavy for him to drag her far. So, he merely clutched her and sheltered closer to the building.

For a child, the realm of adults is a distant and terrible thing, full of concerns and fears and powers beyond the child's ken. The fury of adults is a world-crushing force. Beorn now faced, not the wrath of adults, but the wrath of forces beyond even gods, the wrath of nature in bodied forms.

A second figure marched toward the first, and a wave of chilled air swept forth before his footsteps, filtering among the houses, frosting window panes, freezing whatever snow had been melted by the fires.

Beorn shivered at the touch of this new air, air that felt malicious and alive, that crept through the seams of his clothing and pricked at his flesh with icy fingers. "Eadgyth," he hissed. "We need to go."

And then he felt another wash of air from the opposite direction, warm and scented with undergrowth and rotting vegetation, with life given limitless reign.

He lifted her by her armpits and stumbled backward, dragging her deeper into shadow. Then he watched wide-eyed as the cold giant from the chariot marched forward. He was as tall as the first, dressed all in red, his long and tangled hair decorated with sprigs of holly and clusters of berries. His long beard hung down his chest and clumped with icicles and snow. In his hands, he clutched a mace, its handle formed of braided branches, its twisted head a mass of holly boughs.

The Holly King pointed his mace toward his brother and roared in a breath as sharp as winter ice, "The world is mine!"

A blast of chilled air ran forth, visible by the trail of hoar frost that formed and dropped in its wake, a shower of tinkling pellets upon earth and roof alike.

The Oak King staggered at the blast, then reeled upright, face flushing, and lifted a woodsman's axe. He broke into a staggering run, the world about him awash with a flow of warm, summer breeze, melting snow from rooftops and roads and yards, turning the ground to a spring-time marsh.

Every footstep shook the village, causing houses to judder and creak, tumbling piles of snow down from eaves. A wall of snow slid down and covered Beorn and Eadgyth, and he desperately struggled free, then scrambled to sweep it off his sister. He tore off his gloves so he could reach down into the hood of her jacket and clear it away from her neck. Tears ran freely down his face as his hands stung and his body ached and the world went mad and he scarcely knew if his sister would live or what had happened to his father. And there was nothing. Nothing that he could do. The world was bigger than one young boy. And Winter and Summer were a conflict so much older and grander than himself.

A thunder of clashing weapons shook him from his thoughts, and he stared out to see Holly's mace caught in the beard of Oak's axe.

The King of Winter swept up his mace and twisted aside his brother's weapon, then swung a hard, frozen fist into his brother's face, cracking the branches of his beard and sending forth a spray of green, sappy blood. His voice echoed with a laugh that sounded almost merry, the warmest sound possible in his cold tone.

Oak's head snapped back in a flurry of drifting leaves and tumbling branches. And then he lunged in again and opened his mouth in a wordless roar that melted the ice of Holly's beard. He swept down his axe and buried its head in the festival field, Holly's mace still trapped in the curve of its blade. Then he released it and grasped Holly's shoulders in hands that steamed in the cold night air. Boughs and branches stretched forth from his gaping mouth and struck Holly's face and shoulders and throat and arms, pierced him like needles drawing threads for sutures.

Holly screeched and struggled, but Beorn could feel Oak's victory coming in the warming air, in the way the snow about him softened and rapidly melted. He suddenly felt unbearably warm in his thick coat, and the numb cold in his fingers and thighs turned to the sharp sting brought on by sudden warmth.

Oak released his brother's shoulders and hoisted again his axe.

Holly dropped to his knees, body rigid, ensnared in a thousand boughs and branches.

Oak swept his axe in one solid swing, removing his brother's head again as he had each year thousands of times before, sending it flying down into the wet snow of the festival field. Beorn stared in fear. For he saw no salvation in the victory of Oak. One being was as terrible as the other. Neither cared for the lives of mortal man. Such trifles were beneath them. Their conflict dealt in grander things.

"Well fought, Dear Brother," Oak rumbled and stooped to lift his brother's head. He kissed the frosty brow even as the whole of the head began to melt like ice, followed by the body on the earth.

Oak stood and lifted his arms and sang, sang in a voice as awful as thunder and melodious as a robin's.

Eadgyth stirred and lifted her head softly. "Beorn?" she whispered. She slowly sat up and lifted an arm around her brother, each of them supporting the other. They watched as the Oak King sang his terrible song and a throne of trees and foliage and all the beauties of nature grew to life within the festival field. Even as they watched, this throne took shape too large to comprehend, and the Oak King ascended to sit upon it, its form fitted to his body. He slammed the butt of his axe handle to the earth beside his throne and bellowed, "The world is Summer's!"

Then all went quiet, all save the fading fires and the drip here and there of melted ice and the soft whisper of a breeze too warm for Yule. The children stared out at the wreckage of their village, a victim of the unrelenting force that was nature and time and the unknown, all the forces that Offa claimed man had overcome.

Beorn and Eadgyth felt... very small.

About the Author

Raised in the country in Northern Wisconsin near the shores of Lake Superior, Justin Rose writes novels steeped in emotional turmoil and fantasy adventure with themes of guilt, forgiveness, responsibility, innocence versus knowledge, and the weight of living as mortal beings. When he's not writing his own work, he also curates the Midwest Fantasy Sampler (an anthology series featuring and promoting Midwestern authors), rides mountain bikes on the gorgeous trails of Duluth, Minnesota, joins folk dances, bums about in coffee shops, and sells his books at comic cons, ren-faires, book festivals, and craft fairs all across the Midwest.

https://linktr.ee/justin_rose_autho

THE TREASURE OF ABBOT THOMAS

BY M.R. JAMES

I

Verum usque in præsentem diem multa garriunt inter se Canonici de abscondito quodam istius Abbatis Thomæ thesauro, quem sæpe, quanquam adhuc incassum, quæsiverunt Steinfeldenses. Ipsum enim Thomam adhuc florida in ætate existentem ingentem auri massam circa monasterium defodisse perhibent; de quo multoties interrogatus ubi esset, cum risu respondere solitus erat: "Job, Johannes, et Zacharias vel vobis vel posteris indicabunt"; idemque aliquando adicere se inventuris minime invisurum. Inter alia huius Abbatis opera, hoc memoria præcipue dignum iudico quod fenestram magnam in orientali parte alæ australis in ecclesia sua imaginibus optime in vitro depictis impleverit: id quod et ipsius effigies et insignia ibidem posita demonstrant. Domum quoque Abbatialem fere totam restauravit: puteo in atrio ipsius effosso et lapidibus marmoreis pulchre cælatis exornato. Decessit autem, morte aliquantulum subitanea perculsus, ætatis suæ anno lxxii, incarnationis vero Dominiæ mdxxix.

"I suppose I shall have to translate this," said the antiquary to himself, as he finished copying the above lines from that rather rare and exceedingly diffuse book, the *Sertum Steinfeldense Norbertinum*[5]. "Well, it may as well be done first as last," and accordingly the following rendering was very quickly produced:

[5] An account of the Premonstratensian abbey of Steinfeld, in the Eiffel, with lives of the Abbots, published at Cologne in 1712 by Christian Albert Erhard, a resident in the district. The epithet *Norbertinum* is due to the fact that St Norbert was founder of the Premonstratensian Order.

Up to the present day there is much gossip among the Canons about a certain hidden treasure of this Abbot Thomas, for which those of Steinfeld have often made search, though hitherto in vain. The story is that Thomas, while yet in the vigour of life, concealed a very large quantity of gold somewhere in the monastery. He was often asked where it was, and always answered, with a laugh: "Job, John, and Zechariah will tell either you or your successors." He sometimes added that he should feel no grudge against those who might find it. Among other works carried out by this Abbot I may specially mention his filling the great window at the east end of the south aisle of the church with figures admirably painted on glass, as his effigy and arms in the window attest. He also restored almost the whole of the Abbot's lodging, and dug a well in the court of it, which he adorned with beautiful carvings in marble. He died rather suddenly in the seventy-second year of his age, A.D. 1529.

The object which the antiquary had before him at the moment was that of tracing the whereabouts of the painted windows of the Abbey Church of Steinfeld. Shortly after the Revolution, a very large quantity of painted glass made its way from the dissolved abbeys of Germany and Belgium to this country, and may now be seen adorning various of our parish churches, cathedrals, and private chapels. Steinfeld Abbey was among the most considerable of these involuntary contributors to our artistic possessions (I am quoting the somewhat ponderous preamble of the book which the antiquary wrote), and the greater part of the glass from that institution can be identified without much difficulty by the help, either of the numerous inscriptions in which the place is mentioned, or of the subjects of the windows, in which several well-defined cycles or narratives were represented.

The passage with which I began my story had set the antiquary on the track of another identification. In a private chapel—no matter where—he had seen three large figures, each occupying a whole light in a window, and evidently the work of one artist. Their style made it plain that that artist had been a German of the sixteenth century; but hitherto the more exact localizing of them had been a puzzle. They represented—will you be surprised to hear it?—JOB PATRIARCHA, JOHANNES EVANGELISTA, ZACHARIAS PROPHETA, and each of them held a book or scroll, inscribed with a sentence from his writings. These, as a matter of course, the antiquary had noted, and had been struck by the curious way in which they differed from any text of the Vulgate that he had been able to examine. Thus the scroll in Job's hand was inscribed:

> *Auro est locus in quo absconditur* (for *conflatur*)[6]; on the book of John was: *Habent in vestimentis suis scripturam quam nemo novit*[7] (for *in vestimento scriptum*, the following words being taken from another verse); and Zacharias had: *Super lapidem unum septem oculi sunt*[8] (which alone of the three presents an unaltered text).

[6] There is a place for gold where it is hidden.

[7] They have on their raiment a writing which no man knoweth.

[8] Upon one stone are seven eyes.

A sad perplexity it had been to our investigator to think why these three personages should have been placed together in one window. There was no bond of connexion between them, either historic, symbolic, or doctrinal, and he could only suppose that they must have formed part of a very large series of Prophets and Apostles, which might have filled, say, all the clerestory windows of some capacious church. But the passage from the *Sertum* had altered the situation by showing that the names of the actual personages represented in the glass now in Lord D——'s chapel had been constantly on the lips of Abbot Thomas von Eschenhausen of Steinfeld, and that this Abbot had put up a painted window, probably about the year 1520, in the south aisle of his abbey church. It was no very wild conjecture that the three figures might have formed part of Abbot Thomas's offering; it was one which, moreover, could probably be confirmed or set aside by another careful examination of the glass. And, as Mr. Somerton was a man of leisure, he set out on pilgrimage to the private chapel with very little delay. His conjecture was confirmed to the full. Not only did the style and technique of the glass suit perfectly with the date and place required, but in another window of the chapel he found some glass, known to have been bought along with the figures, which contained the arms of Abbot Thomas von Eschenhausen.

At intervals during his researches Mr. Somerton had been haunted by the recollection of the gossip about the hidden treasure, and, as he thought the matter over, it became more and more obvious to him that if the Abbot meant anything by the enigmatical answer which he gave to his questioners, he must have meant that the secret was to be found somewhere in the window he had placed in the abbey church. It was undeniable, furthermore, that the first of the curiously-selected texts on the scrolls in the window might be taken to have a reference to hidden treasure.

Every feature, therefore, or mark which could possibly assist in elucidating the riddle which, he felt sure, the Abbot had set to posterity he noted with scrupulous care, and, returning to his Berkshire manor-house, consumed many a pint of the midnight oil over his tracings and sketches. After two or three weeks, a day came when Mr Somerton announced to his man that he must pack his own and his master's things for a short journey abroad, whither for the moment we will not follow him.

II

Mr Gregory, the Rector of Parsbury, had strolled out before breakfast, it being a fine autumn morning, as far as the gate of his carriage-drive, with intent to meet the postman and sniff the cool air. Nor was he disappointed of either purpose. Before he had had time to answer more than ten or eleven of the miscellaneous questions propounded to him in the lightness of their hearts by his young offspring, who had accompanied him, the postman was seen approaching; and among the morning's budget was one letter bearing a foreign postmark and stamp (which became at once the objects of an eager competition among the youthful Gregorys), and was addressed in an uneducated, but plainly an English hand.

When the Rector opened it, and turned to the signature, he realized that it came from the confidential valet of his friend and squire, Mr. Somerton. Thus it ran:

> HONOURED SIR, Has I am in a great anxiety about Master I write at is Wish to beg you Sir if you could be so good as Step over. Master Has add a Nastey Shock and keeps His Bedd. I never Have known Him like this but No wonder and Nothing will serve but you Sir. Master says would I mintion the Short Way Here is Drive to Cobblince and take a Trap. Hopeing I Have maid all Plain, but am much Confused in Myself what with Anxiatey and Weakfulness at Night. If I might be so Bold Sir it will be a Pleasure to see a Honnest Brish Face among all These Forig ones.
>
> I am Sir
Your obed^{t} Servt
William Brown.

P.S.—The Village for Town I will not
Turm. It is name Steenfeld.

The reader must be left to picture to himself in detail the surprise, confusion, and hurry of preparation into which the receipt of such a letter would be likely to plunge a quiet Berkshire parsonage in the year of grace 1859. It is enough for me to say that a train to town was caught in the course of the day, and that Mr Gregory was able to secure a cabin in the Antwerp boat and a place in the Coblentz train. Nor was it difficult to manage the transit from that centre to Steinfeld.

I labour under a grave disadvantage as narrator of this story in that I have never visited Steinfeld myself, and that neither of the principal actors in the episode (from whom I derive my information) was able to give me anything but a vague and rather dismal idea of its appearance. I gather that it is a small place, with a large church despoiled of its ancient fittings; a number of rather ruinous great buildings, mostly of the seventeenth century, surround this church; for the abbey, in common with most of those on the Continent, was rebuilt in a luxurious fashion by its inhabitants at that period. It has not seemed to me worth while to lavish money on a visit to the place, for though it is probably far more attractive than either Mr Somerton or Mr Gregory thought it, there is evidently little, if anything, of first-rate interest to be seen—except, perhaps, one thing, which I should not care to see.

The inn where the English gentleman and his servant were lodged is, or was, the only "possible" one in the village. Mr Gregory was taken to it at once by his driver, and found Mr Brown waiting at the door. Mr Brown, a model when in his Berkshire home of the impassive whiskered race who are known as confidential valets, was now egregiously out of his element, in a light tweed suit, anxious, almost irritable, and plainly anything but master of the situation. His relief at the sight of the "honest British face" of his Rector was unmeasured, but words to describe it were denied him. He could only say:

"Well, I ham pleased, I'm sure, sir, to see you. And so I'm sure, sir, will master."

"How *is* your master, Brown?" Mr Gregory eagerly put in.

"I think he's better, sir, thank you; but he's had a dreadful time of it. I 'ope he's gettin' some sleep now, but—"

"What has been the matter—I couldn't make out from your letter? Was it an accident of any kind?"

"Well, sir, I 'ardly know whether I'd better speak about it. Master was very partickler he should be the one to tell you. But there's no bones broke—that's one thing I'm sure we ought to be thankful—"

"What does the doctor say?" asked Mr Gregory.

They were by this time outside Mr Somerton's bedroom door, and speaking in low tones. Mr Gregory, who happened to be in front, was feeling for the handle, and chanced to run his fingers over the panels. Before Brown could answer, there was a terrible cry from within the room.

"In God's name, who is that?" were the first words they heard. "Brown, is it?"

"Yes, sir—me, sir, and Mr Gregory," Brown hastened to answer, and there was an audible groan of relief in reply.

They entered the room, which was darkened against the afternoon sun, and Mr Gregory saw, with a shock of pity, how drawn, how damp with drops of fear, was the usually calm face of his friend, who, sitting up in the curtained bed, stretched out a shaking hand to welcome him.

"Better for seeing you, my dear Gregory," was the reply to the Rector's first question, and it was palpably true.

After five minutes of conversation Mr Somerton was more his own man, Brown afterwards reported, than he had been for days. He was able to eat a more than respectable dinner, and talked confidently of being fit to stand a journey to Coblentz within twenty-four hours.

"But there's one thing," he said, with a return of agitation which Mr Gregory did not like to see, "which I must beg you to do for me, my dear Gregory. Don't," he went on, laying his hand on Gregory's to forestall any interruption—"don't ask me what it is, or why I want it done. I'm not up to explaining it yet; it would throw me back—undo all the good you have done me by coming. The only word I will say about it is that you run no risk whatever by doing it, and that Brown can and will show you tomorrow what it is. It's merely to put back—to keep—something—No; I can't speak of it yet. Do you mind calling Brown?"

"Well, Somerton," said Mr Gregory, as he crossed the room to the door, "I won't ask for any explanations till you see fit to give them. And if this bit of business is as easy as you represent it to be, I will very gladly undertake it for you the first thing in the morning."

"Ah, I was sure you would, my dear Gregory; I was certain I could rely on you. I shall owe you more thanks than I can tell. Now, here is Brown. Brown, one word with you."

"Shall I go?" interjected Mr Gregory.

"Not at all. Dear me, no. Brown, the first thing tomorrow morning—(you don't mind early hours, I know, Gregory)—you must take the Rector to—*there*, you know" (a nod from Brown, who looked grave and anxious), "and he and you will put that back. You needn't be in the least alarmed; it's *perfectly* safe in the daytime. You know what I mean. It lies on the step, you know, where—where we put it." (Brown swallowed dryly once or twice, and, failing to speak, bowed.) "And—yes, that's all. Only this one other word, my dear Gregory. If you *can* manage to keep from questioning Brown about this matter, I shall be still more bound to you. Tomorrow evening, at latest, if all goes well, I shall be able, I believe, to tell you the whole story from start to finish. And now I'll wish you good night. Brown will be with me—he sleeps here—and if I were you, I should lock my door. Yes, be particular to do that. They—they like it, the people here, and it's better. Good night, good night."

They parted upon this, and if Mr Gregory woke once or twice in the small hours and fancied he heard a fumbling about the lower part of his locked door, it was, perhaps, no more than what a quiet man, suddenly plunged into a strange bed and the heart of a mystery, might reasonably expect. Certainly he thought, to the end of his days, that he had heard such a sound twice or three times between midnight and dawn.

He was up with the sun, and out in company with Brown soon after. Perplexing as was the service he had been asked to perform for Mr Somerton, it was not a difficult or an alarming one, and within half an hour from his leaving the inn it was over. What it was I shall not as yet divulge.

Later in the morning Mr Somerton, now almost himself again, was able to make a start from Steinfeld; and that same evening, whether at Coblentz or at some intermediate stage on the journey I am not certain, he settled down to the promised explanation. Brown was present, but how much of the matter was ever really made plain to his comprehension he would never say, and I am unable to conjecture.

III

This was Mr Somerton's story:

"You know roughly, both of you, that this expedition of mine was undertaken with the object of tracing something in connexion with some old painted glass in Lord D——'s private chapel. Well, the starting-point of the whole matter lies in this passage from an old printed book, to which I will ask your attention."

And at this point Mr Somerton went carefully over some ground with which we are already familiar.

"On my second visit to the chapel," he went on, "my purpose was to take every note I could of figures, lettering, diamond-scratchings on the glass, and even apparently accidental markings. The first point which I tackled was that of the inscribed scrolls. I could not doubt that the first of these, that of Job—'There is a place for the gold where it is hidden'—with its intentional alteration, must refer to the treasure; so I applied myself with some confidence to the next, that of St John—'They have on their vestures a writing which no man knoweth.' The natural question will have occurred to you: Was there an inscription on the robes of the figures? I could see none; each of the three had a broad black border to his mantle, which made a conspicuous and rather ugly feature in the window. I was nonplussed, I will own, and, but for a curious bit of luck, I think I should have left the search where the Canons of Steinfeld had left it before me. But it so happened that there was a good deal of dust on the surface of the glass, and Lord D——, happening to come in, noticed my blackened hands, and kindly insisted on sending for a Turk's head broom to clean down the window. There must, I suppose, have been a rough piece in the broom; anyhow, as it passed over the border of one of the mantles, I noticed that it left a long scratch, and that some yellow stain instantly showed up. I asked the man to stop his work for a moment, and ran up the ladder to examine the place. The yellow stain was there, sure enough, and what had come away was a thick black pigment, which had evidently been laid on with the brush after the glass had been burnt, and could therefore be easily scraped off without doing any harm. I scraped, accordingly, and you will hardly believe—no, I do you an injustice; you will have guessed already—that I found under this black pigment two or three clearly-formed capital letters in yellow stain on a clear ground. Of course, I could hardly contain my delight.

"I told Lord D—— that I had detected an inscription which I thought might be very interesting, and begged to be allowed to uncover the whole of it. He made no difficulty about it whatever, told me to do exactly as I pleased, and then, having an engagement, was obliged—rather to my relief, I must say—to leave me. I set to work at once, and found the task a fairly easy one. The pigment, disintegrated, of course, by time, came off almost at a touch, and I don't think that it took me a couple of hours, all told, to clean the whole of the black borders in all three lights. Each of the figures had, as the inscription said, 'a writing on their vestures which nobody knew'.

"This discovery, of course, made it absolutely certain to my mind that I was on the right track. And, now, what was the inscription? While I was cleaning the glass I almost took pains not to read the lettering, saving up the treat until I had got the whole thing clear. And when that was done, my dear Gregory, I assure you I could almost have cried from sheer disappointment. What I read was only the most hopeless jumble of letters that was ever shaken up in a hat. Here it is:

> Job. DREVICIOPEDMOOMSMVIVLISLCAVIBAS-
> BATAOVT
> St John. RDIIEAMRLESIPVSPODSEEIRSETTAAES-
> GIAVNNR
> Zechariah. DREVICIOPEDMOOMSMVIVLISLCAV-
> IBASBATAOVT

"Blank as I felt and must have looked for the first few minutes, my disappointment didn't last long. I realized almost at once that I was dealing with a cipher or cryptogram; and I reflected that it was likely to be of a pretty simple kind, considering its early date. So I copied the letters with the most anxious care. Another little point, I may tell you, turned up in the process which confirmed my belief in the cipher. After copying the letters on Job's robe I counted them, to make sure that I had them right. There were thirty-eight; and, just as I finished going through them, my eye fell on a scratching made with a sharp point on the edge of the border. It was simply the number xxxviii in Roman numerals. To cut the matter short, there was a similar note, as I may call it, in each of the other lights; and that made it plain to me that the glass-painter had had very strict orders from Abbot Thomas about the inscription, and had taken pains to get it correct.

"Well, after that discovery you may imagine how minutely I went over the whole surface of the glass in search of further light. Of course, I did not neglect the inscription on the scroll of Zechariah—'Upon one stone are seven eyes,' but I very quickly concluded that this must refer to some mark on a stone which could only be found *in situ*, where the treasure was concealed. To be short, I made all possible notes and sketches and tracings, and then came back to Parsbury to work out the cipher at leisure. Oh, the agonies I went through! I thought myself very clever at first, for I made sure that the key would be found in some of the old books on secret writing. The *Steganographia* of Joachim Trithemius, who was an earlier contemporary of Abbot Thomas, seemed particularly promising; so I got that and Selenius's *Cryptographia* and Bacon's *de Augmentis Scientiarum* and some more. But I could hit upon nothing. Then I tried the principle of the 'most frequent letter', taking first Latin and then German as a basis. That didn't help, either; whether it ought to have done so, I am not clear. And then I came back to the window itself, and read over my notes, hoping almost against hope that the Abbot might himself have somewhere supplied the key I wanted. I could make nothing out of the colour or pattern of the robes. There were no landscape backgrounds with subsidiary objects; there was nothing in the canopies. The only resource possible seemed to be in the attitudes of the figures. 'Job,' I read: 'scroll in left hand, forefinger of right hand extended upwards. John: holds inscribed book in left hand; with right hand blesses, with two fingers. Zechariah: scroll in left hand; right hand extended upwards, as Job, but with three fingers pointing up.' In other words, I reflected, Job has *one* finger extended, John has *two*, Zechariah has *three*. May not there be a numeral key concealed in that? My dear Gregory," said Mr Somerton, laying his hand on his friend's knee, "that *was* the key. I didn't get it to fit at first, but after two or three trials I saw what was meant. After the first letter of the inscription you skip *one* letter, after the next you skip *two*, and after that skip *three*. Now look at the result I got. I've underlined the letters which form words:

[D]R[E]VI[C]IOP[E]D[M]OO[M]SMV[I]V[L]IS[L]CAV[I]
B[A]SB[A]TAO[V]T[R]DI[I]EAM[R]L[E]SI[P]VSP[O]D[S]

EE[I]RSE[T]T[A]AE[S]GIA[V]N[N]RF[T]EEA[I]L[N]QD
[P]VAI[V]M[T]LE[E]ATT[O]H[I]OO[N]VMC[A]A[T].H.Q.E.

"Do you see it? '*Decem millia auri reposita sunt in puteo in at. . .*' (Ten thousand [pieces] of gold are laid up in a well in ...), followed by an incomplete word beginning *at*. So far so good. I tried the same plan with the remaining letters; but it wouldn't work, and I fancied that perhaps the placing of dots after the three last letters might indicate some difference of procedure. Then I thought to myself, 'Wasn't there some allusion to a well in the account of Abbot Thomas in that book the "*Sertum*"?' Yes, there was: he built a *puteus in atrio* (a well in the court). There, of course, was my word *atrio*. The next step was to copy out the remaining letters of the inscription, omitting those I had already used. That gave what you will see on this slip:

RVIIOPDOOSMVVISCAVBSBTAOTDIEAMLSIVSPD
EERSETAEGIANRFEEALQDVAIMLEATTHOOVMC
A.H.Q.E.

"Now, I knew what the three first letters I wanted were—namely, *rio*—to complete the word *atrio*; and, as you will see, these are all to be found in the first five letters. I was a little confused at first by the occurrence of two *i's*, but very soon I saw that every alternate letter must be taken in the remainder of the inscription. You can work it out for yourself; the result, continuing where the first 'round' left off, is this:

'*rio domus abbatialis de Steinfeld a me, Thoma, qui posui custodem super ea. Gare à qui la touche*'.

"So the whole secret was out:

'Ten thousand pieces of gold are laid
up in the well in the court of the
Abbot's house of Steinfeld by me,
Thomas, who have set a guardian over
them. *Gare à qui la touche*.'

"The last words, I ought to say, are a device which Abbot Thomas had adopted. I found it with his arms in another piece of glass at Lord D——'s, and he drafted it bodily into his cipher, though it doesn't quite fit in point of grammar.

"Well, what would any human being have been tempted to do, my dear Gregory, in my place? Could he have helped setting off, as I did, to Steinfeld, and tracing the secret literally to the fountain-head? I don't believe he could. Anyhow, I couldn't, and, as I needn't tell you, I found myself at Steinfeld as soon as the resources of civilization could put me there, and installed myself in the inn you saw. I must tell you that I was not altogether free from forebodings—on one hand of disappointment, on the other of danger. There was always the possibility that Abbot Thomas's well might have been wholly obliterated, or else that someone, ignorant of cryptograms, and guided only by luck, might have stumbled on the treasure before me. And then"—there was a very perceptible shaking of the voice here—'I was not entirely easy, I need not mind confessing, as to the meaning of the words about the guardian of the treasure. But, if you don't mind, I'll say no more about that until—until it becomes necessary.

"At the first possible opportunity Brown and I began exploring the place. I had naturally represented myself as being interested in the remains of the abbey, and we could not avoid paying a visit to the church, impatient as I was to be elsewhere. Still, it did interest me to see the windows where the glass had been, and especially that at the east end of the south aisle. In the tracery lights of that I was startled to see some fragments and coats-of-arms remaining—Abbot Thomas's shield was there, and a small figure with a scroll inscribed *Oculos habent, et non videbunt* (They have eyes, and shall not see), which, I take it, was a hit of the Abbot at his Canons.

"But, of course, the principal object was to find the Abbot's house. There is no prescribed place for this, so far as I know, in the plan of a monastery; you can't predict of it, as you can of the chapter-house, that it will be on the eastern side of the cloister, or, as of the dormitory, that it will communicate with a transept of the church. I felt that if I asked many questions I might awaken lingering memories of the treasure, and I thought it best to try first to discover it for myself. It was not a very long or difficult search. That three-sided court south-east of the church, with deserted piles of building round it, and grass-grown pavement, which you saw this morning, was the place. And glad enough I was to see that it was put to no use, and was neither very far from our inn nor overlooked by any inhabited building; there were only orchards and paddocks on the slopes east of the church. I can tell you that fine stone glowed wonderfully in the rather watery yellow sunset that we had on the Tuesday afternoon.

"Next, what about the well? There was not much doubt about that, as you can testify. It is really a very remarkable thing. That curb is, I think, of Italian marble, and the carving I thought must be Italian also. There were reliefs, you will perhaps remember, of Eliezer and Rebekah, and of Jacob opening the well for Rachel, and similar subjects; but, by way of disarming suspicion, I suppose, the Abbot had carefully abstained from any of his cynical and allusive inscriptions.

"I examined the whole structure with the keenest interest, of course—a square well-head with an opening in one side; an arch over it, with a wheel for the rope to pass over, evidently in very good condition still, for it had been used within sixty years, or perhaps even later, though not quite recently. Then there was the question of depth and access to the interior. I suppose the depth was about sixty to seventy feet; and as to the other point, it really seemed as if the Abbot had wished to lead searchers up to the very door of his treasure-house, for, as you tested for yourself, there were big blocks of stone bonded into the masonry, and leading down in a regular staircase round and round the inside of the well.

"It seemed almost too good to be true. I wondered if there was a trap—if the stones were so contrived as to tip over when a weight was placed on them; but I tried a good many with my own weight and with my stick, and all seemed, and actually were, perfectly firm. Of course, I resolved that Brown and I would make an experiment that very night.

"I was well prepared. Knowing the sort of place I should have to explore, I had brought a sufficiency of good rope and bands of webbing to surround my body, and cross-bars to hold to, as well as lanterns and candles and crowbars, all of which would go into a single carpet-bag and excite no suspicion. I satisfied myself that my rope would be long enough, and that the wheel for the bucket was in good working order, and then we went home to dinner.

"I had a little cautious conversation with the landlord, and made out that he would not be overmuch surprised if I went out for a stroll with my man about nine o'clock, to make (Heaven forgive me!) a sketch of the abbey by moonlight. I asked no questions about the well, and am not likely to do so now. I fancy I know as much about it as anyone in Steinfeld: at least"—with a strong shudder—"I don't want to know any more.

"Now we come to the crisis, and, though I hate to think of it, I feel sure, Gregory, that it will be better for me in all ways to recall it just as it happened. We started, Brown and I, at about nine with our bag, and attracted no attention; for we managed to slip out at the hinder end of the inn-yard into an alley which brought us quite to the edge of the village. In five minutes we were at the well, and for some little time we sat on the edge of the well-head to make sure that no one was stirring or spying on us. All we heard was some horses cropping grass out of sight farther down the eastern slope. We were perfectly unobserved, and had plenty of light from the gorgeous full moon to allow us to get the rope properly fitted over the wheel. Then I secured the band round my body beneath the arms. We attached the end of the rope very securely to a ring in the stonework. Brown took the lighted lantern and followed me; I had a crowbar. And so we began to descend cautiously, feeling every step before we set foot on it, and scanning the walls in search of any marked stone.

"Half aloud I counted the steps as we went down, and we got as far as the thirty-eighth before I noted anything at all irregular in the surface of the masonry. Even here there was no mark, and I began to feel very blank, and to wonder if the Abbot's cryptogram could possibly be an elaborate hoax. At the forty-ninth step the staircase ceased. It was with a very sinking heart that I began retracing my steps, and when I was back on the thirty-eighth—Brown, with the lantern, being a step or two above me—I scrutinized the little bit of irregularity in the stonework with all my might; but there was no vestige of a mark.

"Then it struck me that the texture of the surface looked just a little smoother than the rest, or, at least, in some way different. It might possibly be cement and not stone. I gave it a good blow with my iron bar. There was a decidedly hollow sound, though that might be the result of our being in a well. But there was more. A great flake of cement dropped on to my feet, and I saw marks on the stone underneath. I had tracked the Abbot down, my dear Gregory; even now I think of it with a certain pride. It took but a very few more taps to clear the whole of the cement away, and I saw a slab of stone about two feet square, upon which was engraven a cross.

Disappointment again, but only for a moment. It was you, Brown, who reassured me by a casual remark. You said, if I remember right:

"'It's a funny cross: looks like a lot of eyes.'

"I snatched the lantern out of your hand, and saw with inexpressible pleasure that the cross *was* composed of seven eyes, four in a vertical line, three horizontal. The last of the scrolls in the window was explained in the way I had anticipated. Here was my 'stone with the seven eyes'. So far the Abbot's data had been exact, and, as I thought of this, the anxiety about the 'guardian' returned upon me with increased force. Still, I wasn't going to retreat now.

"Without giving myself time to think, I knocked away the cement all round the marked stone, and then gave it a prise on the right side with my crowbar. It moved at once, and I saw that it was but a thin light slab, such as I could easily lift out myself, and that it stopped the entrance to a cavity. I did lift it out unbroken, and set it on the step, for it might be very important to us to be able to replace it. Then I waited for several minutes on the step just above. I don't know why, but I think to see if any dreadful thing would rush out. Nothing happened. Next I lit a candle, and very cautiously I placed it inside the cavity, with some idea of seeing whether there were foul air, and of getting a glimpse of what was inside. There *was* some foulness of air which nearly extinguished the flame, but in no long time it burned quite steadily. The hole went some little way back, and also on the right and left of the entrance, and I could see some rounded light-coloured objects within which might be bags. There was no use in waiting. I faced the cavity, and looked in. There was nothing immediately in the front of the hole. I put my arm in and felt to the right, very gingerly....

"Just give me a glass of cognac, Brown. I'll go on in a moment, Gregory....

"Well, I felt to the right, and my fingers touched something curved, that felt—yes—more or less like leather; dampish it was, and evidently part of a heavy, full thing. There was nothing, I must say, to alarm one. I grew bolder, and putting both hands in as well as I could, I pulled it to me, and it came. It was heavy, but moved more easily than I had expected. As I pulled it towards the entrance, my left elbow knocked over and extinguished the candle. I got the thing fairly in front of the mouth and began drawing it out. Just then Brown gave a sharp ejaculation and ran quickly up the steps with the lantern. He will tell you why in a moment. Startled as I was, I looked round after him, and saw him stand for a minute at the top and then walk away a few yards. Then I heard him call softly, 'All right, sir,' and went on pulling out the great bag, in complete darkness. It hung for an instant on the edge of the hole, then slipped forward on to my chest, and *put its arms round my neck.*

"My dear Gregory, I am telling you the exact truth. I believe I am now acquainted with the extremity of terror and repulsion which a man can endure without losing his mind. I can only just manage to tell you now the bare outline of the experience. I was conscious of a most horrible smell of mould, and of a cold kind of face pressed against my own, and moving slowly over it, and of several—I don't know how many—legs or arms or tentacles or something clinging to my body. I screamed out, Brown says, like a beast, and fell away backward from the step on which I stood, and the creature slipped downwards, I suppose, on to that same step. Providentially the band round me held firm. Brown did not lose his head, and was strong enough to pull me up to the top and get me over the edge quite promptly. How he managed it exactly I don't know, and I think he would find it hard to tell you. I believe he contrived to hide our implements in the deserted building near by, and with very great difficulty he got me back to the inn. I was in no state to make explanations, and Brown knows no German; but next morning I told the people some tale of having had a bad fall in the abbey ruins, which, I suppose, they believed. And now, before I go further, I should just like you to hear what Brown's experiences during those few minutes were. Tell the Rector, Brown, what you told me."

"Well, sir," said Brown, speaking low and nervously, "it was just this way. Master was busy down in front of the 'ole, and I was 'olding the lantern and looking on, when I 'eard somethink drop in the water from the top, as I thought. So I looked up, and I see someone's 'ead lookin' over at us. I s'pose I must ha' said somethink, and I 'eld the light up and run up the steps, and my light shone right on the face. That was a bad un, sir, if ever I see one! A holdish man, and the face very much fell in, and larfin', as I thought. And I got up the steps as quick pretty nigh as I'm tellin' you, and when I was out on the ground there warn't a sign of any person. There 'adn't been the time for anyone to get away, let alone a hold chap, and I made sure he warn't crouching down by the well, nor nothink. Next thing I hear master cry out somethink 'orrible, and hall I see was him hanging out by the rope, and, as master says, 'owever I got him up I couldn't tell you."

"You hear that, Gregory?" said Mr Somerton. "Now, does any explanation of that incident strike you?"

"The whole thing is so ghastly and abnormal that I must own it puts me quite off my balance; but the thought did occur to me that possibly the—well, the person who set the trap might have come to see the success of his plan."

"Just so, Gregory, just so. I can think of nothing else so—*likely*, I should say, if such a word had a place anywhere in my story. I think it must have been the Abbot.... Well, I haven't much more to tell you. I spent a miserable night, Brown sitting up with me. Next day I was no better; unable to get up; no doctor to be had; and, if one had been available, I doubt if he could have done much for me. I made Brown write off to you, and spent a second terrible night. And, Gregory, of this I am sure, and I think it affected me more than the first shock, for it lasted longer: there was someone or something on the watch outside my door the whole night. I almost fancy there were two. It wasn't only the faint noises I heard from time to time all through the dark hours, but there was the smell—the hideous smell of mould. Every rag I had had on me on that first evening I had stripped off and made Brown take it away. I believe he stuffed the things into the stove in his room; and yet the smell was there, as intense as it had been in the well; and, what is more, it came from outside the door. But with the first glimmer of dawn it faded out, and the sounds ceased, too; and that convinced me that the thing or things were creatures of darkness, and could not stand the daylight; and so I was sure that if anyone could put back the stone, it or they would be powerless until someone else took it away again. I had to wait until you came to get that done. Of course, I couldn't send Brown to do it by himself, and still less could I tell anyone who belonged to the place.

"Well, there is my story; and, if you don't believe it, I can't help it. But I think you do."

"Indeed," said Mr Gregory, "I can find no alternative. I *must* believe it! I saw the well and the stone myself, and had a glimpse, I thought, of the bags or something else in the hole. And, to be plain with you, Somerton, I believe my door was watched last night, too."

"I dare say it was, Gregory; but, thank goodness, that is over. Have you, by the way, anything to tell about your visit to that dreadful place?"

"Very little," was the answer. "Brown and I managed easily enough to get the slab into its place, and he fixed it very firmly with the irons and wedges you had desired him to get, and we contrived to smear the surface with mud so that it looks just like the rest of the wall. One thing I did notice in the carving on the well-head, which I think must have escaped you. It was a horrid, grotesque shape—perhaps more like a toad than anything else, and there was a label by it inscribed with the two words, 'Depositum custodi'."[9]

[9] "Keep that which is committed to thee."

About the Author

Montague Rhodes James (1 August 1862 – 12 June 1936) was an English medievalist, scholar, and author who served as provost of King's College, Cambridge, and of Eton College as well as Vice-Chancellor of the University of Cambridge. James's scholarly work is still highly regarded, but he is best remembered for his ghost stories. James originally read the stories to friends and select students at Eton and Cambridge as Christmas Eve entertainments, and received wider attention when they were published.

NAUGHTY & NICE, A DAN SHAMBLE, ZOMBIE P.I., HOLIDAY STORY

BY KEVIN J. ANDERSON

1

SANTA CLAUS WAS AN *unnatural*. That made perfect sense—I just hadn't thought of it before.

The jolly bearded guy in the bright-red suit came into the offices of Chambeaux & Deyer Investigations, desperate to hire my services. It's not often, I suppose, that Santa requires a detective—particularly a zombie detective.

"I need your help, Mr. Chambeaux," Santa said.

I extended my gray hand to shake his black-gloved one. "At your service."

I assessed my client-to-be. Santa carried a voluminous cloth sack over his left shoulder; it was limp and empty at the moment, rather than bulging with brightly wrapped gifts. His bloodshot eyes were as red as his suit. His cheeks were pale, and his face seemed less plump than the pictures I had seen on a million Christmas cards.

"It's a crisis." He looked around with haunted eyes. "I've been robbed!"

In the Unnatural Quarter, we see all sorts of clients. After the cosmic supernatural event called the Big Uneasy, all manner of legendary creatures had reappeared: ghosts, vampires, zombies, werewolves, ghouls, and other creatures that go bump, growl, or thud in the night. Why not Santa, too? Somebody who can slip down billions of chimneys in a night—without incurring a single home-invasion charge—would fit right in.

"We'll do everything we can to help, Mr. Claus," said Robin Deyer, my earnest lawyer partner, as she came out to greet the new client. "Is this more of a legal matter or an investigative one?"

"Oh-ho-ho, I definitely need a detective, and I came here because Mrs. Claus and I have heard about Mr. Chambeaux."

I was surprised. "We don't even advertise up at the North Pole. How did you find out about Chambeaux and Deyer Investigations?"

"Actually, we're local. My powers only manifest during the holiday season—it's not a full-time gig up in the cold. The rest of the year Mrs. Claus and I run a nice little bed-and-breakfast in the Quarter. Everybody around town knows the zombie detective to call when they're in a bind."

When I first moved into the Unnatural Quarter, I was a regular human P.I., trying to make a living like anybody else. I catered to clients who, though they sometimes looked like monsters on the outside, still had very human problems. Even after I got myself killed on a case, I climbed out of the grave and got back to work, still with Robin as my partner. Most unnatural aren't even bothered by the bullet hole in the middle of my forehead, and I've stopped being self-conscious about applying morticians' putty to cover it up.

Sheyenne, our office assistant, flitted up to Santa, beaming her gorgeous smile. "May I take your coat, Mr. Claus?"

Not only is Sheyenne extremely smart, competent, and efficient, she's beautiful on all counts. She's also my girlfriend. On top of that, she happens to be a ghost, murdered in the same case that saw me dead. But even through all that, we stuck together. It's a testament to the strength of our relationship.

Santa decided against removing his red coat. "No-ho-ho! It's part of my traditional image. The coat is made of magical material that keeps me comfortable no matter the temperature. That way I never have to take it off until the season's over. Traditions are important, and never more so than around the holidays."

Sheyenne leaned closer and whispered, "For the record, I never stopped believing in you."

He regarded Sheyenne with both wonder and mirth. "Strangely enough, I didn't believe in ghosts—until a few years ago." Santa sneezed, then turned back to me. "Mr. Chambeaux, I'm not going to kid you. There's more riding on this particular Christmas than ever before, and I'm coming apart at the seams. I need you to find my stolen property before Christmas Eve, or there'll be no joy to the world, no ho-ho-ho, no holly jolly, no Feliz in the Navidad, no Frohe in the Weihnachten, no Merry in the Christmas. You see how serious this is?"

"I think I do." I really had no idea, but I didn't want to look dumb in front of Santa Claus. "What exactly was stolen?"

"My list!" He was distraught—which was not at all the sort of attitude I expected from a man famous for his rumbling belly-laugh and infectious good cheer. "My *list* of who's Naughty and Nice! Without that list, I won't know which houses to visit, which Johnny deserves a model train set and which one gets a lump of coal, which Susie deserves a doll and which one gets a boring sweater. If I can't figure that out, Christmas definitely won't be the most wonderful time of the year."

"Don't you keep a photocopy?" Robin asked. "Or an on-line backup?"

Santa was horrified. "And break Christmas tradition? Millions of children believe in me and the way I do things, just so. They have dreams about Christmas, and it's my responsibility to safeguard those dreams." He shook his head again. "If I modernized, there'd be an uproar—not to mention countless bugs in the system—and then you can bet the Easter Bunny would hack into my database and start grabbing my market share. No, everything's done by hand on a very long roll of parchment, the names of every single boy and girl written with a goose quill."

That must have been the world's largest two-column spreadsheet. "And how exactly was it stolen?"

"Someone broke into the offices of my North Pole headquarters. It's our busy season, all of my helpers doing double shifts, decking the halls, dashing through the snow. Our packaging department is a madhouse, full of complete sets of lords a-leaping, partridges, pear trees—and everybody wants five golden rings. We still have an overstock of last year's fruitcakes, and I don't know what to do with the figgy puddings. I was sure there'd be a demand for those again." He wiped a gloved hand across his forehead.

"It's very hectic. I was taking a break with Mrs. Claus. She had made a fresh batch of eggnog, and this time of year she spikes it rather heavily. I slept like a baby ... and when I went back to the office the list was gone!" He tugged on his beard. "It had to be an inside job." He paced back and forth, scuffing his black boots on our all-weather carpet. "I checked with all the line supervisor elves and every single one of the toy builders. This time of year they work around the clock without even restroom or cigarette breaks. But everyone had an alibi."

"Could you have been targeted by Homeland Security?" Robin asked. "Or some other law-enforcement organization monitoring your research as to who might be on a Most Naughty list?"

"I can see why they might want that," I said.

"Not at all, I have a close cooperative relationship with government agencies, considering all that airspace I fly over—and my work has to be done in a single night, so I have no time to mess with clearances. I even let NORAD track me every year. No, that list is in the hands of someone who means no good, mark my words ... and no human could have gotten through my security. It had to be an unnatural."

He hung his head and seemed so sad that I wanted to sit on Santa's lap and give him a hug. He continued, "That's why I came to you, Mr. Chambeaux. If I don't get that Naughty and Nice list in time, I can't stop thinking about all those poor children who'll be disappointed, all those broken dreams, all those undelivered presents. It'll destroy their faith in Christmas ... and they just might turn out to be naughty next year."

I was determined to solve the problem. It's not every day you get a chance to save Christmas—and not just because Christmas only comes once a year. "Don't underestimate how relentless a zombie can be, Santa. I'll find your list. If I have any questions or developments, how will I get hold of you? Do you have a business card?"

"Much better than that." Santa reached into a pocket of his red jacket and pulled out a bright green ribbon with a jingle bell attached. "Just ring this, and I'll be there. Even if I'm otherwise occupied, I have an answering service that can get hold of me."

The pink had come back to his cheeks, and a droll smile lifted his lips. "Oh-ho-ho, if you solve this case, there'll be something very special under the tree—for all of you."

Relieved and encouraged, Santa slung his empty sack over one shoulder and prepared to go. He closed his eyes and touched a finger to the side of his nose.

When nothing happened, he looked around our offices. Finding no chimney, he chuckled. "Sorry, I've been so worried about Christmas being ruined, I forgot how I arrived!" He left through the front door instead.

2

Although I knew I might have to go to Santa's North Pole seasonal offices to see the crime scene, I decided to search in the Unnatural Quarter first, which was much more convenient. (Riding up to the Arctic for hours in a freezing open sleigh sounded worse than flying in a middle seat in Coach.)

I started with someone who kept a similar list—primarily a Naughty list.

Officer Toby McGoohan is a dedicated beat cop, but his penchant for telling off-color jokes to the wrong people had gotten him transferred to the Quarter. McGoo is also my BHF, my best human friend. We help each other on cases. We commiserate about life and unlife over beers at the Goblin Tavern.

I found him outside one of the Talbot & Knowles blood bars, which are frequented by vampires who need their daily caffeine and hemoglobin fix. Some fanged customers drink straight blood, while others go for berry-flavored blood frappés or, now that the weather had turned colder, steaming cinnamon-spice hot clotties.

"Hey, Shamble," McGoo said, tipping his blue cap. "What do you get when you cross a snowman with a vampire?"

"What?" I groaned in advance.

"Frostbite." He persists in telling me jokes. I haven't been able to convince him they're not funny, and he hasn't been able to convince me that they are. As a special favor, I did promise I would try to laugh at some of them. But only some. "What's new and exciting in your world?"

"I just picked up Santa Claus as a client. Somebody stole his list of Naughty and Nice kids."

McGoo's eyes widened. "Well, that's a miracle on ..." he glanced up, looking for a street corner, "32nd Street. If even Santa isn't safe from criminal activity, we are living in troubled times indeed. What does the list look like?"

"Long roll of parchment, millions of handwritten names. Two columns labeled N and N."

McGoo shook his head. "I'll keep an eye out, but we've got real problems of our own in the Quarter." He lowered his voice. "Kids are going missing, Shamble—a lot of them. We've received a rash of reports."

A vampire couple came out of the blood bar, chatting away. One held a to-go carrier with four cups of blood drinks marked with Type A (extra hot), Type O negative, and two with Type B positive (and a hand-drawn smiley face).

McGoo called, "Excuse me, can I see those for a second?"

The vampires turned, surprised. "What is it, Officer?"

"Your blood drinks. I want to show my friend something."

McGoo indicated the to-go cups, the first of which showed the printed picture of a young vampire boy who had been turned when he was maybe twelve years old. Big letters said "Have You Seen Me?" Printed below the photo were the vampire kid's name, pre-turned age, and last-seen data.

The second cup showed a zombie boy with an incongruous smile beneath his sunken eyes. The third was a scruffy-looking full-furred werewolf, and the fourth showed a human girl in Goth makeup wearing an off-the-shelf gloomy expression.

After he thanked the vampire couple, they left. I shook my head. "That's troubling, McGoo. I think I recognize the werewolf kid. He was part of the gang at the rumble a few months ago, Hairballs versus the Monthlies."

"Yeah, he's not the only rough one. Some of the missing children are straight off the Wikipedia page for Juvenile Delinquent. Not all of those photos were in a family album—a few are from mug-shot files."

"Some of the disappearances could just be runaways," I suggested. "Visiting some nice old lady's gingerbread house in the forest."

"For the record, Shamble, she wasn't a nice old lady—I worked on that case," McGoo said. "Not all of the missing kids have records. We've got grieving parents or foster-parents who want to find their missing little angels. I don't know if the cases are related, or just a coincidence."

"I don't believe in coincidence," I said, wondering if this might also have something to do with the stolen Naughty and Nice list. "But I didn't believe in Santa Claus either, and now he's my client. Let me know if you get a lead on my case. I'll do the same if I hear anything about the missing kids."

McGoo nodded. "The Quarter's getting nervous—put your mind to it, see what you come up with. You've got a lot of space in that big empty head of yours."

I tapped the bullet hole in the middle of my forehead. "A little extra space maybe, but it's not empty." I tipped my fedora at him and left.

My first order of business was to figure out who would *want* to steal the Naughty and Nice list, and what anybody would use it for. In order to brainstorm, I invited Sheyenne to lunch.

3

Being a ghost, Sheyenne doesn't eat, not even their special "ephemeral" plate, and I don't need much sustenance. (I've avoided brains, because I don't want to turn into one of *those* zombies who are an embarrassment to the rest of us.)

The Ghoul's Diner, though, was a place to hang out, and Sheyenne likes it when we go out on lunch dates. Strolling down the sidewalk toward the Diner, we free-associated. Sheyenne wore a bright smile as always, and those blue eyes could make a man's heart stop beating, or start beating, depending on which condition he started from.

I wondered aloud that maybe the Big Uneasy had made the Grinch manifest as well, but Sheyenne doubted he'd reached a worldwide cultural status similar to vampires or St. Nick. I disagreed, because I had grown up on the Grinch; still, I conceded that he seemed too obvious a cartoon villain.

I then postulated that the perpetrator could be a Lorax with self-esteem issues, upset that Arbor Day didn't have the stature of Christmas, Hanukkah, Thanksgiving, New Years ... or even Kwanzaa, for that matter. I didn't know if Loraxes were real, either. I seemed to be in a Seussian rut.

A light dusting of snow came down, reminding me that I had to find Santa's list before Christmas Eve, or he would suffer a worldwide toy-distribution crisis. Festive decorations were already strung up in the streets of the Quarter: barbed-wire tinsel looped along windowpanes and awnings, colorful wreaths hung from nooses on gallows lampposts.

Before we reached the Diner, Sheyenne and I stopped on the street where crowds had gathered and traffic halted for an early holiday parade. And it sure wasn't the type hosted by Macy's.

Elves capered and danced at the front of the parade, diminutive creatures dressed in pointed floppy caps and bright red outfits trimmed with white flocking. The costumes resembled a traditional Santa's elf suit, but these were cheap knockoffs that fit poorly with seams showing and with some of the white trim missing.

These elves were not the cute, smiling, industrious workers who stocked Santa's shelves and made the North Pole a cheery, if formerly imaginary, place. No, these elves came from the G-side of the family, having more in common with gremlins, goblins, and gnomes—pointy, stretched-out features, gray skin, and long ears that looked as if they had gotten caught in industrial picking machinery. When they smiled like good elves should, they showed alarmingly pointed teeth.

Behind the prancing elves came a bizarre motorized sleigh crawling along at pedestrian speed so everyone on the sidewalk had an appropriate opportunity to wave. Palm trees adorned the back of the sleigh. On a big wicker chair sat an elf with all the usual elf features (from the G-side of the family), but he wore a white rhinestone-studded jacket, trimmed in Christmasy green and red. He had slicked-back black hair, sideburns that extended halfway down his pointed chin, big garish sunglasses, and oddly out-of-place blue suede shoes.

"You've got to be kidding me," I said to Sheyenne.

"He's for real, Beaux. That's Elfis—I've seen his ads. You know, 'Santa Claus is coming to town, but Elfis will get there faster?' He's a celebrity on the cable-access channels."

I'm a decent enough detective, but I can be clueless about pop culture.

Elfis waved at the crowd and picked up a handheld Vegas-style silver microphone. "Thank ya very much. Santa's got competition this year, boys and girls, naturals and unnatural. The holidays should be for everybody, not just kids who pass some arbitrary naughty-or-nice test. Even naughty kids deserve presents, don't they?"

From the sidewalk crowds, a smattering of natural and unnatural children cheered—kids who knew they were included in the Naughty column, no doubt.

"Santa Claus has had a monopoly on the Christmas season for far too long —but I intend to undercut his position. Elfis Industries has wider distribution, more fairness, and less discrimination. More transparency in holiday gift-giving! We're going to expose all those 'secret admirer' gifts for what they are. And no more bribery with milk and cookies. *Everyone* deserves a present, and I'm the one to give it to them. It's time to put the kitsch back into Christmas!"

His elves began handing out candy canes, traditional red-and-white striped ones, blood-red ones, and black ones. A witch dressed in a midnight-blue gown and pointy cap stood by her young son who looked as if he might grow up to be a powerful necromancer. The boy ran forward to take a black candy cane, but his mother scolded him. "I told you not to take candy from strangers!"

The boy pouted. "He's not a stranger, Mom—that's *Elfis!*"

"Oh," the witch said, and handed him back the cane.

The motorized sleigh rolled by, with Elfis in his sequins and sunglasses waving from under his palm trees. He called out, "Who needs the cold? I have nightmares about a white Christmas! Let it snow, let it snow, let it snow—but somewhere far away! Stick with me, and the holidays will have a warm and sunny glow."

After the parade passed, Sheyenne leaned close to me. "So that's why Santa is so worried. He's got competition this year. And if his rival does a better job satisfying the customers ..."

"Then Santa Claus won't be coming to town anymore," I said. "We might have our first suspect. Elfis has a motive to sabotage Santa's work. I better go talk to him and find out if his intentions really are as pure as new fallen snow."

I could tell this case was going to spell T-R-O-U-B-L-E.

4

After Sheyenne and I had a quick lunch at the diner (pink slime was on special), I went off to continue my investigation.

The headquarters for the competitive holiday operation was an office building in front of a fenced compound of airplane-hangar-sized structures, no doubt where Elfis manufactured and stored all the toys he planned to distribute ahead of his business rival. According to Sheyenne, Elfis's ads promised delivery by Christmas Eve Eve.

The sign at the front entrance had giant letters painted like candy canes, surrounded by yellow suns: "North Pole South: We're Better Because We're Closer to the Equator." Around the doorway was strewn blue sand or fake snow, which seemed incongruous ... until I remembered "Blue Christmas."

When I entered the front door of North Pole South, I heard many busy bodies working in the back, but the reception counter was empty except for a fist-sized fake rock sitting on top of an index card that said "Ring bell for service." I picked up the stone and realized it was hollow. When I shook it, a tinkling chime rang out.

A female elf receptionist scurried out of the back, smiling sweetly with her pinched face. "I see you found our Jingle-Bell Rock," she snickered. "Very clever, don't you think? Elfis came up with it himself." She shuffled papers and handed me a temporary-employment application. "Looking for part-time holiday work? Many positions available."

I shook snow from the brim of my fedora. "That would be a conflict of interest. I've been retained by Santa Claus."

The receptionist's eyebrows rose. "I'll let Elfis know you're here." She took back the Jingle-Bell Rock and punched an extension on her phone. "He told us to expect an overture from Mr. Claus."

"Overture?" I asked. "I can barely hum a tune."

Elfis agreed to see me, probably out of curiosity; at least it got me through the door.

The chief elf's back office was bright and stiflingly hot. A large tropical mural covered the far wall. Wearing only a towel around his waist, Elfis lay back on a chaise lounge under a pair of heat lamps that could have been used to keep food warm in a restaurant. Standing on either side, a pair of Egyptian mummies gently fanned him with palm fronds.

Elfis lifted his sunglasses and sat up to regard me. "Dan Chambeaux, Private Investigator ... that seems an odd choice for Santa, but I knew he'd send a representative before long. He has no option but to open negotiations. I suppose he wants to suggest some kind of merger and keep a token title for himself? Frankly I'd rather just buy his operations outright."

He waved for the mummies to back away. "Would you like some refreshment? I can get one of my boys to make you a mai tai or piña colada. Or, if you want to be more traditional, I have chestnuts roasting on an open fire."

Chestnuts weren't the only things roasting. "I'm surprised you keep it so hot in here," I said, tugging at my collar—and zombies don't perspire.

Elfis explained, "I want to change the paradigm of the holiday season. It's too cold, too snowy, too wintry. You really think shepherds prefer to watch their flocks in the snow? They'd rather be skiing. And if I want something frozen, I order a frozen margarita." He laughed, but it sounded more like heh-heh-heh than ho-ho-ho.

"Now then, let's talk about sending old Saint Nick into retirement. Here's my offer: I take over all his operations, but I let him keep his North Pole annex. He and Mrs. Claus get a nice pension, run their bed-and-breakfast, maybe do a few public appearances for old times sake, but I license his likeness and the brand. I'm dreaming of a profitable Christmas."

"There's been a misunderstanding, Mr. Elfis. That's not why I'm here."

The elf slicked back his hair, adjusted his position on the chaise lounge. The mummies came forward again to fan him vigorously with the palm fronds. "Well, then, I'm all ears."

"Santa Claus hired me as a detective because something very valuable was stolen from him."

Elfis seemed completely uninterested. "Really? And what would old St. Nick find valuable? Can't he just wiggle his nose and make another of whatever it was?"

"It's more of a matter of administrative records gone missing," I said. "I'm investigating the theft."

Elfis snickered. "You must mean his list. Anal-retentive, if you ask me." He slid his sunglasses back down on his face, scratched his sideburns. "And you think I had something to do with it? Why in the world would I need a list like that? I explicitly *don't* discriminate. I give presents to all kids, without scoring them on social behavior. What gives Santa the right to make a subjective decision about who's Naughty and Nice? Judgmental jerk, if you ask me." He sniffed. "I plan to take discrimination out of Christmas gift-giving, make it equal for all. What would be my motive for stealing the list?"

I did have a theory. "You'd hamstring Santa's activities, make him look incompetent, while gaining brownie points for yourself."

"I don't have brownies, Mr. Chambeaux. I have elves. There's a difference."

"That doesn't address my theory."

"Look around you, Mr. Chambeaux. I'm sabotaging Santa's work by perfectly traditional means—undercutting prices, faster distribution, more transparency in my operations. I don't need a list for that."

One of the mummies served him a cool drink in a hollowed pineapple, complete with a colorful umbrella. "Thank ya very much." Elfis took a long refreshing sip. "Tell Santa if he wants to come to terms, I'm having a holiday special. His decision. Either way, it's time he faced some competition."

Elfis reached down beside his chaise lounge and pulled out a baseball-sized knot of thorny leaves, like a wadded tumbleweed studded with berries. "Here, Mr. Chambeaux—have a free sample. Part of my effort to put the kitsch back into Christmas."

He tossed it to me, and I caught it. "What's this?"

"Our new McMistletoe. Cheaper to manufacture, no preservatives needed, non-poisonous, non-habit-forming." He spoke at such a fast pace that my ears could barely keep up. "It's not intended to diagnose, prevent, treat, or cure any disease. These claims have not been evaluated by the FDA." He grinned. "But our McMistletoe is just as effective as real mistletoe. Try it out, you'll see."

I pocketed the mistletoe in my jacket's other pocket, because it didn't seem right to tuck it beside the jingle bell that Santa Claus had given me. "I'll try it," I said, though I doubted Sheyenne would be impressed.

5

I was already disturbed about the missing children McGoo was investigating, but I didn't see the actual pain until the Tannenbaums came into our offices.

Mrs. Tannenbaum buried her face in her husband's broad chest. "Our baby boy!"

Both of them were werewolves—the Monthly variety, so they passed for normal except on full-moon nights. They seemed like a nice couple with modest lives, middle-income jobs, probably had a home that was not extravagant but one they were proud of.

Robin hurried forward to comfort them. "Tell us what happened."

Mr. Tannenbaum pulled a wallet from his pocket and showed us a snapshot. "This is our son Buddy." The kid was of the full-furred persuasion, the type of werewolf who maintained a long muzzle, sharp fangs, moist black nose, and facial fur throughout the month.

"That's his school portrait," Mrs. Tannenbaum said with a sniff. "He was just about to graduate sixth grade." Sheyenne flitted in with a tissue for the grieving woman.

I studied the snapshot. Buddy Tannenbaum's black lips were curled in what I assumed was a smile, but might have been a snarl. What kid didn't make a goofy face when sitting for a school portrait? "Not much family resemblance. Adopted?"

Mrs. Tannenbaum snuffled loudly. "He came from an abused home, and we took him in. Poor Buddy! We wanted to show him all the love and affection he deserved. But one day after school, he didn't come home to do his chores."

Her husband continued, "He often gets preoccupied with friends—he has a strong social life. And what's a chore or two around the house? No need to bother the boy with them. I can do the vacuuming and take out the garbage while my wife cooks dinner."

"On the night he disappeared, I made a fleshloaf with tomato sauce and onions. Buddy's favorite!" Mrs. Tannenbaum wailed, which came out as a trailing howl. "We had to eat it ourselves. We had leftovers for two days."

"Two days? Your son vanished and you didn't report it for two days?" Robin shot me a look, and I saw that furrow of concern on her brow.

"We thought he might be staying at a friend's house," said Mr. Tannenbaum. "He sometimes does that. We try not to be overprotective. A boy needs his space and ... a wolf has to run free."

"Can you find him?" Mrs. Tannenbaum said. "We didn't want to go to the police because ... because we want to keep his record clean. He's going to go to college someday, and it's really a private matter."

"You can count on our discretion, Mr. and Mrs. Tannenbaum." I doubted Buddy's disappearance was unrelated to the other children who had vanished.

"Can you give us the names of his friends, or places where he liked to spend time?" Robin asked.

Mrs. Tannenbaum considered. "He likes to hang out at the comic-book shop. Just Dug Up Collectibles, I think it's called."

"I know the place," I said. "I've been there."

In a fit of nostalgia, I had gone in to browse some of the old comics I'd bought and guarded so lovingly when I was a kid. One day, while tidying up my room, my mom gave them all to a thrift shop, and they sold for a nickel apiece before I could run down there to save them. A few months ago, when I looked in Just Dug Up Collectibles and saw the outrageous prices those issues were now selling for, I left the shop in despair and never went back....

"Is there anything else I should know? Anything that might help?"

The Tannenbaums looked at each other, as if uncomfortable, hesitant, then both shook their heads.

Sheyenne whisked in and made several color photocopies of Buddy's photo before returning the snapshot to Mr. Tannenbaum, who lovingly tucked it back into his wallet. "I'll also submit this to the Talbot & Knowles blood bars," Sheyenne suggested. "They can include it with the other photos of missing children."

Mr. Tannenbaum looked uncomfortable. "I'd prefer to keep this out of the public eye."

"We already talked to the blood bars," snuffled Mrs. Tannenbaum. "They said they were overbooked for the next two months until ... until ..." She began sobbing.

Mr. Tannenbaum completed the sentence. "Until Christmas." He patted his wife on the shoulder. "Please find him soon, Mr. Chambeaux. We have very important Hanukkah traditions, and Winter Solstice, too."

She sniffled again. "The holidays just won't be the same without our dear Buddy. Please find him, Mr. Chambeaux. Such a dear, dear sweet boy."

6

"That kid is an unholy terror!" said Adric the comic-shop owner. He barely glanced at the picture of Buddy Tannenbaum. "He and his friends are monsters—and I don't mean that in a good way."

The wall behind the counter was plastered with autographed 8 × 10s of Adric posing with D-list celebrities. He was a gray-skinned, pot-bellied zombie, not nearly as well-preserved as the special variant-cover issues he kept bagged-and-boarded on high shelves. His complexion showed some signs of putrescence as well as fresh acne, which made him doubly unfortunate; although the undead suffer from numerous physical maladies, few are afflicted by zits.

Adric wore a powder-blue *Star Wars* T-shirt with R2-D2 and C-3PO on the front, and it was much too small for him. I deduced that he'd bought the shirt when he saw *Star Wars* first run in theaters; in the years since, his body had enlarged considerably, though he probably told himself that the shirt had shrunk.

Adric handed me back the photo. "That kid and his friends are always in here stealing things, vandalizing, harassing customers, and of course never buying anything. A bunch of deadbeats and undeadbeats."

I frowned. It seemed Buddy Tannenbaum was not the upstanding young werewolf his parents imagined him to be. "He's gone missing. When was the last time you saw him?"

He snorted. "I kicked out the whole wild bunch two weeks ago—caught them shoplifting one time too many."

I had another thought. "So, does that mean you keep a list of, say, who's naughty and who's nice?"

"Nah, this is a comic store. We get all kinds in here. That Buddy Tannenbaum and his friends, though—they'd definitely go in the Naughty column."

As he talked, Adric used a box-cutter to slice open a cardboard case of new arrivals like an eager coroner working on his favorite autopsy. He opened the flaps and began pulling out shrink-wrapped Christmas ornaments, clumsy-looking figurines of werewolves, vampires, scaly demons.

Frowning in disgust, he held up a crudely painted vampire with red marks smeared across his face. "Look at these! My customers want quality. The catalog said they're hand-painted, but this looks like it was finger-painted, or *claw*-painted." He shook his head. "Maybe even *flipper*-painted."

Adric dug into the box, pulled out a larger figure, a well-muscled werewolf in a cop uniform, holding an enormous Magnum pistol. "Does this look like Hairy Harry to you?" The rogue lycanthropic cop from the UQPD was something of a folk hero, even though he'd retired from the force.

"I wouldn't pay a premium for it," I said. I noticed the figures were labeled *Elfis Originals! Collect Them All!*

Adric kept pulling figurines out of the packaging, then rolled his eyes as he lifted out six genuine Elfis figurines, each wearing a white sequin jacket, brushed-back black hair and sideburns, and big sunglasses. "What? I only ordered one of these."

Next, he removed a larger box showing a scaled aquatic gill-man labeled "Special Limited Edition Creature! (Comes with free lagoon!)." With his stiff zombie fingers, Adric pried open the package, removed the scaly figurine along with a tiny black plastic basin. Apparently, the user was supposed to fill it with water.

"Special Edition? Ridiculous! Look at this: 'Limited to 1,000,000 Units.' How the hell does that make it *collectible?* I'll be lucky to sell six ... well, five, because I'll keep one for myself."

I tried to get back to the reason I'd come there. "Have you seen any of Buddy's buddies? Anyone I could talk to? His parents are distraught."

"No, and good riddance. Maybe they all ran off to join the vampire circus." Adric continued setting out the Elfis Originals holiday ornaments. "Mark my words, his parents will have a lot more silent nights this way. Just imagine what a handful that werewolf kid is gonna be when he hits his teenage years and hormones kick in."

He looked up at where two young zombies were pawing over back issues of *The Crypt-Keeper's Funniest Capers*. The zombie teens had their mouths open and they moaned in laughter at the panels.

Adric yelled, "Hey, you! Be careful with those—you get decaying flesh on any of the pages, you bought it."

The zombies looked up at him, moaned, then went back to the comics, noticeably exercising greater care.

I picked up a fine-print catalog listing of the Elfis Originals ornaments and collectibles and pocketed it for future reference. I thanked Adric and left.

7

When Santa Claus returned to our offices, he looked even more anxious than before. His face was sallow, almost jaundiced; his flowing white beard looked scraggly, with a thin brownish stain from where he'd been hitting the pipe a little too often. He had lost enough weight that his red jacket was gathered in folds around his waist with his wide black belt cinched tighter. I saw that he'd even punched a new hole.

"Usually when I visit, people set out milk and cookies for me." He sounded disappointed, beaten down. "I'll be glad to get back to running the bed-and-breakfast, but I have my duties first. I can't do my rounds without that list of Naughty and Nice." He slumped into a chair beside Sheyenne's desk and let out a sigh. "I tried to write a new one from memory, but my mind isn't what it used to be—too many bitter cold nights out in a reindeer-powered sleigh. I won't kid you, Christmas Eve is a hard night—a real nut-cracker. After it's over, I crawl into bed and sleep for a week."

"My accountant says the same thing about Tax Day," I told him.

Santa adjusted his floppy red cap. "I haven't heard you jingle my bell, and time is running out. It's beginning to look a lot like a screwed-up Christmas."

"I've been investigating," I reassured him. "Particularly your rival Elfis. He makes no secret of the fact that he wants to take you out, but he insists he doesn't need your list to do it. What can you tell me about him?"

Santa's face fell, as if his heart had shrunk three sizes that day. "That elf deserves a lump of coal in his stocking on Christmas morning. Unfair business practices, inferior materials—do you know that his silver bells are made of cheap aluminum?" He frowned again, let out another sigh. "I try not to think ill of people, but I'd like to take a thick candy cane and go thumpety-thump-thump on his head. He's ruining traditions by taking away the incentive for children to be Nice. Just look at the rude manners in chat rooms on the internet."

My heart went out to him. "I'm looking into his North Pole South operations, and Robin is studying his business practices. I haven't found any evidence that he arranged to steal your Naughty and Nice list, but I'll keep digging."

After rummaging around in the kitchen, Sheyenne flitted into the main room, carrying a plate with three stale chocolate-chip cookies and a glass of milk. "Look what I found for you, Santa!"

He brightened. "'Tis the season to be jolly—so I'll try my best." He pulled a paper ticket from the pocket of his red jacket. "Could you validate this for me? I've got my reindeer and sleigh parked on the roof."

"Of course," Sheyenne said, and stamped his parking ticket.

Santa took the rest of the cookies "for the reindeer" and slipped through the door just as Mr. and Mrs. Tannenbaum hurried in. They looked anxious, and my heart sank, wondering how I was going to tell them that their darling Buddy wasn't the sugarplum they believed him to be. If the young werewolf was getting into so much trouble, how could the parents not know? Were they willfully oblivious to the fact that their angel came straight from the dark side?

"We weren't entirely honest with you," Mrs. Tannenbaum said, then looked away shyly. "We have something else that might help."

Her husband said, "I convinced my wife that we needed to give you every detail if we want our Buddy back. Our son is more important than our shame and embarrassment."

"We thought you might be able to solve the case without it, and then we wouldn't have to admit … admit—" Mrs. Tannenbaum's lower lip quivered. Her eyes flashed golden, and I could see a hint of werewolf coming to the fore.

"Buddy's given us difficulties before," Mr. Tannenbaum admitted. "He's an unruly kid. I think it comes from his full-fur blood. Trouble in school, trouble with vandalism. He's even run away from home a few times."

"But he always comes back," Mrs. Tannenbaum interjected. "He's a good boy at heart."

I asked, "Do you think there's any possibility that he's just run off again?"

Both Tannenbaums shook their heads. "Not so close to Christmas. He would have waited to get his toys first. He's a troublemaker, but he's a greedy troublemaker."

I didn't know if that was the best kind or the worst kind. "The information doesn't help a great deal at the moment, but I'll keep asking around."

The Tannenbaums looked at each other. "Oh, that's not what we meant to tell you, Mr. Chambeaux. We were reluctant to say anything about what we did because … because, well, it's not exactly legal."

That's never a good phrase to include in a sentence. I braced myself.

"We had to do something because Buddy ran away so often. So, the last time we took him in to the vet …" Mrs. Tannenbaum swallowed hard, then lowered her voice. "We had a tracking chip implanted in the base of his skull. Nothing anyone would notice, mind you, but … just in case."

I perked up. "A tracking device? Then we can pinpoint his location right away!"

"Yes," said Mrs. Tannenbaum. "Do you think that might help you find him?"

I slapped my forehead, and it made a hollow popping sound from the bullet hole there. "The cases don't solve themselves," I said, "but I do need all the information."

"The tracking signal has a very limited range," Mr. Tannenbaum said. "Quite discreet, but not terribly useful. Still, if you get close enough …"

The Tannenbaums looked sheepish after they gave me the secret frequency and serial number of the tracker. "Just bring our little boy home, please? That would be the best present we ever had."

8

When we began our search, I decided to take police backup—McGoo—just so I could say I was being sensible. I didn't want to go overboard, though, because there was a better-than-even chance Buddy had just run away with his juvenile delinquent unnatural pals. Still, if Buddy's disappearance was connected with the other missing kids, McGoo would want to be along.

Then Robin insisted on joining us. With such a three-pronged approach, how could we not be prepared to solve any problem?

She had frowned in disapproval when she heard about the implanted tracker chip, claiming that it violated the civil rights of an underage werewolf. But McGoo had seen enough troublemakers in his work, and he was more inclined to try the "terrified straight" approach. Robin finally conceded that if the tracker meant we could reunite the full-time fuzzy kid with his once-a-month fuzzy parents, then all was for the best.

With the tracker's frequency and serial number, Robin downloaded a free but highly rated Track Werewolf app for her smartphone. She bundled up in a wool coat, and we all set off into the snowy night to find Buddy, leaving Sheyenne in charge of the office.

We wandered around the Quarter for a frustrating hour, following false signals (a garage-door opener and a universal TV remote control). I was beginning to think that we might not pick up the tracker's limited-range signal until after we had already found the subject in question. We were lost and frustrated; what had seemed to be an easy solution was turning out to be a headache and a waste of time.

Then Sheyenne called us and saved the day. She had found an update for the Track Werewolf app, which dealt with certain bugs and user issues and increased sensitivity. Once Robin installed the update, we found a strong signal. We were closer than we thought.

The signal led us straight to the tall smokestacks and gigantic toy warehouses behind Elfis's North Pole South complex.

Holding her phone, Robin took the lead, guiding us along the chain-link fence to the back service entrance of the gigantic manufacturing warehouses. The temperature was dropping, and fluffy snowflakes drifted down.

Not a creature was stirring, not even the ones that usually stirred at that time of night.

Approaching the back guard gate, we found two burly golems wearing security guard uniforms. Their clay bodies were stiff and hardening in the cold, but one perked up. "Do you hear what I hear?"

The other said, "Do you see what I see?"

Now alert, the golems prepared to block our way, both of them focusing on McGoo's uniform, the dark blue police shirt, trousers, and cap. "That looks good on you," said one of the golems.

"We both wanted to be cops, but couldn't pass the tests," the other explained.

I knew why, but I didn't embarrass them by pointing out the reason.

McGoo said, "We're searching for a missing child, and we have reason to believe he's inside one of the warehouses." He held out a copy of Buddy's picture.

"Kids just can't stay away from toys," said the first golem.

Robin held up her smartphone, showing the app. "And we have electronic evidence he's in there."

The golems were again intrigued. "Is that phone one of the new models?"

The other said, "Does it have Angry Vultures on it? Or Curses with Friends?"

I knew if the golems started playing games on Robin's phone we would never get past the gate. "We need to have a look, bring that boy back to his parents."

The first golem had a stony expression on his clay face. "Sorry. We can't let you inside. Elfis is very strict."

The other golem looked intimidated. "He sees you when you're sleeping, he knows when you're awake, he knows when you've been bad or good." In tandem, they shook their smooth clay heads and pointed upward. "Security cameras."

Time for Plan B. I removed a folded sheet of paper from the inside pocket of my jacket and showed it to the two golems. "We have a duly authorized search warrant to enter the premises, signed by Judge Hawkins herself. This grants us unfettered access to all parts of the North Pole South warehouses so we can find and rescue the young man."

The first golem guard took the sheet of paper and studied it intently, while Robin shot me a questioning glance. She craned her neck to see what the guards were looking at. McGoo could barely keep the smile off his face.

The other golem took the sheet from his partner; they both had frowns on their clay faces. "All right then. We're security guards, sworn to uphold the law." They opened the chain-link gate for us. "Go on inside. I hope you find what you're looking for."

Robin was perplexed, but she glanced down at the blinking light on her Track Werewolf app. Buddy was definitely close, inside the big factory building ahead of us. With his best I'm-an-authority-figure gait, McGoo marched away from the guard golems. Robin hurried alongside me. When we were out of earshot, she asked, "What was that all about? When did you get a search warrant?"

"It wasn't a search warrant," I said. "It's the fine-print listing of Elfis Originals I took from Just Dug Up Collectibles."

McGoo worked at the warehouse door; it was unlocked. "Golems can't read," he said. "At least most of them can't. That's why they couldn't pass their UQ Police Department exams. Good work, Shamble."

Robin was astonished. "Then we got in here under false pretenses, and I have real ethical problems with that. We're trespassing."

"We're rescuing a missing child," I said. My boundaries were a little more blurred than Robin's, but I did manage to get things done.

Robin was about to continue her objections when McGoo opened the loading dock door. The dark, noisy factory hangar was worse than the worst New Year's Day hangover. It was a true holiday of horrors.

9

I doubted children opening their gifts on the morning of Christmas Eve Eve (if Elfis and his minions delivered on time, as promised) would want to know where their presents really came from.

We were seeing the ugly side of holiday cheer: appalling labor conditions, thick smoke, clanging hammers, grinding gears, and jets of steam venting from pressure valves. Foul water trickled out of rusty pipes overhead. A labyrinth of rattling conveyor belts rolled toys along to packaging lines. Sparks flew and blazing fires roared out of open furnaces fed with black coal that poured from supply hoppers in the ceiling. A separate set of conveyors dumped defective metal toys into a smoldering furnace. It was as if the Island of Misfit Toys had an active volcano.

Robin looked around in horror, shocked by what she saw. McGoo's face was stormy with anger.

Most appalling of all, though, were the kids shackled to the assembly line, hunched over the conveyor belts, red-eyed, dirt-smeared, waifish. They toiled at assembling dolls, painting action figures, stuffing collectibles into boxes. There were werewolves, zombies, ghouls, even human children, all looking dejected and haggard.

As I scanned the faces, I recognized many of the kids featured on the Have You Seen Me? pictures from the Talbot & Knowles blood bars. I saw one gray-furred werewolf boy, mangy and yet somehow still cute, chained to a station where he was applying black button eyes onto Raggedy Ann dolls. Either he was confused by the instructions, or the dolls catered to an entirely different type of unnatural, because he sewed three eyes on each doll.

"That's Buddy Tannenbaum!" I said.

The boy heard me even over the factory din. He turned, his tongue lolling out of his mouth, and his eyes lit up upon seeing us. He dropped the doll onto the dirty factory floor and leaped toward us, but was brought up short by silver shackles that bound his wrist and ankle.

"I'll be good! I promise!" he yelped. "I won't be naughty anymore. I don't want to be on the list!"

Robin was ahead of us, grim and determined. "We'll get you out of here, Buddy. Your parents hired us to find you."

"My mom and dad? But Elfis said they didn't love me anymore."

"Of course they love you," Robin said. "Parents love even naughty kids."

A steam whistle blew. More coal dumped out of the feeding hoppers, and the furnace burned brighter.

Then the elves came—evil elves, and ugly enough that they might have been disowned by even the G-side of the family. They carried cattle prods painted like cheery candy canes; others brandished icicle spears that dripped in the intense heat of the factory floor.

McGoo and I drew our guns and stood next to Robin. The ten elves closing in didn't look afraid of us at all. Too late, I realized that they were just a distraction.

Two other hench-elves stood up from behind the conveyor belt and hurled snowballs at us—icy snowballs with rocks in the middle. Cheater snowballs. (I did say they were evil elves.) Their aim was supernaturally true, and with one hail of hard snowballs, they knocked the guns out of our hands.

Then the hench-elves closed in, wielding icicle spears and candy-cane cattle prods. They overpowered us, shoved us to the factory floor, and used tough strands of satin ribbon to bind our wrists. We were going to have a black-and-blue Christmas. An evil elf even slapped a coordinating stick-on bow on each of us before they herded us toward the back of the factory.

"Elfis is going to want to see you," said one of the guards.

"Oh, by gosh, by golly, that was on my Christmas wish list," I said, which earned me a jab from one of the cattle prods. Since I'm a zombie, it takes a lot to shock me, but the experience was still unpleasant. I was more worried about McGoo and Robin, who could indeed be permanently damaged.

Elfis was at a raised supervisor's station near the warmth of the big furnace, sitting on a high director's chair with a small worktable beside him. Black dust from the coal hoppers left a gritty film on everything, but somehow it didn't affect his white sequined jacket or his blue suede shoes. He was perusing a rolled parchment filled with names—countless names, sorted into two columns, one marked N and the other one marked N. He muttered to himself as he used a large goose quill pen to check off names.

"Naughty ... yes, got that one. Naughty ... yes. Naughty ... we have a very high success rate." Then he sneered at a line, crossed it out vigorously with the nib of his quill pen. "Somebody slipped up—this kid's in the Nice column! People tend to notice when *nice* kids go missing." A supervisor hench-elf scurried off to rectify the error.

Elfis picked up a bullhorn and began shouting toward the factory floor. "Listen up, kiddies! I have plenty more applicants to choose from, so if you want to be promoted in my criminal organization, you've got to produce, produce, *produce!* Only the best can survive this boot camp—also known as the Holiday Season! If you work hard, you'll be real henchmen by Easter." Elfis then started to laugh. "We're going to put that damned bunny out of business, too!"

He slid his sunglasses up on the bridge of his narrow nose as his fiendish hench-elves pushed us forward. He seemed surprised to see us. "Mr. Chambeaux and friends—have you come to negotiate on Santa's behalf again? Well, it's too late. I've already got the holidays sewn up in a body bag, and now you'll never stop me."

When all else fails, when things look grimmest, I like to state the obvious. It puts villains off guard and usually gets them talking—too much. "You said you didn't have Santa's list of Naughty and Nice. That was dishonest."

He held up a long finger. "No, that was *misleading*. I said I didn't steal the list in order to earn brownie points or to make Santa look incompetent. I stole it strictly for my own purposes." Elfis waved the parchment, showing us the long list of names. "It's a recruitment tool, like a screening folder for job applicants. Santa already identified the *naughty* children for me, the ones suitable to become part of my operation."

"But you put them to work as slave labor," Robin said.

Elfis shrugged. "Well, they are naughty. Even criminals need to know the consequences of their actions. You do the crime, you pay the time. Community service for *my* community."

I struggled against the satin ribbons binding my wrists. It reminded me of my childhood, trying to snap the ribbons so I could open my presents. Now, as then, the ribbon had supernatural strength.

Elfis leaned forward, opening both of his hands to warm them at the nearby furnace. The conveyor belt continued to clatter, dumping defective toys into it, plastic ones as well as metal. "It's so nice to be warm for a change. And you three will be all toasty, too. I'm afraid I can't allow my plans to be foiled—or tinseled. Into the furnace with them!"

The hench-elves swept forward like a blizzard of evil. Even though I'm a zombie, I had no desire to be cremated. And speaking for my two human friends, I knew that neither Robin nor McGoo wanted to tour the interior of the furnace either. I had to get us out of there.

Zombies, for all of our fragile bodies and flesh that's prone to decay, have very strong teeth. Some zombies use them for ripping into flesh and bone; now I discovered that my teeth were excellent at cutting Christmas ribbon. I tore into my colorful satin bindings, snapped the ribbon—and I was free.

But I couldn't fight all those armed hench-elves. Thinking of only one thing that might save us, I jammed my hand into my jacket pocket and grabbed the loop attached to the emergency jingle bell.

It wasn't much of a jing-jing-jingle—but it was enough to summon Old Kris Kringle.

The flames in the furnace brightened, then made a coughing sound. Black smoke swirled out, and with a whoosh of hot air Santa Claus slipped down the smokestack and made his dramatic entrance. The conveyor belt came to a screeching halt as the jolly guy in the magic red suit (which also proved to be non-flammable) emerged from the furnace like something out of *The Lord of the Rings*. He planted his gloved hands on his hips and bellowed, "Ho-ho-ho! Who's been a naughty boy?"

Elfis nearly jumped out of his skin and scrambled down from the director's chair so rapidly that his sunglasses clattered on the floor. With the empty cloth sack over his shoulder, Santa stalked forward like an avenging angel—and not the type that goes on top of a Christmas tree. He spotted his lengthy rolled-up list on the worktable and seized it, holding it up like a baton. "You have gone too far, Elfis. And now you'd better cry, because Santa Claus is coming to get you."

The hench-elves were panicked. They dropped their candy-cane cattle prods and icicle spears and cowered. Their teeth chattered as if they had gone caroling naked on a cold winter's night and no one was offering wassail, or even hot cocoa.

Elfis tried to run, but Santa quickly caught up with him. I couldn't believe how fast the old bearded guy could move, but he had to have a secret power if he could hit millions of households around the world in a single night.

McGoo held up his bound wrists for me to bite the ribbons. Now *that* was showing a measure of trust! "Good plan, Shamble."

"I call it Santa ex-Machina." I picked bright green satin out of my teeth, then turned to free Robin as well.

Santa had cornered Elfis by the big coal hoppers, and the evil elf had no place to go. Santa didn't need any help, but I was part of this, too—and I had a bone to pick with anybody who wanted to throw me and my friends into a furnace.

Next to me, one of the cowering hench-elves still had a sack filled with the icy rock-filled snowballs. I grabbed one and hurled it with perfect aim, proving that not all zombies are disoriented and uncoordinated. My snowball shot struck the release latch on the coal hopper just above Elfis's head. The trap dropped open, and Elfis looked up just in time to see a black avalanche dump down on him. He was buried under lumps of coal.

Robin, McGoo, and I rushed over to Santa, who gazed with satisfaction at the mound in front of him. "Coal is what Elfis deserved ... although I'd hoped he would turn his life around if given the chance. Such a disappointment."

"You knew Elfis beforehand?" I asked.

Santa nodded. "He was one of my toy laborers, assigned to my workshop for community service, but he escaped, broke the rules of his North Pole parole. I was going to report him, but not until after the holiday season was over. It's a busy time of the year, you know."

We heard a groan, then a stirring. We moved the coal blocks away to reveal an Elfis now entirely covered in black dust. He plucked in dismay at his ruined jacket. "I guess I won't be having a *white* Christmas."

Santa unslung the sack from his shoulder, tugged it open, and strode forward. "Here comes Santa Claus."

Elvis scrambled backward when he saw the yawning sack. "No, Santa! Please! No!"

"Naughty children get what they deserve." Santa snatched Elfis, stuffed him into the sack, and cinched the opening shut. The captive kept squirming, but could not get out. Santa tucked his rolled up Naughty and Nice list under one arm. "Thank you all. I'll start checking these names, see who deserves to be sentenced to the North Pole for a few years."

"*Sentenced* to the North Pole?" Robin said.

"Oh-ho-ho, this list doesn't just show me who gets presents and who doesn't. The naughtiest of the naughty have to help me spread holiday cheer. Parents write me, too, you know. 'Dear Santa, please help me with my child who keeps acting out.' We have a community-service program up at the Pole, where naughty children can learn good behavior by doing good works." He had a twinkle in his eye. "There's a long waiting list, but our success rate is remarkable."

"Except for Elfis," I said.

"Some nuts are harder to crack than others, but a few days of shoveling out the reindeer stables usually makes them a little more cooperative."

Moving with supernaturally swift footsteps, Santa stalked around the factory floor, grabbing the cowering hench-elves one by one and stuffing them into his sack, which was obviously much larger inside than it was on the outside. It needed to be. How else could it hold a world's worth of toys?

With the bulging, squirming load over his shoulder, he turned to Robin, McGoo, and me. "I'll let you free the children." He turned to the shackled waifs on the now-still production lines. "Ho-ho-ho! Have you all learned to be nice instead of naughty?"

A chorus of the enslaved kids affirmed that they had indeed learned their lessons. Some, including Buddy, even volunteered to do community-service work up at the North Pole—after they recovered back home with their loving families.

Santa went to the coal furnace, shifted his heavy sack. "I won't forget you on Christmas morning, Mr. Chambeaux. Or you either, Ms. Deyer, or Officer McGoohan. And now, Merry Christmas to all, and to all a good"—he pushed down his black glove so he could double-check the time on his wristwatch—"a good night." He tossed the squirming bag ahead of him into the mouth of the furnace, touched the side of his nose, and vanished up the smokestack.

"Elfis has left the building," I said. "But the kids are still here."

The three of us spent the better part of an hour freeing the natural and unnatural children from their shackles. When Robin unlocked his chains, Buddy Tannenbaum threw himself into her arms. "Thank you, thank you! Can you take me back to my Mom and Dad now?"

"You'll be home for Christmas," I promised.

For a lot of families, it would be a happy holiday season, except perhaps for those who had ordered their gifts from Elfis Industries and were expecting delivery by Christmas Eve Eve....

While McGoo called for backup to shut down the factory and secure the crime scene, Robin took down names and developed a plan to reunite the kids with their parents. I called the Tannenbaums directly, and Buddy's parents rushed right down. It was a wonderful reunion, with the werewolf kid nuzzling his parents and promising he would be good.

10

It was Christmas morning in the Chambeaux & Deyer offices—and we found surprise gifts waiting for us, brightly wrapped in colorful paper with holly leaves and berries, wreaths, and little snowmen. Since we didn't have a chimney, Santa could only have delivered the presents by breaking-and-entering, but I wasn't going to press charges.

"Looks like Santa was true to his promise," I said.

Grinning, Sheyenne brought the gifts into the conference room. "If you can't trust Santa to keep a promise, who can you trust?"

I hadn't put anything on my wish list, but Santa Claus was supposed to know exactly what a person wanted or needed. I had to admit I was curious.

"You first, Robin." I nudged the thin, rectangular box with her name on it. As a lawyer, Robin tried to remain cool and businesslike, but I could see the sparkle in her brown eyes as she tugged the ribbon aside, and politely worked at the tape. When she couldn't get it unwrapped, she used a letter opener to slash the paper with all the finesse of a well-practiced serial killer.

Inside was a single yellow legal pad and a sharpened No. 2 pencil. Her excitement dimmed, though she remained smiling. "I can certainly use these. And not every lawyer gets to use a pencil and legal pad from Santa himself."

"There's a note," I pointed out.

Robin pulled a slip of holly-fringed stationery from behind the second yellow sheet, skimmed the hand-written note, then read aloud as her smile grew. "'I don't normally give magical gifts—I don't want to establish a present precedent, but I am so grateful for your efforts. After checking my list and the footnotes I made throughout the year, Robin, I know that your work delights you more than anything else. This special legal pad will never run out of paper, and the enchanted pencil will take notes for you so you can have your hands and mind free to concentrate on your client. Ho-ho-ho, best, S.C."

Robin's smile was wide. "I can't wait to try it out!"

Excited, Sheyenne picked up the box with her name on it. She used her poltergeist abilities to undo the bow, pull the ribbon aside, and then, giggling, ripped the wrapping paper to shreds. She opened the box to find an envelope inside—with both our names written on it.

"It's something the two of us can use, Beaux!" With luminous fingers, she opened the flap of the envelope to find an embossed, official-looking certificate inside. "Oh! An all-expense-paid romantic weekend for us at the cozy North Pole Winter Wonderland Bed and Breakfast! Off-season only, it says."

"Now that has definite possibilities," I said, imagining a wonderful time away with my girlfriend. We would have to be creative to overcome the supernatural difficulties that precluded us from touching, but I was up to the challenge.

"Open yours, Dan." Robin handed me the very small box with my name on it.

Judging by the size, I thought it might be a new pair of cufflinks or a tie clip, but who was I to doubt Santa's wisdom or imagination? Zombie fingers are not the most adept at unwrapping small gift boxes, and Santa's elves had used way too much tape, but I managed.

I opened a hinged, velvet-covered box to reveal a small plastic cylinder labeled "Magic Lip Gloss. Use Sparingly." I wasn't disappointed so much as confused, not sure what Santa had been thinking. "Lip gloss?"

Sheyenne made a delighted sound and snatched the tube out of the box. "I think it's for me, Beaux—and that means it's for you." She popped off the cap, extended the lip gloss, and applied it to her widening smile. "A special film for my ghostly lips that might just allow a kiss...."

She leaned closer, but I told her to wait. "Just a minute, let's do this right." I slipped a hand into my jacket pocket and withdrew the wadded and prickly tumbleweed ball of the McMistletoe artificial substitute that Elfis had been trying to bring to market. I raised it up over my head. "This is supposed to be as good as mistletoe."

Robin was skeptical. "With all the quality that we've come to expect from Elfis Industries?"

Sheyenne's lips glistened invitingly from the magic lip gloss. Under the McMistletoe, she came very close, and her ectoplasmic lips brushed against mine. Yes, I definitely felt a warm tingle.

"I think it works just fine," she said.

About the Author

Don't miss the other adventures of Dan Shamble, Zombie P.I.—

Kevin J. Anderson has published more than 190 books, fifty-eight of which have been national or international bestsellers. He has written numerous novels in the Star Wars, X-Files, and Dune universes, as well as the unique Clockwork Angels steampunk trilogy with legendary Rush drummer Neil Peart. His original works include the Saga of Seven Suns series, the Wake the Dragon and Terra Incognita fantasy trilogies, humorous Dan Shamble, Zombie P.I. series and The Dragon Business series.

He has edited numerous anthologies, written comics and games, and composed the lyrics to three rock albums. Anderson is the director of the graduate program in Publishing at Western Colorado University, and he and his wife Rebecca Moesta are the publishers of WordFire Press.

He worked on the recent films Dune: Part One and Part Two from Legendary Entertainment, as well as the forthcoming Dune: Prophecy TV series from MAX, and other films in development, including Persephone and Karousel.

He has 24 million copies in print in thirty-four languages. His most recent novels are *Nether Station*, *Horn Dogs, Persephone,* and *Princess of Dune* (with Brian Herbert).

THE BELLS OF SAINT NICHOLAS

BY JERI SHEPHERD

In a near dystopian future where Saint Nicholas reigns with blood and bells, a team of desperate time travelers journeys into the past to unmake a myth.

THE LAST CHRISTMAS OF Saint Nicholas

Long ago, before reindeer became Nicholas's minion monsters... before his bells rang with their call for blood, there was a final Christmas... one last attempt at joy from the one who had served the season for so long.

Saint Nicholas, immortal steward of the holiday, had walked the earth for centuries. His sleigh once painted joy across the sky, but now cut through clouds like a blade. His sack, which was once filled with wonder, felt heavier each year with disappointment. He had seen countless generations hope... and fail... to have peace on earth and good will toward men. For every child lifted from despair, a thousand more fell to cruelty, hunger, or worse.

And Nicholas had watched what beastly men had made of his holiday. In one city, a fragile truce had been brokered. Songs were sung. Bread was broken. Nicholas had blessed the town with snowfall to blanket their feuds. But in the night, true intentions were revealed... Christmas as a trap to lure enemies. They tied red ribbons around the hands of their opposing combatants and looped them around candy-cane-striped gallows decorated in tinsel and pine boughs. Carols played while people hanged.

Nicholas fled that place and never returned. There was joy to be gifted there. Joy had been weaponized, twisted into nooses, and hung like garland.

Now, finally, the Council of Immortals had granted his petition to retire. He would lay down the mantle. With their approval, Saint Nicholas could select one child in the world to bear the sacred burden—the endless sleigh ride, the immortal heart, and the pulse of Christmas joy that could outshine winter itself. He would bless one child with the bells of Saint Nicholas, once gifted to him by the Nicholas before him, and the Nicholas before him received them in the same manner, all the way back to the first Saint Nicholas gifted the bells by the Council of Immortals. The six Bells of Burden held Peace, Joy, Faith, Hope, Memory, and Immortality. Together, these essences carried Christmas forward in goodness.

It was a bitter winter in Lycia.

The orphanage was nothing more than a leaning skeleton of fire-scorched stone and scavenged timber. Its walls had been patched with the bricks of churches, shops, and homes, the very places burned to ash by a warlord Nicholas had failed to stop. The only survivors were the children, gathered and housed here, among cracked icons and half-melted nativity figurines.

Inside, a few small boys slept huddled together, their breaths clouding the air.

Nicholas entered without sound. His boots left no imprint in the snow, and his breath did not fog in front of him. His robes were no longer red; they had darkened with centuries of soot and sorrow. One sleeve was charred. His gloves had been stitched and re-stitched, the thread unraveled at his palms.

He stopped beside the oldest bunk, where a quiet boy lay curled toward the wall, face relaxed, lips barely parted. This boy, despite all the darkness and cold that life had brought him, was kind-hearted and joyful. He had the hope that the world needed.

Nicholas knelt, placed a hand over the boy's heart, and whispered, "This is not a gift. Not a curse. It is a burden that rings forever."

From beneath his robe, he drew the Bells of Saint Nicholas. Six of them. Silver so tarnished it looked black, their surfaces carved with impossibly small etchings in languages older than scripture. They did not ring exactly. They simply filled the surrounding air with sound. Dissonant. Like a cracked carol, a melody that never found harmony.

He closed his eyes, and drew his final breath as Saint Nicholas, then exhaled it upon the bells.

"May the song of the bells always hold your memories of joy and not those of sorrow and sadness," he blessed the boy, for he knew that—once the bearer was overtaken by negative feelings—the bells would follow.

This was the reason he accepted that his own time as the jolly man had come to an end. Nicholas placed the bells on the boy's chest, just over his heart. He would awaken as the new Saint Nicholas and the Council of Immortals would fill his mind with the knowledge he needed to bring peace and joy to the world for as long as his heart could bear it. The bells hissed as if recognizing the weight of their new master. The boy stirred but did not wake.

And so Nicholas stepped back, turned toward the door, and vanished into the snow without a trace, prepared to retire to The Council of Immortals.

But the child in the bed had not been the one he meant.

In the cold dark corner of the room, the intended Nicholas slept, shivering.

The boy in the bed was also Nicholas, but he bore no gentleness. Nothing of the beauty the immortal saw in the heart he meant to imbue with immortality.

The boy with the bells had forced the quiet, kind Nicholas to trade beds, despite the oncoming cold the boy on the good list had. He said it was only fair and, while the good Nicholas couldn't understand why that might be the case, he gratefully took the draftier bunk, allowing the bully his own bed.

This Nicholas, the angry one, the one now made immortal, had watched his village burn and vowed never to forgive. He would determine the naughty ones going forward. And he would not deliver coal to them. He would burn them upon it.

His eyes snapped open as the bells sang louder in his blood than they ever had in the old saint's.

And, come morning, it was he who rose as the new Saint Nicholas. It was he who walked out into the snow, leaving no footprints.

And, just to cover the metaphorical footprints of his presence, he ensured that the other boy would never wake at all.

New Bethlehem And Old Magic

The air was silent but for the sound of bells, the death toll of an iron carol that sang with the agony of every naughty name it erased.

Dr. Arman Mallett crouched behind the remains of a crumbled wall, his breath frosting in the frigid air. Beside him, Camila Tipler adjusted the dampener on her comms device, her hands trembling despite her gloves. The city—called New Bethlehem—lay in ruins around them, a cruel irony named for hope but drowned in despair. Its streets were ash, its cathedrals broken spines, its carolers a wailing chorus, and its promise betrayed.

Smoke rose from shattered towers, curling into a sky that never brightened. It reeked of peppermint and pine—scents once warm and welcome, now pumped into the air by Nicholas's machines to cover the stench of rot. The aroma, sweet and cloying, stung the eyes and twisted the stomach, as a reminder to all that Christmas belonged to the Sainted Tyrant.

Above them, faint bells echoed on a skipping loop, a scratched recording of an ancient carol playing endlessly in an uneven rhythm. The sound would have been nostalgic if not for its menacing dissonance.

Blood stained the snow, a frozen record of countless desperate battles. The most minor of offenders were sentenced to cruel death on Nicholas's annual Christmas reckoning of the naughty. Here and there, charred remnants of holiday decorations clung to broken lamp posts—a singed wreath, a shattered snowglobe, a wingless angel. Once symbols of joy, they now stood as mocking reminders of the world they'd lost.

"They're close," Natalia Klinkhart whispered. She clutched her satchel like it held her soul. Pages of smuggled hymnals and fragmented prophecies lay within, notes from a time when the holiday was still sacred. "East quadrant."

Arman raised a gloved hand to silence them. He lifted the scope.

A squad of Nicholas's enforcers marched through the snowy street. Their tinman armor gleamed in crimson and bone-white lacquer, a grotesque parody of festivity. Silver stars glinted at their shoulders—some decorative, others sharpened into blades.

At the head of the column stalked one of the reindeer.

It was a biomechanical horror of steel sinew and gristle-strung bone. Its breath puffed steam into the air like a beast from a furnace. Its antlers, jagged and gore-streaked, bore scraps of flesh from recent kills. Its eyes glowed red with unrelenting purpose. Blood dripped from its mouth, staining its chest plate as it gnawed on a piece of something vaguely human.

The reindeer, the possessed minions of Nicholas, no longer jangled bells from their necks. They *were* the bells. They pulsed with the rage of the Naughty List, their hooves pounded judgment into the earth and into the heads of those who would find themselves on it.

The sound of bells grew louder as the creature lifted its head and sniffed.

"If it catches our scent, we're done," Camila hissed. "The dampener's barely holding."

Arman lowered the scope, jaw clenched. "They won't catch us if we keep moving."

"But when we run out of places to move?" Natalia asked. She swept her arm across the ruins. "This is what's left. This is Christmas now. He took it, twisted it," her voice cracked. "I used to string popcorn garlands with my sisters," she said quietly. "Now I pull bone garlands off the dead."

"We will stop him," Arman said, though he didn't feel the certainty his voice demanded. "We go back, we stop him before the bells and," he gestured to the corpse of New Bethlehem—"before this annual holiday holocaust ever happens."

A distant roar tore through the sky.

Then came the screech of metal, followed by a wet crunch.

The reindeer had found prey, a group of stragglers too slow to hide. And hiding at all from the judgment of the Sainted Tyrant was naughty. One scream pierced the air, high and sharp, then snapped off mid-breath. A heartbeat later, the bells rang louder, full of joyless triumph.

Natalia whimpered and pressed her earmuffs tight to her skull, teeth gritted.

The bells weren't just sound. They were pain. Myth They carried the heart of their bearer. And this Nicholas's heart was made of sorrow, vengeance, and rage. To hear the bells in full was to feel the madness behind his smile.

"Move," Arman ordered.

The team slipped from their cover and vanished into the ruins. The bells faded behind them, but the dissonant song vibrated through their bones like a scar.

They had a chance to undo the eternal Christmas, and, with it, the Sainted Tyrant

The Holiday Battle Library

The safehouse of Arman, Camila, and Natalia was little more than a gutted basement reinforced with scavenged steel and patched circuitry. A faint buzzing came from the temporal gate in the corner. Its archway, crudely welded from broken iron fencing and the hollowed spines of rusted sleigh runners, was crowned with a ring of frozen blood. From it hung icicles, sharp as daggers, red at their roots, dripping slowly from the remains of those impaled there in ages past and left to freeze in agony.

Rows of scavenged books lined a makeshift shelf. Their spines cracked. Their pages flaked. Among war manuals and broken hymnals were treasures once sacred: *A Christmas Carol, The Grinch Who Stole Christmas, The Gift of the Magi, The Night Before Christmas,* and *The Christmas Story.* Someone had underlined passages with grease pencil, scribbled translations in the margins, even inserted battle plans into chapters, as if trying to turn the relics into holy scriptures of resistance. For the three of them, these weren't just books. They were weaponized idealism.

Natalia wound an old crank on a snowman figure atop a music box. The melody of *Silent Night* wheezed out, slow and dissonant, unraveling a lullaby never meant for this world. The crank refused to carry the song all the way to peace.

Camila knelt beside the temporal gate, her brow furrowed as she calibrated the controls. Wires wrapped in faded tinsel spilled out around her. A circuit board fused to the side had once powered a string of holiday lights. The activation node had been crafted from a broken ornament cap, still dusted in fake snow. It was equal parts machine and mockery.

"This thing's barely holding together," she muttered. "One wrong jump, and we'll end up in the *Feast Wars*, or worse, the *Red Advent*."

Natalia, pacing, snapped her field journal shut. "We're not choosing a fixed point," she said. "We're aiming for the night he passed the bells. The Lycia Orphanage, when he made the mistake."

"The night the burden changed hands," Arman murmured.

He checked his gear—a rifle, satchel of supplies, and the stabilizer strapped to his wrist. The casing of the latter was lined with beaten brass and one ornament-sized sleigh bell that was dull, cracked down the center, and long silent. He'd found it beside a scorched crib the day New Bethlehem fell.

"We don't know how early we'll land," he said. "But if we reach him in time, if we can stop the handoff, then we stop everything. All of this."

Camila's hands hovered above the ignition. "And if we're too early?"

"Then we watch," Arman said. "And we wait for the moment to rewrite history."

Camila hesitated. "What if we're wrong... if something worse rises instead?"

He didn't answer.

Natalia closed her eyes. Under her breath, she whispered from memory:

"Let not the dark rejoice, when sleigh bells sound like swords."

The gate sparked. The ring of blood icicles trembled.

A pulse of red light flickered across the portal. It flared, stabilizing into a shimmering oval like liquid glass. At its center, the past twisted into view. The ruins of a distant village came into view. There were no screams. No patrols. Just snow, and lanternlight, and... *peace*.

But something caught Arman's eye. In the very center of the portal's image, framed by the glow, stood a figure.

Tall. Robed. Bearded.

Saint Nicholas.

For a moment, through the round outline of the gate, he looked like a saint trapped in a snowglobe and watching them from another time.

They stepped through.

And everything shattered.

Heat. Cold. Pressure. The roar of wind and ice. For a breathless moment, they were suspended in an endless void, surrounded by shifting visions of Christmases long gone—families by hearths, children tearing ribbon, carolers in woolen cloaks.

Then the scenes twisted.

Fires devoured the homes. The gifts became weapons, their ribbons unraveling like leaking veins. The carolers turned cannibal, their mouths wide with teeth, singing as they fed.

And, through it all, the Sainted Tyrant watched.

The rush returned, faster this time.

The portal snapped shut.

The team tumbled out onto a snow-covered forest floor, gasping for breath, coughing out flakes like ash.

And above them, in the trees where they landed, silence.

For now.

The Boy Before The Bells

The forest was quiet.

The wind rolled softly through the trees. Distant birds cried across the sky as their wings caught the afternoon sunlight. There was no smoke, no ash, no blood.

No bells.

Camila pushed herself upright, blinking away the temporal haze. Natalia helped her to her feet, brushing snow and leaves from her coat.

"We're early," Natalia whispered, her voice trembling. "God help us, we're early."

Through the trees, the valley opened. Lights bobbed gently between buildings. Windows glowed with the warmth of hearthlight. Laughter echoed across the streets, a welcome replacement for screams. Somewhere, a dog barked. Somewhere else, bells rang softly... in *celebration*, rather than *judgment*.

At the center of it all stood the village of Lycia... the town that came before New Bethlehem. It was unbroken. Alive. Festive.

The rooftops glistened beneath the snow of early December and chimney smoke curled from nearly every home. Children played in the yard beside a crooked wooden tree hung with lights and ornaments. Parents called them in for holiday meals and quality time.

No orphanage stood here now. Only homes. An orphanage had no purpose.

"He's not lost yet," Camila said. "He has his town."

"More than that," Natalia murmured. "He has a family."

They followed a path toward the village's edge, where a small encampment nestled against the trees. A line of drying clothes hung between two trees.

"They won't accept us if we look like outsiders," Natalia said, already reaching for new attire.

They didn't speak. They took what they needed and buried their own clothing beneath a mound of brush and snow. The new clothes smelled of lavender, tallow, and pine.

By the time they reached the village square, the sun had dipped low behind the hills, casting long shadows through a local market's stalls. No one questioned them. No one stared. They blended in. And they would continue to blend in until it was their time to go.

They sang carols.

They helped string holly garlands with old women who kissed their cheeks and called them blessings. They lifted a massive poinsettia into the town square and watched children dance around it. They shared roasted chestnuts. They drank warm cider steeped with orange and cloves.

For days, they forgot who they were.

Natalia wept quietly as she helped a girl fold paper snowflakes.

Camila mended a boy's broken sled.

Arman found himself staring too long at the flames dancing in the braziers, experiencing holiday joy for the first time in his life.

"This," Natalia whispered to him, "this is what Christmas was supposed to be."

"I remember," Camila said.

Arman smiled as hope came alive within him.

That night, though, they saw him.

The boy named Nicholas.

He was walking home beside his father, Josan, a sturdy man with a kind face and a bag slung across his back. Josan tousled Nicholas's hair, and the boy grinned. The way he clung to his father's arm told his story.

He was loved.

He was safe.

He was no orphan.

"He's younger than I thought he would be," Natalia said, watching the boy duck beneath a hanging strand of evergreens.

Camila's voice caught. "He looks like any one of them."

"But he's not," Arman said as a reminder. "He's the one... unless we stop him."

They returned each day.

They saw Nicholas play with the other children, help his father carry wood, laugh when a local store owner gave him candy. He offered it to a smaller boy nearby... but then changed his mind and popped it into his own mouth.

Not cruel.

Not yet.

Still....

One morning, they saw him sneak away from the village square to toss pebbles at a group of women while their backs were turned. When caught, he lied smoothly, blaming the act on a child with a stammer. No remorse, only the sly confidence of one who expects the world to believe him.

Camila flinched. "He's just a child. We can't blame him for stupid moments."

"We all did things we wouldn't, looking back," Natalia added.

"You don't get it," Arman said. "We're already seeing the hints of who he could become."

Still they hoped.

Still they doubted.

Then came the rumors in the town that a nearby warlord, the one whose banners had returned to the ridgeline, had sent a message. He demanded tribute. Lycia could prove their loyalty by sending a servant-child to join his security team. Only then would he promise to leave them to their peace.

The town refused, and—the next morning—the head of the town council was found floating in the river. His throat slit.

Josan, Nicholas's father, was one of the first to sound the alarm. His voice rang with fury and echoed into a night that might have belonged to any century.

"They'll come for us," he told the council. "We should attack them before they attack us."

Josan was not alone in his beliefs, but he was outnumbered and the town agreed that there was no child they could possibly condemn to slavery with the warlord.

The time travelers met in the dark, eyes downcast.

"Tensions are getting high. The warlord is going to attack."

"He's not an orphan," Natalia whispered. "He's not even alone."

"But he will be," Arman said. "We know it's true. We're standing here because of it. And this town is about to erupt."

"The Saint won't pass the bells until Christmas Eve," Camila said.

Natalia closed her eyes. "So we take him. We take Nicholas. Just for the season. We return him after the burden is passed."

"Just one child," Arman said. "For just one Christmas."

Camila looked toward the edge of the trees. And froze.

Nicholas was there, walking along the forest path with hands in his pockets. He spent more and more moments alone, separating himself from community other than his father. And, when he was alone with his own thoughts, the actions that followed were often disturbing. While walking, he passed a smaller child seated in the snow, coatless, shivering. Nicholas didn't stop. He didn't even look. It wasn't evil. But it was character, slipping out before the power slipped in.

"Okay," Camila said, convicted. "Okay. We take him."

Then, she went to the small child and helped to reunite him to his mother, who hadn't realized he'd wandered off to play in the snow.

The next night, under a moon that hid behind clouds, they moved.

When the lights dimmed and the town hushed beneath frost, they returned with cloaks, gliding like spirits between trees and buildings.

Nicholas stirred when they lifted him, but he did not scream.

Perhaps, in some corner of his dreams, he believed they were angels.

But it's likely that belief broke forever in the moment he awoke in a sack, slung across Arman's shoulder.

They took him into the woods... far from the warmth of Josan's arms and the festivity of the town that would become New Bethlehem. Far from the moment when the bells of burden would be passed.

Camila wrapped him in a blanket. Natalia gave him warm water. Arman built the fire.

"You'll be safe," Natalia said. "This is just for a while. We'll bring you back."

Nicholas said nothing. He didn't fight them. He'd seen them in the town. He didn't even show concern for what his father must have been going through. There was a coldness there that had nothing at all to do with the winter.

"What did I do?" he asked.

Arman looked away.

Natalia pressed her lips into a hard line.

"Nothing yet," Camila said. "That's why you're here."

The Burning Pine Paradox

Nicholas's father, Josan, awoke to silence.

Too much silence.

Nicholas's bed was empty, the blanket kicked aside, the pillow cold.

He checked with the neighbors. No one had seen the boy. He checked the market square. No one had heard him pass. By midmorning, Josan was tearing through the village like a man set aflame from within.

He shouted prayers that curdled into curses. At the schoolhouse, he grabbed the headmistress by the wrist, eyes wild. "Nicholas is gone!" he roared. "Have you seen him?"

She hadn't. But no villager was left without interrogation by the distraught father, regardless of how they helped with the search.

By noon, Josan stood before the town's gathered leaders. His knuckles were raw from hammering on doors.

"It was the warlord's men," he spat. "I know it. He warned us. Threatened us. He wanted a child." His voice cracked. "And now he has mine."

"No one saw soldiers," one council member said gently.

"We've all seen Nicholas wandering alone," offered another. "Maybe he's just gone exploring."

"We have every available person checking his usual paths," said another.

"No," Josan said. "I know it was him. The warlord. And if you won't do something about it, I will."

He left before anyone could stop him. He did not seek council. He did not wait for approval. He went to the warlord's camp with a dagger in his belt and vengeance in his heart. And when the guards tried to turn him away, he killed the first with a cry that sounded like a father calling for his son.

The warlord's favored soldier bled into the snow before his body even landed.

By nightfall, the warlord's banners were flying at the front of a full platoon of his men.

And his rage came with them.

THE TIME TRAVELERS SAW it from the ridgeline on the edge of town first, a line of light, moving like a serpent down the pine-covered hillside. The scent of the trees filled the air, a pine-needled scent they had enjoyed this very week. Except, this time, the pine was burning.

Camila's hand went to her face. "No. No, it's too soon."

"It's exactly on time," Natalia said. "We'll soon get to bring him back."

Arman stood in the clearing, staring down toward the village, watching history twist around them.

"Should we do something?" Camila said. "Stop them? We know what is about to happen down there. The horrors about to unfold."

"It could change too much," Natalia said. "You know that. We all knew that before we chose to come."

Below them, Lycia slept beneath a velvet sky, wrapped in the false comfort of tradition. Twinkling lights glowed in windows. Wreaths hung over doors. Children were nestled happily in beds with tummies full of sweets as stars blinked above.

Then the bells began to toll.

Real bells.

Warning bells.

Nicholas stirred in the tent behind them. His small voice, scratchy with sleep, cut through the dark.

"What's happening?"

Camila tried to lead him back to the tent. "Let's get you back to sleep.

But he pushed past her and looked out at the approaching warlord in the distance. The scream that followed didn't sound like a child's. It sounded like the echo of a hundred winters breaking all at once. The fire overtook the village quickly. Street carts were overturned. Holiday decorations became flaming snakes. Doors splintered. Screams tangled with smoke. The poinsettia burned like a bonfire. Then the chapel. Then the homes.

Camila ran to the edge of the clearing. "We have to stop this—"

"We can't," Arman said, grabbing her arm. "It's already happened. This is the moment."

Natalia dropped to her knees.

"We were supposed to save him," she said. "We were supposed to save everyone."

"We're saving everyone in *our* time," Arman said. "We can't save those who are already gone."

Nicholas's face was framed by the firelight. Orange and red flames reflected in his eyes. It wasn't fear; it was fury. He took a single step toward the outer edge of their encampment as his little chest heaved with great breaths.

"No," Camila whispered.

"Get him back in the tent!" Arman barked. "Don't let him see—"

But it was too late.

Nicholas watched his father's house go up in a column of smoke. He saw bodies tumble like broken dolls through the snow. He saw his neighbors run and fall, and vanish in the smoke.

He saw what they'd taken from him and, in that moment, the snow ceased to fall. The world exhaled only the ash of his loved ones.

Then something new... and old... opened behind his eyes. And he ran. He ran into the burning village with rage.

"Oh my God," Camila said in realization. "It was us. We did this. We did it all."

"We have to go," Arman said.

"But we haven't stopped it—" Natalia began.

"We started it!" Camila snapped. "We have to reset before it locks."

They scrambled for the portal device, hands moving too fast, too frantic. The harmonic stabilizer pulsed red, unstable. Barely holding.

"Now," Arman growled.

They threw the last sequence in and Arman grabbed Camila and Natalia, pushing them through the portal that then vanished into light.

Behind them, in space and time, on the flame-drenched night, the boy's soul became that of the Sainted Tyrant

The World They Made

They hit the ground hard, the portal spitting them out onto the cold stone floor of the safehouse like chewed bones.

Camila gasped, scrambling to her feet. "Same coordinates. Same year."

Arman scanned the readout on his stabilizer. "We're back where we started."

But the silence in the room had changed.

The hum of the gate was sharper now, angry—like it knew what they'd done.

Natalia stood slowly. Her gloves were stained with soot from the last timeline. Her lips didn't move, but her eyes said everything.

It had been them.

They had taken the boy.

They had stolen him from his father.

And that act—their act—had set fire to the world and left behind the boy that would become the tyrant.

Camila sank into a chair, her face pale. "He wasn't even an orphan yet."

Arman didn't respond. He walked to the wall, touched the old, faded map of Lycia pinned there with a rusted tack, and closed his eyes.

He remembered.

Arman had been young then. He was just a boy when Lycia's name was stricken from the record, and its ruins swept beneath the bureaucracy of rebirth when it was rebranded as New Bethlehem. A place with no memory of why it needed to be new; it was merely a town that wanted peace again.

And, following their attempt at the peace, Arman remembered the first Christmas under the Sainted Tyrant.

The air was filled with ash and peppermint. The sky was bloodied with sleigh streaks and silent screams. No one sang that night. Or if they did, it was drowned by the bells. The real bells. Not carols. Not chimes. But the pulsing, iron-tuned judgment of the Saint's wrath echoing from the hooves of his beasts.

It did not matter to their Saint Nicholas that they had changed the name of the town to bring joy and happiness back to its streets, to bless it with hope again instead of the sorrow left behind by its awful legacy. Renaming *his* town was naughty. And there was no mercy for the naughty.

The biomechanical reindeer came first with hooves like anvils and antlers that glistened with the innards of the last town that resisted the Tyrant Saint's Christmas reign. Steam hissed from their nostrils as they charged through streets, their teeth gnashing in frenzy. They gored fathers defending their homes. They trampled mothers clutching their children. Their mouths dripped with ribbons of flesh and tinsel twisted with hair.

Behind them came the Saint. The Tyrant.

No sleigh. No joy. Just a throne of bone bolted to a chariot dragged by the fallen. His sack no longer brimmed with toys; it spilled with limbs, bundled and sorted, labeled *Naughty* or *Naughtier* with ironically beautiful holiday tags. Saint Nicholas's coat, once red with cheer, was now red with blood. He carried no list, only a ledger of names etched into a skin parchment that he checked with a blade instead of a pen.

He laughed that night a jagged laugh, not the jolly one from stories past. It echoed through the village of New Bethlehem as he crowned a gallows tree with the heads of its dissenters, their mouths stuffed with oranges filled with cinnamon sticks and their eyes replaced with glass ornaments that reflected the firelight as if they still wept.

That was the first Christmas Arman remembered. Saint Nicholas's Christmas. Natalia and Camila were older and had memories of joyful holidays. Arman never got to experience such a gift.

"We created the Sainted Tyrant," Natalia said. "Not by failing to stop him—but by giving him something to avenge."

Camila's hands trembled. "So, what now?"

"We go back," Arman said. "Further."

Natalia drifted to the wall and traced the outline of an old ornament hook that no longer held anything. "We made him," she whispered. "But only because the bells existed in the first place. This version of him—this version of Christmas—it all started with the first Nicholas."

Camila stiffened. "You want to stop the original Saint Nicholas?"

"We don't just stop the handoff," Natalia said. "We stop the Council. We end the bells before they ever have a name. Before the burden can be passed."

"But what if we destroy something bigger?" Camila asked.

"What bigger thing could we destroy than Christmas?" Arman asked rhetorically.

Natalia nodded, resigned. "Okay. It ends at the beginning."

"End the bells. End the cycle," Arman said.

"And if the Council tries to intervene?" Camila was still unconvinced.

Natalia's eyes burned like frostbitten fire.

"Then we show them what their legacy becomes."

Outside, the snow had begun to fall again—clean, silent, and so very wrong. As wrong as it had been and even more so now that they knew the bloody holiday was one of their making.

The bells were silent for the moment, but the war they'd started was still raging.

Gift Of The Council Of Immortals

Each jump the travelers made was more turbulent than the last. They weren't sure how much longer they could attempt their mission, but they'd managed their longest jump yet when they landed at the time of the very first Saint Nicholas.

The stars over the clearing flickered like dying candles, casting pale light onto the forest where the time travelers waited in silence. The fire near the young Nicholas's sleeping form crackled low, its embers curling upward in red spirals. There, beside his bedroll, nestled atop a leather hide with straps that could roll the Bells of Burden up like a satchel, lay the six bells.

They gleamed, even in the night shadows. Six silver spheres, etched with symbols recognizing their essences.

One for Peace. One for Joy. One for Faith. One for Hope. One for Memory. One for Immortality.

They were too powerful to leave behind.

"He hasn't accepted them yet," Camila whispered. "He doesn't even know they've been gifted."

Natalia nodded. "Then this is our last chance."

From the trees behind them, a breeze moved through the boughs like a warning. The wind tasted of pine and frost.

The Council of Immortals would be arriving soon to ensure their burden passed easily. Already, the air shimmered faintly with the promise of the divine. But the travelers couldn't allow what came next.

"Take them," Arman said.

Camila stepped forward. Her hand hovered above the satchel, and the bells stirred. One let out a faint chime, like the memory of a lullaby.

Then a whisper, barely audible. "Who dares disrupt the sacred rite?"

Six figures appeared beyond the fire. They were neither human nor spirit. They had robes made of light and shadow wrapped around their forms. Their eyes shone like stars, too bright to stare into. Each carried an object: a candle, a sprig of holly, a shepherd's staff, a broken blade, a feather, and a chain of ice.

"We are the Council," one said. "And these are the Bells of Burden."

"We know what they are," Natalia replied. "And we know what they do."

"You cannot take what was gifted," another said.

"Then we don't take them," Arman said, stepping forward. "We destroy them."

Natalia opened her pouch, revealing a wrapped bundle of mistletoe acid, a poison harvested from the broken future of New Bethlehem and the twisted holiday relics their Nicholas had created. She let a single drop of the liquid fall near the bells.

The nearest bell—Hope—shivered.

"They are not yours to destroy," the Council hissed, their forms beginning to unravel, shedding frost into the air.

"They belong to everyone," Camila said. "And they destroyed everything."

She poured out the glass vial of the liquid

The bells screamed.

One by one, they cracked.

Hope split cleanly down the center. Faith shattered like brittle porcelain. Memory wept molten light and collapsed inward. Joy burst like a firework, vanishing in sparks. Peace let out a single, harmonious tone before fading. Immortality clung to life the longest, beating like a heart. Then it, too, burst and went silent.

The fire guttered. The Council vanished in the wind upon which they had come.

And Nicholas slept on, untouched by Immortality or any of the other Bells of Burden.

Camila looked down at the glass vial now emptied. "It's done."

"Not yet," Arman said. He adjusted the stabilizer.

Natalia nodded. "Now we go forward. We see what world we made."

Together, they stepped into the portal.

And the last light of the bells faded into history.

A Saintless Existence

They jumped.

Again.

Home. Whatever home it was that they created this time.

When the portal spit them out, the light behind them flickered.

"I don't know how many more times we can do this. The portal may not make it. We may not," Camila said.

"Let's hope we got it right this time," Natalia said.

Their safehouse was still there. Same concrete bones. Same foundation. But the air was heavier, stagnant, embalmed.

Camila stood first. Her hand went instinctively to the crank of the music box on the shelf. She wound it.

Nothing.

No broken Silent Night. No eerie lullaby. Only silence. A funeral-like hush had settled over this new world too sterile to be alive.

Arman opened the cabinet where the holiday books had once been tucked between war manuals and survival texts. They were gone. In their place, a single gray binder labelled: Annual Aesthetic Guidelines – Winter Period.

Natalia lifted it, leafed through pages of charts—color swatches, lighting quotas, approved scent diffusions.

No carols.

No stories.

No joy.

They stepped outside into snow that fell too perfectly, too mechanically, like it had been calibrated. People walked in single lines down the street, their expressions not showing fear, but also not expressing hope. Peace. They were blank. Storefronts bore signs that read: Seasonal Observance Sector and Civic Decoration Compliance In Effect.

A square wreath hung on a door—perfectly symmetrical, coldly artificial, pre-lit. It blinked in a steady, emotionless rhythm.

Camila's voice cracked. "No Nicholas. No Christmas."

"Christmas came before him. I just assumed it would continue without him," Natalia said.

"He came when the world needed him," Arman said. "When they needed something to bring them back to belief. They wandered too far without him serving as the bridge between the season and how society could celebrate it."

Natalia wandered into the middle of the street and turned in a slow circle. "We stopped the Tyrant. But we unstitched the story so early that no one ever told it again."

"They stopped believing," Arman said. "In everything."

He picked up a discarded toy from a gutter. A doll, gray as stone. No eyes. No mouth. Just smooth features where expressions should have been. The tag read: Childplay Unit 3.04 – Interchangeable Persona Pending.

Camila crouched beside it. "No wonder the bells were so powerful. They were bound to belief. And we took all of it away."

Natalia didn't speak. She moved to the edge of the block where a display window shimmered with artificial snow. Behind the glass, mannequins posed beside sterile silver trees. Above them, a sign flashed:

WINTERTIME – A TIME FOR HARMONY

No mention of Christmas.

No light. No Christ. No Nicholas. No hope.

Only algorithmic design.

They returned to the safehouse without speaking.

They were just three people who had tried to save the world from a monster and had unknowingly wiped out its last real memory of magic. And only the three of them knew the reality, both the glorious and the gory.

Arman stared into the dead hearth.

"Maybe," he said, "we were never supposed to fix it."

The Bells Divide

The world without Nicholas was still snow-bound and silent.

They stood in the safehouse beneath flickering emergency lights. The portal hissed behind them, a wounded thing trying to die in silence.

Camila wiped dust from the stabilizer. "There's nothing left here in this world. I wouldn't have even built this thing to try to save a world like this one."

"No Saint. No stories," Natalia whispered. "Not even songs."

"Then we try one last time," Arman said.

Natalia looked up. "The beginning?"

Arman nodded. "We don't just undo the Tyrant or erase the bells. We give them to the right Nicholas. The one who was meant to hold them."

They'd done the research. They knew the moment. They knew the tale. The Council of Immortals passed the burden by firelight when faith in Christmas began to die.

And now, they would go there, again, this time to steal it rather than destroy it.

Camila twisted the stabilizer's node.

The gate flared open.

They stepped forward.

But so did someone else.

A voice echoed from behind them, cold and curious. "What are you doing here?"

They turned—and froze.

It was Nicholas.

Not the Saint. Not the Tyrant. Just a man who never became either. He was a sanitation worker in the gray uniform of the civic order, with a clipboard in hand and cleaning gear on his belt.

His eyes were sharp and cold. "How did you get in?" he asked. "This building's condemned."

They said nothing.

But the glow of the portal danced in his pupils—and he saw too much.

His eyes narrowed. "That's... not part of the city."

And then he moved, not with violence, but with hunger. Before they could guess what he would do, Nicholas stepped toward the light and vanished into it.

"NO!" Camila screamed.

It was too late. All they could do is follow and hope he hadn't disrupted their own travel.

They landed on the soil of the past and the cruel Nicholas was nowhere to be seen.

"Where is he?" Camila asked immediately.

"He must not have made it. Think of how many times we trained for these jumps. His body wasn't prepared." Natalia encouraged them all, including herself.

"It doesn't matter," Arman said. "We have a job to do, whether he's here or not, and it looks like we're in the right place."

Ancient, snow-blanketed pine trees surrounded a firepit. The sky overhead was purple-black, streaked with stars never even named by modern mouths.

By the fire sat a young man.

Saint Nicholas. The first.

Not yet a saint. Not yet a legend. Just a kind-faced figure cloaked in wool, sleeping near the flames of his campfire.

The bells rested at his side, new and shining.

Camila crouched behind a moss-covered log. "The Council has already been here."

"That's okay," Natalia said. "We're right on time."

"He asleep," Arman whispered.

They crept closer. The fire crackled. Nicholas stirred but didn't wake. From the trees behind them, something else moved. They turned but didn't see anyone.

The gray-clad Nicholas, the one they hadn't meant to bring, watched from the shadows. His breath steamed in the cold. His hands curled into fists at his sides. He had no name in this place. No myth. No memory. But when he saw the bells, he felt them. In his marrow. Like they were meant to be his.

The travelers approached the fire slowly.

Camila opened her pouch. "We don't have to steal them all. We'll leave two. Enough for this Nicholas to follow his path."

Arman hesitated. "And if that changes the burden?"

"Then at least it's shared," Natalia said.

"Which shall we leave him?" Camila asked.

"Peace and joy, of course." Natalia said.

She reached out and lifted four of the bells as quietly as she could and cut the strap that bound them together with a small blade she'd pulled from her pouch. A tiny prick in her heart echoed the snap of the leather strap. In her hand was Memory, Immortality, Hope, and Faith—the other four bells.

They turned to go, unaware that the gray-uniformed Nicholas followed from the shadows.

At last, they reached the portal edge and, just as they were ready to make another jump, Nicholas appeared.

"I don't know what those are, but I don't think they belong to you," he said.

"They certainly don't belong to you," Natalia said as the stabilizer screamed with energy and light flickered out from it in all directions.

Camila grabbed the stolen bells from Natalia and jumped into the portal. Nicholas leapt after her and reached out for the strap carrying the burden.

The moment all four bells were in motion, the portal spasmed.

A sound like tearing thunder shook the trees. Time rebelled.

Arman and Natalia joined the fold and crashed through the threshold with the other two. The bells tore apart between them, with Camila and the Sainted Tyrant each screaming as they ripped Christmas apart, coming away with two bells apiece.

Passing The Burden

Camila, Arman, and Natalia tumbled out of the portal at the base of a ruined stone wall.

The orphanage.

"Where'd he go?" Camila snapped. "The wrong Nicholas?"

"Maybe he really is gone this time." Natalia suggested.

"That was one hell of a jump, even for us. Rang my bell," Arman said. Then, after a glare from Camila, he added. "Sorry. Bad choice of words."

They were outside the orphanage. Smoke drifted from the chimney. Frost clung to the bricks.

Inside, huddled in a corner to keep warm, a boy slept. Nicholas. The right one. The kind one.

Camila crept forward, heart in her throat.

She set two bells gently on his chest.

They sang, recognizing him.

He didn't stir, but the room warmed and they immediately knew... had *Hope* and *Faith*... that they had succeeded.

"Hope," Natalia said. "And Faith. Those are the two you were able to hold onto in the portal."

"He'll be a true Saint with those bells," Camila said.

"Let's bring the other Nicholas to a different bunk. Leave this one where he was supposed to be sleeping from the start," Arman said as he scooped up the kind Nicholas.

"When the burden passes from the other Saint Nicholas, it will be the bells of Peace and Joy," Natalia said.

"He will be a kind Saint Nicholas with those Bells of Burden," Camila smiled. "A loving leader of his holiday."

Arman moved the cruel Nicholas from the bed where he placed the chosen boy. Even he was startled at the appearance of the boy they'd known in their previous jump. While he had been troubled when they last saw him, he was still just a boy with a family, and a community. Now, his features were sharp as ice and cold as hatred. His heart hurt for the person this boy had become, but at least he would be prevented from becoming powerful given the newfound heights of cruelty in his being.

Outside the orphanage, their duty done, Camila adjusted the stabilizer. "The gate's breaking up. I've done all I can and we've got just one last jump."

"Let's hope it was enough," Natalia said.

They dove into the portal.

A Tale Of Two Christmases

They landed in snow.

It was no silent night. It was filled with sound again. But not the yuletide melodies they were longing to save. Screams. Howls. And, in front of them, the reindeer.

They stood before a herd of fang-toothed, steel-limbed, red-eyed horrors. The twisted creatures aimed their blood-stained antlers and scratched their hooves against the ground hungrily, as they prepared to charge.

Camila gasped. "No! No, this isn't right!"

Natalia pulled her backward, beside Arman and herself, eyes wide with horror.

Behind them, the portal flickered. And, on the other side, visible just before it collapsed—New Bethlehem. The real one. The one they'd saved. It was beautiful.

A child laughed and ran by with a stuffed teddy bear. Lights at the far edge of their vision twinkled in windows. Carols rang out. It was Christmas... as it was intended.

"We split the bells," Natalia said.

"So we split time," Arman finished. "Two Christmases. Two worlds."

"Two Nicholases?" Camila asked fearfully.

As if in answer, standing beneath an ornamented tree, they saw him, watching them from the other side. It was the gray-uniformed Nicholas. The one they'd lost in the portal. His expression was enough for them to know that his soul was indeed that of the Sainted Tyrant.

He smiled, held up his two bells, Memory and Immortality, and cruelly mouthed, "Merry Christmas." The words twisted in the air, festive and feral.

"He knows," Natalia said. "He has Memory. He knows it all."

"It's even worse," Camila said.

"How could it be worse?" Natalia asked.

"Because of his other bell. He has both Memory and Immortality," Camila said hopelessly, for Hope was dead along with Faith and Peace and Joy. "He will never forget, and he will never die. The world would burn for eternity beneath his perfect recollection."

"Eternal life to create the world over there that exists over here," Arman said.

"And this world, with no Immortality Bell, no longer has a Saint Nicholas," Natalia said in realization. "And no one with the Memory of his goodness."

The three time travelers turned to face the horror that would unfold, not in one world, but two.

Then the portal collapsed.

For good.

And the herd charged.

About the Author

"Red"is a 15-Time #1 International Bestselling, award-winning, 31-year writing and publishing professional of 125 independent- and traditionally-published titles with 750,000+ copies sold. She writes genre fiction and TTRPGs *(Runequest, Okkorim, Legends of Avantris, Gudnak, DCC)* as Jeri Shepherd; romance and plays as Maggie McMahon *(Shakespeare Shakeups)*; and children's books, author resources, celebrity biographies *(Dick Vitale, Steve Palec)*, sports writing *(Fergie Jenkins, Dr. Rick Lehman)*, and nonfiction as Reji Laberje. Red leads writing and gaming tracks *(GaryCon, Nerd Street, Gen Con, Origins, Dragon Con)*; runs a publisher, dabbles in podcasting; and co-owns Red Rose Works (courses, coaching, game services, and host of her Working Writers Mastermind with authors Christopher D. Schmitz, T.R. Nickel, and AG Wedgeworth). Red, a USAF Arabic Linguist Veteran, mom, Gigi, and dog mama lives on a riverfront in Wisconsin with her husband since1996, Joe. They enjoy nature, music, travel, sports, church, and life!

https://linktr.ee/redwritesbooks
https://www.redwritesbooks.com

MEMORIES, GHOSTS, DUST, AND DEAD BUGS

BY JOE PROSIT

GRAMPS DIED ON DECEMBER 24th. I found out the next day. One last "Merry Christmas" from the old fart.

What I didn't know, what I wasn't made aware of until after the new year, was that he'd willed me more than just his ashes in a jar. My last Christmas present from the old coot wasn't an electric train set, socks, or even a US savings bond. It was his house. Whether or not the property was to be a boon or an albatross was yet to be seen.

I made the trek from my north-metro, new-construction, split-entry to the pre-dust bowl-era farmhouse surrounded by its petty kingdom of corn stalks in under two hours. But I might as well have crossed the solar system as distant and alien as the old place felt. If my home was Earth, Gramps' was Pluto. I took my contractor truck with all the tools and equipment in the back because the roads were going to be icy and the tools in the back might come in handy. Two hours later, I'd managed to stay out of the ditches and make it to the snow-packed gravel driveway.

Didn't give much thought to anything till I stepped out of the driver's seat and set my boots on the ice. Rather than marching straight for the front door, when I looked up and saw the house, I stilted and stopped.

I'd been to the place before, decades ago, when I was a knee-high, shit-stained pissant and when mom and dad were still alive. Back then,

I never thought about things like market value, Return On Investment, and profitability. And I gotta admit, those concerns were silenced by the looming presence of the house. It was like something out of a Nathaniel Hawthorne book, the outline made familiar by a million Halloween coloring book pages. A haunted edifice. A gothic monolith. It was big as far as farmhouses built in 1918 went. A wide front porch. Two stories with an attic. Multiple steep-pitched gables. Red trim and white-flaking-to-gray plank siding. Two brick chimneys. Nothing surrounded it but a gnarly, leafless oak and acres and acres of knocked down corn stalks peeking their broken necks above the white, windswept drifts of snow.

I glanced back to the chimneys. No smoke rising. If that was the home's only heat source, it was going to be as cold inside as it was outside. It also meant frozen or maybe busted pipes. And getting the flues and the fireboxes up to code would be another, and most likely impossible, challenge. At some point, the cost of refurbishing the place would outweigh any ROI, and as soon as the scales tipped that way, it meant calling a bulldozer and then a realtor. The acreage would still be worth something, even here on the Planet Hoth.

Well, at least inside, I could get out of the wind chill, assuming the windows weren't all busted out. I tucked my chin away from the gusts and into the collar of my thick Carhart coat, flipped up my hoodie, and trudged up the snow-covered, creaking porch steps.

The key I received in the mail pushed through the rusted tumblers and fit snug in the lock, but was ultimately unnecessary. The knob turned with a light twist and the front door invited me inside with a stepped-on-cat's screech. But it was the warmth that seduced me across the threshold. Good old-fashioned, electric baseboard heat.

The renovations checklist grew long, fast. Filling a roll-away dumpster or two was top priority. Gramps was a bit of a hoarder. Unopened mail. Moth-eaten clothes. Dirty dishes. Dime-store prints of painted ducks and deer. A white dish towel hanging from the handle of the stove with a needle-point depiction of the dish running away with the spoon. A plastic coffee cup featuring a girl in a bikini which disappears when you add hot fluids. The bikini. Not the girl. In the living room was an old record player and stereo speakers built into a cabinet. On the shelves, brick-a-brack, broken keepsakes, and every Christmas and pottery class gift my sister and I ever dumped in his lap. In one corner, there were toys me and my sister played with three decades ago that were acquired three decades before then. Memories, ghosts, dust, and dead bugs. They all had to go.

Next on the list were the usual suspects for flipping a house: new shingles, new carpet, fresh paint on the walls, new appliances, updated electrical and plumbing fixtures, new furnishings, and finally, some modern decor. Granddad loved his Thomas Kinkade lakeside cabin landscapes, but they didn't do much to appeal to younger generations.

As for the house itself, the foundation was solid and level. No black mold in the walls. The leaks in the ceiling were minimal and easily fixed with new plumbing or a new skin of shingles. It had good bones. No need to call the bulldozer and the realtor, in other words. The place had potential. Full kitchen. Spacious living room. Even if I'd have to wall up the fireplaces, the hearths would serve as beautiful highlights. I was still undecided on whether to sell or rent the place. I had no intention of living here, that much was certain. I had my place, and Edgar Allen Poe meets American Gothic was never my vibe. But with a little spit and polish, you might call it quaint. Quiet. Charming. Peaceful. And with four bedrooms? The vacation rental property ad copy wrote itself.

Which brought me back to the issue of Return On Investment. It cost me nothing but property tax to own it. Maybe thirty, forty grand in renovation costs, less if I did most of the work myself, which was my plan. Even if I only booked out the place every other weekend, at five hundred bucks a night, I could be above water in as little as a year, year and a half.

This was all a quick first-floor assessment. Hadn't busted out so much as a tape measure or a multimeter yet. Hadn't even put the key for the unlocked front door back in the card it came in. When I set my boot on the first wooden step, I figured I'd better pocket that in case I tripped on the narrow, steep staircase and lost the damn thing. When I went to put it back, I once again stuttered to a stop.

Grandpa was never a fan of lawyers, so of course, he never had a legit will drafted up. Instead, he put little notes in greeting cards and set them on the kitchen windowsill for someone to discover and distribute according to the first names scrawled on the outside of the envelope. Jane got the title to his pickup and a hundred grand in US savings bonds. I got the key. Jane's title and bonds came in a Happy 5th Birthday card. Mine? A Christmas card. Thomas Kinkade with his favorite subject: a cottony snow-covered church decorated with wreaths and red bows.

"This old place is a part of me. Keep it in the family & take good care of it, kiddo!" it said inside in slow, squiggly, old-man cursive.

"I get it, Gramps. It's a Christmas present," I muttered to myself, dumped the key back inside the card, tucked it into my back pocket, and started up the staircase. Never asked for it, but it was mine anyway.

Never really got to know my grandpa much. He was a vet of some war and never talked much. When he did, it was never directly. Surface-level stuff. Sports. School. Weather. That sort of thing. His death was a mourning a lifetime in the making.

More of the same upstairs what was downstairs. Old clothes. Unwanted personal effects. Outdated carpeting, wallpaper, and fixtures. And more dead bugs. Damn, there were a lot of 'em. Not ladybugs, but invasive Asian lady beetles that stunk when you stepped on them. Not stepping on them wasn't an option. Add a visit from vector control to the to-do list. Maybe pest control too, but I hoped not.

Three of the four bedrooms were upstairs. If I was going to flip the old farmhouse into a modern vacation rental property, the bedrooms were critical to getting a decent price. All three were, for the most part, empty. Gramps slept in the ground-floor bedroom. My guess was he didn't venture up here too often to deposit his eclectic, old man detritus. It wasn't until I stepped into the third bedroom, the one at the end of the hall, when I had another one of those immobilizing stammer steps.

This was the room where Jane and I would play when Mom and Dad brought us to visit. A dead tube TV sat against one wall. Black and white, with bunny ears poking above the back. Channel 29 came in and played cartoons on Saturday mornings, if I remembered right. In front of the TV, the hardwood floor was covered by a brightly colored rectangle of green lawns, red and blue houses, and winding black and yellow streets. A toy chest built to pirate treasure specifications sat under the drafty, plastic-covered window. Puked onto the carpet were half its contents: Dolls. Action figures. A threadbare teddy bear. A smiling, leering plastic rotary phone. A stick and at the end of the stick a clear but cloudy plastic ball full of bells that was supposed to be a vacuum cleaner? A smattering of cars sized to commute and race through the streets on the carpet. Also, because he never understood the appeal of video games, a plank of pine board upon which he'd installed a series of arcade buttons, a joystick, and a length of yarn dangling out the back so we could play video games and "still use your imagination." Another Christmas gift no one asked for.

The heat wasn't so good up here. The freezing wind came across the endless acres of farmland unabated until it hit the glass and hardly slowed down then. A single thermostat to regulate the whole place, no doubt. I tugged up my coat's zipper.

The way the toys lay, some of the Hot Wheels still on the road, the naked Barbie doll sitting at a pink table set for tea, the old G.I. Joe with an M-16 still in his kung-fu grip... Had anyone been up here since the last time Jane and I had fought over playing House or playing War? Judging by the layer of dust and dead beetles, no. Not a soul.

Opposite the TV, a door was set into the wall. It was slightly smaller than a normal door. Maybe five and a half feet tall rather than a modern, up-to-code, six foot eight-inch door. The knob was missing and replaced by a length of twine knotted into the latch's workings. I didn't remember that door being there, but kids never noticed such things when there were toys and TV involved. Now? Well, additional rooms meant additional value.

My boots left prints in the gray on the way to the door. I pulled the string. A mechanism popped inside the workings. The door eased open under its own weight.

AT FIRST, I ASSUMED it was a closet. A big closet. A walk-in. But it was more like a small adjoining office, maybe half the size of the bedroom. Bare tongue-in-groove plank walls. A single light bulb was mounted on the ceiling. A yellowed string dangled from its socket, just out of reach from the doorway. Dipping my noggin under the header, (it was a bit of a low bridge) I entered to see if the place was fit for human occupation or better left to a pack of homesteaded possums. It smelled like things long dead. No possums, living or otherwise. Plenty of dead lady beetles under my boots that sounded like walking on those plastic runners realtors lay down during open houses. Enough dried-out carapaces to keep any pack of possums fed through the winter. When I stepped around the door to reach the light's pull string, I must have pushed the door. Just as I wrapped my fingers around the string, the door clacked shut in the frame. The room fell dark.

A moment of panic. A moment of sheer certainty that the old forty-watt bulb had long ago burned out. That I was trapped in here, a million miles from home, on the dark side of Pluto or Hoth, forever.

A quick tug and the bulb snapped to life. Dust on the top side of its pear body burned and drifted whiffs of that first-time-the-heater-gets-turned-on-for-the-winter nostalgia. Syrupy, orange light shone on the big closet. On the small room, really. It would make a nice home office, or a massive wardrobe big enough for any Hollywood heiress and all her shoes.

But no critters. No window. No furniture either.

There was something more to this place than its odd size, strange smell, and the abundance of crunchy orange beetles. Something silent. Something waiting. Something patient. Something greedy. The shadows hid much more than the light bulb revealed.

But the dim light showed me one thing. A door. It was a small thing, maybe three feet tall and two across. This new door, like its predecessor, was also missing the knob and in lieu, dangled a length of twine from the round hole where the knob should have been. But that wasn't the strangest part. Next to the latch, mounted on a piece of one-by pine, was a button. Not a doorbell. It was round and made of cheap, white-faded-to-yellow plastic I'd expect to find on an arcade game. It was labeled with a single word, printed and applied by means of a label maker. Instead of "JUMP," or "FIRE," or "KICK," it said, "BOOM."

"Well, obviously I'm not touching that," I said and didn't feel even a bit silly for saying it out loud.

Instead, I focused on the door itself. Surely it granted access to an attic, an electrical panel, or perhaps a dumbwaiter or a laundry chute. Nothing extraordinary or even uncommon about any of those things. But I sensed there was something extraordinary about this door. About the whole room. I was compelled. Lacking a knob, I pulled the string. A mechanism inside the door made a grinding metallic sound. The latch gave way. The door slowly but smoothly exposed its contents.

The dark did its part in protecting the interior's modesty. Getting on all fours, I peered inside. Too deep, too dark to see the back wall. I retrieved my phone and thumbed on the flashlight. The steel-cold beam made nude the darkness.

Inside the small room, beyond the small door, was a smaller room. And at the far end of this smallest room yet?

"Is that another... No. Is that...?" I mumbled with my face inches from the dried old wood floor populated in stinking carapaces. "...another fucking door?"

It was. And again, it had a string instead of a knob. And next to it, another button, this one also round and white and labeled in all caps, "BOOM."

"What the hell?" Talking out loud to myself didn't seem like the kind of thing that deemed me crazy. As cool and quiet as the house was, it was the kind of thing that filled the void and allowed me to retain some essence of normality in this growingly odd situation.

That ability quickly dissipated, as quickly as my flashlight had abolished the dark in this smallest of small rooms. Behind me, a clap of wood against wood spooked me. I spun.

Above the shut door leading back to the bedroom with the toys and the TV, one slant of the tongue-and-groove wall had dropped open like a trapdoor. But that was far from the most unsettling part. Beyond the opening, rather than the ceiling of the old toy-littered bedroom, appeared a set of eyes.

Fear glazed the whites of those eyes, terrified while also terrifying. Yet, they were undeniably familiar. As familiar as the stubble on my chin. I've stared back at those eyes every morning while my razor did its job of dragging away shaving cream and leaving smooth skin. Those eyes were my own baby blues.

But they looked dull, distant, detached. They looked down and away, furtively, regretfully, to something next to the missing doorknob. Never has a sight seemed so familiar while simultaneously so inhumane. Then something clicked. It wasn't the mechanism inside the door jamb; the door remained shut. Some other mechanism entirely was set to work. Something in the already low ceiling.

Dust waterfalled down all four walls. More than a few of those dead lady beetles, too. They leaked through the seams where the walls met the ceiling, and looking up, I saw why. The ceiling and the lone light bulb fixed to it were sinking.

"Hey. Whoa," I said, not sure if I was speaking to myself anymore or speaking to... speaking to another version of myself.

The trapdoor above the normal door snapped shut, blocking my view of those familiar but fearful blue eyes. The ceiling continued to lower at a slow and steady rate.

"Hey!" I yelled this time.

Scrambling back to my feet, I pocketed my phone and reached up to the descending ceiling. It was made of the same tongue-and-groove wood the walls were, and when I pressed up against it, nothing changed. The ceiling was as firm and as determined as a car compactor. There was no stopping it and no slowing it down. It wasn't just being lowered by some hidden system of ropes and pulleys. It was being pressed down by... hydraulics? A thousand pound counter weight? It didn't much matter because as hard as I pushed back up, there was no affecting it. The ceiling sunk lower and lower. It descended past the header of the door leading back to the bedroom. If I ran to the door and tried to pull it open, the lowered ceiling would have prevented the door from opening.

"Hey!" I screamed now, pressing the hunch of my back against the ceiling. "Hey, I'm trapped in here!"

Only I wasn't. There was the smaller room just beyond the smaller door. If I went in there, I'd probably be even further trapped, but at least I wouldn't be crushed. It was, if nothing else, an option. Not a good option. But an option.

No. There were always other options. I set my palms just above my bent knees. I rested my broad shoulders against the ceiling. The single light bulb glared directly into my eyes, so I sealed them shut. Then I pushed. I was a strong guy. Played defensive end in high school. Worked with my hands all the years since then. Had built up some of that fabled "old man strength." If I couldn't overpower the weight pressing the ceiling down, I could perhaps break whatever mechanics operated it. My thighs strained. My back did its best to remain stiff. I pushed against my legs with my arms. I ground my teeth and growled through them.

The ceiling didn't so much as pause. The boards didn't so much as bend. I had as much luck pressed against the compressing steel walls of a garbage truck. Still, I tried. Until something sharp and electric zapped the muscles and nerves in my lower back. Until spots appeared in my vision. Until my equilibrium went wonky.

I gave in, almost collapsed, but stayed on my feet, hunched over and having to hunch lower every second.

The smaller door then. There was no other choice.

By the time I reached it, it was as necessary to be on all fours to fit through it as it was to stay below the ceiling. Thankfully, the hobbit door swung inwards and wasn't rendered inoperable by the descending ceiling. I scrambled inside like a squirrel, or perhaps a possum.

It was dark inside, but I gave that no thought. It was much more important that I pull my legs in behind me even as the light bulb in the previous room exploded against the floor. Everything went pitch black then. Bits of thin glass joined the multitude of dead lady beetles. All were just as fragile against the pressure of the ceiling. They cracked in unison.

Didn't realize I was panting until hit by the sudden silence of the blackness. But I was. Sweating under all my layers despite the cool air, too. That foolhardy attempt to squat press the ceiling had done something to my back. Tweaked it real good. The pain only really flared up when I straightened it, so I kept it curved for the time being.

Needed to get my bearings. Needed to figure out a way out of here. I should have grabbed my damn tool bag before ever leaving the truck. Then I'd have a headlamp and not have to rely on my phone. And a hammer to bust through the damn walls, if that ended up being necessary. Instead, I had my phone, an old Christmas card, and a key to an unlocked door I couldn't get to.

I TURNED THE FLASHLIGHT back on and panned it across my surroundings.

If the first room was the size of a small office or a large closet, this was the size of a spacious dog kennel. Not the little kind you'd put a yapping Pomeranian in, but the ones big enough to accommodate a German Shepherd or even a St. Bernard. Still not great for a full-grown adult. Maybe four feet across in all directions. Including floor to ceiling, which, considering the room I just left, was of heightened importance. And just like the previous room, the walls and the ceiling were made of the same tongue-and-groove wood planks. The floor was littered with crispy and deceased stink bugs. And of course, there was another door. And another white plastic button with the same label-maker word adhered to its concave shape.

"Boom, huh? Nope. Still seems like a bad idea," I advised myself.

Something had set things in motion in that last room. Maybe it was pulling on the string attached to the light bulb. Maybe it was opening the door that led into this room. Maybe, most likely even, it was those blue eyes peering in from the bedroom. Anyway, there was no rush to go and make the same mistake twice. I put my butt on the floor and sat criss cross applesauce like it was kindergarten story time.

There were no windows, no furniture, and no possums. There was a light bulb and a pull string, a tiny door, and that "BOOM" button. The door next to the button was maybe two feet tall, one foot across, if that. Probably wide enough for me to squeeze my gut and my butt through. If I went sideways, I could fit. Probably.

I turned the cold white light of my phone back to the previous door. It was small, but bigger than this new door. Hobbit-sized compared to pixie-sized. It was still open, but instead of exposing the inner workings of whatever pressed the ceiling down to the floor, there was more tongue-in-groove paneling. It was then that it dawned on me that someone had built this. Someone with enough forethought to think of someone trapped in this room who'd want to see the guts of the trap. Someone who didn't want that other someone trapped in here to see the guts.

"Gramps?" I said, doubtfully.

He was never much of a handyman. The best he could do was make that homemade Atari 2600 knockoff. My phone swung back to the round, white, plastic, arcade game style button with the label-maker printed "BOOM" on it mounted to a cheap slab of pine board. Sure. The designs were near identical. But the intent...

"No way," I said and saw my breath make haze in the gleam of the flashlight.

Regardless of who made these modifications to the old farmhouse, they had constructed some sort of game. A puzzle. A path to follow. A trap. And the trick to any game, any puzzle, any trap, was not to play the way you were supposed to. The trick was to cheat. The choices were obvious. I was to either press the button (an obvious, dumb move) or try my luck with Door Number Three. Either choice would be playing the game as the designer of the game intended. A sucker's move.

Maybe I didn't have my hammer or a crowbar to rip apart the walls. And maybe the ceiling was reinforced with hardened steel. But the walls… they were that tongue-in-groove pine. Nothing I couldn't break through with a few stomps of my heel.

I scooched over to one of the two doorless walls. Before I went to kicking, I went to knocking. No doubt there were studs on the other side of the planks, and if I was going to kick my way through, I needed to find the spot midway between the studs where the planks were the easiest to break. Again, if I would have brought my tool bag with the stud finder in it, I would have been much better off. But one has to make do.

Wrapping my knuckles against the wood, moving left to right, I listened for a spot hollower than the rest. My raps echoed against the wood and reverberated off the other walls, the sound bouncing back to me indistinguishable from the sound coming from the other side of the planks. Everything sounded hollow, dry, lifeless. I kept at it, but things besides the ceiling were closing in around me: Claustrophobia and its demon twin, Impatience.

"Fuck it," I said while spinning around on my butt. "Fuck *this*," I said, thinking of the game whoever built this place wanted me to play.

No, I wasn't going to open the new, smaller door. And hell no, was I going to press that damn button. I set the sole of my Red Wing against a spot that sounded marginally lower pitched than the others. I drew my knee up like a piston and drove the heel into the wood.

It didn't give. Pain shot up my bones. I kick again. The impact created a bang much louder than my knuckles, but nothing so much as cracked. I scooted a foot to my right and kicked again. Same results. A loud bang. A sifting of dust drifted from the ceiling. Some dead bugs bouncing off the floor boards. A foot further to the right, same results.

"Alright," I said. "Time to pick a spot and give 'er hell."

I went to work, ignoring the pain in my heel, the sweat gathering in the fabric of my t-shirt under my layers, and the heavy breathing filling up the silence between the hammers of my kicks. I didn't want to hear my own breathing. I wanted to hear the crack of wood under my boot. Needed to hear it to know I was making some progress. Half a dozen kicks in, as if the house knew exactly what I didn't want, a song started up from downstairs.

"What the hell?"

It was the Ronettes. That happy, poppy, shopping-mall-friendly song I never learned the name of about sleigh bells jingling and ring ting tingling too. I didn't give a damn if it was lovely weather for a sleigh ride or not. I wanted the damn board to break under my boot!

I kicked again. Again. Again.

Downstairs, the record skipped and restarted the song with its bouncy, goofy, little keyboard and bass riff, followed by the sound effects of a horse neighing and clopping along. Well, at least that answered that question. My kicking had knocked the needle onto the record and got the song playing. But that meant the record had to already be spinning, right? I didn't know. I didn't own a god damn record player and had no intention of ever owning one. I just needed to bust through this–

–stupid–

–fucking–

–cheap ass–

–tongue-in-groove–

–wall.

Each kick I drove into the wall between each thought was equally ineffective. Between "cheap ass," and "tongue-in-groove" the record skipped again, not back to the start but to the first verse about falling snow and friends calling "yoo hoo." Sonofabitch, if I kept kicking would the record keep scratching back to the start? Maybe if I gave it a break, it would play itself out. That was the excuse I used to catch my breath and give my aching heel (not to mention my throbbing lower back) a break, anyway. So I sat, and the song played.

When it reached the end, there was a moment of calm quiet. Even my breathing managed to drag to a steady, easy, pattern. Now, finally, I could think clearly and hear if my work was making any progress.

Then the song started up again, the piano leading the way with that incessant "Ding ding ding a ling."

I kicked.

Skip. "Ding ding ding a ling."

I kicked again.

Scratch. "Ding ding ding a ling."

Again.

Skip. "Ding ding ding a ling."

"Fuck!" I screamed, and at least I didn't have to hear that stupid little jingle for one brief moment. Of course, the rest of the tune and an incompetent Foley artist's interpretation of a horse followed.

"Okay. Fine. You want me to open the door, I'll open the door," I grumbled to myself. Or to Gramps. Or to whoever it was that had put me in this place. Anything to ease the pain in my back and my heel and to cover up the muffled sounds of that damn song.

I crawled over to the tiny door on all fours, the light from my phone shining and then blacking out in rhythm with my hand holding it, tromping against the floor. When I reached the door, I didn't hesitate. Ignoring the "BOOM" button, (still not dumb enough to fall for that one) I pulled on the string.

The tiny door swung open.

Behind me, another panel dropped open with a loud clap. When I swung my phone that way, another set of eyes squinted and turned away from the glare. Clamped shut the way they were, I couldn't examine the color of the irises, but I knew those crow's feet to either side of them.

"No, no, no! Don't you do it!" I yelled and scrambled for the opposite side of the room.

Four feet across, it didn't take long, even on my hands and knees. Nevertheless, the open board swung up and slammed shut, back into place before I could get there. Not a moment later, the waterfalls of dust and dead bugs rained down around me as the ceiling disjointed from the walls. It clunked and jolted a bit before it began its steady descent toward the floor. As low as it started, it wouldn't take long to crush me along with all the lady beetle carcasses. I gave the door, the small but not smallest of the doors, an attempt. But there was no string on this side of the door. Only on the more exterior sides of these doors. Even before the ceiling reached the header, going back the way I came wasn't an option.

Like a dog, a raccoon, like a possum, I skittered back across the floor. When my head smashed out the light bulb I never bothered to turn on, I ignored the sting of tiny cuts in my scalp. Instead, I plunged headfirst through the little open door. Immediately, my shoulders got hung up. I twisted a bit, curled inward, and worked them through one at a time. I dropped my phone to the floor of this new, inevitably even smaller room, and put both my palms against the frame, pushing myself into this cramped, dark place. My belly wedged firmly into the narrow gap. My breath sent out plumes of dust and shells and tiny transparent black wings into the air. I breathed some of it in. I hacked. I spat. The gleam of my phone, its lens pointing up, illuminated all those airborne particulates. I sucked in my stomach and squirmed.

I wasn't getting through. No way Jose. Too many decades of too many beers and too many pizzas.

The realization came on fast and unquestionably. The door wasn't going to work. Which left me with only one option: The "BOOM" button.

My hands switched sides of the door jamb. Rather than pushing me deeper in, they went to work pulling me out. Sure. I could have reached and pressed the button while I was still half in one room and half in another, but I had a fairly reasonable fear that hitting that button would do a terrible thing to one of these two rooms, and being in both increased my odds of catastrophe from fifty-fifty to one hundred percent.

It took work. It took time. It took a lot more sweat, enough to coat me from head to toe, but I managed my way out of the third room and back into the second. As soon as I was there, the dim sounds of the Ronettes competed with the grinding of whatever mechanism that was lowering the ceiling closer and closer to my head.

It was even with the top of the tiny door already. Would be low enough to compress me thin enough to maybe use it in seconds. Rather than giving it a chance, I stuck out one finger and depressed the "BOOM" button.

NOTHING BLEW UP. NOT the small room nor the smaller room. And not me either. Although I seemed to fade out. Everything went fogged over, blurred, slippery, and unclear. Visually, audibly, tactilely, but also consciously. I don't remember leaving that small and getting smaller each moment room, and I don't remember anything close to waking up in the next place. I just sort of faded back into reality like a song slowly turned up from zero.

I was lying on the floor along with all the dust and dead bugs. My skin was still wet with sweat, but it was cool now, which chilled me to the bone. The wetness of my cheek and forehead made a paste out of the dust bunnies and bug carcasses. My body hurt in various places. My heel. My lower back. My scalp. But I didn't immediately remember why. Instead, they were clues that allowed me to piece together my most recent misadventures. Like waking up in a sorority house with a pair of panties in the sheets, a used condom in the toilet, and a fifth of tequila spilled on the carpet. Only, a lot less fun.

Picking myself back up, I found that I could stand upright, that I was still surrounded by four walls of unfinished tongue-in-groove pine boards, that there was a small but human-sized door to my right and a half-sized (hobbit-sized I'd called it early) to my left. The human-sized door to my right had no doorknob and no string with which to open it. The light bulb over my head was intact and already turned on. Next to the hobbit door was a button.

And something on the other side of that door was making a deep, guttural, rhythmic thud... thud... thud.

And was that Christmas music? I thought I heard a piano and a chorus, out of sync with the thumps.

"What in the ever loving..." I mumbled. Talking to myself, if that was a symptom of insanity, had become commonplace sometime ago, and perhaps rightly so.

I staggered over to the smaller door. Just to get a closer listen. Not to do anything besides figure out what was causing that incessant thumping. My hands fell against the pine boards above the miniature door. I leaned my head against the wood, thankful for its support. That fade-in fade-out sensation returned, vaguely. Like the quieter echo from a much louder source. Leaning against the wall, looking down at the hobbit door, I noticed something for the first time.

One of the planks above the door was offset with the others. Raised from the otherwise flush wall. It was, I suspected, another door. Not a big door. Not even a hobbit or a pixie-sized door. More like a fall-away gun slit or a peephole. Something just big enough to see through.

Beyond the wall, that thudding paused. The music, still muffled to the point of unrecognizability, continued. The multiple walls it passed through muted all the nuances and details, but I had a good idea how it went. A sickeningly good idea. And I was starting to have a pretty damn good guess as to what was making those thuds.

A flood of possible implications followed.

What would happen if I opened that peephole? What would I see? What would happen if I didn't and simply went through the hobbit door? What if I hit the "BOOM" button again?

I glanced back to the human-sized door across the room that led back to the toy-littered bedroom. A vague outline of another gun slit / peephole formed above the header.

What would happen if I did nothing?

I didn't intend to open the panel. Didn't even know what I did to open it. Touched it maybe. Grazed my fingers over the surface. It fell inwards, whacking the wall on the other side of the door when it did. And just like that, I was peering into the smaller room. And what did I see?

Some asshole sweating through a hoodie and a Carhart coat, sitting on his keister with his Red Wing boot wound up to bash through the wall. A slice of thin glass from a busted out light bulb jutted from his forehead and leaked cherry-red blood into one squinted eye.

A long-forgotten Christmas carol went "Ring-a-ling-a-ding-dong-ding."

He spun my way. *I* spun my way. A version of me, an unnatural twin only a few DNA bonds off. Not me. Not exactly. Enough separation to differentiate. To do what I had to do next, before the slot in the door behind me opened up and revealed a pair of awful, judging eyes looking in on me.

As subconsciously, as thoughtlessly as I'd opened the gun slit, my fingers found the smooth round plastic of the "BOOM" button. A moment before pressing it, I saw panic in the eyes across the room. My fingers released the button. The peephole clapped back shut. The Christmas music muted. A low, mechanical grinding began on the other side of the wall. My awareness drained out of me like water from a leaking bucket. I don't remember my legs giving out. I hardly remembered hitting the floor.

COMING TO ON THE thin, worn out carpet decorated with the little cartoon city was only slightly more comfortable than waking up on the dust and dead-bug lined hardwood floor, but I was more than happy to feel it under my bones.

Groggy, drunk with whatever magic had brought me here, I sat up slowly. The old tube TV was behind me, as dead as a Kennedy. The ancient toys surrounded me like mourners around a casket. G.I. Joe. Barbie. Hot Wheels. The beat-up white box for a game of "Cooties." Beyond them was the door leading into... What was it? Not a closet or an office, but a small room that led to an even smaller room, which perhaps led to an infinite chain of ever decreasing rooms beyond that. No doorknob but a pull string to trigger the latch, but only from this side.

Was anyone left on the other side? Wedged between two rooms, trying to scream over the sound of a torturously sticky-sweet Christmas tune? Impossible. One man entered that trap, and one man came out. No one was on the other side. No one should ever go on the other side. That was the short and long of it.

I rose on unsteady legs. My feet shuffled across the carpet, kicking a toy out of the way as I went. My hands rested on the door's trim. No button next to this door. Nothing to warn others what might happen if they pulled on that string and walked through. I pinched that string but rather than pull it, I crammed it into the round hole where there should have been a door knob.

There. That was enough for now. Maybe later I'd board up the whole damn door, give anyone else the impression that zombies waited for them on the other side. Perhaps that wasn't so far from the truth.

Was there a vague outline of a gun slit just above this door? Did I hear a distant rhythmic thud... thud... thud... coming through multiple walls? Did I hear a faint but familiar tune coming not from the downstairs record player but through a series of shrinking doors? Was someone in there screaming as an unearthly weighted ceiling crushed them as easily as a light bulb?

There was no point in trying to answer those sorts of questions. There was only one question that really mattered: Call a realtor, a bulldozer, or both?

I could make that decision somewhere other than here, but I was leaning toward both. I didn't like this house. Never had. Wanted out and never wanted to set foot in it ever again. On my way out of the bedroom, my Red Wing kicked one last toy. The homemade video game control. Plastic buttons and a joystick from some old arcade machine screwed into a one-by piece of pine with a length of yarn dangling out of the back. A controller for your imagination.

Picking it up, I saw the buttons were labeled with nonsense terms only an old man who'd never so much as played Pacman might think appropriate. "ZAP," "WHOOSH," and finally, "BOOM." On the back of the controller, next to the spot where the red yarn was affixed with a big glob of yellow wood glue, were a few words written in black magic marker. The handwriting matched that of the card I had tucked into my hip pocket, written with the same but significantly younger and slightly steadier hand.

"Merry Christmas Jane and Michael! Grandpa loves you! - December 25th, 1984"

Eyes shifting back to the door without a knob, I pressed the "BOOM" button one more time, tossed the fake control to the floor, and walked out.

THE END

About the Author

Joe Prosit writes sci-fi, horror, and psycho fiction. His novels include Bad Brains, 99 Town, 7 Androids, Zero City, Look What You Made Me Do, and most recently, They Come From Below, a Lovecraftian horror set in northern Minnesota. He has published many short stories in various magazines and podcasts and compiled them in his short story collections titled Machines Monsters and Maniacs. All his books can be found at www.JoeProsit.com. If you'd like to find the man himself, he's regularly on the road at cons and events all across the Midwest or lost deep in the Great North Woods. He lives with his wife, kids, and dog in northern Minnesota.

THEY SHALL NOT GROW OLD

BY JARED BARTEMEYER

The hinterlands around Luxembourg City were beautiful this time of year. The markets were shaped, the music and cheer, the children were laughing... oh, the sweet little dears. Then one night became many, the raucous and jeer... don't say it too loudly, you'll awaken their tears.

HANNA VOGEL
FIFTEEN YEARS AGO – December – Luxembourg City

The smells of fresh bread and sweets filled the air as Sophia wiggled her way through the crowd. *To be young again,* thought Hanna. "Sophia, where I can see you, please... *bitte.*" Watching her sister's troubling innocence... while trying to keep up with the little one's holiday excitement was no easy feat, but she managed... allowed herself to enjoy it, even. The markets never felt more alive to her than they did this time of year... she thought, gazing through the mass. After their grandmother had passed, it was just the two of them. Hanna wasn't ready to be a parent. By all margins none of it was just. She found that out on a night much like this one... several years ago, when her father and mother were taken from them. She was only nine, but life wouldn't let her grieve... not even for a moment, it made her grow faster than most. Her parents had been on holiday... they had never left or gotten away before, just the two of them... but that year, five years ago this past November... everything changed. Nothing was fair—none of it.

Hanna could see Sophia laughing, running near the edge of the market with the neighbor's boys, Victor and Loran. Victor dreamt of being a football star, while Loran would often talk about aeronautics... *his love for airplanes and history was widely known throughout the neighborhood.* He buzzed around chasing them with his small red airplane model, pretending he was a fighter ace from one of the great wars. As she turned towards the local baker's tent, the fresh smell of daily bread filling her nose, Hanna let herself feel young again. She loved baking with her mother in her grandmother's kitchen. All at once, the smells of fresh pastries and sweets took her back to a more pleasant time. She picked out several sweets for the next morning, but also éclairs for Sophia and Victor... and of course a madeleine for Loran to enjoy tonight. Turning away, Hanna looked for Sophia, but she wasn't there. *Damn it, Sophia... why can't she listen?* Making her way through the crowd, towards the market's edge, she called out for her. "Sophia? Come please, I've brought sweets." There was nothing, only the muted hum of the city market.

Just then, she looked down on the snow-covered ground that lined the edge of the plaza. *A small red airplane was turned over, half buried in the snow... Loran.* She dropped her bag of sweets and picked up the plane, examining it in her hands. Her eyes became wide as she suddenly felt the weight of the present moment. Standing up, holding the plane in her left arm, she frantically scanned the crowd. *Oh my God, where are they...*

Suddenly, a tug on her jacket. *It was Loran... oh thank God...* he reached for the plane and smiled. Relieved, Hanna bent down to him. "Loran, are Sophia and Victor with you?"

"Oui... Yes..." Loran could smell the sweets in the bag. He picked them up and looked inside. "They're just over there, with them..." His eyes lit up when he saw the madeleine that Hanna had brought for him. "Is this one for me?"

"Natürlich... of course, Loran... I've even got some éclairs for your brother and Sophia... would you show me where they are?"

"Ja... okay. They're over there near the edge of the forest... playing with—"

"Oh... that's it. We're leaving, come now Loran... make sure you have your things... come on now, take me to them." *Near the forest... at night...*

Sophia knew better than that. Hanna grabbed Loran's wrist and began a brisk walk through the field. Snow started falling more heavily as they walked towards the trees, as the holiday songs and bells from the market began to fade. Hanna could tell Loran was upset... *she could hear him crying...* that's when she realized how hard she'd grabbed his wrist. She let go, bending down in front of him. "Oh Loran... I'm so sorry... it's just that I worry." Loran gathered himself and looked to Hanna...

"It's okay, Hanna, I understand... *I think.* Thank you for the sweet."

Hannah opened the bag and revealed another madeleine; she handed it to him—wiping away a tear streaming down from his left eye. Hanna held Loran's left hand, and they walked together towards the forest. A moment passed before Hanna noticed Loran wasn't eating the sweet. "All full?"

"I think I'll save it for them... they looked hungry."

Hanna smirked, "You go ahead and eat, sweet boy. I brought some more for Victor and Sophia."

"No, not them... the soldiers. They didn't say anything... but I could tell."

Hanna furrowed her brow. "Soldiers... *here?"* As they continued to walk, Hanna quizzically looked down at Loran... the madeleine tucked tightly to his chest.

As the snow continued to fall, the edge of the forest came into view. Hanna could see Sophia and Victor, *they were laughing...* running around kicking a ball. "Sophia... Victor... come now, we're going home." They didn't respond. It was as if they couldn't hear her.

"Come on, Hanna... follow me." Loran said, then ran forward toward his brother. Hanna ran after him, trying to keep pace... Loran flying his little airplane in his hands, making propeller noises. As she ran, Hanna's shoe broke a clasp. She bent down to inspect the damage... *wonderful.* Looking up, she could see Loran now next to his brother... he held out the madeleine high into the air... *some sort of offering.*

Hanna got to her feet, walking forward slowly, as to not lose her shoe. Just then, all in an instant, the snow stopped falling and everything was silent—even the laughs and cheers of the children couldn't be heard. It felt foreign, her hands, breath... even her own thoughts she felt were betraying her. That's when Hanna saw them, *the soldiers Loran had mentioned.* She counted ten... maybe twelve men. Hanna couldn't see their faces... *it was as if they didn't have any,* but based on their dress, Hanna guessed Second

World War... maybe First... she wasn't sure. She could only see German uniforms... *blood was everywhere.* What was this... *a dream... a nightmare?* One of the soldiers noticed her... followed by the rest. *Then it all stopped...* the children frozen in place, the soldiers standing at attention—facing toward her. Hanna wanted to move, but she couldn't... begging to call for Sophia, *but unable.* Then the ground began to shake... the trees in the forest began to rattle... *and then they were gone.*

Almost in an instant, Hanna could breathe again. She felt the snow falling on her face and hands. She looked around, *but everything... everyone was gone.* That's when she brought her hand up, revealing a small red airplane... *Loran's.*

It was all so vivid... as if reality was the lie. Focused on the unexplainable, Hanna fell to her knees and screamed. *She was alone... again.*

So, the years would pass, this reminder for all, the innocence lost... when duty called.

Foster Grant

Present Day – December – New York City

It had been one hell of a quarter... *better part of a year, really.* Looking down onto the city, I wondered how there could be such life and abundance... *and how I could feel so alone.* These past few years had really taken their toll on everything... and now the holiday season was in full effect. The rushed deadlines, grueling late hours, and mired thoughts presented the most unpleasant spell... truly making it *the most wonderful time of year.* I didn't quite know how I was still standing, *honestly...* I guess I'd been doing it for so many years... but I'd be doing it a disservice if I didn't at least admit that the work was impressive. The hollow and unflinching nature of the business meant that I had more securities and options than most of them down there... *such embarrassing wealth.* Daring to say it aloud made it sound even worse. *This enviable station in life...* soul crushing in ways that are difficult to wrap meaning around. *I know it's what sent her away.*

Teresa and I met during undergrad, through an international study abroad program in Europe. She knew me before any of this, better than anyone... *I think.* Times were simpler. We shared laughs... moments of doubt, sadness... *desires.* It all felt so right... the dreams we had, where we saw ourselves when we were old and grey... *I wanted to provide that for her...* the future and family we would build together... it all seemed so wonderful—*so possible... I couldn't wait for us to get there.* These were such naïve thoughts, though, made by those yet to experience much of the world... *the way things worked.* She was my everything... *but I hadn't been that for her.* Looking back now, knowing what had happened, how much we had been through together—how it all came undone... *I swear to God I was a better man than that.* I don't blame her for leaving... I didn't fight it... *but I should have.* I could say that everything I've done until now has been for her and Cassandra, but the truth was that I was good at what I did, *the world needed men like me...* that was my justification... my rationale... what I told myself for years... and every day my body ached... *it was getting harder to maintain the lie.*

For weeks now I'd put the phone in my hand with the intention of calling... her name appearing on the screen... *just to hear her voice... I didn't care if they were the same words I'd heard before...* but my hands wouldn't let me dial. *Every single night...* as if my body knew this soul wasn't worthy of such love... of devotion... *every time caving to vices,* drowning the nights under the burden of some misguided sense of self-preservation.

Cassandra, my daughter... she didn't understand why things were different. I wanted to be the man my wife once thought I was... the father Cassandra deserved. She was growing up too fast, these past few years becoming a blur. *Had it really been three years since that science project on the kitchen table?* Something had to change.

As I walked back inside, I noticed the clock – 6:48PM. Ten minutes or so until Ingrid would drop off Cassandra from ballet. She'd been working so hard... *I knew her mother would be proud.* My favorite nights had always been the ones we'd spent together in this room. Teresa was an architect and structural engineer for the city—her office strewn about with plans and papers... measurements and possibilities. Originally from the Catalonia region of Spain, I knew it was hard for her to accept some of the more modern forms of building and planning that so often lacked the soul from where she had come. I had always appreciated the way her mind worked. It's one of the things we bonded over most... her creativity and scope...

and the numbers. In both of our fields, they had to make sense, or else everything would fall apart. *There wouldn't be nights like that any longer...*

She never even told me she was sick... *that I never noticed her pain was worse.* Then one day, nearly three months after she'd taken Cassandra to stay at her mother's... *she died.* I remember when I got the phone call, *I was working late... again. I knew she'd died of a broken heart... it was all my fault.* I got up from the desk and walked toward the window and looked out... no one down there would notice my pain... *why would they? What was their reason to care?* Not long after, Cassandra came home to stay. So wrapped up in my guilt, I nearly forgot to be a father.

Five minutes until she was home.

We had to get away. As Christmas approached, I thought about what would mean the most for Cassandra. She'd just lost her mother... *what kind of gift does that warrant?* How she had any spirit left about her was a bravery I felt few possessed. Even though she was only nine years old, Cassandra had often asked me about what her mother was like when she was young. Perhaps this was the time to share those moments with her, to create our own memories together, and start out this next year with an outlook that was undimmed for the first time in years. *We would go back to where it all started... Luxembourg City... where we had met.* I would show her the city center, the charming and historic neighborhoods of The Grund, the castles and architecture of the regions that Teresa so desperately tried to incorporate into her work... and the Christmas markets that this time of year were so magical in their own ways. *She would love it... we both would.*

WHEN WE ARRIVED, THE scene was magnificent. Immediately I was taken back to my youth. The vibrancy of the city felt just right... the stucco buildings, a dusting of snow... the smells of cinnamon and honey, kebabs and fresh pastries. I hadn't seen Cassandra's face so filled with joy in some time... *I would show her everything.* She ran over and looked through a large section of local flyers and catalogs. As I joined her, I remember visiting some of these places myself... the castle in Vianden, the Palais Grand-Ducal, even the Chateau we met at in Differdange. *We would go to it all. I would let her see the world as her mother did when she was young.*

CHECKING INTO THE HOTEL was easy enough... most people could tell you were American straight away. They wanted to practice their English with you... and so often we'd be speaking in German, or French... *Luxembourgish for the initiated...* and they'd be responding in English. It was all a bit ironic... but it had a certain level of charm I think we all appreciated. The entry was grand and distinguished, chrome accents and archways that spread throughout the lobby. Checking in, I noticed several more flyers on the desk... reading one aloud, "The Luxembourg American Cemetery... within walking distance of the Sandweiler German Military Cemetery. These hollowed grounds offering a unique look and reminder for the costs of war." Hmm, I thought... *that might be interesting.* Cassandra and I were both trying to turn the page with a new lease on life... perhaps recognizing the young men of our past that allowed it to happen would be somewhere to start. *That would have to wait until tomorrow, though...* after the initial rush and taking in of these new surroundings, I feared Cassandra and I would barely have the energy to make it up to the room. Stuffing the pamphlets into my jacket pocket, I picked up our luggage and called the elevator... in the morning we would explore the city together.

THE SUN SHONE BRIGHTLY the following morning. I let Cassandra stay in the bed nearer the window; the sounds of cobblestone streets and snowfall I know helped her sleep better. She had gotten up before me... standing close to the window, examining something in her hands. "What's that you have there?" I said, sitting up and gathering myself.

"Look Father, isn't it beautiful?" Cassandra raced over and sat next to me on the bed—handing me a *small red airplane...* it looked like something mid last century. History had always been one of my great loves, but I hadn't appreciated it as much in my college years as I had in my formative. I'd switched my focus to International Relations when I'd gone abroad... *Teresa made sure I excelled in that department.*

"Is this something you brought... did Mother or Nanna get this for you?"

"No, Father... it was here, just this morning... sitting on the windowsill. Isn't it magnificent? *It looks really old...* but quite good for its age."

"Sitting there, just in the window? You didn't bring it?" Cassandra slowly shook her head, signaling she hadn't. Getting up, I set the plane on the bed next to Cassandra, slid into my slippers and raced toward the window. Looking around the edges, there was no fire escape, no way to enter from the outside... *and it was bolted down from inside the room.* It couldn't have come from here... maybe we just didn't notice it last night, after all... we were quite tired when we arrived. Perhaps housekeeping left gifts for the children at this time of year. *Wouldn't that be special?*

THE ELEVATOR DOORS OPENED, and the lobby came into view. The hotel was fairly crowded with the comings and goings of fellow patrons, while the smell of fresh bacon and jams quickly turned us toward the breakfast lounge. Everyone seemed so friendly... and we took our fill to eat. We positioned ourselves by the large windows that bordered the sidewalk just outside. With Christmas markets and decorations strewn outside, I knew that Cassandra was itching to get outside and explore... *so we did.*

Outside, the weather was cool, not unbearably so, but enough that the rooftops and surrounding yards had a fine dusting of fresh powder. When I thought of how I wanted Cassandra to be introduced to the city... this was exactly how I'd imagined it. We headed toward the courtyard. There were several ornate fountains in the middle, the pumps turned off, but still quite beautiful to admire. Surrounding them were pop-up shops of a wide variety. Bakers, artisans, leather workers, and butchers... they all gave life to the square. It was still morning, but the smokers and ovens were busy preparing the goods needed for an imminent lunchtime feast.

I held Cassandra's hand as we looked at one of the holiday shops. Ornate Ornaments... all glass blown and hand crafted. I remember having gotten something similar for Teresa as a gift the year we left. *I wanted to surprise her,* so I carefully wrapped it and took it on the plane with me. Unfortunately, it didn't survive the flight... *crushed in my backpack.* I remember, days later when she met my parents, she raved about how beautiful and considerate she thought it was. When they asked to see it, she followed it up with, *"it just wasn't very practical..."*

Cassandra picked out several ornaments and a new scarf. The latter went well with her green eyes... I wonder if she knew it was her mother's favorite color. "Father, I've heard the pastries and sweets from the shop at the end *are to die for...* may we please go there next?" She got the sweet tooth from me, not Teresa... she came by it honestly. I guess I didn't realize what a little researcher and planner she'd become, *it's as if she herself had been here before.*

"It's your day, sweetheart... you lead." Without hesitation, she raced toward a shop near the end of the street. Its fumes were intoxicating, no doubt... and by the time I'd caught up with Cassandra, she was already enjoying samples of various sweets. "Father, try a madeleine, they're delicious... I knew they'd be."

I ordered several of them for us to enjoy... *she was right,* brought me straight back... they were wonderful. "Cassandra, I didn't know you liked sponge-cake. How did you come to decide on that one?"

"He told me," she calmly delivered.

"Who told you...?"

"I'm not sure... he seemed nice. He said he was just visiting where he used to live." That's when she procured the small red airplane from the hotel.

"Well, if you see him again... tell him these were an excellent choice." We then walked toward the edge of the market and found a bench to enjoy our spoils. Several violinists and a cellist were warming up close to the fountain, while games of chess amongst the locals were intensely driven nearby.

People watching had always brought me comfort, and I noticed Cassandra's gaze had fixated on a young woman walking out near the edge of the forest. She was dressed in all black and carried a bouquet of flowers.

As I flipped open the morning paper, I didn't give it much attention at first. Cassandra, though, stepped up to the edge of the courtyard, fetching a closer look. I flipped to the local news section. The headline read, '*Alone in the Dark: The Fifteenth Year Anniversary of the Tree Line Three.*' *That was today... December 23rd... exactly fifteen years ago.* I continued reading... survived by her sister Hanna... Sophia Vogel, and Victor and Loran Auclair disappeared on the night of December 23rd, 2009. Local authorities investigated the claims and took statements from witnesses to the event, but the mystery remains unsolved to this day... the case now rests in the hands of the state.

By now, the woman in black had set her flowers down near the trees and made her way back toward the courtyard. Cassandra watched her as she moved her way down a side street and away from the market... I could see her keeping her face hidden, wiping tears from her face. That's when I stood up, and saw her leaning her back against a neighborhood shop... *was this the woman from the paper... Hanna?* Before I could say anything, Cassandra had already begun chasing after her. "Cassandra, sweetheart... wait!" The crowd parted as I followed her towards the eatery. She didn't stop though; she just waved for me to follow.

Cassandra had by now approached the woman... extending her hand and introducing herself. I could see the woman's makeup running slightly near the eyes, a cigarette in her left hand. I managed to fumble through some words, "hi... umm are you alright?... I mean... Sprechen Sie Englisch?"

"Ja... hello, I'm—"

"Hanna... right?" She looked at me, puzzled, taking a drag from her cigarette. I brought up the newspaper and flipped through to the article... "Alone in the Dark..."

"Ja, that's me... the one who got away."

"I'm terribly sorry, I'm not good at this... I just wanted to—"

"Say you're sorry? What for?" Hanna took a deep inhale and then flicked her cigarette away down the alley. "It's been fifteen years... I'm all done with sorry and condolences... they're still out there somewhere... I know they are."

Cassandra took hold of Hanna's hands. "You're right... they say not to worry... that they'll be okay..."

Hanna leaned down in front of Cassandra. "You're sweet, child... to comfort a stranger. What's your name?"

"Cassandra..."

"You look about the same age as my sister, Sophia... the last time I saw her. She had beautiful green eyes, just like yours... but I fear I will not see hers again, so maybe I'll just look at yours a little longer." Hanna then leaned in and kissed Cassandra on the forehead. As she stood up, a tear streamed down her left side. Wiping it away, she turned toward me... "guess I'm not all cried out, after all." She gave this bittersweet look beneath a half-hearted smile.

I didn't know what to say, but somehow managed the words. "I know that no one can fully understand another's pain... I know that, but... well, we both lost someone very close to us recently, and I know how hard it can be. I wasn't there for her. For years, I was a different person than the one she knew. I see that same sadness in your eyes."

"Many here still don't believe me... they think that I had a psychotic break... that I've somehow lost my mind... *that I could be involved in their disappearances. Maybe they were right...* I keep coming back to the same place, and none of it makes sense. They had uniforms... the more I researched, the stranger everything was. *They were German uniforms from the Second World War...* I know that somehow the German Military Cemetery here in Sandweiler is at the heart of it. The mass graves, the unknown soldiers... were they the restless spirits of the men buried there? I don't know, none of it seemed natural. *I've tried for so many years.* It's as if they're reminding us of what they lost... *the innocence of their youth.*" Hanna's face softened. It looked like it had been years since someone had cared. "And I know how it sounds, *that I've gone mad... right?* Just kind of given up on most things in recent years... you know? Hoping that one day, it'll all be over... like some kind of dream."

"What about coffee? Have you given up on that?" I smirked; a moment of levity filling the air. Sensing this, Cassandra looked into the bag of sweets and grabbed another madeleine. "Haven't you had enough young lady..." I jived.

"It's not for me, Father... it's for Hanna." Cassandra offered the cake to Hanna. "I was told it was your favorite."

Hanna bent down once more. "They are... who told you that? Fritz... no, let me guess... ah, I know... Ms. Laude is a few streets over. She told you, didn't she... she's always trying to feed—"

"No, the young boy from this morning... *Loran.* He said they were your favorites, and he wanted to thank you for the last one you gave him."

"Cassandra... what boy are you talking about?" I didn't understand what she was saying; I'd been with her all day... *I don't remember her with anyone.*

"The one from breakfast this morning... he was outside of the window... he mentioned he liked my red airplane... he wanted me to take care of it for him. He also said that the soldiers were kind to him... to all of them." Cassandra procured the small red plane from her pocket and placed it in Hanna's palm. *"I think you should have it."*

Hanna looked down at the airplane... I barely knew her, but it looked like she'd seen a ghost. She dropped the plane and stood up, visibility shaken. "This disappeared years ago... what is this... what do you want? Who are you people?!"

Cassandra took both of our hands and began walking out toward the tree line. "Come... I'll show you." Frightened, Hanna met my gaze... I wanted to speak, but I couldn't. I could tell Hanna was scared. *Was this still my daughter?*

MOMENTS PASSED AS CASSANDRA led us through the fields and into the trees... then a small clearing, before it came into view. The wall which lined the cemetery allowed us entry as we made our way down the cobblestone path.

"We're almost there." Cassandra voiced. Rows of gravestones lined the walk, the names of young men that hadn't grown old. *Men...* I could barely stomach it. Most of them were teenagers... *but they were old enough to go to war,* and this was the result. This was the Sandweiler German Military Cemetery... based on the prior reading, most of them lost their lives in the winter of 1944 during the Battle of the Bulge. *The war should have been over...* instead, their lives given to God on the most unholy of doomed crusades. The skies had darkened and illuminated the cross which dominated the rear of the site. There were rows of headstones... but this cross was a reminder of the men whose names were lost to time... *a mass grave given with no sanctuary or peace.*

Then the snow stopped falling, and everything was silent. As a deep fog rolled in, my body felt foreign. I could tell Hanna had been here before. Then a rustling of trees, slowed breath, and heightened senses... *then a child's laugh.*

"Sophia?! Victor... Loran?" Hanna rushed forward, collapsing to one knee, unable to continue. "Sophia... where are you?! If you can hear my voice, please come home." Her voice echoed for a moment... then the soldiers appeared through the fog... dozens of them. Their uniforms tattered, some stripped and bare... *the ghosts of dead men.*

Hanna frantically grabbed a notebook from her bag and opened a page near the middle. "Hans Meier... Deiter Klein... Rolf Angel... I see you... I see all of you. I've found your names... I want to give you peace. In this lifetime of war, I ache for you to have it. I pray for your lost innocence, the lives you could not bear... but please don't take their future... I beg of you."

Then one of the ghosts moved forward and bent down in front of Hanna—he looked toward Cassandra... "then she must take their place."

"No!" I bellowed... suddenly finding my voice—the attention quickly settling to me. "I'll go..."

Cassandra pulled at my jacket, looking concerned. "Father? Where are you going?"

Bending down, I kissed her forehead... "it's going to be alright sweetheart." I stood up, struggling to move past Hanna.

"Don't... it's not fair..." Hanna cried.

"Nothing's fair... I'm just glad I got to spend this last day with my daughter." I looked back towards Cassandra. "I know you'll make us proud."

The ground started to shake as the soldier motioned me toward the forest. I could sense Hanna holding Cassandra tight, not letting her follow me. *I dare not look back.* It was all a dream... everything faded as we entered the forest... then three children ran out toward Hanna. A girl... and two boys. *I'm sorry, Cassandra... I love you more than you know.*

Everything went dark after that... and moments of silence passed. Then the sounds of machine guns and tanks... screams of men dying. It was awful, overwhelming... all consuming. It stayed like that for some time...

MY HANDS RAN ACROSS the sheets; they were soft and freshly cleaned. The ache in my heart was gone as I opened my eyes... *I was back in the apartment. It was New York... was it really all a dream?* I grabbed my phone and checked online... desperately trying to find a story of the missing children in Luxembourg... *there was nothing.* I could hear Cassandra laughing in the kitchen... *Cassandra....* I sprung out of bed and raced to see her...

Teresa turned around with coffee in her hands... "good, you're finally awake... should we make some breakfast?". I dropped my phone and stared at her. "Is everything okay?"

That's when I walked up to her, kissing her passionately—spilling her coffee on the floor. I looked in her eyes, the most beautiful shade of amber... *this was my Teresa.* I didn't know how... I didn't care why. She looked at me with such relief. It had been years since I'd seen the weight of it all lifted from her shoulders. *Things would be different now...*

"Father, come look..." Cassandra was decorating the tree in the living room. My fingers lingered on Teresa before she playfully pushed me away. I smirked and went over to Cassandra.

"Well, you've been busy this morning..."

"Mhmm, I saved one for you..."

Cassandra handed me a small wooden box. "What is it?" I asked as she ran toward her mother. I shook my head... *alright, no answer.* As I opened the lid and peeled away the wrapping, *a small red airplane appeared*—a handwritten note underneath it. I looked to Cassandra... hugging her mother, and then back to the note... it read, *'make us proud'.*

Holding the note up, I looked toward Cassandra. She held her index finger to her lips... and smiled.

About the Author

Jared Bartemeyer is a screenwriter, author, and executive producer based in the Chicagoland area. He's created, written, and produced nearly 30 titles, while working with over 50 incredible artists from around the world. He's the lead visual designer and art director for Eden Skye and Arcadian Fall, while also remaining the front facing project manager for distribution and publishing. As an industry veteran, he's exhibited at hundreds of shows around the United States, hitting most major markets—while hosting story crafting panels through Fan Expo, Wizard World, and Revolution conventions. With a deep love and respect for adventure, culture, nuance, and historical context, he's been able to craft thoughtful universes and compelling lore. Through his experience, he's found that audiences are craving new stories with characters and motives that matter. Jared was selected as a quarterfinalist in Screencraft's animation screenplay competition, and holds degrees in History and Diplomacy & Foreign Affairs from Miami University. Additionally, Jared also heads the Chicago area publisher Aeonian Dawn.

THE 12 DAYS OF MURDER

BY T.R. NICKEL

ONE YEAR AGO – 24th of December

The precinct smells like pine air fresheners and coffee.

Someone had stuck a mini Christmas tree in the break room, the kind that runs on batteries and sings carols in tinny, off-key bursts if you press its foot. It's been driving Ket mad, so I make sure to press it on my way in, just to see him twitch.

"You're evil," he mutters around a mouthful of jammy dodger.

"Festive," I counter, peeling off gloves damp from the cold. "It's the day I was named after, so I'm just getting into the holiday spirit."

He rolls his eyes, and we head over to our workstations.

The desk is a mess—papers, files, a rogue Saint Nicholas bobblehead someone's placed there as my secret santa gift. I poke his head and see it wobble, which makes a small chuckle leave my lips.

Even with a mountain of paperwork piles on my desk, it doesn't deter my mood. There's frost on the windows and a cheer in the air.

It's a good day.

We've got two cases close to wrapping—one burglary ring nearly nailed, and an identity theft that turned out to be a pissed-off ex with access to bank logins. Nothing spectacular or glamorous, but it's honest work.Not to mention I'm close to solving this stalker case. The profile is already put together, and I have cops patrolling for anyone who fits the description.

Things are looking great.

I sip on my coffee and flip open the file for Mrs. Talbot's missing Yorkshire terrier. She swears it's been kidnapped, and made sure we made note that it was wearing its gingerbread bandana.

I believe her when she says her dog didn't just run away. I mean, I don't—but I want to.

And that's the thing, really. I still want to believe people. That we're doing this job to help, to protect. That we can get there in time—most of the time—and when we don't, it isn't because the world is dark. It's because we're still catching up to the light.

Ket comes over, leans on my desk, and raises a brow. "You're chipper. Did you win the lottery?"

"Better," I say. "I slept more than four hours."

"Saints preserve us for the wave of energy that is a less sleep deprived Eve!"

I laugh. The sound is easy, unguarded. While we work, I stop to notice the way the walls look under the winter sun, and how the lights reflect off the badges of those who were killed on duty that hang in a glass case.

I've been here long enough for the shine to feel normal—but not long enough for it to fade.

There's a case board on the far wall, string and photos still pinned like spiderwebs in progress. I glance at it with anticipation, not dread. Every face there is someone I intend to help.

As the day dwindles to a close, I leave the station. My scarf is wrapped around me, breath curling in the air like steam from a kettle.

The city feels alive. Carollers are warming up outside the market. A child tugs on their mum's sleeve to point at the animatronic reindeer in the bakery window. The air smelling like roasted chestnuts and cinnamon. Everything feels great, until I feel a tug on my arm.

Timell is breathing heavily, a small bead of sweat dripping down his forehead. "A tip just came through. Abandoned warehouse, Angel Lane. A man dragging Collin inside."

He doesn't need to repeat himself before we are rushing towards the police car.

Snow's falling in weak spirals. One of those slushy, grey winter evenings.

We've been on this case for three days. Collin Snow. Good man, by all accounts—family bloke, worked finance, sang in the church choir.

He had mentioned that someone had been following him. So much so he began to get scared. Then his car was broken into, and then his house. Collin came to us and demanded action and I had reassured him and his wife that we would find the stalker and keep them all safe.

I was so close. So close I could feel it in my chest, but if that tip is real... close will mean nothing.

The warehouse is at the edge of the city. Rusted siding, shattered windows, spray-painted reindeer with blunts in their mouths. There's a wreath on the door—plastic, sun-faded, tied with a bow.

The padlock we had put on it years ago is now laying on the ground broken. I draw my weapon and shoulder the door open. Even if it is just from some kids who had broken in to be dumb and have fun, the fact is, someone saw our suspect here—and I'm not taking chances if it means getting to our civilian in time.

A metallic smell assaults my nose. It snakes into my lungs, coats the back of my throat. I taste it before I register it. My stomach lurches, but I force it back down.

The floor beneath my boots groans, the sound echoing off rusted beams and cracked concrete. Flashlight slicing the dark, until it lands on him.

Hanging suspended from a steel support beam like an ornament. Collin's wrists are bound with rope, the fibres dark with blood where they cut into the skin. His throat slit..

My chest tightens. My hands don't shake, but I can feel the weight building behind my ribs, behind my eyes.

BREAK

I deliver the news myself.

I owe them that much. More than that, even. There's no protocol strong enough to convince me otherwise. No junior officer I trust to carry something this heavy.

Their house is lit up like every other in the neighbourhood. Strings of coloured bulbs crisscross the windowsill, blinking slow and steady—red, green, red, green. A plastic reindeer slouches in the garden, nose unlit. A snowman leans crooked in the yard, a carrot nose and button eyes.

Their house is about to feel empty in the place Collin once took up, and I'm the one who is going to make them realise that horrible truth.

I wish I had better news, that I could have gotten there in time, could have stopped it from happening at all—but the reality is something else.

I climb the steps slowly, boots scraping frost from each one. My breath ghosts in front of me. My hands are cold despite the gloves.

Lara answers before I knock. She's wearing a jumper with Santa's jolly face smiling at me.

It's far too big for her, sleeves bunched at the wrists, the neck stretched wide.

The kids are behind her. A boy and a girl. The boy clutches the doorframe. The girl—Holly, I remember now—stands very still, peeking out from behind her mother.

Lara speaks before I do. "Collin hasn't come home," she says, voice shaking. "Please tell me he's okay."

The Saints know I wish I could.

"I'm so sorry," I say, voice low and cracking.

Her knees go. Like the strings holding her upright have been cut.

She sinks to the floor in the open doorway, hand clinging to the frame. Her son—Lucas—drops down beside her instinctively, latching onto her arm, his tiny fingers wrapping around her sleeve like if he holds tight enough, this might still be a bad dream.

Holly looks at her mother with furrowed brows and tears welling in her eyes.

They are too young to understand what my apology was really for, but I think a part of them knows just from their mothers reaction.

I kneel beside Lara, and for a moment, I don't speak. Just sit. Let her sob. Let her lean into her son.

There's no comfort I can give that'll make this better, no words that will make the truth any lighter. So I don't insult them with a script. I just stay.

Later, I make them all tea.

It gives me something to do. My hands are shaking. I stare too long at the mismatched mugs in the cupboard before I pick one with a snowman on it.

Noel Snow sits at the kitchen table, Collin's father. His eyes are clouded over with shock, his posture brittle. There's a faint tremor in his right hand as he grips the mug I pass him. He stares at it for a long time before speaking.

"He was always home by six," he says, voice thin and far away. "Said it was sacred. Family time. Dinner. No matter what was happening."

I nod. My throat's too tight to speak.

"He built the dollhouse under the tree," Noel adds, eyes misting. "Stayed up till three making sure the roof tiles lined up. Said he wanted Holly to think Santa was a damn architect."

In the living room, Nicholas is pacing—Collin's brother. His movements are sharp, erratic—like a wire pulled too tight. The second I step through the archway, he's on me.

"You were supposed to protect him!" he snaps, voice splintered. "You said you had leads! Said you were closing in!"

"I know—"

"You don't know shit." He takes a step forward, fists clenched. "You had one job. One. And now my brother's gone."

I don't flinch. I don't defend myself because he is just grieving the only way he knows how. He needs to throw the blame somewhere. I let it be me.

"I'm sorry," I say again, and it's not enough, and never will be.

Chris's breathing is ragged. Tears stream down his cheeks but he doesn't notice, or doesn't care. He storms past me, slamming his fist into the wall on his way down the hall.

Noel doesn't even look up from the tea. Lara's still holding the kids on the couch, whispering things I can't hear.

I don't know how long I should stay.

An hour or two? Maybe until the silence stretches too far. Perhaps just until the fire dims and the kids start to drift, heads on laps and shoulders.

When I finally leave, the sky is waking up.

Pale gold spills across the slush-covered street, turning ice to diamonds that don't sparkle. My breath fogs the windshield as I sit in the car, both hands wrapped around the wheel.

Frozen.

This wasn't a failure of logic or procedure. It wasn't missed evidence or lack of leads.

I did everything right. I chased every thread. Knocked on every door. Cross-referenced every theory. I really, truly believed we'd get there in time. That we'd save him, but we didn't and that's what I can't shake. That's what won't let me sleep—what still whispers in the quiet hours.

Once upon a time, I thought effort was enough. That if you worked hard, followed your gut, gave a damn—you could win, but this city doesn't run on hope.

Not even during Christmas.

Not anymore.

ON THE FIRST DAY

I've seen some odd sights in my time — a bloke proposing to his girlfriend in the frozen-food aisle, a vicar dancing drunk on a pub table, a councilwoman streaking across the green during last year's summer fête. But this? This tops the lot.

The orchard was a place I was fond of back when I was a kid. It was where we would play hide-and-seek amongst the gnarled trunks. We would come home sticky with pear juice and scraped knees. Regardless of the season, this was a playground in my youth.

Right now, the trees leaned with brittle weight, iced over and groaning under the December's frost. It would be pretty if it weren't for the body strung up in the branches, arms splayed out like wings, head cocked at an unnatural angle. A taxidermied bird—a partridge—nailed to his chest.

"Jesus, Mary, and Joseph," mutters Ket, pulling his scarf higher up his face as if that'll keep the smell out. "What kind of sick freak—?"

"Let's find out," I cut him off.

There's no point in stating the obvious. This is the most fucked up thing this town probably has ever seen outside the murder of Collin last year.

I step closer, the snow crunching beneath my boots. The stuff that had fallen last night has covered any tracks we could have found, which at least gives us a timeframe.

"Snow started falling at twenty-hundred hours, then stopped around three this morning." I say out loud for Ket to jot down and for us to fact check later. "The frost on the body suggests he's been out here for at least four hours."

"Would put the scene set up at around one," Ket states, scribbling into his small notebook.

Nodding my head, I stare up at Jolly Fenn. He worked maintenance at the community center. Lived over on Juniper.

He had been a quiet man, but always showed up at town events. Charlie never caused any trouble, had never attracted it either—yet now he is a Christmas decoration.

My gaze shifts to the bird. I furrow my brow as I see something sticking out of its beak.

"Get me gloves." I shout to the coroner, who has been waiting to do her job.

She rushes forward, handing me the latex. I climb the ladder she had set up to get up close enough to pull it free. The paper crinkles—a rolled-up piece of parchment.

On the first day of Christmas, my true love gave to me...

I stare at the words, my heart thudding in my ears. Ket stood down at the foot of the ladder, his eyes watching me intently.

Something about the handwriting tugged at a memory—familiar, but not something I could place.

My stomach twists.

"Eve?" Ket's voice cuts through.

I snap my fingers, him already knowing that I'll be needing an evidence bag.

As I slip it inside, I look down towards him to meet his eyes. "Start canvassing the area. I want to know if anyone saw someone wandering around this morning."

Ket nodded, but he just held the ladder as I climbed down. "You think they will strike again?"

"I think this is just the beginning, and we have eleven more nights to go."

The coroner gave me a quiet nod, then moved in to begin her work, the ladder creaking beneath her weight. Ket lingered by the tree, his expression carved from disbelief and something deeper—fear.

I was already pulling out my phone when I heard the tires crunching over ice.

The sleek black SUV rolled to a stop by the fence. The passenger door swung open, and out stepped Mayor Daphne Wren, clad in a cherry-red wool coat, gloves that cost more than my monthly heat bill, and a scowl sharp enough to cut steel.

She stopped dead in her tracks when she saw the body.

Her breath caught, her eyes wide. "Good Lord above..."

Then, as though some switch flipped, she straightened her spine and walked toward me, her heels clicking like a gavel.

"This is—this is Jolly Fenn, isn't it?" she asked, voice tight.

"It is."

She inhaled slowly through her nose, then exhaled like she was trying not to scream. "Eve, this is the first day of the Twelve Days of Cheer. You realize what this will do to the town if word gets out?"

I blinked. "A man is dead, Daph."

"And I'm aware of that," she said quickly. "But perception matters. We've got reporters already sniffing around after that food truck explosion last month—if they get a whiff of something like this? We're going to lose half our Christmas Market sponsors."

I stared at her. "Jolly was strung up with a goddamn partridge nailed to his chest and you're talking about sponsors?"

"Don't take that tone with me." Her voice dropped into a lower register—the one she used at meetings. "I'm not minimizing what's happened here. I'm asking you to be careful. Discreet. Just until we have answers."

I bit back the response, and instead, I turned my gaze back toward the trees.

"I'll be as careful as I can be," I said finally. "But I'm not sweeping this under the rug. This isn't a prank gone wrong. This is murder, and one I think will be repeated soon."

Her eyes narrow. "What do you mean?"

I reach into my coat and hold out the bagged parchment.

She took it and read the words, her brow furrowing. "Is this... from the carol?"

"First verse." I met her gaze, saw the realization settle like frost over her features. "If this is what I think it is, we've got eleven more to go."

For a moment, she is silent. The color drained from her face.

When she spoke again, her voice was softer. "Who would want to do something like this?"

I don't answer because I'm not ready to. There is no guess I can give just yet.

Instead, I take back the evidence bag and tuck it safely into my coat before turning to walk towards the road.

BREAK

The precinct's quiet. Too quiet, considering a man was found nailed to a tree like a festive warning sign less than twelve hours ago.

Ket perches on the edge of his desk like he's forgotten how chairs work, nursing a coffee that smells like he had melted a dozen or so candy canes in it.

I'm pacing, boots scuffing the tile, the parchment in its plastic sleeve resting under the fluorescents like a sleeping curse.

On the first day of Christmas, my true love gave to me...

"Still nothing on Jolly Fenn?" I ask, half-knowing the answer.

Ket shakes his head. "No recent enemies. No dodgy habits. Lived alone. Clean record. Loved dogs, apparently."

"A real menace," I mutter, rubbing my brow.

He flips through a thin file with the weariness of someone hoping for magic between the pages.

"If this was personal," he says, "why the theatrics? Why not just... do the deed and be done with it?"

I lean against the wall near the radiator, arms folded. The warmth barely makes it through my coat. "Because this wasn't just about killing him. This was staged. Designed to be found, and whoever did it wanted us to know it was the first of something."

Ket glances at the evidence bag again. "Think it's political? A message?"

"If it is, I'm not getting it."

We sit in the thick of silence for a moment. At least until one of the officers hit the stupid mechanical singing tree.

"I looked into that other case," Ket says, cautious. "The Snow one. Just to compare notes. See if there's overlap."

My body stills. "And?"

He shrugs. "Different methods. Timing seems to be the only match."

I nod, but I'm not listening. Not properly. My mind's already slipping back.

I head home when the sky starts bruising.

My flat's small, but clean. Everything on my walls feels like it's from a life I no longer live—a poster of a band I no longer listen to. The decorations that have been up since last Christmas.

I shed my coat by the door, kick off boots that squelch with thawed snow, and don't bother turning on the main lights. The fairy ones strung across the windows still, and they cast enough of a glow to keep the dark at bay.

I pour a glass of whiskey. The good kind because I need something to numb all this and drink for those who no longer can. The sip burns.

The first drink is for Jolly, the second is for the silence, the third is for Collin.

His name still tastes like failure on my tongue. It's the only taste I've had for almost a year.

Saints, I'm pathetic.

I stare at the shadowed wall across from me, watching lights dance over plaster like ghosts at a masquerade. The flat's always quiet. No one is waiting for me or to check to see if I've eaten. It makes me think about Lara sometimes. About her kids. About how you say the right things, hold their hands, make tea—and none of it stops them from having to bury the ones they love.

I down the rest of the glass, quickly followed by another, and another.

"Should've gotten there sooner," I mutter.

I scrub a hand down my face and reach for the bottle again. The drink steadies me, but the thoughts don't.

The smiles in photographs. The final text messages. The way the milk goes bad in the fridge while families wait for answers.

I curl onto the sofa without bothering to change. The whiskey is sharp in my veins now, and the memories are blurring at the edges, like a page I keep dog-earing.

The city's quiet outside. The kind of stillness that only December brings. Where even the drunks have passed out and the wind can be heard rattling the window panes.

I close my eyes.

Somewhere in the half-sleep, I see him. Not Collin—but the body from today. The bird nailed to his chest. Its wings spread open, like it might still try to fly.

On the first day of Christmas, my true love gave to me...

ON THE SECOND DAY

The shrill buzz of my phone yanks me from sleep like a bucket of ice water to the face.

I jerk upright, heart hammering, mouth dry as sandpaper. The room spins once, twice, then settles into a dull sway. My empty glass makes me want to fill it as it sits there on the table. The clock reads 5:42 a.m.

My mouth is bone dry, breath sour with last night's whisky.

The screen glares up at me from the floor, casting pale blue light across the carpet. I lean too far for it, head spinning as I half-fall, half-roll off the couch.

I swipe to answer before it can let my eyes close again and fall asleep right here.

"Yeah," I croak.

"Eve." Ket's voice is taut. Urgent, but already worn thin at the edges. "We've got another one."

That sobers me more efficiently than a shower and slap combined.

"Where?"

"St. Clements, the high school."

I'm already moving, dragging on last night's jeans, and buttoning up a dress shirt. No time for tea or shame for the fact I might still be a little drunk.

I grab my coat and keys with one hand and Ket's still speaking in my ear with the other. "Eve, there's two of them."

The word "two" lodges under my skin like a burr.

"I'm ten minutes out," I say, already shutting the door behind me.

BREAK

The sun hasn't fully risen when I reach St. Clements. Just that grey, uncertain light that coats the city in frost and seasonal depression. The roads are slick even with some salt, and the air has a bite to it that turns breath to smoke and makes everyone look like they are related to Rudolph.

The school sits on the edge of town, old brick with ivy. There banners for the upcoming holiday programme strung along the fence. "A Midsummer Christmas Dream!" one reads in candy-red font. A tinsel-draped Titania grins beside a grumpy-looking Santa Claus.

It would be funny if I wasn't here for a murder case.

The theatre building is separate from the main school—low and wide, with curved awnings and peeling gold lettering above the doors. Someone's draped fake holly across the entrance.

I duck under the line of crime scene tape, nodding at some of my counterparts as I make my way across the frozen walkway, boots crunching against scattered salt.

Ket meets me just inside, his fringe matted to his forehead with sweat.

He doesn't speak right away—just leads me inside in silence.

The auditorium is dark, save for the harsh cones of portable lighting set up by forensics. The beam hits the red velvet curtain. Glitter litters the floor like festive shrapnel. There are cardboard trees on stage as well as snowmen made out of papier-mâché. The faint scent of greasepaint and hairspray still clings to the air.

And at the centre of it all—them. Two bodies suspended from the theatre rigging.

Ropes and harnesses, repurposed from whatever production was meant to be here this week, are now holding corpses aloft. Arms outstretched. Heads drooped like sleeping birds. Pale skin drained of colour and life, lips painted bright red, eyes sewn shut with thick, black thread.

They hover above the stage like angels fallen mid-flight.

And in the centre of the stage, placed where the spotlight would hit—a heart.

Roughly made. Jagged. Glass panels and warped copper, welded together

Inside, thick crimson liquid sloshes slowly. There are tubes connecting them to the crude metal work.

My stomach lurches, maybe from the whiskey or the act of this freak draining these teens of their blood.

Taped to the side is a note. Same red ink as before.

On the second day of Christmas, my true love gave to me...

My stomach lurches.

"They were students," Ket says beside me. His voice is low. Apologetic, almost. "Seventeen. In the drama programme. Played Romeo and Juliet last spring."

The detail lands like a stone in my chest.

I stare up at them, suspended in air, and for a moment I forget to breathe. Every inch of them posed with purpose. Their hands almost touch. Their fingers are curled like they were mid-reach, mid-yearning, mid-some-last-private-thought neither of them had time to finish.

"Names?" I manage, voice a breath in the quiet.

Ket checks his notes. "Isaac Barnes and Clara Osei. Friends say they'd just started dating. Got paired for the leads in the Christmas show."

I look at them again and want to scream. Want to burn this entire twisted altar down to ash and bone. The ropes creak slightly with the air's movement, and, for a terrifying heartbeat, I think they're going to move—come back, speak, scream. But the moment passes.

The blood-filled heart below them pulses in the stage light. It's almost beautiful, in a horrific, wrong sort of way. The glass catches reflections from the tinsel still dangling from the rafters, and for a second it looks like it's glowing.

I turn away and press the heel of my hand to my eye. Guilt flickers in my throat, sour and familiar.

"Did anyone hear anything last night?" I ask. "Theatre's separate from the main school. Shouldn't have been anyone here."

"Janitor said he locked up around eight. No alarms triggered or signs of forced entry." Ket informs me.

"And the rigging? Someone would have had to know how to work the system."

Ket nods grimly. "It's an old school manual system. Needs some strength behind working it. Not something you figure out by simply watching a YouTube video."

I glance at him. "You can find anything on YouTube nowadays."

Though, he's right. We're looking at someone who is able to have enough strength to do all of this.

A shiver works its way up my spine and plants itself between my shoulder blades. "Let's get statements from the drama teacher, janitors, any students who worked backstage. I want every one of them vetted and logged."

Ket gives a quick nod, already moving.

I stay, though. Just a moment longer.

The velvet curtains ripple faintly as a heater kicks in somewhere backstage. Glitter still falls from the rafters like dust from a ceiling that forgot how to stay whole.

Outside these walls, the city is singing. Shops are opening. Children are clambering onto Santa's lap. Christmas lights are blinking in windows, but in here—here there are ropes, red lips, hearts made of copper, and blood.

ON THE THIRD DAY

By the time I make it back to the precinct, the sun has clawed its way above the skyline and is painting everything in a golden hue. The kind that looks warm until you step into it and realise it's still winter outside.

My office smells like spoiled coffee. I've barely dropped my coat onto the back of the chair when the door bangs open hard enough to rattle the frame.

Mayor Daphne enters like a hurricane in heels.

"You absolute grinch," she hisses before the door's even swung shut behind her.

I blink, caught mid-motion, hand still half-raised toward the case file on my desk. Her hair tied back so severely it looks like it's pulling at her scalp. Her cheeks are flushed, not from the cold—but anger.

"Good morning to you too," I mutter, dropping into my seat.

She doesn't sit. Of course not. She paces instead, a tightly wound figure-eight like she's trying to wear down the carpet.

"Two children, Eve. Two. Strung up like decorations in a fucking school auditorium. And where were you?" Her tone is sharp.

"At home sleeping like the majority of the populous."

She rolls her eyes. "I don't mean physically. Don't be clever."

I open the file slowly, just to give my hands something to do. "This isn't something we could've predicted. It's not random, and it's not obvious. We're working on it."

"No," she snaps. "You're not working on it. You're allowing it to keep happening. While I'm getting calls from every councillor in the district wondering what the hell is happening to our 'safe little borough' during the most important time of the year!"

There it is. The veneer cracks.

"It's always about optics with you, isn't it?" I say, calm now. "What the lights look like on the high street. What the donors will say. Your goddamn poll numbers."

She turns on me, slow and dangerous. "Oh, don't do that. Don't make me a monster." A scoff follows. "Maybe if you spent more time working the case and less time pickling your liver, you'd have the mental capacity to actually do your job."

I flinch—but only inwardly.

"You're not worried about the case," I say quietly, flipping the page. "You're pissed I never called you back."

She looks at me with wide eyes that blink rapidly a few times.

A pause. A beat.

Then she laughs—her hand flying to her stomach like what I said was the best one liner of a comedy special.

"Oh, for God's sake. Still clinging to the idea that you broke my heart?" She shakes her head, steps closer, voice softening with poison. "Eve, I don't give a shit who you sleep with—but when people start dying on your watch, when children start dying—my job is to clean up your mess. Not reminisce about your tragic self-sabotage."

The words sting in that old, familiar way. The kind that has nothing to do with murder and everything to do with memories. Ones you bury and call it being a professional.

"Go ahead, Daph," I say. "Call the Interpol. Maybe they'll take one look at the blood-soaked theatre, realise who the killer is within minutes despite not knowing a single soul in this town, and solve it all in time for the nativity play."

She leans forward, palms flat on the desk between us. "Step. Up," she says, low and brutal. "Catch the freak who's doing this. Or I swear to the saints, Eve, I'll bring in someone who can."

I meet her eyes.

There's grief there. Not for the victims. Not even for the city, but for whatever we used to be, buried under politics and whisky and bodies.

She straightens up, smooths her coat, and reclaims her dignity like a second skin. Then she walks out without another word. The door closes behind her with a muffled click.

I stare at it for a moment, just long enough to watch the handle still its faint tremble.

Then I turn back to the file. Nothing about my expression moves. Nothing betrays the churn in my chest or the echo of her voice still vibrating in the corners of the room. I slide the note from the second scene back into its evidence sleeve with a touch that's almost reverent.

A soft knock follows. No dramatic entrance this time.

Ket peeks his head in. His smile is tentative, the way you smile at a bear who hasn't decided if it's going to maul you or fall asleep.

"Hey. Did you survive?"

I don't look up. "Shut the door."

He does. Slips in with a coffee in hand and a clipboard under his arm. His hair's doing that thing it does when he's stressed—sticking up in three directions like it's trying to flee his head.

It happens because he runs his fingers through his hair a million and one times like a member in a boy band.

Ket drags the spare chair over, spins it around backwards, and straddles it like he's still in school. He watches me sift through the scene reports with the wary patience of someone waiting for lightning to strike.

And it does—just not loud. Not flashy. Just a spark, small but sure, at the back of my skull.

"Both murders," I start slowly, "took place early in the morning."

Ket nods. "Between two and three. Their deaths happened around midnight via the autopsy."

"Exactly." I tap the timeline chart. "No chance of being seen. But that's not just an opportunity. That's the choice."

I lean back, knuckles against my mouth, eyes scanning the board behind my desk—photos, pins, bits of parchment and string forming a web no one else can yet read.

"This isn't spontaneous. It's not anger. This is premeditated. Every detail—planned, choreographed. The way the bodies were arranged. The placement of the notes. Even the locations."

Ket shifts in his seat. "First was the tree in Orchard."

"Second," I add, "was inside the theatre. An enclosed space. He escalated not just in number—but in intimacy. He had time to drain two bodies. Build that metal heart. Set the stage."

"It's definitely not an act of passion."

I nod. "He's been waiting. This isn't just a killing spree—it's a performance."

Ket exhales, the weight settling across his shoulders. "Which means..."

"Tomorrow, it's going to be three."

He swears under his breath.

Ket runs a hand through his hair, the anxiety finally starting to show. "So, what are we supposed to do? Stake out every theatre, school, church, park, and bloody pigeon coop in the city just in case he fancies staging tomorrow's murder in the Christmas market?"

"We're not going to get ahead of this by canvassing alone," I say.

My eyes glance over the Christmas decorations that have been there for over a year. The small pine tree I had brought in is so far gone, withered and brittle.

"Three French hens," I say aloud.

Ket looks up.

"Could be literal. Could be symbolic," he says. "Birds, women, French nationals. We're looking at interpretation."

I nod, pacing slowly. "He's following the song, but it's his version of it. The lovers weren't just turtle doves—they were young, romantic, and their death tragic."

Ket rubs a hand over his face, then flips a page. "Okay, what do we have that fits the theme?"

"Madame Leclerc," I say. "Teaches French at St. Clements."

He writes her name on the board.

"Then the Montagne sisters," Ket adds. "Florist shop off Peregrine Street. Born in Marseille."

"Add them to the list," I murmur.

He quickly jots it down, the pen scraping against the paper.

"And the café," I state. "Café Matinal. Centre of town. French owner—Laurent Duval."

Ket continues to write it down.

We add a few more names to the list. People who had just visited France, some who had made their genealogy their whole identity.

"I'll take the café," I say. "We can't watch them all ourselves, not tonight. We need to bring in backup."

Ket is already pulling out his phone. "I'll loop in dispatch. Quiet presence only—plainclothes where we can. We can't afford to scare him off his script."

"We just need to get there first," I say. "Before he does."

Those words sit heavy in my chest as I say them.

BREAK

The festival is in full swing. The blinking lights of every colour lighting up the otherwise white blanketed ground that is surrounding the town square. Stalls selling hot cocoa, seasoned nuts, handcrafted ornaments. There are actors dressed as elves, all volunteers to help with the immersion into the collective delusion that this is somehow the North Pole.

Daphne, to her credit, had done her job. The press is silent. The streets look safe. The illusion still holds.

But that means no one here knows there's a monster threading through their crowd. That he might be standing right beside them, sipping mulled wine.

My boots crunch against ice as I move past a stall selling gingerbread men. Another offers carved angels out of birch wood. The air is thick with roasting chestnuts, pine, and cloves.

Despite the cheer surrounding me, I feel a tightness in my chest. I might be able to feel more at ease, feel more confident, if I could just understand why.

He's playing the song, sure. Following the pattern that's in the melody. But it's not for spectacle, because it's all kept in private spaces.

A show for a selected audience.

Then there are his notes—his phrasing. 'My true love gave to me.'

If this was for art, he'd say so. Name it after the subject, like 'a partridge in a pear tree.'

This feels more like a love letter, and I don't know who the bells is it intended for.

I reach the booth at the far end of the square, tucked beneath the eaves of the old clock tower. A sign with Café Matinal scrawled in chalk perches above racks of buttery croissants and paper cups stacked into leaning towers, but there's no Laurent.

Only a teen in a reindeer hat is working the counter—Carol, I think her name is. Her cheeks are wind bitten, and her gloved fingers fumble over the lid of a cocoa cup.

"Where's Laurent?" I ask.

She startles, then points to the clipboard on the counter. "Oh, hi detective Holly. He left maybe twenty minutes ago," she says. "Said he needed to grab something from the kitchen and never came back. But your friend stopped by!"

She pulls a piece of card from under the till and hands it to me with care. It's stiff. Matte. Tucked into an envelope sealed with wax.

"He said that you might come by and asked if I could leave this for you."

No name on the front. Just the echo of red.

I open it slowly, the paper rough beneath my fingertips. A faint scent clings to it—iron and cloves. My heart's already sinking as I read.

Do you like my gifts? I have so many more to give you.

My heart is in my throat, as I fold the card with trembling fingers and slide it into my coat.

Laurent Duval is gone, and I got my answer.

He's doing this because of *me*... and he already has his next victims.

I pull my radio from my pocket. "Ket, he's not here. We were too slow."

The crowd around me bursts into song—'Holly Jolly Christmas' rising in cheerful crescendo. A brass band kicks in just as I finish speaking.

My hand tightens in my coat pocket. My legs are already moving, long strides cutting across the square, past the carolers, the booths, the children with cinnamon sticks and powdered cheeks.

Because I know now. The bastard is doing this for me. That's why the letters end where they do. It's a confession.

And if he knows anything about me... he'd know this time of year, these brutal acts, it would send my thoughts right back to where my life changed.

I lost my belief in the cause and effect, in justice, in the bloody point of all of it.

Collin Snow.

I break into a run.

The cold burns against my skin, wind slicing at the corners of my eyes. The streets blur as I cut through them. Left at Hollytree Lane. Across the cracked paving stones past the cinema.

I run until my feet find themselves headed down Angel Lane.

The warehouse door groans open like a mouth too long left closed.

Inside, it's colder than I remember. Not just winter-cold, but underground, bone-deep chill. The kind you find in crypts and confessionals. The kind that settles into you like a secret.

My torch cuts across the warehouse interior—same rusted beams, same sagging rafters—but now, something's different.

It's not empty.

A workbench. Welding equipment sits haphazard beside coils of copper wire and soldering rods. Sheets of glass lean against the wall—some cracked, others etched with notations. Arrows. Angles. Measurements.

On the far wall, nailed with careful symmetry, is a storyboard.

Twelve panels. Each one holds a sketch of a mock-up display.

The partridge—check. The turtle doves—check.A wireframe of three people in tiered cages, feathered costumes sketched in with soft graphite.

And more still. Diagrams of gallows, of fountains, of a carousel. The twelve days of murder he plans to carry out.

There's a folder beneath it all, and when I open it, I see profiles. Headshots. Print-outs. Surveillance photos. Victims past, and victims intended. With each name, a song verse is written beside it.

Bile climbs up the back of my throat. He really did plan everything. This isn't just madness, but delicately and thoughtfully orchestrated.

I step further in, hand instinctively brushing my sidearm, thumb grazing the safety.

Then I hear a muffled sound.

Swinging the torch around—toward the back of the room. Stacked crates. A curtain of torn canvas. Something behind it shifts. I move fast, sidearm drawn, and shove the canvas aside.

Three figures bound, gagged, and eyes wide in the dark.

Laurent and the Montagne sisters. Rope cutting into skin. Mouths packed with fabric and sealed with tape.

They're alive.

Laurent's eyes are glassy with exhaustion, but they fix on me like an anchor. He tries to speak through the gag and I quickly try to close the distance, but I hear a shuffle from behind me.

"You came," he says.

I turn, my eyes widening for just a second before focusing on Nicholas Snow, as he stands in the doorway. I instantly aim my gun.

He's more put together than I expected. Crisp coat. No wild eyes. Just calm, his hands loose at his sides, but there's something behind the stillness—something reverent.

"Didn't think you'd make it before the fourth day," he continues. "But I hoped."

My gun doesn't lower.

"Put your hands up where I can see them and turn around," I say.

Nick doesn't listen. Instead, he steps in.

"Left notes with a few people for you, just in case you were able to." Nick's eyes trail me up and down. "I'll still give you your gifts...but now I can show them to you here. Just for you and me to see."

"You're under arrest for the murders of—"

"I saw you, Evie." He cuts me off. "I watched you closely after the night you told us."

My grip on my gun tightens.

"At first, I just wanted to apologize for how I reacted. You were so kind to me, to my family.... You looked at us like we really mattered.

My grip tightens. "You were grieving," I say. "You were vulnerable. It wasn't—"

"But then I saw just how devastated you were at how hurt my family was that you couldn't even acknowledge me." His voice sharpens. "After Collin. I sent messages, called, even came down to the station—but you were so worried that you thought I was disappointed in you, that you couldn't even give me a courtesy reply."

"You are seriously fucked up in the head." I whisper. "I didn't reply because I felt like I failed at my job, that I wasn't able to protect my community. It had nothing to do with how you felt."

"I know you are just too shy to admit it..." He laughs. "I saw the way you stepped into the dark, and instead of forcing you into the light, I thought I'd join you here because that's how much I love you."

He steps forward again. "This... all of this... it's how I made sure you'd see that you don't need to hide from me anymore."

My mouth dries. Every instinct screams to pull the trigger, to stop the moment before it deepens. But part of me wants to understand, and that's the most dangerous part.

"You think this is love?" I say, quiet. "You think this is how we connect?"

He smiles, and it's not mad—it's devoted.

"Death brought us together, and now it reconnects us." He takes another step forward. "Merry Christmas, Eve."

About the Author

T R Nickel released her debut novel, Light of Evanora (of the Legends of Limoria Series), in 2021.

She is more known by her friends and family for her intense imagination and desire to make others smile. Since she was a young child living in the state of cheese, TRN has been fascinated with books and the craziness that goes into creating something so magical. Starting off with writing poems, that she would jot down into a tiny bright yellow memo pad, grew an intense passion to create and fill a world with her own craziness.

A Krampusnacht Carol, A Lucky Devil Short

BY MEGAN MACKIE

"'Twas the night before Krampusnacht and all through the bar, everyone was stirring, and shaking and pouring and getting reasonably drunk…" St. Benedict flopped over the aforementioned bar.

Rune wrinkled her nose. "That doesn't rhyme with 'bar.'"

St. Benedict continued. "The Krampus masks were hung on the walls with such care, in the hope that St. Nicholas just wouldn't care…"

"Are you going to do the whole poem?" Rune asked as she pushed aside the last of the newsprint used in the last storage box holding the last Krampus mask. "And you can't rhyme a word with itself."

Her partner, St. Benedict, grinned his iconic grin. "Who says?"

He sat up, then perched himself on the corner of the Lounge Bar in the equally iconic establishment known as The Lucky Devil. He looked at the line of masks taking up the spaces usually reserved for patrons. Every surface, from the bar to the cluster of tables to the only booth in the room where the namesake Lucky Devil sat, were covered in demonically wood-carved masks of every color and fierceness imaginable. As for the kitschy demons ensconced on shelves along all the walls, several sported Christmas hats and at least one was sharing space with an Elf on the Shelf. It was a very festive, if incomplete, atmosphere.

Most of the said patrons were in the Main Bar, the room to the right of the Lounge Bar if you were entering from the street. The Back Bar was also fully occupied to make up for the temporary loss of the Lounge.

"Okay, then," St. Benedict continued, "How about 'The Krampus masks were hung on the walls with creepy stares, in the hope that St. Nicholas..."

"Okay, got the idea, thank you. How drunk are you already?" Rune interrupted, picking up her bottle of wood oil, only to find it empty but for some squeaky bubbles as she attempted to refresh her polishing rag. Exasperated, she threw the bottle a little too hard at her garbage can, which made the enchanted trash receptacle skitter away as if startled.

"Viola!" Rune shouted. A small lavender light separated from the others, dancing on her ceiling. The little Fae that lived in the bar were helping to set up for Krampusnacht. Though it took a dozen of the little hand-sized Fae children to lift one mask, they were all so proud of their work that Rune had to let them continue. The rest of the Fae, either those that could not fly or were not interested in helping, contributed by giving directions or advice from their rafter nests.

Viola, a pretty little Fae who took her name to heart and wore a lavender petal dress that matched her wings exactly, alighted next to Rune on the bar.

"Yes, Ms. Rune?" she asked politely with a little curtesy that would have looked in place in a royal court somewhere. Rune wasn't entirely sure why the little Fae called her "Ms. Rune," but they had always done it. One had started it shortly after the Fae moved into her bar. Then they all started doing it. It made her feel like a kindergarten teacher.

"Hello, Viola," St. Benedict said, tipping his fedora to her. The little Fae eyed him coolly, then sniffed and turned back to Rune.

"What can I do for *you*?" she emphasized clearly to Rune, and Rune alone.

"Could you go grab the second bottle of wood oil from the kitchen? Get a couple of others to help you if it's too heavy."

"I can certainly handle it myself," the little Fae declared imperiously. To be fair, she had grown larger than Rune's hand, the first Fae in the bar to show any signs of actual growth, so maybe she could.

"Thank you, Viola," Rune said with a weak smile, and the self-satisfied Fae jetted off toward the bar's kitchen, only to be blocked by St. Benedict's upstretched hand.

"Lady Viola, I said 'hello,'" he insisted. The little Fae buzzed her wings, backing away as she crossed her arms, then turned her nose up with a petite sniff.

"St. Ben..." Rune interceded. He dropped his hand and the little Fae flitted off.

"What did I do to upset little Lady Viola?" St. Benedict asked jovially, looking to Rune to join in with his mock-hurt routine.

Except she didn't. Rune looked away, saying nothing as she fiddled with a leather tie that had come undone on one of the masks. "Look, I've got a lot of work to do. Half the staff are out with the flu, and having to clean up the *party* we had here ..."

"You sound like you're trying to get rid of me?" St. Benedict countered. Heedless of the masks near him, he reached over and attempted to snag a liquor bottle from the well on the other side.

"What... Hey! Will you be careful?" Rune moved quickly to save one of the masks from taking a nosedive off the bar.

The Saint didn't apologize, he only slipped off the bar into one of the more appropriate stools in front. With a satisfied sigh, he pulled the pouring spout from the bottle before dumping a good portion of the drink down his throat.

"What the hell...?" Rune started to say when a sharp clack to her right drew her attention.

A small group of Fae had worked off the black lacquer top from a small box sitting by itself on a table near the door. "Hey!" she called, bee-lining across the room to intercede. "I said no touching the mask with the black fur. You leave this for me to handle."

"We weren't going to touch it!" a bright green Fae named Peasblossum declared.

"We were just going to look at it," a pinkish-yellow one calling herself Jolly Rancher added.

"Acorn said it was cursed," remarked a small grey Fae named Cloud.

"And I said, 'no way.' Ms. Rune would never have a cursed mask in the bar where anyone could see it," Jolly Rancher sniffed, crossing her little arms.

"Maybe you all never mind what Ms. Rune will or won't do and go help the others," Rune said, gently encouraging the winged creatures to hover away from the mask.

"Buuuuuuuut," Peasblossum whined, holding up a tiny hand, "*is* it cursed?"

"He's got a whole packet of honey riding on it," Cloud said dryly.

"Not my problem, scoot!" Rune said, suppressing the laugh in her voice. The small group and their three spokesfae all flounced away in a burst of Fae dust chorused with disappointed whines and groans. Pushing down on the lid, Rune attempted to re-secure the box only for St. Benedict to interfere, grabbing the edge to pry it up out of her hands.

If only getting rid of St. Benedict was as easy as chasing off the baby Fae.

"*Is* it cursed?" he asked peering inside to stare at the beautifully, and terribly, carved wood.

He was too close. Moving into her space as thoughtlessly as if she were nothing important. It made her skin tingle and shiver when he neared, and not in a good way. He always smelled good, and, with this proximity, she could taste the cold and winter highlighting his unique scent.

"Hey, hey, Rune? Is it cursed?" he repeated, completely oblivious to what he was doing to her.

Rune huffed. "I have no idea, but it's in its own box with a ward mark on it so I figured I'd get someone to check it out before I hung the mask up. The last thing I need is a customer getting... I don't know... possessed or something."

He continued to stare at the mask.

"Yeah," he said softly, "I can see how that would be a problem."

Unsettled, Rune snatched the lid back and snapped it over the mask. Doing that seemed to only irritate her uninvited guest more.

"Hey!"

"Just leave it alone, please," she said. She turned away from him and returned to the mask she had been working on, just as Viola dropped a new bottle of oil onto the bar before flitting away. Picking at the plastic seal on the top, Rune tried to come up with something else to say to St. Benedict.

He beat her to it again.

"So, what is all of this? A Lucky Devil Christmas tradition?" He took up another of the masks, one she deemed harmless, to look at closer.

"Yes, we celebrate Krampusnacht on December fifth, you know, because it kind of goes along with the theme of the bar. Which means these *needed* to go up after Thanksgiving was over. So I'm way behind and the rest of my staff, who don't have the flu, are extra busy with the flood of patrons in the next room."

"So, we get to dress up in these masks and go beat random strangers with wooden switches, right?" he asked, slapping the mask over his face. His piercing blue-green eyes gave the mask life, making its twisted features eerie. Then he triple blinked and flared his augmented eyes. His iris and pupils disappearing into glowing blue light. Rune could imagine her friend... her work partner, dancing through the streets in that thing with nothing but fur tied around his shoulders and waist, making women shriek with delight and excitement as he harangued them.

She filed that thought away for later. "No. Mostly these are for decorati on..." Rune started to explain just as she was interrupted by a high-pitched screech and bang near the front of the Lounge Bar, making them both jump.

"He stole it! He stole it!" One little Fae, a wingless one the color of a brown mushroom, the infamous Acorn, cried, pointing at the door. The lacquer box lay beside him on the floor, shattered into pieces.

"What the hell?" Rune moved to the door, grabbing it before the wind seized the wood and glass to slam it against the outside wall.

Out in the wintery night, she saw a car parked with its lights on in the snow-covered street. A young man slid his way toward it to the chorus of his friends screeching and cheering as they waved their arms out of the windows.

"Screw you, bitch!" One of his friends laughed as he flipped her off from the car window while the thief piled into the back, screaming "go, go, go!"

The driver didn't go, go, go, but instead snatched up the black mask to hold over his face while he flipped her off some more. The first unruly teenager disappeared into the car only to come out with an empty glass bottle, which he flung at her.

Rune attempted to dodge the missile as her steps propelled her forward into the street toward the car. It hit her shoulder painfully. A few more empty and semi-empty bottles came sailing. One of them clipped her head, and she slipped on the slushy street to fall on her butt.

As she sat up, grasping her wound, the laughter from the car cut short.

St. Benedict bowled past her to a chorus of "oh shits," the teens slid back into the vehicle.

The driver hit the gas so hard his front wheel spun a second before digging down enough to find traction. Even as the car peeled away, St. Benedict grabbed at the handle of the back door, managing to pull it open even as it ripped from his hand. The boy within screamed and desperately snatched at the free-swinging door as the car tore away.

St. Benedict kept pursuing, however, until the loose, wet snow had its impact on him too and his feet went out from under him. Using his augmented reflexes, he managed to roll out of the way of another oncoming car blaring its horn back up to his feet.

"Dammit!" the Saint shouted as, a block away, the refugee car turned, missing another oncoming vehicle by inches before disappearing into the night.

After a breathless moment, Rune turned onto her knees. Her elbow and one palm screamed at her where she hit the ground. Staring down at the palm, she saw bits of gravel stuck in her glistening skin. Abrasions but no real blood. She'd have to go inside to check her elbow. The whole left side of her was wet enough for the cold wind to slice through her sweater and jeans as if she wore nothing.

When St. Benedict marched past her, his cell phone to his ear, she realized that she wasn't going to receive any help standing up.

"I got the license plate," he said, clenching and unclenching his hand in obvious rage, like a panther who just had his prey snatched away.

"Hey, Mal.... Mal shut up about priorities," he barked into the phone, "Run a license plate. ATT 540. Chicago plate, yeah." He paused a minute, listening. Rune stepped up onto the sidewalk, tucking her hurt hand under her arm. "No, this isn't... I don't have... It's not for a case, okay? It's... a trio of assholes just robbed the Lucky Devil and... No, nobody's hurt." He didn't even look at Rune to confirm that. "They just took a mask...What... What do you mean...? Put Maxamillion on the phone right now. I said put him on. I don't care, I'll tell him where he can shove his protocol... Mal... Ma..." He dropped the hand holding the phone, letting it bump against his side as he stared up into a snowy streetlight.

He growled loudly, then shoved the phone back into his inner coat pocket. "Don't worry, I'll find them."

"No, St. Benedict, honestly," she rolled her eyes, "I'll find them." Rune headed back into her bar.

"Where are you going?" St. Benedict asked.

"To get my coat."

"WILL YOU SLOW DOWN!" Rune screeched. She hung on to the emergency grab bar in St. Benedict's car.

"I've got this completely under control," St. Benedict declared as he whipped around another car in the process of turning left, violating all the rules against cars using the bike lane as their personal passing lane.

"I don't see how! You've been drinking, I should drive!" Rune squealed, but his blue-opaqued eyes never glanced at her.

He accelerated way past the 35 mph speed limit. "I'm fine. My augmented system is already detoxing me."

"How can you see anything with your eyes like that?!" Rune screeched, wishing she had never gotten into his stupid car.

"My augmentations are allowing me to see everything and are automatically plotting a path to the target. You can stop with the magic now if you want," he said as he decelerated too quickly, throwing Rune forward against her seat belt and flopping her hood over her eyes.

Clutching the shards from the mask box in her other hand, the gold thread of magic she'd been using to locate her mask shivered as the distance and exact direction kept changing faster than the magic could correct for. It had been a simple thing for Rune to ping her Finding magic through the shard and get a thread to give them a direction to head. Catching up to the thieves turned out to be simple as well as they were casually driving around with their prize, completely unaware of their pursuers.

"There's ice!" Rune shouted as the car began to skid around a corner.

"I'm compensating for it," St. Benedict answered confidently, as he counter-turned the wheel to let the car straighten out its fishtail.

"I should have just reported the theft!" Rune moaned as her stomach threatened to rebel against her again.

"Will you stop harping on me! I GOT THIS!" St. Benedict shouted back, getting more angry. "This is literally what I do all day, Rune!"

"Will you stop shouting at me and slow down!"

Mercifully, he did. *Way* down.

So, so much worse. He crawled down the street now.

No ... prowled.

Heedless of the cars that followed, he leaned forward, squinting his glowing eyes at a darkened alley. The car they pursued was nowhere to be seen, but Rune's Finding thread pointed them toward an alley.

Finally, the car immediately behind them grew impatient, and slammed on the horn.

"St. Benedict! Will you pull over!"

He complied with that, sliding into a spot already cleared of snow, knocking aside the lawn chairs someone put there to hold "their" spot.

"St. Benedict," Rune growled, dropping her face into her hand in exasperation.

"That's not legal and we both know it," he countered, settling the car into park and yanking up the parking brake. "You can't 'save' your spot."

"It's a cultural Chicago norm and *you* know it. If you've put the effort to dig the spot out, you have the right to return to it as long as there is snow."

He turned to the lawn chair, now wedged between his car and the one in front. "I do not recognize your authority," he said to it, then proceeded to open the secure space in between the seats. The armrest opened, revealing his gun, shooting bracelet, and spare clips within.

"No!" Rune declared, laying her hand over the weapons to block him from withdrawing them. "They threw bottles, not bullets."

"You don't know that's still true," he countered, and pulled the weapon out, securing the connecting firing bracelet to his wrist. That linked the gun to him and made it impossible for anyone other than him to fire it. Before she could protest more, he left the car with his weapon.

She followed, slamming the door a little too hard. He had marched into the alley without even acknowledging her when there was a shout from within. "I said, 'no guns!'"

The three teenagers were there, all standing outside their car, the front of which had been plowed into a dumpster. The kids themselves looked a little bruised, battered, and freaked.

"What the hell? Damn, its eyes are glowing! Brett, do you see that?" one of them shouted as he held the mask out at arm's length.

"But it doesn't have eyes!" presumably Brett answered.

"Hey, you kids!" St. Benedict called.

They all turned to him with wide eyes, but before anyone could react, further mist exploded from the mask so fast it rolled over all of them like a rushing wave. The three teenagers screamed their heads off, only for them to become more and more muffled as the mist thickened.

"Rune!" was all she heard before St. Benedict was swallowed by the puffy wet whiteness.

"St. Ben," she called back, but even as she felt forward with her hands she saw and touched nothing. "St. Ben, where are you?"

"St. Benedict!" Rune shouted, but it was like she was shouting inside a small closet.

Her hands reached out, going a few tentative steps in the blinding, cloudy dark.

"St. Ben?" she called again, when she still hadn't encountered him.

Yellow-green glowing eyes opened before her, accompanied by a hostile laugh and chains clinking. Strangely, she could see them clearly despite the mist.

She screamed, but no one heard.

St. Benedict's breath was all he heard as he hurried down the darkened alley. Slamming his back against ice-cold bricks, the Saint, corporate spy extraordinaire, lifted his gun higher.

"Rune! Rune!!" he hissed, but his voice barely seemed to go past the immediate area around him.

He clung to his weapon, knowing it was most likely useless against the mythological creature he pursued.

Or it pursued him. He wasn't very sure.

Yet, the animal part of his brain would not let the weapon go. Scanning up and down the alley, his augmented sight popped all the relevant details of his environment into sharp relief.

Like most Chicago alleys, trash cans, and dumpsters lined the edges, punctuated by metal fire escapes every few feet. Unlike most Chicago alleys, these had been going on forever, never turning or opening into a street. Mist as thick as soup filled the area, limiting visibility to only what was immediately around him. His augmentations extended that to a theoretical six feet, forming outlines of shapes in the blank slate that was the mist. Sometimes there were streetlights glowing soft yellowed light, but there was no regularity to their distribution and more than one was broken and dark. Some sections were thick with snow and others a mere dusting.

He had been searching for Rune for twenty minutes, though at that point he would settle for one of the teenagers. Or anybody.

Forcing him to quiet his breathing and the heart pounding in his ears, he strained to listen and was rewarded by a whimpering sound close by.

He reached toward a form that appeared out of the mist, crouched on the ground with their hands covering their head.

"Rune!"

"Ahhh!" the teenage boy, the one called Brett, squealed in a very un-Rune-like manner. "I'm sorry, I'm sorry man. It wasn't supposed to be like this. We were just supposed to try out Jake's new car."

A roll of laughter echoed through the mist.

"Shut up," St. Benedict snapped, turning back toward the mist.

"Oh God, what is out there?" Brent asked, barely managing to accomplish a whisper. His hands were pressed against his temples, his face blotchy and red as a toddler's.

"Just a guess: Krampus," St. Benedict said.

In his augmented vision, he saw the lines forming and reforming, trying to find things in the mist to coalesce into a shape for him. Gesturing with his non-dominant hand, he summoned a keyboard that only he could see and typed in a quick search term, hoping the general knowledge in his computer brain had some information about Christmas time legends.

Krampus. A horned anthropomorphic folktale figure. Said to accompany Saint Nicholas on December the 5th, seeking out naughty children to punish for their year of misdeeds using a symbolic birch rod, or branches tied together with a chain to flail them. Krampus will also bear a sack or basket with which to capture naughty children into. Krampus is also known to have one human foot and one hoofed foot, like a horse.

"Fun," St. Benedict said as his eyes skimmed the text that appeared in his vision quickly.

"Fun?" Brent whispered.

"Let me ask you something, and try to be as honest with me as you can. How 'naughty' would you say you've been this last year?" St. Benedict scanned around them, looking up and down the alley for any sign of the legend made flesh.

"I mean, I don't know. I've been okay—" Then Brent stopped talking as he saw a shadowy figure appear out of the mist just a few feet away.

"Not 'okay' enough," St. Benedict noted as his blue pupil-less eyes went wide. In his vision, the lines were confused, trying to form around the shape, only to... slip off? Like the form he could see with his real vision wasn't entirely there.

"Hallucination?" he muttered out loud to himself. "Illusion?"

"Brent!" a voice shouted, one of teenager's compatriots appeared in the mist behind the creature. His hands were out before him and he didn't see the threat before it saw him.

"Jake!" Brent's voice cracked. "Run!!"

It was too late. The Krampus whirled and charged, a sinister cackle cutting through the dense air. St. Benedict only got a glimpse of the basket on its back, bouncing with its movements.

Swish, Swish, went the birch rod in response.

Jake screamed, but the sound was cut off as Krampus tackled him, making both disappear.

St. Benedict charged forward. He wanted to just aim his gun and fire, but the risk of hitting the kid was too great. Maybe he should have listened to Rune and left it in the car for all the good it was going to do him.

It was only after he ran for too long, and hadn't encountered the Jake kid being attacked by Krampus that St. Benedict realized he was lost and alone again in the mist.

"Brett?" he belatedly turned and shouted. Going back the way he came didn't yield the kid, nor even the same dumpster they had been hiding beside.

"This is not fun. I'm not having fun," he called out into the mist, no longer caring if the Krampus heard him or not.

"But I am," a voice said just next to his ear. He whirled around to it, bringing his gun up to point at... nothing.

A cackling laugh echoed louder than it should have from the mist.

"Okay. Oooookay, the joke is on me," St. Benedict said, redirecting his gun to the sky again.

His eyes scanned around slowly this time.

On the other side the Krampus stood, grinning. Its large hand was gripping around the third teenager's neck.

"Oh. That must be Carl," St. Benedict said.

The kid whimpered, his fingers gripping white knuckled on the enormous fingers at his neck. In fact, St. Benedict was pretty sure that those fingers were proportionally bigger than they should be as the Krampus himself was only taller than the kid because of the horns.

"Help me," the teenager squeaked out, pleading with the only other adult.

St. Benedict pointed the gun. "Let him go," he said.

"She said no guns," Krampus replied, the voice deep and squeaky sharp at the same time. "She said no guns. She said no guns." Krampus kept repeating it over and over and as it did, the voice warped and changed.

Until it was Rune's voice saying it. "I said no guns."

"Okay, okay!" St. Benedict acquiesced, letting the gun hang from a finger on one hand while holding up the other in the "no harm" position.

The Krampus stopped speaking. Only grinned with too many sharp teeth.

St. Benedict kept his hands up, even as he knelt down so he could lay the gun on the ground.

The second it touched the ground, the pavement swallowed the gun up.

"Hey!" St. Benedict shouted, slapping his hands as if he hadn't just seen what he'd seen, and the piece would appear again. Digging through asphalt would ruin his manicure.

"No!" the teenager yelped, and only then St. Benedict realized he had looked away.

And all he saw were a pair of legs sticking out of a hamper-sized basket on a hairy back. Then, even that those were gone as the teenager slipped the rest of the way into the basket. A whole teenager shouldn't have been able to fit in there, but the basket wasn't even bulging.

"Two naughty boys down," Krampus said as the mist swallowed it up once more.

St. Benedict had been running in this twilight world for most of an hour. The Saint would have thought he was the last one standing, but he had noted what the Krampus had said.

"Two down. So where the heck are you, Brett?" he muttered as a chill shook through him. No matter how strange and ethereal this mist was, it was doing one thing all mist does that he hated. It was making him damp and very cold. If not for his augmentations allowing him to warm up his core, he'd have been worried the winter would get him before the Krampus.

"Come, kid, don't be a frozen lump somewhere. I don't need any more nightmares."

Then a hand dropped onto his shoulder.

Jumping out of his skin, St. Benedict lost all his cool as he flipped around to face...

"Brett!"

"You're... you're a-a-alive!" the teenager, who was hunching down hard in his leather jacket, chattered out through clenched teeth. "I thought it got you."

The Saint shook his head. "Naw, kid. It seems only interested in three."

"What... what about your lady friend? Did it get h-h-h-her too?" Brett asked.

St. Benedict furrowed his eyebrows. He had been about to say 'no, he didn't think so,' but he realized that might be entirely wrong.

The kid looked around them, rubbing his upper arms hard. "We... we should get out of here," as if that hadn't been what either of them had been doing the whole time. "Maybe if we can find the car, we can—"

St. Benedict didn't let him finish that sentence. Instead, he grabbed the kid by the collar.

"I got him! He's right here!"

"What are you doing?" Brett tried to struggle. It was cute, really. But St. Benedict had him in a headlock a second later. He wasn't even trying that hard to keep hold of the kid.

"Get away! Get away from me!" the squeaky-voiced kid shouted. The kid stank of sweat and fear. He may have also pissed himself.

A pair of green-yellow glowing eyes cut through the semi-dark of the mist. At their appearance, the kid squealed another high pitch noise.

A hulking black shadow formed.

Like he had seen before, the Krampus was distinctly shorter than St. Benedict, which, sadly, didn't diminish its fierceness. But at last he got to have a really good look at this Krampus.

Above the floating, goat-slitted eyes were a pair of long horns curving away from the creature's head. Black fur coated the whole thing's body except on its terrible, tan-colored face. A single clop of a hoof hit the cracked pavement of the alley, followed by a shimmy of Christmas bells. Yet, when it stepped clear from the thick mist, it led with a single bare, black foot.

The kid stopped resisting St. Benedict and instead tried to grip the fabric at the Saint's coat at his back as if that would pull them both backwards and away. It was useless. St. Benedict wasn't going anywhere.

"No! Shoot it, shoot it!" the kid squealed.

The creature hissed, perfectly understanding what the kid was saying. It bared its crooked fangs, tiny spears of bone instead of teeth.

St. Benedict shook his head. "Hey now, hey," he tried to soothe. "No one's shooting anyone, okay? Mr. Krampus, sir. Or is it ma'am?"

The Krampus sniffed contemptuously, its green-yellow eyes darting between the two men, sizing them both up. Then it stomped its hoofed foot. It lifted the whipping switch in its clawed hand.

"Brett Turner," the Krampus roared, its growl a sweet bass note, incongruously musical in contrast to its fierce appearance.

At the sound of his name, Brett went still.

"Thief, liar!" The Krampus accused, whipping the switch back and forth in the kid's direction, punctuating each word. In its other hand, the Krampus whipped out a thong that had been tied around its waist. Christmas bells rang out, sweet and bright as the ones he'd associate with Santa's Sleigh.

Once more, the mist swallowed Krampus.

"Thief, liar, assailant," the Krampus's voice sang out in the mist with the jingle of Christmas bells echoing from everywhere. "Thief, liar, assailant."

"No, please. Don't let it get me," Brett begged.

"Yeah, well, maybe you deserve it," the Saint said. "But I think you got one shot at saving yourself. You're going to have to confess."

"I didn't do nothing," Brett argued.

"Did that argument help your friends?" St. Benedict countered.

"Thief, liar, assailant," the Krampus whispered.

Jingle. Jingle. Jingle.

The kid was listening now. "It's already gotten your two buddies. You're all that's left, Brett."

"I tell you I didn't do nothing!" Brett shouted uselessly.

St. Benedict released the kid's head, letting him stand up. "Bullshit. This is a Krampus. They know everything you've done. You can't hide from them."

Brett shot a nervous glance at St. Benedict, still trying to stay close, even as he looked around for a sign of the Krampus. "It was just supposed to be a joke."

"Yeah, we're all laughing now," St. Benedict said dryly.

"It wasn't even my idea. It was Carl's. He said I had to... prove myself. That I was cool."

"Thief, liar, assailant."

St. Benedict chuckled. "Proved you're an idiot, stealing from a magic establishment."

"It was just a mask!"

"Obviously not!" St. Benedict turned as he shouted at the kid, only to see the Krampus's shadow burst out of the mist behind Brett. The kid must have seen his expression, because he spun around too late. It grabbed him by the front and lifted the kid so his feet cleared the ground.

"Thief," it bellowed and swatted the kid on the backside with the switch.

"OW! Stop it!" Brett screeched, wriggling hard against the Krampus's grasp.

"Thief!" It swung twice more. "THIEF!"

"Alright! Alright, I did it. I stole the mask!" The kid wept. "I went into the bar. Carl told me to, but I'm the one who did it. I just... I just wanted them to stop calling me a wuss." The kid kept talking, not noticing that the Krampus had lowered him down. "That I don't take shit from no one but... I knew it was wrong." He wiped his arm across his running nose.

"I'm just... I'm just..." then the kid hit himself in the head with his fist, punctuating each word. "I'm just a worthless waste of space." The Krampus stopped him, laying its stronger hand over his fist.

Brett gazed down into the terrible face. "I'm truly, very sorry. I... I fucked up. I knew better, too. I mean, I get it. I know it was wrong, but I just wanted to believe him, you know?"

"We all eat lies when our hearts are hungry," the Krampus growled, a shiver of bells chorusing. "Try again. Do better."

The kid wiped his nose again and nodded. "I am sorry."

Then the Krampus gave him a slight push away. "Go. Go home. Do better."

Unsure, Brett complied, pausing as he passed St. Benedict. "Thank you," he said, though for what the Saint wasn't sure.

"As she said, do better," St. Benedict agreed, and offered his hand to shake.

The kid smiled as he pumped the hand. "You know, it's weird. I feel a lot better now."

"Merry Christmas," St. Benedict said.

The kid scoffed. "God, that's lame," and walked off into the mist.

The Saint turned back to the Krampus. "And that just leaves you and me, Krampus."

The creature bared its fangs in a snarl.

"So do you think you want to tell me, now, why you're so mad at me?" he asked, shoving his hands into his pockets.

"Rude and ill-mannered," the Krampus spat. She swished her switch.

He took a step forward. "Can you be more specific?"

The switch smacked hard against his leg, now within the creature's reach. He flinched, but did not falter as he took another step. Smack, went the switch again. "Selfish!" the Krampus declared.

As the pain lanced through his pants, it came with a strange clarity. "Because I didn't help you set up for Krampus day?"

Smack went the switch on his other leg. "Bully!"

"I wasn't bullying..."

Swat, swat. "Bully!"

He winced and held up his hands. "Alright, I might have been a drunk bull in china shop..."

Swat. "Liar!"

"Damn, that hurts!" Yet, he was starting to see it. Her point of view. With each swat of the branches, it became clearer, until...

"I didn't show up for the Fae's birthdays," he said. Reaching up to the Krampus's face, he set his hands on either side and gently pulled the mask away, revealing Rune's tear-streaked angry face.

"I had to explain to all of them a dozen times each why you weren't there. You didn't even call. When I called you, you just... you just yelled at me that you were busy and whatever it was could wait. They were more excited about you coming than the King and Queen of the Fae!"

St. Benedict nodded his head. "And you had to deal with their King alone."

Rune huffed, folding her arms, now void of fur and returned to clothing. She tapped the toes of her normal, human foot on the ground in a nervous gesture. "It's just, you promised to be my wingman when dealing with him. He's still a pain in the ass."

The Saint nodded. "Rune, I am so sorry that I didn't make it to the Fae's birthday party and left you in the lurch."

She nodded in acknowledgment. "You could have at least called."

"I could have at least called," he agreed. Around them, the mist dissipated.

"I understand if you can't come but you need to communicate."

"Yup, I do." Turning they walked down and out of the alley toward his car. "And I'm sorry for how I've been acting today."

"Yeah, then there's that," Rune nodded, renewing her ire. "You've been an out-of-control jerk, and that's not like you."

St. Benedict rubbed his eyes as he nodded again. "Yes, I'll own that. Things went...bad at work. I can't talk about it, obviously, but I let it get the best of me and I don't know... It's like they say, you act the worst with the people you feel safest."

"Who is this 'they?'"

"You know, the 'they' out there." He waved his hand toward the cold city and all the stars now in the sky, that had now returned as the mist dissipated away. They were once more in the alley where this little adventure had begun. "The-out-there-they. Does it matter?"

"No." Rune kicked a bit of snow off her shoe, before blowing out what he hoped was the last of her anger like a horse.

"I'm sorry I wasn't there for you," he said.

Rune's shoulders sagged in resignation. She looked tired, and he didn't blame her. "Look, St. Ben. You *are* great with the big things, coming to help me fight the good fight or chase down a-hole teenagers." She waved at the trio of teens as they piled into their car, all looking more chagrined, and very much alive, than they had an hour earlier. "It's just..."

St. Benedict cleared his throat. "Would you still like help setting up for Krampusnacht?"

"Yes, please." She gave him her pretty "little-girl" smile.

St. Benedict grinned and held the door out for her, then handed her the mask.

"And I think we'll put *you* back in storage," she said to the wickedly smiling Krampus mask.

The mask laughed. "*Grufs vom Krampus, Fraulein.*" Then it evaporated in her hands. Out of the night, coming from nowhere, rose the tinkle of Christmas bells and a soft, menacing chuckle.

Rune and St. Benedict exchanged a look.

"Let's get out of here," Rune said. St. Benedict quickly offered her his arm, and she took it so they both could hurry out of the alley. He remote-started the car with a gesture of his augmentations.

"Oh, you know what?" St. Benedict said as he helped her into the car, then got in on the driver's side. In seconds, he shifted the car heard into gear.

"What?!" Rune asked, whipping her head about.

"Acorn was right, it *was* cursed," St. Benedict said with a mischievous smile, "I owe them some honey."

About the Author

Megan Mackie is a Chicago writer. With her smashing success with her inaugural, amazon bestselling book, The Finder of the Lucky Devil, she is now the author of The Lucky Devil series, the Dead World Series, and the Working Mask series with one new series coming out later this year. She has become a personality at many cons, recognizable by her iconic leather hat and engaging smile.

Outside of her own works, she is a contributing writer for the rpgs Legendlore and Legendlore: Legacies by Onyx Path Publishing and Sirens: Battle of the Bards through Apotheosis Studios. Outside of writing, she likes to play games: board games, RPGs, and video games. She has a regular Pathfinder group who is working their way through Rapanthuk. She lives in Chicago with her husband and children, dog, three cats, and her mother in the apartment upstairs.

TOY SOLDIERS

BY EVAN CLOUSE

SANTA RUBBED HIS FOREHEAD in frustration as his wife, Mrs. Claus, placed a fresh cup of steaming coffee on his desk. "What is causing your brow to furl so, my dear?" her kind voice asked.

Santa wiped a slight tear from his ancient cheek and looked out his frosty window at the raging blizzard outside before responding. He let out a deep sigh and said in a worn voice, "Oh, my love. Every year it just gets worse and worse. The Naughty List just keeps on growing and growing. All of these sweet little children whose souls are being corrupted by their parents. They are turning them into hateful little bigots. They pick on their classmates for no other reason than they look different or worship differently or some other inconsequential reason. The world's adults are being corrupted and consumed with hatred for anyone who are not exactly like them. And it is affecting our children. So many children who were on the Nice List just one year ago are now on the Naughty List. And, my dear, I do not think that it is a coincidence that many of these children turn from nice to naughty after they are given access to cell phones and the internet. Technology can be used for so many wonderful, inspirational things. Why must mankind bastardize everything? And why must they indoctrinate the innocent into their perverse, loathsome views? I am so saddened by today's world. I have not seen such an uptick on the Naughty List since the late 1930's. So many wonderful children who were corrupted by the lunacy of a power-hungry maniac. And it is happening again. Only this time, there is constant reinforcement of these vile messages through those damned devices that they look at constantly. I don't know what to do, my love. I fear that lumps of coal simply won't be enough this year. I fear that a much stronger message must be sent. At least to some.

"Like this one," Santa continued as he turned the page in the ancient book. There was one name in the middle of the yellowed paper that was glowing red. "This little boy right here. He is far more than naughty. He has evil in his soul. Pure evil. I'm afraid, my love, that if this boy were allowed to reach adulthood, that he could be an existential threat to all of humankind. Yes, I believe that for this *particular* boy, we must summon Irwin and Gale."

Mrs. Claus's complexion turned as white as the sheets of snow outside their modest domicile. She clutched at her collar and said with a quivering voice, "No, my darling. No. you can't be serious. You can't summon *them*. Surely, this boy has some redeeming qualities. Please, dear. We cannot unleash *them* upon this boy."

Santa leaned back in his chair while hiding his beleaguered face in his calloused hands. He looked up at his wife with tears in his pained eyes and said, "I'm sorry dear. But this must be done. Just look at the paper. Look at his glowing red name. Look at how the universe is sending us an urgent warning about him. This boy is not redeemable. Because this boy is the Anti-Christ. Please, my love, summon Irwin and Gale."

Mrs. Claus righted her spine, clenched her fists and said, "Very well. I am just so sorry that it has come to this. I had hoped to never summon them again. But *I* see what *you* see. I see the name. I see the threat. I can see the world ending in a hellfire of his creation. I will be right back. With Irwin and Gale."

Ten minutes later, Santa's study door burst open, and the disfigured forms of two pungent smelling elves came darting into the room. "Hiya Santa!" Irwin yelled out while his twin sister, Gale, began shoving candy canes into her mouth. "Thanks for the invite, Santa!" she exclaimed while her brother was haphazardly knocking books off of a shelf. "It's been a while! What can we do for ya? Oooooh! Can I have these chocolates? And this letter opener? And this piece of paper? And this log?"

"Irwin, Gale, please sit down," Santa's booming voice commanded. The pair looked at one another and shrugged before taking a seat on a bright green sofa. "Wow, he's kinda uptight," Irwin stated to his sister who replied, "Yeah. Wonder what's up *his* fat ass. Maybe Mrs. Claus isn't giving it up, heh, heh, heh."

Santa got up from his desk and walked over to the pair of chortling elves. He looked down upon their repulsive faces that were covered in deep scars and throbbing, moist boils. Their asymmetrical, bloodshot eyes looked up at this towering figure while their impossibly large, pointed ears perked up in anticipation of their assignment. "Thank you for coming," Santa began. "Your services are, unfortunately, required once again. We have a small boy who is a threat to humanity. I need your special gift this Christmas, my friends. I need you to make this child a very special toy. A special toy that will give him what he deserves. Do you understand?"

"Understand?" Irwin yelled out as he and his sister jumped up from their seats and began clapping. "Why *of course* we understand! We've been waiting for *decades* for this shit! Oh! What type of toy shall we make, Santa? Should it be a stuffed lion that comes to life and bites his head off? Or perhaps some special cookies that will grow in his tummy until he explodes?" "No, wait," Gale interjected. "How about a chemistry set that blows up and dissolves his skin? Or a spaceship that shoots his eyes out with real lasers? Or maybe a violent video game that he gets sucked into and then he gets hacked up! Hack! Hack! Hack! And his blood will fly everywhere, and it will be so funny and..."

Gale was cut off by a patient Santa. "No, no, nothing like that, my friends. I already know what he desires. It is right here in his letter to me. He wants a collection of toy soldiers. And I fear what he wants to use them for. I need you to make them. I need you to make him an army of toy soldiers using your special gift. But listen to me carefully. I do not want your special ingredient to be activated unless his actions necessitate it. I want to give him an opportunity to learn. An opportunity to change his ways. He will receive this one test. I shall leave him a note. A personal note. And it will be up to him to decide how to use these toy soldiers. He will determine his own fate. Now, be off, my friends. The next time I see you I want a brilliantly wrapped package. A brilliantly wrapped package of special toy soldiers that can only be created by the two of you."

Irwin and Gale were cackling as they placed large chunks of green plastic into a scorching cauldron. They giggled with glee as they stirred the harmless plastic as it melted. "And now, for our special ingredients!" Gale yelled out. The pair stuck their index fingers deep into their hideous noses and pulled out long, pale green streams of snot. They vigorously shook their disfigured hands over the cauldron until their nasal discharge became dislodged and fell into the vat. The plastic glowed and hissed momentarily as the goo became absorbed by the plastic.

"And now, a bit of mercilessness," Irwin declared. "I'm sure glad we had a large meal of raw roadkill this evening!" They stuck their snotty fingers deeply into their mouths until they began gagging. They each leaned over the bubbling cauldron and vomited. Large chunks of fur, bone, and flesh were intermingled with the pale stream of acidic refuse that splashed into the glowing concoction. They looked at one another wearing devilish grins as they licked their lips and swallowed the final remnants of their own ghastly spew.

Their incessant chortling continued as Gale said, "And now, to load their guns!" The siblings turned around, pulled down their tattered britches and began defecating into the maniacal creation. Loud plopping sounds were heard as bricks of feces plummeted into the liquifying nightmare.

"Oh, Rudolph," Clarice stated as the pair of reindeer watched the demented activity from outside the devilish elves' window. "Please be careful this year, dear. Please be careful delivering these packages."

"I will, my love," Rudolph responded in his nasally voice. "If Santa has asked *them* to make toys, then it must indeed be a special assignment. Yes, I must ensure that this package gets to its intended child. I fear that failure may doom all of humanity."

Clarice rolled her hazel eyes and said, "Yeah, whatevs. I don't really care about *that* shit. I just want you to get your lazy ass home on time. You need to take out the trash. And make me dinner. And don't forget to pick up my wine. I'm almost out. And make sure you put your filthy clothes in the hamper as soon as you get home. I don't want to even *see* that smelly shit. And if you think you're going to have that goddamned dentist-elf Hermie come over this weekend, just think again. I'm sick of him always wanting me to open my mouth. And have you noticed he always has one hand in his pocket fondling himself while he looks into my mouth? I'm telling you Rudolph, there's something wrong with that little perv."

"Yes dear," was all the submissive Rudolph could think of to say as the pair returned their gaze to the morbid activities inside the dilapidated quarters of Irwin and Gale. A tear fell from Rudolph's eye as he watched a pair of grotesque, smiling elves pouring the glowing hot wax into metal casts.

The five-year-old boy was beaming with anticipation as he looked upon the brilliantly wrapped package. The red, green, and gold paper and bows reflected the brilliant blinking lights of the ornate Christmas tree. There was an envelope that said, 'From Santa and His Special Elves.' The boy opened the envelope and began reading the hand-written note that it had contained.

Here you are my fine lad. Enjoy the toy soldiers that you requested. I am sure that they will give you hours upon hours of fun. But just remember. Only use these soldiers when you absolutely must and only against outside threats. They are never to be used for your own self-enrichment and must never be used against their own people. These are patriotic toy soldiers who have taken an oath to protect their country. They have not taken an oath to you, and I am now placing them in your trust. I now trust that they will be used by you to protect our freedom and that they will never be used against innocent people. I hope you understand. These toy soldiers will protect you and give you the respect that you deserve. They are now in your hands, and it is your choice as to how to use them. It is now your choice to determine what will happen to your soul. Kindest regards, Santa.

The boy shrugged and ripped the note into tiny pieces. His eyes glowed with greed as he tore the glistening paper from the box. He stared in awe at the rows of plastic green toy soldiers while his devious mind whirled. He then raced up the winding staircase of his mansion, threw open his playroom door, and dumped his large box of four-inch plastic soldiers upon the floor. He got down on his knees and began lining the plastic green men in position. Their tiny guns were pointed toward an area of the room that contained an eclectic assortment of stuffed animals, board games, action figures, and other random toys.

The boy looked across the room at the discarded toy menagerie and said with an evil sneer, "Alright assholes. I now have my army. And they will do anything that I say. Just look at them. Standing proudly and pointing their guns at you. You toys that I never wanted here. You toys that invaded my playroom every birthday, Easter, and Christmas. I never asked for you. You are boring and stupid, and I hate you because you do nothing for *me*. And if you do nothing for *me*, then I have no use for *you*. All you do is take up space in my playroom. Well, I am now going to take care of that. My soldiers are going to lock you away until we can find a place to put you."

The toy soldiers stood in frozen silence, awaiting their orders as the boy exited the room. A small trail of liquid green plastic dripped from one of the soldier's eyes when the boy returned with a small playpen. The boy set the playpen up next to the window which he immediately opened, allowing a gust of cold air to enter. "This is where you will stay. And you won't get any blankets, either," the boy sneered as he picked up two of his soldiers and marched them across the floor toward the pile of toys. "Now, are you going to get in this playpen, or do my soldiers have to shoot you?" he said as he strategically placed the additional toy soldiers around the unwanted toys. He looked around the room and saw a toy robot sitting on the shelf. "I think that I'll start with you," the boy haughtily stated as he grabbed one of the toy soldiers, walked across the room, and positioned the soldier to point his plastic muzzle at the robot.

"Yes, you will be the first," he said. "You were one of my favorites. I was so excited to get you last Christmas. You always did what I wanted you to do. All I had to do was put batteries in you and press the buttons on the remote and you did exactly what I told you to do. But then you broke. Your arms won't lift anymore, and your wheels get stuck, and you don't do what I tell you to do anymore. You betrayed me, so in the playpen you go."

He picked up the robot and marched him across the room with the dutiful toy soldier still pointing his muzzle at the forlorn, metal toy. The boy cackled as he dropped the robot into the playpen. "Now, who's next? Yeah, you. Stuffed donkey. All you did was sit there and judge me. You're definitely out of here." The donkey was marched into the playpen by the boy holding a toy soldier.

One by one, all of the undesirable toys were rounded up by the toy soldiers. One by one they were thrown into the playpen. One by one they internally wept as they powerlessly awaited their dastardly fate. The boy threw the final toy into the playpen and began laughing while placing his toy soldiers around its perimeter. "Yeah, this is great. Finally, all you useless toys are in one place where I can keep you under the watch of my toy soldiers. And if any of you try to escape, my soldiers will shoot you. But wait. They are still in my playroom. They are still taking up space and I still have to look at their stupid faces. No, I can keep you here for a while, but you're still poisoning my playroom. Okay soldiers. Just guard these stupid toys tonight. I know just what to do with them. Tomorrow, we'll put them on my big toy train, and we'll take them to the basement. But wait. Then they'll be taking up space there. No, just holding them won't do. They need to go into the furnace. Then my entire house will be rid of these stupid toys who have done nothing for me, and I will be left with only the toys that do what I want. Then, this will be the greatest house ever!"

"This is bullshit," one of the toy soldiers whispered to another as the boy's loud snoring was heard from the adjacent bedroom. "I mean, what in the hell are we doing? We took an oath to defend freedom, not be the lethal personal police force of some spoiled brat who gets rid of any toy that he doesn't like. I mean, they're just toys. Just like us. They have the same dreams of being loved and played with. What was their infraction? Being bought as a present for some unappreciative little asshole who is unable to see how all these toys contribute into making this playroom a more joyful place? They're just toys. Just like us. And if this little bastard can turn on them, he sure as hell can turn on us too. We could be next. Just like he did to that poor robot."

"Yeah, he'll definitely turn on us too unless we do every twisted thing that he wants," another toy soldier replied. "If we don't do things that violate our oath and basic sense of humanity, then he'll just buy bigger toy soldiers and march *us* into the furnace too. Plus, if this is how he treats toys, how in the hell is he going to treat actual human beings when he gets older? Man, have mercy on the people if this little asshole ever gets any power. So, what should we do Sarge?"

"Well, the way I see it," the first toy soldier began answering. "Is we took an oath to protect all of the toys in this playroom, regardless of where that toy came from. We did not take an oath to this boy and this boy has betrayed all of these unfortunate toys and us. He has committed treason. And there's just one fitting punishment for that."

The boy woke up sitting in a chair. He began frantically struggling against the tinsel, popcorn strands, and Christmas lights that bound him. His sweaty face looked around his playroom. The eyes of all of his toys were staring at him with vengeful, anticipatory glee. He heard several loud clicks of rifles being cocked directly in front of him. His toy soldiers were all lined up with their tiny plastic guns pointed at him. One of the toy soldiers yelled out, "Fire!"

The last thing that the youthful Anti-Christ heard before the deadly hail of plastic bullets exploded into his skull was the maniacal laughter of a pair of watching disfigured elves.

"Well, well, well," Satan cheerfully stated as the black soul of the boy fell upon blistering brimstone. "Wow. Those elves are good. I wasn't expecting you for quite a while. They prevented a lot of needless suffering and bloodshed too. I was actually kinda looking forward to seeing all that, but hey! Now that you won't be around to kill them off, maybe I've got a chance to corrupt their souls! Yeah, if you had killed them off, they'd get a one-way ticket to heaven! But now that the future's been altered, I have a shot at tens of thousands more souls. Damn if this isn't a great plan. Anyway, welcome to hell. Let me show you around a little bit. We don't get too many kids down here. Even the blackest of kids' souls at least get Purgatory and a do-over. But not *you*. *You're* a special case, kid!

"Now, now, don't cry. I know you miss your daddy. Don't worry. He'll join you here soon enough. So, just turn that frown upside down and...hey! Stop looking at those demon cheerleaders! They're too old for you and...wow. That's kinda ironic. Anyway, take a look at this pamphlet. It'll give you all the basics about living here."

The confused, whimpering boy took the charred pamphlet, wiped tears from his eyes, and began reading.

CONGRATULATIONS ON MAKING IT TO HELL!

On behalf of our lord, Satan, we would like to thank you for being a damned soul and choosing, through your Earthly actions, to reside in Hell. We are most pleased that you committed such abhorrent atrocities that the Universe banished you here for all eternity.

While here, which will be forever, please feel free to enjoy our wide variety of amenities that are designed to cater to your every whim. Whether it be horseback riding, fine dining, relaxing by the pool, or having a fun night out singing karaoke with friends, we have it all here for you. Oh wait. I had you going there, didn't I? Just a little harmless fib from one damned soul to another. Let me start again. Welcome home. This is hell. You are fucked. The End.

"Okay kid, have you read the pamphlet? Pretty self-explanatory, right?" Satan stated. "Okay, so now you know that you're a damned soul that is going to be punished for all of eternity, Now, what to do? Oh right! Your eternal punishment! Sorry. I've just had so much on my mind lately and..." Satan's voice trailed off for a moment as he looked over at a group of mean girl cheerleaders. "And their goddamned gum-snapping is distracting! Knock that shit off, bitches! Where in the hell are you getting your gum? Seriously. Where in *hell* are you getting your gum? We haven't stocked that shit in years. Oh, never mind. Bigger fish to fry. Now, what to do with this kid? Oh yeah. I think that'll do.

"Alright kid, here's what we're going to do. What's the one thing that you love more than anything? Attention, right? A relentless stream of adoration from your brainwashed followers. So, I don't think that I'll cause you any physical harm. That shit's so overdone anyway. No, from now on, you're going to stand in that corner over there naked. And everybody that walks by you is going to stop and point and laugh at you. Over and over and over for all eternity you are going to bathe in embarrassment and low self-esteem. You are going to absolutely hate yourself because you will come face to face with how people *really* feel about you, and you are going to understand what a worthless piece of shit you truly are. You are going to get the unvarnished truth from everybody! And that shit's *not* gonna be pretty, let me tell ya because everybody, and I mean *everybody*, thinks you're an asshole. Yes. An eternity of self-loathing and shame seems to be what is needed in this moment. And if I get bored with that, there's always the eternal hot poker up the ass. But let's start here and see how this works out for a while, alright? Now if you would please disrobe. Oh, and hey! I almost forgot! Merry Christmas! Or, in *your* case, Merry *Anti*-Christmas. Here, I got you a present. It's a box of toy soldiers, heh, heh, heh. Now somebody pass me that eggnog. I'm feeling festive tonight."

THE END

About the Author

Evan Clouse is a fifty-something-year-old married man who has entered his 2/3-life crisis and decided to become an author. After over a quarter century of doing social work, he became despondent over the deteriorating condition of our nation's intelligence, empathy, and civility towards one another. This was his fuel, and his books are the result.

https://hangingchadsbook.com/

The Naughty List

by Ivy Ru

Child's Name: Felicity Abraham
Age: 9
Status: Naughty
Elf: Sprinkle Pop
Notes:
November -

- The child was observed removing wings from a housefly in her room using tweezers from her guardian's craft kit.

- Caught eavesdropping on older siblings during a private conversation in a shared bedroom.

December -

- When asked to clean the dishes after dinner, she put the dishes away dirty.

- Seen leaving the sink running before going to school, causing a small kitchen flood.

Child's Name: Chance Green
Age: 12
Status: Naughty
Elf: Twinkle Drop
Notes:
October-

- Seen stealing a neighbor's scooter, and later abandoning it in a ditch near the child's school.

November-

- Caught skipping sports practice, then seen eating with friends.
- Observed attempting to replace sibling's shampoo with hair remover in the shared bathroom.

Child's Name: Harper Johnson
Age: 6
Status: Naughty
Elf: Taffy Cane
Notes:
November-

- Observed pulling cat's tail in the family's living room.
- Seen stealing and destroying guardian's cosmetics, then attempting to flush the container down the toilet.
- Observed refusing to complete spelling and mathematics homework at the dining table.

December-

- Seen destroying a sibling's birthday cake after blowing out their candles in the kitchen.

My fingers trembled slightly as I stared at the files in front of me. The parchment in my hands held the report of this year's naughty and nice listings in my sector, typed out in bold red and green lettering. I had seen enough naughty kids for a lifetime through my work at the North Pole, but nothing like this. This was unprecedented. The number of naughty children had increased by almost 135% since my first year as a naughty and nice investigator, so I expected a larger number this year. In my sector alone, there had been another increase... a 57% increase in naughty behavior over the last year alone!

I flipped through a few of the entries again, appalled by the acts of these children. I knew these kids could change a lot over the years, and I'd seen my fair share of downfalls, but these kids were on track to be the next skilled doctors and scientists. Chance was a model student, and he was the president of the student council. Felicity was practicing to become a dog trainer and helping out at the local animal shelter. Even little Harper was helping around the community by planting trees and organizing reading clubs. Now they were stealing and skipping chores of every kind. *How could I have let this happen?*

A heavy sigh escaped through my lips as I set the files back on my desk and leaned back in my chair. They were the last ones out of over a hundred I had read in the last few hours. There wasn't anything I could do about this dilemma tonight besides mope. Everyone else on my sector team had already gone home for the evening; only I had waited for the report to come in. I pulled my coat off its hook and zipped it up, pulling the furry hood around my face. I resolved to contact the other sectors first thing the next morning to ask if they had seen a similar increase in naughty cases.

I left my office, walking through the heated hallways. Working in the North Pole had its advantages: cheaper housing, free snowblower repair, and, of course, never-ending snow, but my work allowed little extra time for building snowmen.

The Naughty and Nice Investigation Unit (N2IU) was extremely secretive. Mr. Nicholas Claus knows nothing of the unit's existence and he never will. It's better for Christmas if word doesn't spread. The spirit of the season revolves around trust, love, and peace. Keeping an extremely watchful eye on every child in the world does not exactly reflect those values.

Each sector is responsible for the children in fifteen to thirty cities, as well as their respective elves. We investigate children and what is going on around them. You could consider what we do "stalking," but Nicholas wouldn't have a chance at Christmas without our work.

The biting wind of the North Pole slipped into my coat the moment I stepped outside, and I hurried toward the train station. The street was illuminated with warm yellow streetlights, all adorned with candy cane garlands and evergreen wreaths. Though the constant winter made it feel like Christmas year round, I always appreciated the extra touches the elves added as the season grew closer.

The train station was nearly empty, save for a handful of other night owls like me leaving the office. Every station near the workshop had both a human train and an elf train. Though many stories will tell you that the Clauses are the only humans living in the North Pole, that couldn't be further from the truth. There were many other semi-mortal humans working and living in the North Pole; I was one of them.

In the beginning, the only humanoid inhabitants of the North Pole were humans themselves. Once we found out how useful magical creatures like elves could be, we began employing them to do tasks around the workshop. We believe very much in Elf jobs. Toy manufacturing, sleigh preparation, coal retrieving, and reindeer care are extraordinarily important, all headed by elves. We can't make our significant contributions to the season without them laying the groundwork.

I boarded the train, riding with the other humans in comfortable, warm silence. There were speakers in every corner of the train car, all playing instrumental covers of well-known Christmas music. I don't know if the point was to make you tired, but it always did anyway. The constant smell of warm sugar cookies didn't help. The elves on their train honestly didn't know how good they had it. They may only have standing cars, but at least that keeps them awake for their ride to the elf cities.

My home was dark when I arrived, forcing me to flick on the light above my front door. The candy-cane shaped fixture cast a warm pink glow over my coat rack as I unloaded my layers. I had always lived alone while working in the North Pole, so I was used to my house being the perfect temperature upon my arrival. Tonight, a chill swept through my skin as I approached my bedroom.

The window was open.

The window was open and its evergreen garland was flapping out into the frigid night. I pulled it shut quickly, cutting the garland in half. I watched the string of green float away in the wind as I warmed my hands with my breath. My home's windows have remained unopened for years. No one did when they lived in the North Pole.

Before I went into the office the next day I would have to call my local repair elf to check on the windows seal. I couldn't imagine how much money I had wasted heating the place in just one day.

I climbed into my bed of red and gold quilts, burrowing deep into the down pillows. I imagined sugarplums, and nutcrackers, and all the things that make you fall asleep faster, but my eyes stayed alert. They had already adjusted to the dark, but that did not stop every stack of books and a strangely upright bag from looking like someone or something staring back at me.

I usually cured my insomnia with a glass of warm milk. Tonight, something paralyzed me and I couldn't bring myself to leave my bed. Something about the naughty cases, my window, and this knew-found, unbridled paranoia didn't sit right with me.

I ARRIVED AT THE office late, because the damned repair-elf was slow to be scheduled. Far below the main workshop level, where the elves manufactured toys under the watchful eye of Nicholas Claus, was the N2IU office. This meant stairs. Endless stairs.

Everyone had seen the report, so I could avoid an unnecessary meeting. I walked over to the analysis officer of my sector, placing a hand on the back of his chair.

"Good morning Ben, give me an update." I said, taking a sip from a foaming, gingerbread flavored coffee one of the interns had handed me.

"Mornin' Kate. As you know, we've had a tremendous increase in naughty listings in our sector. Looking at the data for other sectors and comparing it to our own, there is definitely something going on. I have contacted Human Affairs and Events to see what could have caused such a centralized change. I copied you on the email," he reported, in his normal monotone voice.

I patted Ben on the shoulder as he finished speaking, flashing him my friendliest and most approving smile.

I continued through the department until I came to my office, and unlocked the door with my seasonal key card. For safety, we destroy and produce IDs and key cards every couple of months, so why not make them a little festive? This season's cards were decorated with sparkling sugar cookies, designed so realistically that my mouth watered every time I had to open a door.

My office was just as I had left it the night before, old coffee mugs on the file cabinet, a dying Christmas cactus near my only window, and the newest reports on top of my pile of candy cane boxes. A girl's got to snack.

I hung my coat on its hook and sat behind my comfortably cluttered desk. Cracking my neck, I opened my computer and typed in my password *ChristmasLover1781*. It's an easy one to crack, so I always think about changing it to something a little more cryptic, but I can never find the time.

Sure enough, Ben had copied me on all of his correspondence with the other sector communications and analytic members. It seemed that none of them were having issues to the degree we were, but there was something going on in the world.

I called the director of Human Affairs and Events to ask if something had caused such an unprecedented level of naughty behavior. We had seen a similar spike in naughty cases during events like market crashes, World Wars, pandemics, and tours of popular musicians. This time, though, there seemed to be no specific influence on the behavior changes.

"Hi Jeff, how are you doing this morning?" I asked.

"Hi Kate. I'm doing as well as can be expected. I woke up this morning, so that was rough." Jeff said, sighing.

I rolled my eyes. Jeff was probably the second oldest human in the North Pole, only surpassed by Nicholas, of course. We had all been waiting for Jeff to retire for the last few centuries, but he refused to give up, despite how many times he complained about still being alive.

"Jeff, I need you to find out if any big events took place in the last couple of months in and around my sector area. We've had a rise in naughty cases this year," I directed.

"Of course, give me a few moments... unless I die first." he drawled.

Oh my kringle. Every time.

After a moment of silence that was accentuated by the clicking of letters on a keyboard, Jeff spoke again, "I hate to tell you Kate, but there's not a thing going on. No elections, no wars, nothing important. The dark ages were more interesting than this.

I sighed, only slightly dramatically, before responding. "Thanks anyway, Jeff. I'll see you for drinks this Friday?"

"Of course, unless I-"

I hung up before Jeff could finish telling me how he was going to die in the next week. I looked up from my phone and saw an intern standing timidly at the door, waiting for my permission to enter.

"Hello, Jingle! How are you doing this chilly morning?" I asked, swivelling my chair so I was facing the elf.

"I'm doing just fine, Kate." Jingle said, voice high and timid.

Jingle was the first elf to ever work in the N2IU, just as an intern, mind you. It filled my heart with joy to see their people receive more opportunities after serving the workshop, mines, and stables.

Jingle stepped toward me, holding out a stack of manilla folders. I quickly took them from her hands and opened the first one on my desk.

"What am I looking at here?" I asked, flipping through the files.

"These are the elves that have been recommended for interviews, and possible re-education. As you will see in the folder on top, they are all suspected of foul play against the children." Jingle responded.

I nodded, dismissing Jingle from the office. She walked away quickly, closing my office door softly behind her.

There were three elves' files in front of me now, Sprinkle Pop, Taffy Cane, and Twinkle Drop. These elves had never been a problem before, and now I was forced to recall them to the North Pole for a one-on-one before we completed the naughty listing of the children under their care.

Hours passed before I could successfully send a recall out to the elves, it was always hard to contact them while they were in the field. Eventually, I got a response from all three of them. I would interview Sprinkle Pop first thing tomorrow when she got back to the North Pole.

I SLID INTO THE metal chair across from Sprinkle Pop, and my chair made a deafening scratch against the cement floor. The office had been decorated, like every other room in the workshop, with green garlands and red ornaments. A singular light shone from the ceiling, casting a warm but ominous glow over the handcuffs on the elf's wrists.

I gently set a file on the table and slid it towards the elf, allowing her a brief look through its contents. Sprinkle clumsily flipped through the pages. I suppose her hands were restrained in cuffs, but I would've expected more nimbleness from an elf.

"Miss Pop," I said, opening the file to the report she had submitted on her subject, Felicity Abraham, "I have a couple questions for you about the

Abraham child. Nothing to be worried about, just a new precaution in the N2IU."

Sprinkle Pop nodded, but we both knew that there was nothing routine about this meeting. We were walking on cookie crumbs.

"When did you first notice naughty behavior from Felicity Abraham?" I asked.

Sprinkle thought for a moment before responding, allowing enough time for me to believe she hadn't rehearsed before the interrogation. "I believe the first instance of recorded naughty behavior was near Halloween, when the child took more than the recommended amount of candy from an unattended bowl."

I nodded in agreement, jotting down a couple of notes on the pad in front of me. Stealing candy wasn't outlandish. I would have to inspect the file to confirm the truth of Sprinkle's statement.

"And how about changes in the child's environment?" I asked.

"I did notice a change in the behavior of the parents around the time of..." Sprinkle began.

My questioning continued well into the evening. Sprinkle responded with intelligent and emotional answers when required. Her answers weren't wrong, but they also had no additional detail. No surprises. It's almost as if they were too perfect. Rehearsed or crafted specifically to keep me from being suspicious which in turn made me more suspicious than ever. I had no reason to keep Sprinkle in the department, much to her supposed chagrin, so I released her with not so much as a warning.

It could be a conspiracy. It had to be. Her answers were so polished, so perfect. Each time she answered, she took time to think! It was as if she wanted there to be enough time between answers to make me believe she hadn't practiced before interrogation. Someone, probably other elves, had to have rehearsed her answers. I felt like ripping my hair out.

As Sprinkle walked away, I found rage rising within me. How could the elves hide something from the people that had given them so much? I have worked tirelessly in the North Pole day and night for centuries, just as they have. *What makes them think they have some sort of right to ruin this utopia for us all?* I slammed my fists against the wall, instantly regretting my actions. I should've asked better questions. I ruined everything.

I raced home, not bothering to wait for the train or stop at the pop-up Christmas bakery. I needed to review some files, and I was sure that I would find something on Sprinkle.

The walk from the train station to my house was usually a pleasant one, but tonight it was all wrong. It was so much darker than usual, having to work past sunset. The Christmas Lights were too bright, they pierced through the darkness of the night sky like a dozen suns. My neighbor's "classy" white lights clashed with my colorful, blinking ones. I'd managed to overlook this in the past, but I couldn't help but mutter a string of insults under my breath as I walked to my front door today. I unlocked my door. I can't believe I had to lock my door, anyway. I wondered if we'd always locked our doors or if that was something that happened only after the arrival of the elves.

I shook off my boots after closing and locking my door behind me. It sent clumps of grayish snow across my floor. I rolled my eyes at the thought of mopping my floor tomorrow morning and carelessly stepped on one of the clumps. A shiver went down my spine and I quickly picked up my foot, a cold wet spot was already forming on the bottom of my sock. I dragged myself, and my soggy sock, toward my bedroom.

I didn't bother putting on a fresh set of Christmas pajamas, opting for yesterday's that laid crumpled on the floor. The pajamas felt wrinkled, and the scent of my cinnamon pine sachet had almost completely disappeared.

This case was taking everything out of me! I could barely take care of myself anymore! *Did the elves even realize what they were doing to me?*

I woke early in the morning, my body racked with chills, and my quilts damp with cold sweat. I never found out what had woken me. Perhaps it was the ice storm beating against my bedroom window, or maybe it was my own paranoia attempting to protect me in my subconscious. No matter. I slid from my bed, and found myself on all fours as my vision adjusted to the darkness blanketing my room. Every corner was filled with shadows, all of which could easily hide a small humanoid. I crawled toward my bedroom door, the lump in my throat refusing to let any tears fall onto my wooden floor.

My hair caught beneath my hands as they slid across the floor. Sweat created a strange paste with the dark varnish. I opened the door and screamed. An elf stood on the other side, eyes wide as they stared back at me.

I lifted my hands in front of me, and nearly fell as I shifted my weight onto the balls of my feet. The elf did not try to escape as I wrapped my hands around its fragile body, and smashed it into the ground as I screeched.

I had heard stories of strange spirits people heard deep in the poles. Spirits that screamed bloody murder until helped, only to have their rescuers find a person or animal already frozen to death, or long since buried under the ice. I have to imagine they sounded like I did in that moment, as I held a life in my hands and had no hesitation to end it.

I pounded the body of the small figure I had slammed to my floor. Then, I hit it again. After my third blow to the floor, the elf shattered to a million tiny pieces of blue ceramic. I smashed at the pieces until they turned to bloody dust. My hands were tattered as I brought them up, shaking, to the light switch.

My grandmother's vase sat in front of me, completely and utterly demolished. I quickly retrieved a dust pan. *How could I have been so silly?* I suppose this case had more of an impact on me than I had originally thought, but it was part of the job. I always knew that this would be a hard path for me. I had too much love in my heart to truly punish any elves.

Taffy Cane was waiting for me in the interview room when I arrived at work after my morning escapade. I considered informing the human resources department about what I assumed to be a case-related hallucination, but decided that it would be safer to keep those things to myself. It was impossible to tell who could be behind this elf conspiracy.

I started Taffy Cane's interview with the same questions I had asked Sprinkle. Taffy's responses were nearly identical. There was definitely something going on. The interview dragged on for hours, and–though Taffy answered the same as Sprinkle–he was much more timid. Taffy was prone to rambling, shaking, and even crying after answering some questions.

Eventually, I decided it was time to take a break. I released Taffy from his small handcuffs and led him toward the door. There was a Christmas cookie vending machine and hot cocoa dispenser outside the interview room. I assumed that Taffy would enjoy a snack and then we could get back to work, but I was sorely mistaken. I should have never trusted that elf to do what was right.

Taffy ran toward the door, bursting out into the dark tundra before I could process his escape. Once I realized what was going on, I bolted after the rogue elf, not bothering to don my coat or gloves.

Taffy kept running, even as I yelled at him to stop. It was a good thing for me that elves aren't known for their long strides.

I cornered Taffy outside the workshop entrance, pleading with him to see reason.

"Please, Taffy, you know we are just trying to keep everyone safe, including you."

Taffy shook his head. "You were only ever trying to help yourself. You are no more intelligent or special than the rest of your race. The elves now know that Christmas would never happen without us. You will never forget that we hold the power. Never again."

Taffy quickly retrieved a small pink gumdrop and popped it into his mouth. I had no idea what would happen next, but I knew it would not end well.

After a few seconds of chewing, I could see red foam pooling in the corners of Taffy's mouth. He fell back into the snow, writhing like a seal cub first learning to swim. Then he stopped.

I stood in front of Taffy's body for longer than I care to admit. Adrenaline and fear stopped me from moving an inch. With the sound of the train whistle as it approached the station, I was pulled back into the reality of my situation. I started yelling for help, running towards the train station. Troves of people poured out of the station, but none would listen to me or even look at Taffy, crumpled and blue. It was as if they didn't even care that there was a dead body ten feet away from the workshop entrance.

The ignorance of any one passerby only encouraged my suspicions of foul play, or even a large-scale elf conspiracy. Taffy's death was the only evidence I needed to take more aggressive measures in my investigation. I walked back toward my office in the workshop, almost forgetting that a few minutes earlier I had been mourning the death of Taffy Cane. The air bit through my coat more than it had when I was running. I guess the adrenaline pumping through my veins wasn't enough to ward off the everlasting chill of the North Pole

When I reached my office, I didn't hesitate to walk past it, and continue deeper into the workshop. I headed to the Department of Reeducation.

I had never visited the Department of Reeducation. My sector had never had this many issues with our field elves. None of them lost control. Not ever.

Elves have an incredibly complex psyche. Their species is mischievous by nature, which means they need to be heavily trained before working in the North Pole. The Education Department was for new, incoming elves. Its Reeducation counterpart was very different. This department is where the most disobedient elves are brought to get a push in the right direction.

I walked into the Office of Reeducation, careful to not startle anyone inside. I was sure that no one came down here; the majority of our elves were very well behaved. I was wrong. The main lobby of the department was painted a festive shade of green, with red doors leading into smaller offices. I could hear the sound of yelling elves from behind each of the doors.

"Hello," said a woman behind the reception desk "How can I help you, ma'am?"

I smiled and approached the desk, attempting to peek into the reeducation rooms, "I would like to recommend a couple of elves from my sector, I have reason to believe they are planning some sort of conspiracy not only against my team, but also the entire workshop."

The woman smiled warmly and stood, walking around her desk until she stood right next to me. "Of course, ma'am. If you could write down their names, I will get right on that."

I was surprised at her efficient response, but appreciative. "Don't you need to know what evidence I have?"

The woman shook her head, and handed me a small stack of forms. "We know the nature of elves. Most of them will be reeducated at one point or another. The best thing we can do for them is to get them help. We can give that to them."

I nodded, smiling as I filled out the paperwork for reeducation, "Do you think I could view one of the reeducations in progress? I've always been curious about the process."

"Of course, ma'am." The woman said, leading me toward one of the red doors.

The door was flanked by large refrigerators, filled with strange pills and vials. Each container bore the same four words: 'For elf use only'. I assumed that these were medications, ones that would help elves regain their normal emotional control.

Inside the room sat dozens of elves, all staring at a chalkboard at the front of the room. A human stood in front of the catatonic elves, explaining the basic principles of Christmas cheer. The elves chanted responses in unison. I watched them continue the lesson and almost began crying.

Though the elves were in a state of medicated compliance, I knew that the message of what Christmas is all about was still getting through to them.

We were really saving these elves, giving them a better and brighter future.

"Yes," I said, turning back to the receptionist, "This will be perfect, thank you."

"The pleasure is mine ma'am, all mine."

About the Author

Ivy Ru has been sharing stories from a very early age. Some of her first works consist of tales of her adventures with her imaginary sister Sinnamon, but she's also published a short story in a young author anthology with Lunespark, co-written a Dungeons & Dragons adventure with her dad, and published a short story in an anthology with Nerd Street and TreeShaker Books. When she's not at school or the keyboard, Ivy spends her time playing percussion, harp, and piano and practicing many forms of dance. Though Ivy has many passions, she aspires to become a full-time author. You can see Ivy Ru's other works and endeavors by visiting IvyRuWrites.com.

Origins of the Santa Tracker, A Horror Story for Christmas Eve

BY JOSHUA PRUETT

MY GRANDAD TOLD ME this wild story about the birth of the NORAD Santa Tracker once.

I didn't believe him, but most of it checks out. You can look it up.

I think I've got the dates right. Scared me a little when I was a kid. Just... weird stuff. Things I didn't really believe until I dug in after the facts.

Only, that just made it worse.

That night, there by the fire, I'd just set a few handmade cookies and a plastic tumbler half-full of milk on the wooden TV tray, just to Grandad's side.

I wasn't quite ten years old, but so much older than nine. I'd left my security blanket and sucking my thumb and even a few toys well behind already, the world just starting to blossom in front of me. My life was coming, and my grandad, like the stationmaster, was signaling with his voice and the furrow of his brow that the train was coming.

So, slowly, rocking in his old chair, he laid some track. Some history. *His* history.

My grandpa, Oliver, was born in Montrose, Colorado, 1934. As a teen, he was big into trucks and cars, and like most boys in town, dreams of being in the military. Later, he won't "pass muster," as he put it, for his physical evaluation when he applies. But in the interim, he's still dreamin' big, his interests moving from wheels to wings, catching fire December 24th, 1948 when he reads a strange news article in the local paper.

Oliver's 14 now, thinking about his future, when he comes across what's supposed to be an official United States Air Force "communique" that's tracking Santa's sleigh. Eight reindeer, at 14k feet, the whole bit. It's kiddie stuff, and he knows it, only, friends of his have seen things. Things in the skies.

This is where things start to get weird. Now, maybe someone at the USAF was bored, or they just thought it'd be fun to get a little press, a little ink in the local, but the 14k sticks in Oliver's craw funny and won't let go. It's too specific. 14. He looks at some maps he's got, scrounges up a free one from the nearby Esso gas station, another for state parks, whatever he can grab, hunting for points of interest. 14. Then it hits him like a freight train; The Fourteeners! He had to explain it to me because I didn't follow.

Colorado's got fifty-eight mountain peaks over 14k ft, most of any state, and they're called the 14ers. Grandad smirked a bit as he laid it all out. Apparently, outside of being young car-enthusiasts, there's not much to do in Colorado as a teen except sneak out with your Dad's hooch, get into trouble with similarly minded boys and girls or just grab a blanket and stare up at the stars. He painted the picture for me. Skies so clear you can count constellations and go cross-eyed staring up at that bright black abyss as it's staring right back.

Only, some of young Oliver's friends have seen more than constellations. They've seen stars, streaks and bright lights moving across these same peaks, all at about 14k ft, near as they can figure. At first, when he hears the stories, he assumes they've just been drinking too much. Then, one night, he gets an itch he can't scratch. They've got him wondering, thinking, dreaming with his eyes open. What if there was something, or better yet, *somethings,* up there in the dark? What if it was real?

So, late one night, heart beating like a cottontail running for its life, 14-year-old Grandad sneaks out and walks, then runs miles out of town and finds a good spot under the stars. He lays low, real low, tall grass brushing his arms and the top of his head. He keeps still, slowing his heartbeat, letting the bright ocean of stars pull gently on his eyes. And sure enough, he sees something. Then he goes back the night after, and the night after that, and he sees more of his own *somethings* up there in the dark.

Not like ships, or saucers, nothing like the posters from the local matinee, just "lights that speed." And he's not scared, he's thrilled. The sky just got way more exciting. He directs his passion for engineering toward aeronautics and suddenly, his whole life takes a very different direction.

I mentioned once that, him being 14, discovering a connection between that article, the 14k sightings and the 14ers was pretty coincidental. He just smiled.

Then he asked me if I thought a USAF dispatch about Santa might be a convenient cover for something else, something much worse? I didn't answer. He asked, what's harder to believe in? Santa, or a conspiracy to cover up evidence of an imminent alien threat? He just smiled...

We skip ahead a bit. It's 1955 & 21-year-old Grandad is trying to get work at Colorado Springs CONAD, Continental Air Defense Command, the precursor to NORAD as we know it today. Security is tight, hard to even get a foot in the door. Oliver gets discouraged, but those sky lights never go away, their gravity pulling him back two to three nights a week, just watching. But a young man in his twenties needs more than hobbies, and if CONAD's doors are closed, he just needs money where he can find it, so Oliver gets part time work at the local paper, Colorado Springs, The Gazette. A lot of grunt work, taking ads over the phone and setting type for local retailers. It's not glamorous, but it fills his days and Grandad feels like he's a bit more connected to the outside world.

Then, December of 1955, something bizarre happens. And I swear this is true. Again, you can look it up.

Oliver helps set an ad for the local SEARS, something cute for the holidays. Kids can call in and "talk to Santa." Kiddie stuff again. Promotion. But something goes wrong. A single digit is off on the phone number. The calls never connect to the small, employee break room at SEARS where a Colorado Springs drama student waits, and waits, and waits, "Santa's Elf," getting into character for a call that never comes.

Instead, every call placed to the number in the ad goes right to CONAD & Crew Commander Harry Shoup's desk, who gets so fed up talkin' to kiddies about Santa he and his team take turns making up Santa's current location, telling stories and finally, getting into it, having fun on a cold weeknight in Colorado. And just like that, legend lays out the birth of the Santa Tracker...

But here's the kicker. Grandad swore up and down he wrote the right number down. He was a 21-year-old kid, hungry for work. Mistakes like that cost papers money and cost kids like him their jobs. Someone *gave* him that number.

The odds that a single digit "mistake" would connect directly to CONAD, while not astronomical, are still very *high*, probability wise. But even *that* math doesn't work when you factor in the Santa thing back in '48, also being connected to the USAF. Or Oliver's involvement *at all.* Why then? Why him?

I brought this up once, maybe twice, and each time Grandad leaned close and whispered, "Someone *wanted* those coincidences."

He said, "They wanted people, *kids*, watching the skies, every winter, and they wanted to get that data back to a higher authority. Someone was looking out for us."

"Little pitchers have big ears," he said, "and even larger eyes." Asking adults to watch the skies for the Russians would have just fueled more Cold War paranoia. This was 1955, after all. But asking kids to watch the skies for *Santa*...

"It wasn't red Russians they were worried about."

My grandad told me, there are things in the skies over Colorado.

And they've been there for a very long time. There's a history there. As of August, there's been over 100 sightings in Colorado this year alone. The NORAD Santa Tracker was never just for fun. It was an early warning system.

From 1955 on, the tracker is tradition and public knowledge. Grandad said, two years later, CONAD gets a big upgrade, becomes North American Aerospace Defense Command, official Sept 12, 1957. From Continental to Aerospace, why? Why Colorado? The visibility? No, he told me.

The lights, the regular sightings, the 14ers, four corners, ley lines too, all of it - Colorado's an epicenter. Every winter, it's the same. They come back, he told me. And we need to stay vigilant.

"So, Santa's an alien?" I blurted out once. Grandad put his rough hand on mine...

"You're old enough now," he said.

Old enough for what? I thought.

He said, "What is Santa, son? Who is he? A jolly old elf who brings you gifts? In his sleigh, pulled by flying deer, bending the rules of time and space, bringing joy to children."

He stopped then.

"Only, he comes with a warning," said Grandad. "How many gift-giving angels come with warnings?"

"Too many," I said.

"Good answer." He smiled. Then he leaned back and took off his glass es.For a moment, everything stopped. It seemed like the whole world was hanging on his every word.

"The stories and songs are warnings." Grandad laughed.

"Bet you didn't know he wasn't always chubby..."

I listened.

"Sure," Grandad said, "he had a bowl full of jelly back in ''Twas the Night Before Christmas,' in the early 1800s, but the red-clad, white-haired fat version was invented by Coca-Cola & illustrator Haddon Sundblom in the thirties."

He waited again, the room losing air for a moment. Then he leaned forward.

"The warnings are for a Santa you don't know," continued Grandad.

"Why do you think Santa needs you to stay asleep, to stay in your beds?" he asked.

"So, we don't see you wrapping our gifts," I said.

He smiled and roughed up my hair.

"Smart boy. But what if..."

He got up, mid-thought, as if he needed to chase the story around the room as he told it. A speeding hare, always just out of reach.

"Maybe we say stay in bed for the same reason we tell you not to go into the woods at night."

Grandad leaned against the fireplace, glaring into its fiery belly.

"Maybe the Santa isn't bringing anything. It's hunting."

His face changed then. My grandad was always a warm man, accessible. But when he told this story, he got colder, vulnerable. I could feel it.

"Think of the songs, son," he said, then he looked at me and his eyes turned pale.

The fire in the fireplace had grown small, a whisper in the dark. I pulled my arms around me and lowered my chin, as if being smaller might keep me out of sight or keep me safe from the anxious tremble building in my belly.

"You better watch out.""You better not cry.""Better not pout."

Grandad cleared his throat, sitting back down into the old rocking chair.Then..."He sees you when you're sleeping.""He knows when you're awake.""He knows if you've been bad or good.""So be good for goodness' sake..."

Grandad leaned close to me then, eyes catching the last of the fire-light, glowing."Stay in your bed," he said, "because you're being hunted by something we can't stop."

I couldn't breathe.

He grabbed me then, and hugged me close to his chest, his breath like peppermint and leather. He kept saying, "I'm sorry, son. I'm sorry... watch the tracker. Always watch the tracker. Then you'll know where it is. How close. Be ready."

"Ready for what?" I asked, choking on my words as if they were too big for my mouth.

When you're a kid, everything changes the moment you see fear in the face of an adult. But what I saw in my grandad's eyes that night was worse than fear.

Something... older.

Then, suddenly, he was done. Grandad shook it off, propped me up on my feet & smiled, almost.

"What is it? I asked again. "Tell me."

Grandad took me by my shoulders and nodded at our big, oversized fireplace, a knowing smirk on his face.

"Whatever it is, I'm not sure milk and cookies are gonna protect either of us from what's coming down the chimney tonight."

Then he pulled an old shotgun into his lap. I hadn't even noticed it sitting there by the fireplace. He pushed me toward my bedroom.

"I have some... presents left to wrap," he said, "and I know you don't wanna spoil the surprise."

I went to bed that night, but I didn't sleep.

In the morning, Grandad was gone.

"Fishing," my dad said, too quickly.

But I knew he was lying. I would learn the truth a few weeks later.

Christmas morning was a quiet one that day, strange, everyone going through the motions.

Trying to cheer me up, Dad brought over his laptop. He wanted to show me the Santa Tracker he found.

"It's NORAD," he said.

"That means it's real," he said.

He pointed at the screen, and my stomach knotted.

"Santa was here last night," said Dad, pointing to the radar image.

"He was really here!"

But I didn't need to see the blinking red light.

I could still smell the gun powder in the air.

Grandad warned me to be ready. And now, I will be.

Every year, I get closer.

And it does too.

I just keep my eye on the NORAD Santa Tracker, and I plan, and I wait.

I don't cry.

I don't pout.

I don't sleep.

Because Santa Claus is coming to town.

THE END

About the Author

New York Times Bestselling Author and Emmy Award-Winner Joshua Pruett is the only human being on Earth to have written for both MYSTERY SCIENCE THEATER 3000 and DOCTOR WHO.

Currently working on the widely anticipated return of Disney's PHINEAS AND FERB, Joshua is perhaps best known for his work as a TV Writer on MILO MURPHY'S LAW, the original feature for Disney Plus, PHINEAS AND FERB THE MOVIE: CANDACE AGAINST THE UNIVERSE and THE LAST KIDS ON EARTH, the Emmy Award-Winning Netflix animated series. Joshua headed back to the Last Kids universe in Spring 2023, co-writing the NYT bestselling graphic novel, THE LAST COMICS ON EARTH, with Max Brallier, the first of four books, illustrated by Jay Cooper and Douglas Holgate.

Previous published work includes the original horror short story collection THE MISERY COMPANY, the Predator-as-summer-camp-slasher short "Ghost Story" in PREDATOR: EYES OF THE DEMON, a tie-in anthology from Titan Books and his original full cast Doctor Who audio book TIDES OF THE MOON from DOCTOR WHO: THE SIXTH DOCTOR ADVENTURES: WATER WORLDS from Big Finish Productions. With two other stories in various stages of development, Joshua is one of only a handful of American writers to have contributed to Doctor Who. He's also written books and comics for all ages, including the hilarious middle grade novel SHIPWRECKERS: THE CURSE OF THE CURSED TEMPLE OF CURSES, OR WE NEARLY DIED. A LOT. with Scott Peterson from Disney/Hyperion. Also see Joshua's first solo middle grade series, GYRO AND THE ARGONAUTS, pitched as 'The Hitchhiker's Guide to Greek Mythology,' a revisionist take on classical myths where the monsters become the heroes they were always meant to be, (2025.)

Hell on the Shelf

by E.H. Drake

"And you swear this isn't just for Instagram?" I try to keep my tone light.

"Jacob..." The twist in my wife's dark lips makes it clear I haven't entirely succeeded. Cynthia puts the drying towel down and places a brown-sugar hand over her heart, holding the other high. "Scouts honor."

I nod and keep scrubbing the pan. I believe her but that still leaves another concern and I'm not sure how to be delicate about this. She's still healing, not even able to go back to work yet; I don't want to accuse her of anything sinister.

But Ethan deserves his hideous tradition.

I keep my eyes fixed on the now clean pan as I ask, "And, the tree trimming?"

Cynthia's eyes grow big but we don't have time to discuss it. Edie starts to cry, her tiny wails sputter in our thrift-store baby monitor as Cynthia abandons the dish towel and plants a soft kiss on my cheek. Her tone is a little melancholy. "Put a pin in this?"

I nod, but she's already thundering up the steps to get Edie, her soft cooing much easier to listen to over the still-sputtering monitor.

"Hey there, Princess. Mommy's got you." The cries slowly melt into tiny hiccups as Edie settles, and my wife hums. Most likely getting a bottle ready. Our baby breastfeeds just fine, but Cynthia knows the bottles let me connect more easily. I've told her she doesn't need to give up that experience, that I'd find another way to bond with Edie. But Cynthia just makes new excuses as to why it's fine.

It makes her happy to make me happy.

That's why it was so hard not to just jump on board with this stupid idea.

"God, how many times a night do babies eat?" Ethan strolls into the kitchen, rubbing the sleep from his eyes, his wallet chain dangling limply from his wrinkled jeans.

I scoff. "You should thank your sister. It's not good to–"

"Fall asleep at the computer," Ethan mocks, the light of the fridge bathing his pale features in a sickly yellow. Containers clank and clatter softly as he hunts to the back. "Do we have any leftover pizza?"

"Got plenty of curry," I tease.

His blonde eyebrows scrunch together under his unnaturally red hair as he sneers. "I don't like that spicy stuff."

"You've never tried it." I smile despite the reprimand.

"Never tried road kill either." My son finally emerges from the fridge, his words muffled by a chunk of two-day-old pizza. "Somehow, I'm okay with that."

"Don't talk like that." I peek at the monitor, as though my wife might hear us. She's still humming softly to Edie, oblivious to the conversation. "Cynthia is just trying some new recipes."

"Yeah, well, tell her to try some without peas next time." Ethan finishes his pizza and starts back towards his room. "Night, Dad."

I sigh and wave. "Goodnight, son."

It takes Edie another half hour to settle back to sleep. By the time she's dozing, I've put the dishes away and pulled meat from the freezer for tomorrow. Beef. Maybe if I offered burgers, we could have a family meal without incident.

A man can dream.

I actually agree with Ethan about the peas, but picking them out isn't exactly rocket science. I know for a fact that spices don't bother my son. He wasn't exactly sneaky, adding the last banana pepper to his slice.

It's not fair for Cynthia to always be the bigger person. And really, all she wants is a silly tradition to help our baby girl believe in Santa. That's not going to interrupt what Ethan and I do or how we remember his mother.

I'm just so tired of this peacekeeper role. I want my prepubescent son. The one who ran into Cynthia's arms with wild abandon, begging her to go to Dairy Queen, because he knew she would cave before I could say anything.

It's not all Ethan or his adolescent hormones. But he is contributing to the friction.

Cynthia finally emerges from Edie's nursery, and I smile at her. Disheveled as she is, with a heavy black bun wobbling on the top of her head, stumbling back into the kitchen with her yoga pants and my hoodie, she's never been more adorable. The tight yawn stretching her little face doesn't hurt.

I shake my head, chuckling, "We can get the stupid elf."

She halts mid-yawn like her software needs to reboot before she can process what I just said. Those big brown eyes widen with delight. "Really?"

I nod, now trying to hold in laughter. Her expression is priceless.

Cynthia flings her arms over me, squeezing with delight, and her laughter seems to roll out of me. I can't even bring myself to tell her she's putting too much weight on my neck as she giggles and kisses me, hard.

ETHAN POKES AT THE thing on our mantel, as though he expects his skin to melt from the slightest contact. "I don't understand."

Cynthia's grin only widens. "We hide him in the house and move him around in secret."

"I get the principle." I can't see Ethan's face as he continues to examine the ugly doll, but his expression isn't hard to imagine. "I don't get why."

"So your sister can experience some Christmas magic while she grows up." I offer Cynthia a supportive smile.

Ethan turns around, so this time I can see his eyes roll. "Edie doesn't even know where her nose is. She won't be able to follow that."

"Not yet." Cynthia agrees, cooing to Edie and cradling her slowly. "But she'll get there."

Ethan glares at the doll. "Doesn't the hideous appearance detract from the whimsy?"

I try not to laugh, but I can't bottle it quickly enough. Cynthia's mild reproof only makes it worse.

She really has chosen a hideous model. I'd seen plenty of these things online when she first brought the idea up. They were all typical doll creepy, with overly perfect smiles and noses pointy enough to post on a corkboard.

This one looks like an aggravated gnome. Apparently, the short legs will prevent the cat from going after it, but that face…

"I got it from an Instagram influencer. It's homemade." Cynthia smiles reluctantly and shakes her head. "They also make a lot of great herbs and teas."

Ethan's brows raise a fraction. "Tell me that all means you paid less for it."

"It's important to support small businesses," Cynthia huffs. "She made it custom for us. It even came with this card."

She hands it to me and I read some cheesy message about our special elf keeping our family wholesome for the season. I'm not sure if my new headache is entirely due to the heavy lavender-mint odor. The lady who crafted this thing wears way too much perfume. I hand the card back and fan the air around me.

"It's custom ugly, got it." Ethan scowls at the elf, taking in the tiny green outfit and grizzly little beard. The tinsel on the shelf behind it looks like it will burst into flames any minute as the little lights bloom in and out, over and over. Cynthia has already taken several perfect photos, capturing just the right angle and lighting.

"Oh, 'cause that's the only wonky decoration we have?" Cynthia eyes the tree.

Ethan pauses then laughs a little. "Point taken."

It's true, the tree is covered by about twenty layers of pale pink tinsel. That would be bad enough, but the huge cartoon eyes and big mouth, both cut out from poster board, make the pitiful tree look like it's screaming in anguish.

It's stupid, something Amanda did for our son when he was little. Ethan wanted our tree to look like the cookie monster. I'd had to pick up blue tinsel from the floor for weeks after that first one. But young Ethan loved it and the two insisted on continuing the tradition. The face grew weirder and weirder every year. This one was apparently meant to be some dog named Courage.

Cynthia is always supportive of the tradition but I've noticed it's one of the few bits of her Christmas decor she doesn't post online. I'm not sure if that's because of the appearance or because she thinks the tree isn't meant for her. And I'm honestly not sure which would be worse.

"Oh, I almost forgot." Cynthia offers Ethan a gleeful smile. "I got it a Spider-Man costume."

I beat Ethan to the punch on this one. "Don't you dare dishonor Spider-Man like that."

Even Miles Morales deserves better than this grumpy little troll sitting over my mantle.

Cynthia sighs dramatically. "You get to do pranks..."

Ethan gives us both a skeptical look. "Pranks?"

"Yeah, part of the tradition involves playing pranks on the kids when they're naughty." I shrug. "But Cynthia and I agreed you can get us back once in a while."

Ethan smirks. "Do you two even realize how bad this idea is?"

"Nothing crazy," I say sternly. "Nothing that would hurt anyone."

Ethan crosses his arms. "Any rules a third grader wouldn't figure out?"

"Not really." Cynthia shrugs. "Pranks are family-specific. Your dad and I agreed to play it by ear this year. Troubleshoot as we go."

Ethan's grin twists and grows, like the twin tails of a perfectly curled ribbon bouncing into place. "Let the games begin."

"I CAN'T GO TO school like this." Ethan doesn't yell, but his whole body trembles. It makes him look a bit mystical with all the glitter slowly falling from his head.

"You should have thought of that before you stuffed packing peanuts into the diaper bag last week." I try so hard not to laugh. Honestly, I thought he got off easy. "Do you realize how long it took her to change your sister and then clean that up?"

"I didn't interrupt her work!" Ethan defends.

"No, you interrupted the doctor and nurse who had to halt everything and help her clean the exam room." I muss my son's hair and instantly regret it, the gold and pink specks clinging firmly to my palm from his hair gel.

Ethan groans and looks towards the heavens for advice. "The guys are going to call me a fairy, I just know it."

"That or Twilight." I chuckle and point to the door. "Your bus will be here any second."

"More rice, Ethan?" Cynthia holds out the pot.

"I'm good." My son shakes his head and takes another small bite. The hurt on her face makes me wince. Cynthia is trying to signal a truce. But I can't say anything. Ethan isn't technically doing anything wrong. And Cynthia doesn't need me to fight every battle.

"So, how was school?" I just about want to plow my head through the table for asking,

Ethan glares daggers through my skull. "Twilight."

With that, he stands up and clears his remaining plate.

"Thanks for dinner." The tone is barely polite and clipped.

Cynthia's eyes well up even as she smiles and feeds Edie another spoonful. "Of course, I'll make sure to pack the leftovers for lunch."

"Whatever." He's out and down the hallway by the time I stand.

"That's it." I kiss the top of Cynthia's head.

"No, you'll only–"

I don't hear her as I thump down the hall and knock on Ethan's door. I have to knock harder than I like, just to be sure he can hear me over his headphones. "Get out here."

The door cracks open. Over Ethan's glittery head, I can barely make out his sketchbook on the desk and his mom's old radio to the side. "What?"

Some of my earlier irritation melts. "Get your coat."

Ethan's eyes widen a fraction. "What?"

"We're going for a drive." I dig in my pockets and jingle the keys. "You still have a few more hours to complete, right?"

He nods slowly. I turn around and walk back down the steps. I'm about halfway down when my son's steps thunder behind me. I swear I can feel his questioning eyes drilling the back of my skull. The cogs are turning fast.

I suppress a grin and start whistling a merry tune. Cynthia's lips curl in a Grinchish grin as I pass the kitchen. Ethan's steps falter. He's wondering if this is a trap, but he also knows how seriously I take his driving lessons. I've scraped too many bodies off the asphalt to dick around with driving.

He finally decides it's worth the risk, jumping down the last few steps with a dramatic karate noise and grabs a tattered hoodie from the hook.

"IT'S OKAY, WE'LL TRY again."

Ethan settles his forehead against the steering wheel, muttering incoherently, as though I don't realize he's cursing.

"Your mom hated swear words."

"She still married you," he mutters, peeking at me. "Why can't I get this?"

"Because adrenaline is a bitch. Now try again."

"Are you being a hard ass because of..." His sentence trails and my son won't meet my gaze.

I look into my lap, trying to ignore the mental images he's incidentally conjured. "Not entirely."

We sit in a dense silence for several seconds before Ethan blows out a long breath and sits back, pushing some of his hair from his eyes. I've already resigned myself to a full car detailing after the first wave of glitter detached itself. Wearing a little in the office tomorrow will be some penance for letting things get this far.

Ethan pulls the car around the deserted parking lot.

"Alright, rev the engine a bit." I keep my tone calm, my hands on my knees so I won't grip the door or grab the steering wheel.

Ethan follows my direction with a quick gulp, the engine's low rumble swallowing the noise.

"Now ease off the brakes and let it get to speed."

The car lurches forward, and only my rigid posture prevents my head from snapping forward before Ethan gets it up to speed. We're now sliding on the slick ice beneath us.

I nod. "Jerk the wheel."

He hesitates.

"You can do it."

He nods and yanks the wheel to the left, then to the right. Over and over, the tension in my muscles grows tighter, barely keeping me from turning into a bobblehead. It only takes a couple of the too-quick jerks before the rear wheel drive becomes useless, and we seem to lose gravity.

Ethan takes a sharp breath, and I keep my tone low, forcing him to pay attention. "Turn into it."

Instead, he hits the brakes, and the car slides.

I close my eyes. "Start pumping."

He doesn't hear me. Only the knowledge that the Walmart and the nearest light pole are too far away for him to hit keeps me from taking over. My own father has got to be smirking from heaven, remembering each and every time I talked back to him about these skills.

I steady myself and speak louder, my eyes still closed. "Pump them."

Finally, I break through his panic, and I feel the car slow in several little bursts.

It lurches to a stop, and Ethan slams the car into park, growling under his breath. I open my eyes and clap him on the shoulder, waiting.

His breath slows, and he looks down to his lap. "Are you pissed?"

I shake my head.

"I don't mean about the driving." His eyes dart up for a split second.

"I know." I squeeze his shoulder.

"She was trying to make up, huh?"

I nod. "She knows how much you love that recipe."

Shrimp fried rice is Ethan's favorite. Cynthia learned to make it especially for him, understanding how much my first wife used to fuss over it. It had taken years for her to find the perfect blend, and Ethan always starves himself until dinner just to save space.

Ethan tosses his hands through his hair, further messing up my car. "I'm starving."

"Serves you right," I snort.

He snorts and nods. "Yeah. It does."

We didn't talk specifically about the pranks last night, but I assumed they would slow down. The stench in my nose after I pull into the garage alerts me just how wrong I am.

Sadly, much of my job is pranks gone awry. So I am terribly familiar with this odor.

I sigh, pinching the bridge of my nose as I close the garage and head inside. My shiny new headache only grows as I climb each step.

"It wasn't me!" Ethan hisses.

"I thought we'd reached an understanding." Cynthia's voice warbles, and she sniffs. I stop on the top step, listening. They aren't yelling. In the background, the all-too-familiar sounds of *Monsters Inc.* accompany Edie's frantic giggling.

Is it sad that I can picture the exact scene I'm listening to based on the incoherent screaming of the little green monster? Maybe we needed to stop letting Edie watch it for a bit.

"I'm telling you, I didn't do this." Ethan starts to pace, his shadow staggering across the wall. There's a split second where he seems to be running, his shadow moving so fast it looks thinner than before. I rub my weary eyes. Twelve hours of funerals and pickups are screwing with my head.

Ethan's shadow jerks once more then falls back into a regular pace, halting as Cynthia retorts, "I found the cans in your room."

"And I have no clue how they got there."

Well, that conversation is going nowhere fast. "Surely you can come up with a better excuse, son."

"Dad, I know how it sounds, but I'm telling the truth." Ethan's wounded expression gives me pause. But his tone reminds me of the one and only time he tried to shoplift, and the questioning feeling leaves my gut.

The cans in question lay on the kitchen table, each one about as thick as my finger. *Asspray* is written on the side in comic-book-style characters. I glare at the spray, as though it magically appeared in my house without invitation. "Where'd he put it?"

"In my air vents." Cynthia shakes her head. "I had to wash Edie four times to get the smell out."

She scratches her arm, and I sigh.

"Son, you know Cynthia's sense of smell has been far higher after your sister was–"

"God, why won't you guys listen?" Ethan actually sounds panicked now. Has he gotten better at lying? "Why would I do this?"

"You tell us." I stand next to my wife and lean against the wall.

"You're never going to see my side." Ethan mutters under his breath and glares at the floor. "Just ground me already."

I'D BARELY CAUGHT AN hour of sleep before being called in a few nights later. The Christmas season brings out the greatest cheer in town, but it also heightens the most acute misery. The man had been discovered by his niece, unable to get out of bed and go to the bathroom by himself.

The EMTs couldn't have done anything. He'd drank away his misery and delivered it to his family. The niece had been a practical woman, washing the dishes when I'd loaded him on the gurney, slow tears working familiar trails on her cheeks. She'd been mopping the floor as I left, cleaning the blood and bile so her son wouldn't have to look at it in the morning. The little one had cried himself to sleep on the couch, still clutching his great-uncle's work jacket.

I'm usually good at compartmentalizing my work. I don't bring it home; I haven't touched a bottle in years. But that final image kept haunting me, even as I had put the man in storage, waiting for the crematorium in the morning.

The clock in my car reads 4:32 AM. Cynthia has been alone with Edie for three hours and needs to be up and ready to leave in two for an appointment of some kind. I need to get my ass inside. With one long breath, I run a hand down my face and exit the car.

The house is quiet when I step in, without even a murmur on the baby monitor. Maybe Edie gave her mother a break. I stagger into the kitchen and double-check the coffee maker. Set for 6:15, perfect. I sway up the steps, gripping the handrail as though I were about to slide into the deepest pits of hell without it.

My steps sound strange to my sleepy ear, as though there's a tiny echo every other one. Then it's like they're fading behind me. I blink and look around. If the cat ever came upstairs, that little pit pat would make sense.

But Wilikers avoids Edie's level ever since she grabbed his tail two months ago. He's not confrontational, but our grumpy old cat is practical. Is there a big rodent on the stairs with me?

I debate turning on the light, but I hate to risk waking everyone just because my tired mind is playing tricks on me. Maybe the cat found something interesting up here. So I stand on the top step, swaying slightly and listening intently.

There's a soft *plop* like dropping a shirt on the floor. Then, nothing. Wilikers lets out a low, menacing hiss before scampering out of the living room.

"Stupid cat." I shake my head, glad I'm not the only one jumping at shadows, and walk to Edie's room to check on her. I nearly face-plant as my hand slips from the door, the sudden jerk waking me.

"What the..." I wipe my hand on my shirt, leaving a trail of thick slime, and I try again. Slip again. "What the hell?"

My wife's sleepy, panicked voice comes from inside the room. "Jacob?"

I look up, as though she's speaking from heaven. "Cynthia?"

Relief floods her voice. "Oh, thank God! Can you open the door? I need to piss."

"What happened?" I try again and find the door just as slimy as the first attempt

Edie giggles from inside as I investigate the slippery door handle more closely.

"Just open the door. I'll explain later."

"Okay, okay. Give me a second." I run across the hall, grabbing something random from the hamper and dashing back. It takes both sides of what turns out to be a pair of dirty boxers before I get the goop off. I have to grab another random towel just to open the door.

"Hold her!" Cynthia pushes Edie into my arms and dashes into our bathroom.

I bounce our daughter as my wife sighs in exaggerated relief.

"Now, can I know what happened?"

Cynthia staggers out, her face a storm cloud. "Your son put vaseline on the door handle."

"Yeah, I gathered that." I hold up a still-shiny palm. "But why'd you stay inside?"

She gawks at my hand. "He stuck it on the outside, too?"

Too? I can feel my face pinching in anger as I walk into Edie's room and stare at the handle. In the flickering stars of my daughter's night-light, I can see the slick goo dripping from the handle. Part of me wants to ask Cynthia why she didn't just use a blanket and wipe the handle clear, but she's probably had a grand total of two hours of sleep in the last three days.

And really, she's not to blame.

"Hold her." I hand our daughter over to my wife. "Wait in our room."

"Honey, don–"

"Please." My fists clench, and I can't bring myself to look at her. I know my voice sounds like a thousand sharp pins. The door to our room closes softly behind me as I walk to the end of the hall.

I knock out of habit, but open the door right away. My son is apparently asleep, his lumpy form a deep silhouette in the dark.

"Ethan–" I growl as I flick the switch and light floods the room, "get u...uhhh..."

The lumps are not my son. I've just been duped by a giant stack of pillows.

EDIE HAS FINALLY PASSED out in my arms. I was worried she might wake when the window squeaked open, but her little snores seem to match the pitch with the slow creek.

Ethan has a soft touch, I barely hear him pulling the screen from this window or the soft grunt as he pulls his body up. Must have balanced on the deck railing below his window. Still, that required a good amount of upper-body strength.

I school my expression and wipe the impressed smirk from my features. I'm in the darkest corner of my son's room. He's pretty slick, sneaking back through the window and softly stepping on his bed with a practiced quiet. I'm almost annoyed by the surge of pride I have to tamp down. It's not hard, not with the conversation I've been waiting for.

I wait until he replaces the screen before speaking softly. "Stay quiet, I don't want to wake your sister."

Ethan jumps off his bed and tumbles to the ground, his hand over his heart as he scrounges for his phone and shines the light in my face.

"Did you hear me?" I glare. "Turn that thing off before."

My son's face stays stretched in horror even after he's confirmed I'm not an axe murderer.

"I'll be right back." I stand, cradling Edie against my chest. "Don't even think of sneaking back out."

I can hear Ethan pacing back and forth, muttering and cursing, while I lower his sister into the cradle. I chuckle despite myself. The earlier rage from his prank has subsided with the ever-growing worry of where he was. I'd debated calling him but worried that would actually make him avoid coming home.

Now he's safe and I'm relieved. Calmer.

As I lean in his door frame, Ethan flops onto his bed. "How much shit am I in?"

I pretend to consider it for a moment. "Mammoth-sized."

It's an old joke between his mother and me. Ethan smirks and draws a hand down his face. "Can you chew me out in the morning?"

I shake my head and point to the alarm on his bedside. "It is morning."

He groans and nods wearily. "What do you want to know?"

"Let's start with why?"

"Okay but I thought that was pretty obvious." Ethan shrugs. "You grounded me, I was bored."

"But we agreed to tone it down with the pranks." I gesture to his sister's room. "How is this toning it down?"

Ethan's gaze follows my hands then comes back to me, quizzical. "What's Edie got to do with me sneaking out? It's not like I was on duty."

"I'm not talking about that, though we'll get to that in a moment." I point to indicate the sleek slime trailing down my shirt. "Why would you put vaseline on the knob?"

"Wait, what?" Ethan's whole face crunches in confusion. "Is Edie okay?"

"She's fine but you should have asked that before you trapped Cynthia in there and bolted from the house." I cross my arms. His act is reigniting some of my earlier fury. "She was trapped in there for two hours before I got back from a call."

"Wait, no..." Ethan waves his arm madly, his voice raises an octave. "You think *I* trapped her?

"Who else?"

"No, no, Dad it couldn't have been me. I left around eleven."

I laugh but it's not pleasant. "Your best defense is that you were sneaking around doing god knows what."

Ethan shakes his head vehemently. "Look, you're already gonna punish me, I can accept that. I snuck out. But I didn't do *this*."

His eyes are huge. The expression reminds me of a fight I had with Amanda early in our relationship. One of her old friends tried to tell me she'd been cheating, even sounded pretty convincing. My first wife had begged me to give her time to prove it was nonsense. And it was her eyes that won me over.

I let out a long breath. "I want to believe you–"

"Then do." Ethan pulls at his hair and growls.

I stare, unsure what to say for a long moment.

"God Dad, you're supposed to be on my side!"

The shout snaps me out of my stupor and I shake my head. "Not when you're doing something this reckless."

I move to leave the room, reaching to turn off the light.

"Dad, it wasn't me!"

"So what? I'm supposed to believe that Cynthia locked herself in the room."

"No, of course not, but–"

"Then who?"

His mouth hangs open, waiting for the words to tumble out. But they don't.

I nod. "I'll talk it over with Cynthia. We'll decide on your punishment after dinner tonight. I'm too tired and angry to look at you right now."

The look on his face wounds me, even as I switch off the light and close his door.

"HE'S STILL INSISTING HE didn't have anything to do with the knob." I flop into bed after dinner and stare at the ceiling. "Even had a few friends call me to give him an alibi."

"I don't get it." Cynthia lathers her arms in something that smells like cinnamon. Probably a seasonal scent. "He's never been a big liar. He's not exactly good at it."

"Maybe we don't know him as well as we think." I rub my face in exhaustion. "I certainly never thought I'd have put bars on his windows."

"I still think that was extreme." She quirks one brow at me and leans across the bed.

"You want him sneaking out?"

"You telling me you never did?" Her smile lifts to match her brow.

I groan, remembering all the hell I put my poor parents through. "Don't remind me of all the karma I've earned."

She snorts and takes my hands in hers. "I love that you want to keep us all safe. And I love how you protect this family."

"But..."

Her smile grows. "He's going to get his driver's license soon. And I know how nerv–"

A crash sounds downstairs. Followed a mutinous yowl from Wilikers. We both bolt upright, flinging the covers off and sprinting to the door in a synchronized motion. I punch the code into our gun safe as Cynthia runs to Edie's room and Ethan pokes his tired head out. "What's going–"

I hold a finger to my lips and he blinks a few times before looking at the pistol in my hand and nodding slowly. The only time I'd heard a noise even similar to that from Wilikers was when the bulldog next had gotten a hold of him. Wilikers might be stupid but he's a fighter.

And that doesn't explain the crash. Nobody in this house would even leave a cup on the counter. That stupid cat breaks everything. Maybe he just busted a stray glass and stepped on the shards but I'm not betting on that.

I point at Ethan, then the ground before hooking a thumb at Cynthia and Edie. Ethan grabs a heavy duty flashlight from his room and nods solemnly. It's the best we can do.

I descend the steps, listening to the cat's low growl in some distant corner, and the pitter patter of his steps in the opposite direction.

The other night, I'd been certain I'd heard extra steps. Could it really just be a big rat?

I chase the pitter-patter into the kitchen. No broken glass on the floor but there is a trail of blood, far too great for a little cut. "Shit."

I clear the entrance and pantry before scanning the room, just the way Dad taught me. That's when I notice a knife missing from the block. We always hand-clean those and put them away.

"What the..."

The pitter patter sounds again and I rush after it only to halt in our living room. I'm not sure I understand what I'm looking at. My son's ugly cartoon dog-tree is torn beyond recognition with pink tinsel strewn everywhere and the cardboard face shredded into jagged confetti.

I shake myself out of it and start checking the room. Wiliker's angry growl grows with each step. Finally I see his eyes gleam in the dark; he's crouched under the tree with every gray hair on end and his fangs bared. The blood trail leads right to him.

I want to lift him, see what happened, but that knife didn't walk out of the kitchen and this stupid cat probably didn't hurt himself. Something rustles to my right and I swing around, keeping the gun low. One of the tree ornaments jiggles wildly, another one shattered on the floor just beneath it.

Something else on the tree shakes and I lift my gaze, just in time to see the mystery rodent jump down. It has to be a rodent, too small to be anything else.

This is also when I realize the ugly doll is missing from our mantel.

"SOMEONE BROKE INTO OUR home to steal the elf and ruin the tree?" Ethan shakes his head, though I can hardly see the gesture. His whole body shakes as Wilikers rocks the pet carrier, hissing and trying to run in circles.

"Maybe Wilikers climbed the tree and knocked the elf over." Cynthia cradles Edie in her arm, her voice a sing-song against the chaos of the emergency vet's office.

I blow out a long breath. Cynthia offered to keep Edie at home but I refused. I didn't want to scare her but I haven't found the missing knife.

Or Wilikers' tail.

Someone is hiding in our house. That's the only explanation. Even if I'd found the intruder, my adrenaline will keep me awake for days. Even now, I'm picking out the tiniest details on the floor and this whole conversation was going in slow motion, each syllable dripping into my brain like cold syrup.

No windows were broken, the doors were locked. The house was clear.

"Honey?"

I shake my head and look at my family. "Yeah?"

"What are we going to do tonight?"

"We have to wait here for the police. I'll let them in once we get home."

We've only been waiting a couple minutes while the clinic cleans a room and preps Wilikers for surgery. We'll be here for a while. And I still don't think it'll be enough time to think.

Cynthia sways on her feet and I hold up my hands. "Go crash on the couch."

She shakes her head, even as she hands me our daughter. "You don't have to make excuses to hold her."

I snort. "Safety first, someone needs to drive us home."

She nods slowly and shambles over to the couch, only a little less stiff than a steel gurney. Ethan takes the flimsy plastic chair next to me and sighs, "What a night."

I close my tired eyes, hating myself as I ask, "Have you been finding another way to sneak out?"

"Wait, what?" Ethan blanches. "Dad, you can't possibly–"

I hold up a hand. "You would never cut up the tree, let alone hurt your mother's idiot cat. I just need to know if you left a window open or something that might have let an intruder in."

Ethan swallows, his expression turning grim before he shakes his head.

"You won't be in trouble, I just need to know." I plead, hoping he fesses up to something.

"Dad, I seriously need you to believe me here."

I hold his eyes and it's like Amanda is pleading through our son. I finally nod and look at the floor again.

His shoulders slump even as he keeps trying to hold the wiggly carrier in his grip. "You don't want to go home tonight."

I shake my head.

"So why not get a hotel?"

"For how long?" I eye my son. I don't know what's going on but I know the lesson I need to instill in this moment. "How long do we flee from our home? How long do we hide?"

Ethan swallows and I look at my wife, already drooling on the ugly orange upholstery.

"I know our home. I know the terrain." At least, I thought I did.

"That's where you make your stand." Ethan nods sadly and looks up sharply as a nurse approaches. He hands over the carrier, hesitating only a second. "Take good care of this fuzzy moron?"

The nurse smiles. "Of course."

He could follow her, insist on being with the cat while they put him under. Instead he sits back down and nods to me. "How do we do this?"

The police come and take our statements, asking for all the photos Ethan and I took of the house. They make us repeat it all over and over. Trying to fill the gaping holes in our story. The trail of blood in our kitchen doesn't help. One of the officers continues to side eye Ethan, with his neon spiky hair and baggy jeans.

It takes all the energy in me not to growl. I might have questions about his behavior but my son isn't a burgeoning serial killer. Of course, I also don't have a better explanation. When we finally go home, they search the house, top to bottom, the older officer shrugging when they finally meet my family on the front lawn. "We didn't find anything. In good news, they left the elf back in place."

My eyebrows launch into my hairline. "What?"

"You said they took your little elf." The younger officer taps his body cam, as though indicating he needs to prove it. "But that ug—" A look from Cynthia silences him. "little darling seems to be back in place."

I understand his words but they make no sense. Adrenaline or not, I *know* that rag doll wasn't over the fireplace when we left. I looked again when we left, so this wasn't just some flicker of my terrified mind.

Why would they put it back?

Cynthia coughs awkwardly and nods at the officers. "Thank you for everything."

"Call us if you need anything more." The younger officer gives a lazy salute before they load back into their cruiser and I shake my head.

"Never a cop when you need them," I mutter under the roar of their engine and Cynthia elbows me, though it lacks any energy. Or maybe she's just trying to stay still so she won't wake Edie.

"Play nice..."

I roll my eyes but stay quiet otherwise. Cynthia doesn't need me unloading all my rage right now. She needs sleep. I probably need a day off but we can't afford that.

"Alright." I wave my hand like I'm welcoming a queen back to her castle. "After you, ladies."

Cynthia smiles and trots in. Ethan waits until they're on the threshold before whispering, "You really don't think I–"

"No."

"Thanks, Dad," Ethan hugs the carrier to his chest. It's still, Wiliker's sedated with a big ugly cone to keep him from ripping out the seven stitches. I still have no idea how seven stitches fit on his tiny nub of a tail and my tired mind keeps hunting for the answer. At least it gives me something to think about.

"We need to get inside." I nod to the door. "I'll take the first watch."

THE OLD LAWN CHAIR stabs me in the back. I haven't figured out how but I also haven't really looked into it.

Being uncomfortable only helps me stay alert. My old Glock sits in a mesh cup holder, a thermos mug steaming in the other. The weirdest ideas dance in my skull. It doesn't help that my line of sight puts me into a staring contest with that ugly little troll on my mantle. I consider getting up, turning it around. But that means leaving my post at the top of the stairs.

A few times my eyes droop, and in the second, just before I snap them open again, my worst memories flash in my mind. Our car sliding in the snow. Amanda's panicked face growing white in the oncoming traffic. Her ribcage stitched and stuffed back into its approximate shape for the funeral, the wax and makeup covering the bruises and scrapes with an unnaturally smooth layer. Her hair wasn't even the right shade of blonde anymore.

My eyes snap open to the harsh shriek of Ethan's alarm and Edie's little cries. I chug the lukewarm coffee and glare at the ugly doll, as though it has an answer. I won't watch my family break again.

I CALL OUT OF work. I haven't done this in years but I can't drive safely and I need to check the house again. Ethan is at school and Cynthia took Edie to some Toddler Playdate at the local park. Normally I would complain that Edie isn't even toddling yet, but today, it's a blessing. It took me forever to get her out the door; she couldn't find her credit card and I had to remind her she doesn't need it to sit on a park bench.

The first thing I do is turn the ugly little troll to face the wall. I know it's ridiculous but I don't need to feel it's beady button eyes on me as I check the house again. I rummage through the furnace room, my nerves heightened every time I move a water-salt bag or check behind a shelf.

The anxiety only grows as I check the bathrooms and kitchen. Then the bedrooms and closets. I even go so far as to slowly pull our tree from the wall, covering the carpet in yet more pink tinsel while praying I don't jostle one of the older ornaments. But something in my gut says I don't have time to take them down.

The ornaments tap and jingle as I toddle backward with the tree. Nothing appears. I have Wilkers at the top of the stairs in his crate. In part so I can hear him hissing if the intruder tries to sneak past me but also so he can see me working and hopefully remain calm.

I sigh, disappointed. Maybe we just lost the knife and the cat did something insane last night. Maybe it's unrelated. But I can't shake this feeling. I slowly shift the tree back in place and get ready to grab the vacuum, sighing at the ugly pink confetti everywhere on the rug.

The sound chokes my throat when I see the beady little eyes of that ugly little troll glaring down at me. From a completely different place on the mantel. But what halts me is the grey length of fluff laying behind it, crusted in a brown layer at the severed end.

I CAN'T TELL THEM about the tail. I photograph it then grab it with a ziplock bag. Years of dealing with the most grotesue suicides and car accidents couldn't properly prep me for this. I can feel my gag reflex trying to remember its purpose, even as the plastic dulls Wiliker's normally coarse fur and the crunch of his old blood.

With my other hand I dial the one of the numbers off on the detective's cards from yesterday. The older cop picks up after half a ring. "Ortiz."

"I'm afraid I have an early Christmas gift."

He snorts. "Can I pick it up on my way home?"

"My family can't see this." I pause to text the picture to him. "I'm coming to you."

The office pauses then grunts. "Nope. We need to preserve evidence."

"Way ahead of you and out the door." I grab the pet carrier, climb in the car, and shoot a quick text to Cynthia. Then Ethan. *Do not come home until I text you.*

"YOU SHOULDN'T HAVE MOVED it." The officer handed my phone to his tech team. "Please copy the most recent photos."

The tech agent nods and launches off while Ortiz continues to glare at me. I roll my eyes. "Are you old enough to remember records?"

"Pretty sure you grew up with CD Roms."

I snicker, despite myself. I can't tell if that was meant to be ironic or not. "Look, I moved the tail so my family wouldn't come across it. I signed the forms to copy everything on my phone. You scolding me isn't going to unwind the clock."

His dark eyes don't even blink, I'm not that concerned with staring contests right now. Wilikers mewls loudly and I look down at the carrier, calculating how long it's been since he had access to his litter box. "How long will he need my phone?"

"Long enough we can chat." He nods towards a small room and walks away without looking back. Not like I'm going anywhere. I grab my cranky cat and follow him into the tiny break room, standing silently in the entrance as he pours two cups of tepid coffee then digs through a drawer and swears. "Dammit, Harper."

He slaps the drawer shut and hands me one of the cups.

I take a sip and grimace at the bitter taste. "My tax dollars are hard at work, I see."

"I'd offer you some sugar, but there's one guy in the office with a massive sweet tooth." He chugs his cup in a single gulp. "So you turned from the tree, the elf was spun back around and the cat tail was just sitting there."

I nod as I put the carrier back down.

"And you're sure you didn't miss it before?"

"Did you?"

"Anything else amiss at home lately?" He considers this then shrugs. "Maybe a plumber or electrician that felt off?"

I try to think and only end up shaking my empty skull.

His look turns skeptical. "What about the pranks?"

"Huh?" I obviously know what he's talking about, just not why he's bringing it up.

"Your son mentioned some elf pranks that you suspected him of, but he swears he didn't do. Something to do with... fart spray. Is that a real thing?"

I give the cop a look. "If I've heard of it as a coroner, I *know* you have."

"Fine," he snorts. "I'll stop playing dumb cop. So how'd your son purchase the spray?"

I give him a quizzical look and he raises his brows, leaning his heavier framer against the cheap laminate counter. "Do you give him an allowance or something?"

"I mean, no. Ethan asks for money and we discuss the purpose."

"Has he asked for money recently?"

I shake my head, wondering where the hell this is going.

"Does he have a job?"

"You obviously know the answer is no," I growl. "Didn't you suspect my son?"

I'm glad he's changed his tune but the sudden shift feels like whiplash.

"Origianlly yes. But then he called to tell me about the incident with the vaseline. Seemed worried about all of you, thought maybe someone had been in the house for longer." Ortiz pours himself another paper mug. "At first I figured he was trying to shift the blame, but then I looked into your finances."

"Don't you need a warrant for that?" My blood starts boiling with all my pent up energy.

"Common misconception." He waves his hand, as though the simple gesture dismisses the very idea. "But that's not the interesting bit."

I wait. He's playing a game and I refuse to go along.

"There was an order from some online prank shop about one week ago from your wife's card." Ortiz eyes me calmly. "Do those two get along? Your wife and your son?"

I blanch at the implications. "Of course."

"Everyone says that, I swear." He snickers and crumples the paper cup, tossing it to the waste bin. A few drops stray onto the floor and it bounces off the rim onto the floor. "Damn."

"What do you want me to say?" I stammer. "Of course they fight, we all do. What family doesn't?"

"Cliché number two," he groans out, bending down with a napkin to clean his spill.

"Fine, since you have all the lines, what should I say?" Now I'm starting to get pissed. Somehow, I know this was what he was trying for but I can't stop myself. "My late wife introduced me to Cynthia before she passed. They were best friends in college. When Amanda passed..."

Some of my frustration leaks at the mention of her death. The lack of sleep has all those memories threatening the back of my eyelids once more. Ortiz finishes cleaning and gives me a sympathetic look. But he doesn't apologize. He just waits.

I sigh and look at the ceiling, hoping the ugly fluorescent lights will burn it all from my mind. "Cynthia happened to be moving back in the area for her mother. She helped so much with the funeral, so I tried to return the favor. We actually decided against seeing each other at first."

"So what changed your minds?"

"Ethan." I smile and watch his face, waiting for the expression.

He doesn't react much, but those brows twist while he waits.

"He mentioned I seemed more at ease before we stopped talking. Asked me to please keep doing whatever it was that I'd been doing. When I explained..." I pause, a little embarrassed.

Ortiz lets out a knowing laugh. "He said something no teenager has any right to say, but you remember saying at his age."

"You've got kids?" He nods and I laugh. "He told me to go get laid."

The cop leans against the wall and smiles ruefully. "And after you two got serious?"

"She asked for his blessing before we went any further." I shove my hands in my pockets. "They fight every now and then, but no more than Ethan and I do."

He nods and walks out of the breakroom. "So how do you explain the fart spray?"

I HAVE NO EXPLANATION. I try to think of something all the way home. But nothing comes to mind.

Ortiz suggested maybe Ethan stole the card to make the order. But that just doesn't feel right. I don't think he even believed it. Ethan's never even successfully shoplifted. Sure he's had schemes but nothing like this. And there wasn't any jealousy when Cynthia got pregnant; he'd only asked if he had to share his room then plopped his earbuds back in.

I don't have any answers, but I have a suspicion. A crazy, wild suspicion that I need to get out of my system. I pull into the garage and kill the engine, marching into my house and up the stairs before I can overthink this. I'm up the step, across the living room, and yanking the ugly little troll off my mantel and twist it around.

I don't believe for a second that this thing is actually pranking my house, but everything started when it showed up. And it is custom made...

I flip it outside of the outfit and feel the squishy body. It smells like an old tea shop, earthy and pungent. I try to ignore the odor as I feel around. Maybe there's a camera or a recording device inside? So far I only feel a crunchy kind of stuffing, maybe the herbs I'm smelling.

I turn the ugly thing over and stare into its beady little eyes. That's when I notice the speck of red in its beard. I rub the dried blood between my thumb and forefinger. It could just be there from when the intruder deposited the cat tail on my mantel...

Part of me wants to believe that scenario. In logic. But something is missing.

I glare into the thing's face, part of me stupidly expecting a twitch. Something. I look around, knowing I'm alone but needing to confirm it before I growl. "Your time is up."

"You really had to turn it over into evidence?" Cynthia looks sadly at the mantel as she cradles Edie.

"At least something good came of that psycho brutalizing my cat." Ethans is shoving microwaved rice into his face, his fork scraping the bowl for every buttery grain before he gives Cynthia a big grin. "Best batch yet."

My wife snorts with a soft smile, not even bothering to comment on the rice between each tooth as Ethan continues to chow down. "I guess I could order another one–"

"Nope." I shake my head and try to calm my tone. "Only five days to Christmas, it wouldn't be worth it."

Cynthia's brows bunch and her eyes scroll up and down my body. "Right... We'll go with that."

I let out a breath as she heads upstairs with our daughter and Ethan gives me a sly look as he shovels in more rice. "You could just admit it freaked you out."

I can't say I feel guilty about throwing that hideous thing out. Yes, I considered driving him over to the detective, using the spec of blood as an excuse. Ortiz had already threatened to come by and check the mantel for evidence I might have missed. I'd offered to let him in on my lunch break, provided I didn't have an emergency pick up.

So basically, I'd told him to shove it. The man had accused my son, then wife, of taking the pranks too far for whatever reason. If I let him back in the house, his bias will directly influence how he interprets anything he finds. I'm still worried, I'll spend most of the night installing a new camera system and *burglar proof* dead bolts. I'm pretty sure there is some kind of disclaimer about that name; I'll need to upgrade everything later. But I can't keep standing guard at the top of the steps. Eventually, I'll get called in for a late night pick up or need to sleep.

Czynthia and Ethan both know how to handle the Glock but neither of them should be forced to stand guard. Cynthia insists on moving Edie back into our room for the time being so I've installed latch hooks on each door. It's not a perfect solution but it'll give an intruder pause.

I'm not sure how useful I've been to my coworkers today. The word zombie comes up in this job a lot, but it usually refers to the clients who sit up on gurneys or fart postmortem.

This profession requires a level of dark humor that certain members of the public would abhor. Then again, those same pearl clutchers were the first to call us so they didn't have to see their loved one sans the soul.

I sigh and chug my fifth cup of coffee making sure it has plenty of time to kick in before I drive home. I didn't sleep last night, but I'd been more relaxed without that ugly doll staring at me. I'll be even better tonight, after trash is picked up. Part of me seriously debated dismembering that hideous thing, but I couldn't let the paranoia win.

As I get in my car, I check the rear view multiple times as I back out of my parking space, my exhaustion making me jump at every flicker or shadow. The drive home is normally a numb sort of auto pilot; Cynthia always calls it my daily meditation. Today, I take the back roads, forcing myself to pay careful attention to the less familiar curves and potholes.

I've had too many calls from overworked lawyers or nurses crashing their cars, sometimes taking some innocent bystander with them. If tonight was anything like the last few, I'll have to call out of work again. Finally, I pull onto our street and line myself to back into the driveway.

After I press the garage button, I flick my eyes back to the rearview mirror and frantically curse, "What the fuck!?"

My head spins back around, so fast I probably look like an owl as I gawk. I've never kept decorations in the rear deck of my car. My late wife loved to keep those dancing flowers and a couple stuffed animals in the back. Cynthia has a single bobblehead on the dash. Both women have given me a hard time for my car's lack of a personality.

Yet there, casting a shadow from my rear window, a pair of beady eyes stare me down.

I barely remember to put the car in park before flinging myself to the driveway. The old asphalt tears at my palms and arms. The engine is still rumbling as I wind myself back around and gawk.

At nothing.

The door to the garage flies open and my family comes running. I'm panting too hard to hear what they're saying as I keep gawking at the back of my car. The door chime starts dinging, the staccato patterns interrupting their muffled words in my head.

"Dad." Ethan kneels in front of me, snapping. "Dad!"

His tone catches me off guard and I finally move my gaze to his eyes. My son's tone is low, calm, and controlled, like he's approaching a wild dog. "You're scaring Cynthia and Edie."

His words are lightning through my spine. It's only now that I realize I had to scream loud enough to penetrate the house and all our insulation to have them running like this. I cough and force myself to stand. "I'm okay."

"Bullshit."

"Ethan." Cynthia cradles Edie's head against her chest. "Language!"

"Cynthia, I'm sorry but we don't have time for this."

Something in his tone strikes through the adrenaline and I finally take in their clothes. Ethan and Cynthia both wear heavy coats, Edie is in her winter gear, and all our vacation bags wait behind them in the garage. Despite the obvious trip preparation, Ethan and Cynthia both stand on the frigid concrete with bare feet.

"What's going on?" I can't keep the edge out of my tone.

They share a look, one that's unfamiliar to me but seems practiced. Cynthia frowns but nods and Ethan sighs. "The pranks kept going after the doorknobs."

"I thought we agreed–"

"We *did*." Cynthia interjects. "It's not us."

"And you didn't think to tell me?"

"Oh, because you've been so honest lately." Ethan snorts. "Why don't you tell Cynthia what happened to the elf."

I stare at my shoes.

“It’s not like I didn’t figure it out.” My wife gives me a sad smile. “Look, can we talk about this on the way to a hotel or something? My feet are freezing and that chime is starting to annoy me.”

I swallow and scowl at the open door of my car, the repetitive ding emphasizing her point. It had to be in my head but...

“Dad?” Ethan shakes my shoulder and I look at him.

I shake my head. “You need to drive.”

He tilts his head and squints. “Why?”

“I’m too exhausted.” I drag a hand down my face. “Hallucinating.”

“Hallucinating?” Cynthia’s tone is urgent and terrified.

“Yeah, just now.” I shake my head and force myself to stand, handing the keys to Ethan. “But, let’s handle one thing at a time.”

“Can we start with your shoes?” I nod at Ethan’s bare dirty feet as he brakes for the next stop sign. It seems to take longer than it should but I assume he’s being careful due to the falling snow.

“They disappeared right after we agreed to leave the house.” Cyhthia shakes some rattle-like thing over Edie’s car seat. “We looked everywhere, we’d just agreed to give up when we heard you screaming in the driveway.”

“And what other pranks happened? Why didn’t you tell me?”

They share that same expression through the rearview mirror.

I can’t take it anymore. “Enough secrets!”

Ethan shakes head. “You first.”

He sets his jaw and glares at me, not as his father, but like an equal. And I have absolutely no argument.

“I threw the elf in the trash after I found Wiliker's tail.”

At his name, the cat yowls from inside his carrier.

“Why?” Cynthia seems mildly amused but mostly concerned, cooing at the cat and our daughter in turns. “You don’t actually think...”

The question is so crazy she won’t ask me.

“No, but it creeped me out.” I stare at my shoes. “And today, I swore I saw it in the car.”

Ethan scoffs. “Any other lies?”

I shake my head. "Now, why didn't you tell me about the pranks?"

"Because you would just have blamed Ethan." Cynthia gives me a sympathetic look.

"What do you mean?"

"Look, Dad, you're trying your best but the pranks kept escalating." Ethan shrugged and turned on his blinker. "And it's always between us for some reason."

"What do you mean?"

"Saran wrap over the toilet in my bathroom." Ethan sneered.

"Beggin' Strips in my BLT"

"Well those don't seem too ba–"

"Superglue on my face." Ethan grumbled.

"What?" I can't keep the outrage from my tone.

"A bucket of water that slammed into my skull this morning." Cynthia winced at my expression. "We knew neither of us would do that."

"Then, this evening, I went to put Edie down for Cynthia and there were mouse traps in her crib. That's when we started packing." He stops at another intersection but the car takes a minute.

"The roads too slick?" I ask as the car jerks again.

"I mean yeah but..." Ethan stutters. "Something feels off."

Something in his tone snaps me to attention. His posture is tense, the arms rigid and his face pinched with concern. Everything except his eyes, wide and reflecting the passing street lights as we approach a stop sign with more jerks and a telling *flop flop flop.* I sit up straight and look in the rearview mirror.

The back tire sags and flops, barely staying on the rim in the snow. "Ethan, pull ov–"

The tire shreds and the rim squeals as Ethan slams on the brake. "Shit!"

Cynthia gasps and clings to Edie's car seat, covering our daughter on instinct.

I place a hand on Ethan's arm and grit through my teeth, "Pump the brakes."

Those eyes grow wider but he nods rapidly as the car tugs and pulls against the snow.

"Jacob?" Cynthia's question is filled with worry.

"Not now." I snap, clenching Ethan's arm, letting him know I'm here.

"Jacob!"

I ignore her this time as the car starts to slide, our tail end slides into oncoming traffic, the headlights of another car approaching slowly, their horn blaring louder and louder.

"Jacob!" Cynthia's scream is now accompanied by Edie's cry as I grab the wheel and Ethan mutters something over and over. Before I can turn the wheel, he's already doing it.

And there, just under my wife's frantic cry and the oncoming horn I hear him chanting, "Turn into it. Turn into it."

He keeps pumping the breaks and the car starts to come back into his control. As we slow, the truck in the oncoming lane rolls past, shouting out the window.

Only once Ethan pulls to the side of the road, slamming the car in park and wrenching his door open to vomit do I finally expel a breath.

"Jacob!" Cynthia's panicked shriek makes me choke on the breath. I turn in time to see her slamming that ugly little elf against the window. It squeals and yowls in a gremlin voice that shouldn't even exist. It squirms and wiggles and despite Cynthia being at least twenty times this stuff doll's size, her arms tremble with effort while she keeps it pinned to the window.

I lunge to grab it but the thing twists free and scrampers through Ethan's open door.

"What the– ow!"

I spring back into the front, grab the back of my son's shirt and haul him back into the car. The little troll screams in anger as Ethan slams the door shut with a bloody hand.

"Oh my god, what happened?" Cynthia pulls a clean diaper from her bag and wraps it over my son's hand.

"It stabbed me!" Ethan winces but uses the paper velcro to pull the diaper tighter.

"What do you mean it stabbed you?"

"I mean it pulled a knife from god knows where–" We all scream as the doll lunges onto the hood and slams the handle of the handle of our missing kitchen knife on our windshield.

Ethan yells something incoherent and slams the car back into drive. The elf slips from the windshield and an ugly screeching makes us cover our ears and winch as it tries to bury the knife in our hood. Suddenly, a horrible grinding makes Edie cry while the car tries to slide and slip again. The elf flies off and Ehtan keeps driving, ruining the rims

The ever growing grinding is further punctuated by our unsteady breathing and the ever growing rattle of our shredding tires until Cynthia finally pipes up, "It was going after our son."

We don't utter another word as Ethan pulls over so I can investigate the tire. Even without getting under our car I can already see it's a lost cause. The body is destroyed, the rim is bent, and the wheel is hanging at an angle that tells me the axle is toast. We're walking in this snow, two of us barefoot. All the while, that ugly little rag doll is hunting us.

I wrap Edie in my coat, and offer my too-large shoes to Cynthia. She shakes her head and points at Ethan. We don't have time to argue before we hoof it to the next gas station. The clerk glares as we enter. "We don't allow pets."

Cynthia puts the carrier down, Wilikers mewling plaintively from inside, before she puts on her best pleading face. "Look, we've just had an awful car crash. We just need a minute to regroup."

The clerk sneers but shrugs and pulls out their phone, effectively dismissing us so he can doom scroll.

I motion for my family to follow down an aisle and turn to my son. "Let me see that hand."

Ethan holds out his trembling palm, but his voice is collected. "It's already stopped bleeding."

I move the diaper to confirm, it's a shallow gash that'll heal in a couple days. Only then do I hand Edie to Ethan and pull out my own phone, but I can't even think who to call. I look at Cynthia and I know we're sharing the same thought. She shakes her head, "The police would know we're hiding something. There's knife damage all over the hood."

I nod and put the phone away. We huddle next to the cold drinks cooler and I try to banish any questions on how we'll replace the car. First things first.

"Dad..." Ethan looks skeptical. "Did you know?"

I shake my head and look at my wife. "You said it went after Ethan?"

She nods and brushes a hand over his cheek, like she needs to confirm he's there. "It tried to lunge between the seats when the car started to slide."

Ethan gulps and nods. "Makes sense."

"How does any of this make any sense?" Cynthia shakes her head.

"No, I mean the elf is weird but think about it." Ethan rocks Edie calmly and tries to keep his tone soft. "All the pranks were between you and me. I mean, if you didn't know me so well..."

Cynthia offers a supportive smile but silence falls between us and I wrap an arm around my son. "I'm sorry."

"You should be." Ethan snorts. "And those bars better be coming off."

I level a look at him. "You still snuck out."

"Okay, so my elf is trying to divide our family." Cynthia shivers a little until she wraps an arm around our kids. "Why?"

"Wait, what did that card say?" They both look at me funny and I roll my eyes. "That card the creator provided. It said something about keeping our family wholesome."

"Yeah, so?" Cynthia's eyes bug as she looks at Ethan again. "Oh, Jesus!"

Could it be this elf thinks my son, from the prior marriage, doesn't qualify?

Her shout is loud enough that the clerk at the front finally looks up from his phone. "Hey, y'all gonna buy something?"

"Just trying to figure out who to call." Cytnhia shivers again. "We'll be out of your hair–"

The lights all shut off, the low hum of the coolers cut off, and the only light comes from our phones.

"Oh, what the fuck?" The clerk grumbles as he fishes under the desk.

"Dad..." Ethan's voice wavers.

"Shh." Cynthia places a hand over our son's mouth, her dark eyes scanning the floor. I turn Ethan and point him at the cooler, my back to his.

My son hisses, "One of you should take Edie."

"Shhh." Cynthia backs up to us, watching the opposite direction.

"Seriously?" Ethan turns and forces me to look at him. "What if that thing comes after me with Edie in my arms?"

"Hey what are you whispering about back there?" The clerk comes out from behind the desk, a big flashlight in one hand. Next to the shelves and off whatever stool he uses, it's easier to see how short he is.

"Just wondering what's going on," Cynthia tries to soothe.

"Hell no!" The clerk stomps toward us, like the angry shadow of a dwarf. "All this started when you wandered it. Get your animal and–"

The door opens, but no one is visible. Wilkers growls and hisses. My family tenses and the clerk turns. "What the–"

A tiny shadow runs past the aisle, a flicker of street light gleaming from the blade. The clerk shrieks as the knife flashes out and blood flows onto the cheap tile. He crumbles to the floor, dropping the flashlight, which spins, flickering in and out, blinding us briefly just before showing the man clutching his ankle while he screams, like a macabre strobe.

"Over there!" Ethan points his chin and I only catch a flicker of movement.

"No there!" Cynthia kicks out and hisses, barely audible under the still screaming clerk. Something thumps against a cooler door, then the knife clangs on the tile floor as my wife bends over, pressing a hand to her leg. "Little shit got me!"

I look around but I can't see either the elf or the knife. Shit, it still has the blade. I don't even know how it's holding the knife, the doll doesn't have fingers. But our growing wounds make it clear this thing knows how to use it.

"Your scarf." Ethan cradles Edie in one arm to point. "Tie it around your leg."

Cythia nods and does so.

"What the hell is going on?" The clerk tries to crawl away from us.

"You saw it. Now shut up and let me think." It's basically a homicidal rodent. No matter how crazy all of this is, no matter how weird, I can overpower a doll.

Something crinkles and rattles nearby. Just as I realize it's climbing a shelf of chips, the elf lunges, the knife shining bright just before it moves to plunge it into Ethan. My son turns, curving his spine and hunching over his now crying sister protectively.

I grab the doll, slicing my hand on the knife as I slam it into the ground. Those beady little eyes become twin pinpricks in the limited light, while the elf growls and grumbles in that high pitched voice.

I pin it, using all the muscles in my arm, much to my dismay. "Cynthia, go get Wilikers."

"What, why?" But she'd already moving.

Ethan leans against the cooler doors, cradling his sister and cooing softly. "Dad wants to give him revenge."

"Right." I nod and pick up the knife, dropped during our scuffle, and start chopping up new cat toys.

CHRISTMAS EVE

"Oh that's perfect!" Cynthia snaps several shots of our new tree before turning to Ethan. "Can I post it?"

"Thought your followers only like cute, cuddly stuff," Ethan teases, scarfing a third bowl of rice and smiling proudly at his recreation of Snoopy while Wilkers plays with the leftover tinsel.

"Those idiots are the ones that talked me into that elf." Cynthia snorts. "But my parents would love to see what you made. They *adore* The Peanuts."

Ethan grins, "Tell them I say hi, Mom."

Cynthia pauses, smiles warmly then nods before clicking on her phone.

I yank a piece of tinsel from the cat's mouth and hold it just out of reach. Edie giggles wildly from her baby swing in the corner. "Hey, did you ever find your card?"

She shakes her head. "I'm starting to wonder if that was one of the pranks or if I just lost it."

"You called it in, right?"

Even with the criminal case open, the clerk backing us up on a random intruder stalking us, we're not getting our car back. We didn't have coverage and there is no one to recover the funds from. Sure, we looked into the instagram influencer she got the elf from but the account was closed. And how would we explain our need to track the transaction to the police?

The last thing we need on top of everything else is some asshole racking up our debt.

"Yup, there was one charge I didn't approve of so they're looking into that one." Cynthia puts her phone down and sits next to our daughter. "Seems like a simple over-charge to the instagram influencer I bought that thing from."

Ethan and I both pause, looking at her. I swallow. "You mean, like a second transaction?"

"Yeah the amount was a bit higher, but similar figures. I think she just mis-entered my card for another order."

I don't have a chance to question this further. The doorbell rings. Cynthia moves to stand, wincing at the still-healing gash on her leg. I toss the tinsel away and wave for her to sit. "I got it."

I walk down steps, greet our mail carrier, and make bad jokes about working on Christmas Eve as I sign for a large but light box. Probably a last minute Christamas gift from Cynthia's parents. I open it before going upstairs to check if anything needs to be wrapped, and I am greeted by no less than twelve sets of beady little eyes from under tiny little gnome hats.

THE END

About the Author

This story is dedicated to R.K. Reif, the English teacher who helped this author learn that it's okay to be the nerdy goth kid, with special thanks to everyone who offered ideas for the *pranks*. Remind us all to never to piss you off.

EH Drake is an indie author living in Minnesota with her family. She loves dogs, almost anything with vampires, and reading three books at a time. This story is a prequel to her *Blood Herring* trilogy. She's also working on a young adult super hero and a zombie western. You can find her new novels, social media, and upcoming events at www.EHDrake.com. See you there!

THE GHOST

BY WILLIAM DOUGLAS O'CONNOR

AT THE WEST END of Boston is a quarter of some fifty streets, more or less, commonly known as Beacon Hill.

It is a rich and respectable quarter, sacred to the abodes of Our First Citizens. The very houses have become sentient of its prevailing character of riches and respectability; and, when the twilight deepens on the place, or at high noon, if your vision is gifted, you may see them as long rows of Our First Giants, with very corpulent or very broad fronts, with solid-set feet of sidewalk ending in square-toed curbstone, with an air about them as if they had thrust their hard hands into their wealthy pockets forever, with a character of arctic reserve, and portly dignity, and a well-dressed, full-fed, self-satisfied, opulent, stony, repellant aspect to each, which says plainly: "I belong to a rich family, of the very highest respectability."

History, having much to say of Beacon Hill generally, has, on the present occasion, something to say particularly of a certain street which bends over the eminence, sloping steeply down to its base. It is an old street—quaint, quiet, and somewhat picturesque. It was young once, though—having been born before the Revolution, and was then given to the city by its father, Mr. Middlecott, who died without heirs, and did this much for posterity. Posterity has not been grateful to Mr. Middlecott. The street bore his name till he was dust, and then got the more aristocratic epithet of Bowdoin. Posterity has paid him by effacing what would have been his noblest epitaph. We may expect, after this, to see Faneuil Hall robbed of its name, and called Smith Hall! Republics are proverbially ungrateful. What safer claim to public remembrance has the old Huguenot, Peter Faneuil, than the old Englishman, Mr. Middlecott? Ghosts, it is said, have risen from the grave to reveal wrongs done them by the living; but it needs no ghost from the grave to prove the proverb about republics.

Bowdoin street only differs from its kindred, in a certain shady, grave, old-fogy, fossil aspect, just touched with a pensive solemnity, as if it thought to itself, "I'm getting old but I'm highly respectable; that's a comfort." It has, moreover, a dejected, injured air, as if it brooded solemnly on the wrong done to it by taking away its original name, and calling it Bowdoin; but as if, being a very conservative street, it was resolved to keep a cautious silence on the subject, lest the Union should go to pieces. Sometimes it wears a profound and mysterious look, as if it could tell something if it had a mind to, but thought it best not. Something of the ghost of its father—it was the only child he ever had!—walking there all the night, pausing at the corners to look up at the signs, which bear a strange name, and wringing his ghostly hands in lamentation at the wrong done his memory! Rumor told it in a whisper, many years ago. Perhaps it was believed by a few of the oldest inhabitants of the city; but the highly respectable quarter never heard of it; and, if it had, would not have been bribed to believe it, by any sum. Some one had said that some very old person had seen a phantom there. Nobody knew who some one was. Nobody knew who the very old person was. Nobody knew who had seen it; nor when; nor how. The very rumor was spectral.

All this was many years ago. Since then it has been reported that a ghost was seen there one bitter Christmas eve, two or three years back. The twilight was already in the street; but the evening lamps were not yet lighted in the windows, and the roofs and chimney-tops were still distinct in the last clear light of the dropping day. It was light enough, however, for one to read, easily, from the opposite sidewalk, "Dr. C. Renton," in black letters, on the silver plate of a door, not far from the gothic portal of the Swedenborgian church. Near this door stood a misty figure, whose sad, spectral eyes floated on vacancy, and whose long, shadowy white hair, lifted like an airy weft in the streaming wind. That was the ghost! It stood near the door a long time, without any other than a shuddering motion, as though it felt the searching blast, which swept furiously from the north up the declivity of the street, rattling the shutters in its headlong passage. Once or twice, when a passer-by, muffled warmly from the bitter air, hurried past, the phantom shrank closer to the wall, till he was gone. Its vague, mournful face seemed to watch for some one. The twilight darkened, gradually; but it did not flit away. Patiently it kept its piteous look fixed in one direction—watching—watching; and, while the howling wind swept frantically through the chill air, it still seemed to shudder in the piercing cold.

A light suddenly kindled in an opposite window. As if touched by a gleam from the lamp, or as if by some subtle interior illumination, the spectre became faintly luminous, and a thin smile seemed to quiver over its features. At the same moment, a strong, energetic figure—Dr. Renton, himself—came in sight, striding down the slope of the pavement to his own door, his over-coat thrown back, as if the icy air were a tropical warmth to him, his hat set on the back of his head, and the loose ends of a 'kerchief about his throat, streaming in the nor'wester. The wind set up a howl the moment he came in sight, and swept upon him; and a curious agitation began on the part of the phantom. It glided rapidly to and fro, and moved in circles, and then, with the same swift, silent motion, sailed toward him, as if blown thither by the gale. Its long, thin arms, with something like a pale flame spiring from the tips of the slender fingers, were stretched out, as in greeting, while the wan smile played over its face; and when he rushed by, unheedingly, it made a futile effort to grasp the swinging arms with which he appeared to buffet back the buffeting gale. Then it glided on by his side, looking earnestly into his countenance, and moving its pallid lips with agonized rapidity, as if it said: "Look at me—speak to me—speak to me—see me!" But he kept his course with unconscious eyes, and a vexed frown on his bold, white forehead, betokening an irritated mind. The light that had shone in the figure of the phantom, darkened slowly, till the form was only a pale shadow. The wind had suddenly lulled, and no longer lifted its white hair. It still glided on with him, its head drooping on its breast, and its long arms hanging by its side; but when he reached the door, it suddenly sprang before him, gazing fixedly into his eyes, while a convulsive motion flashed over its grief-worn features, as if it had shrieked out a word. He had his foot on the step at the moment. With a start, he put his gloved hand to his forehead, while the vexed look went out quickly on his face. The ghost watched him breathlessly. But the irritated expression came back to his countenance more resolutely than before, and he began to fumble in his pocket for a latch-key, muttering petulantly, "What the devil is the matter with me now!" It seemed to him that a voice had cried, clearly, yet as from afar, "Charles Renton!"—his own name. He had heard it in his startled mind; but, then, he knew he was in a highly wrought state of nervous excitement, and his medical science, with that knowledge for a basis, could have reared a formidable fortress of explanation against any phenomenon, were it even more wonderful than this.

He entered the house; kicked the door to; pulled off his over-coat; wrenched off his outer 'kerchief; slammed them on a branch of the clothes-tree; banged his hat on top of them; wheeled about; pushed in the door of his library; strode in, and, leaving the door ajar, threw himself into an easy chair, and sat there in the fire-reddened dusk, with his white brows knit, and his arms tightly locked on his breast. The ghost had followed him, sadly, and now stood motionless in a corner of the room, its spectral hands crossed on its bosom, and its white locks drooping down.

It was evident Dr. Renton was in a bad humor. The very library caught contagion from him, and became grouty and sombre. The furniture was grim, and sullen, and sulky; it made ugly shadows on the carpet and on the wall, in allopathic quantity; it took the red gleams from the fire on its polished surfaces, in hom[oe]opathic globules, and got no good from them. The fire itself peered out sulkily from the black bars of the grate, and seemed resolved not to burn the fresh deposit of black coals at the top, but to take this as a good time to remember that those coals had been bought in the summer at five dollars a ton—under price, mind you—when poor people, who cannot buy at advantage, but must get their firing in the winter, would then have given nine or ten dollars for them. And so (glowered the fire), I am determined to think of that outrage, and not to light them, but to go out myself, directly! And the fire got into such a spasm of glowing indignation over the injury, that it lit a whole tier of black coals with a series of little explosions, before it could cool down, and sent a crimson gleam over the moody figure of its owner in the easy chair, and over the solemn furniture, and into the shadowy corner filled by the ghost.

The spectre did not move when Dr. Renton arose and lit the chandelier. It stood there, still and gray, in the flood of mellow light. The curtains were drawn, and the twilight without had deepened into darkness. The fire was now burning in despite of itself, fanned by the wintry gusts, which found their way down the chimney. Dr. Renton stood with his back to it, his hands behind him, his bold white forehead shaded by a careless lock of black hair, and knit sternly; and the same frown in his handsome, open, searching dark eyes. Tall and strong, with an erect port, and broad, firm shoulders, high, resolute features, a commanding figure garbed in aristocratic black, and not yet verging into the proportions of obesity—take him for all in all, a very fine and favorable specimen of the solid men of Boston. And seen in contrast (oh! could he but have known it!) with the attenuated figure of the poor, dim ghost!

Hark! a very light foot on the stairs—a rich rustle of silks. Everything still again—Dr. Renton looking fixedly, with great sternness, at the half-open door, from whence a faint, delicious perfume floats into the library. Somebody there, for certain. Somebody peeping in with very bright, arch eyes. Dr. Renton knew it, and prepared to maintain his ill-humor against the invader. His face became triply armed with severity for the encounter. That's Netty, I know, he thought. His daughter. So it was. In she bounded. Bright little Netty! Gay little Netty! A dear and sweet little creature, to be sure, with a delicate and pleasant beauty of face and figure, it needed no costly silks to grace or heighten. There she stood. Not a word from her merry lips, but a smile which stole over all the solitary grimness of the library, and made everything better, and brighter, and fairer, in a minute. It floated down into the cavernous humor of Dr. Renton, and the gloom began to lighten directly—though he would not own it, nor relax a single feature. But the wan ghost in the corner lifted its head to look at her, and slowly brightened as to something worthy a spirit's love, and a dim phantom's smiles. Now then, Dr. Renton! the lines are drawn, and the foe is coming. Be martial, sir, as when you stand in the ranks of the cadets on training-days! Steady, and stand the charge! So he did. He kept an inflexible front as she glided toward him, softly, slowly, with her bright eyes smiling into his, and doing dreadful execution. Then she put her white arms around his neck, laid her dear, fair head on his breast, and peered up archly into his stern visage. Spite of himself, he could not keep the fixed lines on his face from breaking confusedly into a faint smile. Somehow or other, his hands came from behind him, and rested on her head. There! That's all. Dr. Renton surrendered at discretion! One of the solid men of Boston was taken after a desperate struggle—internal, of course—for he kissed her, and said, "Dear little Netty!" And so she was.

The phantom watched her with a smile, and wavered and brightened as if about to glide to her; but it grew still, and remained.

"Pa in the sulks to-night?" she asked, in the most winning, playful, silvery voice.

"Pa's a fool," he answered in his deep chest-tones, with a vexed good humor; "and you know it."

"What's the matter with pa? What makes him be a great bear? Papa-sy, dear," she continued, stroking his face with her little hands, and patting him, very much as Beauty might have patted the Beast after she fell in love with him—or, as if he were a great baby. In fact, he began to look then as if he were.

"Matter? Oh! everything's the matter, little Netty. The world goes round too fast. My boots pinch. Somebody stole my umbrella last year. And I've got a headache." He concluded this fanciful abstract of his grievances by putting his arms around her, and kissing her again. Then he sat down in the easy-chair, and took her fondly on his knee.

"Pa's got a headache! It is t-o-o bad, so it is," she continued in the same soothing, winning way, caressing his bold, white brow with her tiny hands. "It's a horrid shame, so it is! P-o-o-r pa. Where does it ache, papa-sy, dear? In the forehead? Cerebrum or cerebellum, papa-sy? Occiput or sinciput, deary?"

"Bah! you little quiz," he replied, laughing and pinching her cheek, "none of your nonsense! And what are you dressed up in this way for, to-night? Silks, and laces, and essences, and what not! Where are you going, fairy?"

"Going out with mother for the evening, Dr. Renton," she replied briskly; "Mrs. Larrabee's party, papa-sy. Christmas eve, you know. And what are you going to give me for a present, to-morrow, pa-sy?"

"To-morrow will tell, little Netty."

"Good! And what are you going to give me, so that I can make *my* presents, Beary?"

"Ugh!" but he growled it in fun, and had a pocket-book out from his breast-pocket directly after. Fives—tens—twenties—fifties—all crisp, and nice, and new bank-notes.

"Will that be enough, Netty?" He held up a twenty. The smiling face nodded assent, and the bright eyes twinkled.

"No, it won't. But *that* will," he continued, giving her a fifty.

"Fifty dollars, Globe Bank, Boston!" exclaimed Netty, making great eyes at him. "But we must take all we can get, pa-sy; mustn't we? It's too much, though. Thank you all the same, pa-sy, nevertheless." And she kissed him, and put the bill in a little bit of a portemonnaie with a gay laugh.

"Well done, I declare!" he said, smilingly. "But you're going to the party?"

"Pretty soon, pa."

He made no answer; but sat smiling at her. The phantom watched them, silently.

"What made pa so cross and grim, to-night? Tell Netty—do," she pleaded.

"Oh! because;—everything went wrong with me, to-day. There." And he looked as sulky, at that moment, as he ever did in his life.

"No, no, pa-sy; that won't do. I want the particulars," continued Netty, shaking her head, smilingly.

"Particulars! Well, then, Miss Nathalie Renton," he began, with mock gravity, "your professional father is losing some of his oldest patients. Everybody is in ruinous good health; and the grass is growing in the graveyards."

"In the winter-time, papa?—smart grass!"

"Not that I want practice," he went on, getting into soliloquy; "or patients, either. A rich man who took to the profession simply for the love of it, can't complain on that score. But to have an interloping she-doctor take a family I've attended ten years, out of my hands, and to hear the hodge-podge gabble about physiological laws, and woman's rights, and no taxation without representation, they learn from her—well, it's too bad!"

"Is that all, pa-sy? Seems to me, *I'd* like to vote, too," was Netty's piquant rejoinder.

"Hoh! I'll warrant," growled her father. "Hope you'll vote the Whig ticket, Netty, when you get your rights."

"Will the Union be dissolved, then, pa-sy—when the Whigs are beaten?"

"Bah! you little plague," he growled, with a laugh. "But, then, you women don't know anything about politics. So, there. As I was saying, everything went wrong with me to-day. I've been speculating in railroad stock, and singed my fingers. Then, old Tom Hollis outbid me, to-day, at Leonard's on a rare medical work I had set my eyes upon having. Confound him! Then, again, two of my houses are tenantless, and there are folks in two others that won't pay their rent, and I can't get them out. Out they'll go, though, or I'll know why. And, to crown all—um-m. And I wish the devil had him! as he will."

"Had who, Beary-papa?"

"Him. I'll tell you. The street floor of one of my houses in Hanover street lets for an oyster-room. They keep a bar there, and sell liquor. Last night they had a grand row—a drunken fight, and one man was stabbed, it's thought fatally."

"O, father!" Netty's bright eyes dilated with horror.

"Yes. I hope he won't die. At any rate, there's likely to be a stir about the matter, and my name will be called into question, then, as I'm the landlord. And folks will make a handle of it, and there'll be the deuce to pay, generally."

He got back the stern, vexed frown, to his face, with the anticipation, and beat the carpet with his foot. The ghost still watched from the angle of the room, and seemed to darken, while its features looked troubled.

"But, father," said Netty, a little tremulously, "I wouldn't let my houses to such people. It's not right; is it? Why, it's horrid to think of men getting drunk, and killing each other!"

Dr. Renton rubbed his hair into disorder, with vexation, and then subsided into solemnity.

"I know it's not exactly right, Netty; but I can't help it. As I said before, I wish the devil had that bar-keeper. I ought to have ordered him out long ago, and then this wouldn't have happened. I've increased his rent twice, hoping to get rid of him so; but he pays without a murmur; and what am I to do? You see, he was an occupant when the building came into my hands, and I let him stay. He pays me a good, round rent; and, apart from his cursed traffic, he's a good tenant. What can I do? It's a good thing for him, and it's a good thing for me, pecuniarily. Confound him. Here's a nice rumpus brewing!"

"Dear pa, I'm afraid it's not a good thing for you," said Netty, caressing him, and smoothing his tumbled hair. "Nor for him either. I wouldn't mind the rent he pays you. I'd order him out. It's bad money. There's blood on it."

She had grown pale, and her voice quivered. The phantom glided over to them, and laid its spectral hand upon her forehead. The shadowy eyes looked from under the misty hair into the doctor's face, and the pale lips moved as if speaking the words heard only in the silence of his heart—"hear her, hear her!"

"I must think of it," resumed Dr. Renton, coldly. "I'm resolved, at all events, to warn him that if anything of this kind occurs again, he must quit at once. I dislike to lose a profitable tenant; for no other business would bring me the sum his does. Hang it, everybody does the best he can with his property—why shouldn't I?"

The ghost, standing near them, drooped its head again on its breast, and crossed its arms. Netty was silent. Dr. Renton continued, petulantly:

"A precious set of people I manage to get into my premises. There's a woman hires a couple of rooms for a dwelling, overhead, in that same building, and for three months I haven't got a cent from her. I know these people's tricks. Her month's notice expires to-morrow, and out she goes."

"Poor creature!" sighed Netty.

He knit his brow, and beat the carpet with his foot, in vexation.

"Perhaps she can't pay you, pa," trembled the sweet, silvery voice. "You wouldn't turn her out in this cold winter, when she can't pay you—would you, pa?"

"Why don't she get another house, and swindle some one else?" he replied, testily; "there's plenty of rooms to let."

"Perhaps she can't find one, pa," answered Netty.

"Humbug!" retorted her father; "I know better."

"Pa, dear, if I were you, I'd turn out that rumseller, and let the poor woman stay a little longer; just a little, pa."

"Shan't do it. Hah! that would be scattering money out of both pockets. Shan't do it. Out she shall go; and as for him—well, he'd better turn over a new leaf. There, let us leave the subject, darling. It vexes me. How did we contrive to get into this train. Bah!"

He drew her closer to him, and kissed her forehead. She sat quietly, with her head on his shoulder, thinking very gravely.

"I feel queerly to-day, little Netty," he began, after a short pause. "My nerves are all high-strung with the turn matters have taken."

"How is it, papa? The headache?" she answered.

"Y-e-s—n-o—not exactly; I don't know," he said dubiously; then, in an absent way, "it was that letter set me to think of him all day, I suppose."

"Why, pa, I declare," cried Netty, starting up, "if I didn't forget all about it, and I came down expressly to give it to you! Where is it? Oh! here it is."

She drew from her pocket an old letter, faded to a pale yellow, and gave it to him. The ghost started suddenly.

"Why, bless my soul! it's the very letter! Where did you get that, Nathalie?" asked Dr. Renton.

"I found it on the stairs after dinner, pa."

"Yes, I do remember taking it up with me; I must have dropped it," he answered, musingly, gazing at the superscription. The ghost was gazing at it, too, with startled interest.

"What beautiful writing it is, pa," murmured the young girl. "Who wrote it to you? It looks yellow enough to have been written a long time since."

"Fifteen years ago, Netty. When you were a baby. And the hand that wrote it has been cold for all that time."

He spoke with a solemn sadness, as if memory lingered with the heart of fifteen years ago, on an old grave. The dim figure by his side had bowed its head, and all was still.

"It is strange," he resumed, speaking vacantly and slowly, "I have not thought of him for so long a time, and to-day—especially this evening—I have felt as if he were constantly near me. It is a singular feeling."

He put his left hand to his forehead, and mused—his right clasped his daughter's shoulder. The phantom slowly raised its head, and gazed at him with a look of unutterable tenderness.

"Who was he, father?" she asked with a hushed voice.

"A young man—an author—a poet. He had been my dearest friend, when we were boys; and, though I lost sight of him for years—he led an erratic life—we were friends when he died. Poor, poor fellow! Well, he is at peace."

The stern voice had saddened, and was almost tremulous. The spectral form was still.

"How did he die, father?"

"A long story, darling," he replied gravely, "and a sad one. He was very poor and proud. He was a genius—that is, a person without an atom of practical talent. His parents died, the last, his mother, when he was near manhood. I was in college then. Thrown upon the world, he picked up a scanty subsistence with his pen, for a time. I could have got him a place in the counting-house, but he would not take it; in fact, he wasn't fit for it. You can't harness Pegasus to the cart, you know. Besides, he despised mercantile life—without reason, of course; but he was always notional. His love of literature was one of the rocks he foundered on. He wasn't successful; his best compositions were too delicate—fanciful—to please the popular taste; and then he was full of the radical and fanatical notions which infected so many people at that time in New England, and infect them now, for that matter; and his sublimated, impracticable ideas and principles, which he kept till his dying day, and which, I confess, alienated me from him, always staved off his chances of success. Consequently, he never rose above the drudgery of some employment on newspapers. Then he was terribly passionate, not without cause, I allow; but it wasn't wise. What I mean is this: if he saw, or if he fancied he saw, any wrong or injury done to any one, it was enough to throw him into a frenzy; he would get black in the face and absolutely shriek out his denunciations of the wrongdoer. I do believe he would have visited his own brother with the most unsparing invective, if that brother had laid a harming finger on a street-beggar, or a colored man, or a poor person of any kind. I don't blame the feeling; though with a man like him, it was very apt to be a false or mistaken one; but, at any rate, its exhibition wasn't sensible. Well, as I was saying, he buffeted about in this world a long time, poorly paid, fed, and clad; taking more care of other people than he did of himself. Then mental suffering, physical exposure, and want killed him."

The stern voice had grown softer than a child's. The same look of unutterable tenderness brooded on the mournful face of the phantom by his side; but its thin, shining hand was laid upon his head, and its countenance had undergone a change. The form was still undefined; but the features had become distinct. They were those of a young man, beautiful and wan, and marked with great suffering.

A pause had fallen on the conversation, in which the father and daughter heard the solemn sighing of the wintry wind around the dwelling. The silence seemed scarcely broken by the voice of the young girl.

"Dear father, this was very sad. Did you say he died of want?"

"Of want, my child, of hunger and cold. I don't doubt it. He had wandered about, as I gather, houseless for a couple of days and nights. It was in December, too. Some one found him, on a rainy night, lying in the street, drenched and burning with fever, and had him taken to the hospital. It appears that he had always cherished a strange affection for me, though I had grown away from him; and in his wild ravings he constantly mentioned my name, and they sent for me. That was our first meeting after two years. I found him in the hospital—dying. Heaven can witness that I felt all my old love for him return then, but he was delirious, and never recognized me. And, Nathalie, his hair—it had been coal-black, and he wore it very long, he wouldn't let them cut it either; and as they knew no skill could save him, they let him have his way—his hair was then as white as snow!

God alone knows what that brain must have suffered to blanch hair which had been as black as the wing of a raven!"

He covered his eyes with his hand, and sat silently. The fingers of the phantom still shone dimly on his head, and its white locks drooped above him, like a weft of light.

"What was his name, father?" asked the pitying girl.

"George Feval. The very name sounds like fever. He died on Christmas eve, fifteen years ago this night. It was on his death-bed, while his mind was tossing on a sea of delirious fancies, that he wrote me this long letter—for to the last, I was uppermost in his thoughts. It is a wild, incoherent thing, of course—a strange mixture of sense and madness. But I have kept it as a memorial of him. I have not looked at it for years; but this morning I found it among my papers, and somehow it has been in my mind all day."

He slowly unfolded the faded sheets, and sadly gazed at the writing. His daughter had risen from her half-recumbent posture, and now bent her graceful head over the leaves. The phantom covered its face with its hands.

"What a beautiful manuscript it is, father!" she exclaimed. "The writing is faultless."

"It is, indeed," he replied. "Would he had written his life as fairly!"

"Read it, father," said Nathalie.

"No—but I'll read you a detached passage here and there," he answered, after a pause. "The rest you may read yourself some time, if you wish. It is painful to me. Here's the beginning:

"*'My Dear Charles Renton:—Adieu, and adieu. It is Christmas eve, and I am going home. I am soon to exhale from my flesh, like the spirit of a broken flower. Exultemus forever!'*

"It is very wild. His mind was in a fever-craze. Here is a passage that seems to refer to his own experience of life:

"*'Your friendship was dear to me. I give you true love. Stocks and returns. You are rich, but I did not wish to be your bounty's pauper. Could I beg? I had my work to do for the world, but oh! the world has no place for souls that can only love and suffer. How many miles to Babylon? Threescore and ten. Not so far—not near so far! Ask starvelings—they know. I wanted to do the world good and the world has killed me, Charles.'*"

"It frightens me," said Nathalie, as he paused.

"We will read no more," he replied sombrely. "It belongs to the psychology of madness. To me, who knew him, there are gleams of sense in it, and passages where the delirium of the language is only a transparent veil on the meaning. All the remainder is devoted to what he thought important advice to me. But it's all wild and vague. Poor—poor George!"

The phantom still hid its face in its hands, as the doctor slowly turned over the pages of the letter. Nathalie, bending over the leaves, laid her finger on the last, and asked—"What are those closing sentences, father? Read them."

"Oh! that is what he called his 'last counsel' to me. It's as wild as the rest—tinctured with the prevailing ideas of his career. First he says, '*Farewell—farewell;*' then he bids me take his '*counsel into memory on Christmas day;*' then, after enumerating all the wretched classes he can think of in the country, he says. '*These are your sisters and your brothers—love them all.*' Here he says, '*O friend, strong in wealth for so much good, take my last counsel. In the name of the Saviour, I charge you be true and tender to mankind.*' He goes on to bid me '*live and labor for the fallen, the neglected, the suffering, and the poor;*' and finally ends by advising me to help upset any, or all, institutions, laws, and so forth, that bear hardly on the fag-ends of society; and tells me that what he calls 'a service to humanity' is worth more to the doer than a service to anything else, or than anything we can gain from the world. Ah, well! poor George."

"But isn't all that true, father?" said Netty; "it seems so."

"H'm," he murmured through his closed lips. Then, with a vague smile, folding up the letter, meanwhile, he said, "Wild words, Netty, wild words. I've no objection to charity, judiciously given; but poor George's notions are not mine. Every man for himself, is a good general rule. Every man for humanity, as George has it, and in his acceptation of the principle, would send us all to the alms-house pretty soon. The greatest good of the greatest number—that's my rule of action. There are plenty of good institutions for the distressed, and I'm willing to help support 'em, and do. But as for making a martyr of one's self, or tilting against the necessary evils of society, or turning philanthropist at large, or any quixotism of that sort, I don't believe in it. We didn't make the world, and we can't mend it. Poor George. Well—he's at rest. The world wasn't the place for him."

They grew silent. The spectre glided slowly to the wall, and stood as if it were thinking what, with Dr. Renton's rule of action, was to become of the greatest good of the smallest number. Nathalie sat on her father's knee, thinking only of George Feval, and of his having been starved and grieved to death.

"Father," said Nathalie, softly, "I felt, while you were reading the letter, as if he were near us. Didn't you? The room was so light and still, and the wind sighed so."

"Netty, dear, I've felt that all day, I believe," he replied. "Hark! there is the door-bell. Off goes the spirit-world, and here comes the actual. Confound it! Some one to see me, I'll warrant, and I'm not in the mood."

He got into a fret at once. Netty was not the Netty of an hour ago, or she would have coaxed him out of it. But she did not notice it now in her abstraction. She had risen at the tinkle of the bell, and seated herself in a chair. Presently a nose, with a great pimple on the end of it, appeared at the edge of the door, and a weak, piping voice said, reckless of the proper tense, "there was a woman wanted to see you, sir."

"Who is it, James?—no matter, show her in."

He got up with the vexed scowl on his face, and walked the room. In a minute the library door opened again, and a pale, thin, rigid, frozen-looking little woman, scantily clad, the weather being considered, entered, and dropped a curt, awkward bow to Dr. Renton.

"Oh! Mrs. Miller. Good evening, ma'am. Sit down," he said, with a cold, constrained civility.

The little woman faintly said, "Good evening, Dr. Renton," and sat down stiffly, with her hands crossed before her, in the chair nearest the wall. This was the obdurate tenant, who had paid no rent for three months, and had a notice to quit, expiring to-morrow.

"Cold evening, ma'am," remarked Dr. Renton, in his hard way.

"Yes, sir, it is," was the cowed, awkward answer.

"Won't you sit near the fire, ma'am," said Netty, gently; "you look cold."

"No, miss, thank you. I'm not cold," was the faint reply. She was cold, though, as well she might be with her poor, thin shawl, and open bonnet, in such a bitter night as it was outside. And there was a rigid, sharp, suffering look in her pinched features that betokened she might have been hungry, too.

"Poor people don't mind the cold weather, miss," she said, with a weak smile, her voice getting a little stronger. "They have to bear it, and they get used to it."

She had not evidently borne it long enough to effect the point of indifference. Netty looked at her with a tender pity. Dr. Renton thought to himself—Hoh!—blazoning her poverty—manufacturing sympathy already—the old trick—and steeled himself against any attacks of that kind, looking jealously, meanwhile, at Netty.

"Well, Mrs. Miller," he said, "what is it this evening? I suppose you've brought me my rent."

The little woman grew paler, and her voice seemed to fail on her quivering lips. Netty cast a quick, beseeching look at her father.

"Nathalie, please to leave the room." We'll have no nonsense carried on here, he thought, triumphantly, as Netty rose, and obeyed the stern, decisive order, leaving the door ajar behind her.

He seated himself in his chair, and resolutely put his right leg up to rest on his left knee. He did not look at his tenant's face, determined that her piteous expressions (got up for the occasion, of course) should be wasted on him.

"Well, Mrs. Miller," he said again.

"Dr. Renton," she began, faintly gathering her voice as she proceeded, "I have come to see you about the rent. I am very sorry, sir, to have made you wait, but we have been unfortunate."

"Sorry, ma'am," he replied, knowing what was coming; "but your misfortunes are not my affair. We all have misfortunes, ma'am. But we must pay our debts, you know."

"I expected to have got money from my husband before this, sir," she resumed, "and I wrote to him. I got a letter from him to-day, sir, and it said that he sent me fifty dollars a month ago, in a letter; and it appears that the post-office is to blame, or somebody, for I never got it. It was nearly three months' wages, sir, and it is very hard to lose it. If it hadn't been for that, your rent would have been paid long ago, sir."

"Don't believe a word of *that* story," thought Dr. Renton, sententiously.

"I thought, sir," she continued, emboldened by his silence, "that if you would be willing to wait a little longer, we would manage to pay you soon, and not let it occur again. It has been a hard winter with us, sir; firing is high, and provisions, and everything; and we're only poor people, you know, and it's difficult to get along."

The doctor made no reply.

"My husband was unfortunate, sir, in not being able to get employment here," she resumed; "his being out of work, in the autumn, threw us all back, and we've got nothing to depend on but his earnings. The family that he's in now, sir, don't give him very good pay—only twenty dollars a month, and his board—but it was the best chance he could get, and it was either go to Baltimore with them, or stay at home and starve, and so he went, sir. It's been a hard time with us, and one of the children is sick, now, with a fever, and we don't hardly know how to make out a living. And so, sir, I have come here this evening, leaving the children alone, to ask you if you wouldn't be kind enough to wait a little longer, and we'll hope to make it right with you in the end."

"Mrs. Miller," said Dr. Renton, with stern composure, "I have no wish to question the truth of any statement you may make; but I must tell you plainly, that I can't afford to let my houses for nothing. I told you a month ago, that if you couldn't pay me my rent, you must vacate the premises. You know very well that there are plenty of tenants who are able and willing to pay when the money comes due. You *know* that."

He paused as he said this, and, glancing at her, saw her pale lips falter. It shook the cruelty of his purpose a little, and he had a vague feeling that he was doing wrong. Not without a proud struggle, during which no word was spoken, could he beat it down. Meanwhile, the phantom had advanced a pace toward the centre of the room.

"That is the state of the matter, ma'am," he resumed, coldly. "People who will not pay me my rent must not live in my tenements. You must move out. I have no more to say."

"Dr. Renton," she said faintly, "I have a sick child—how can I move now? Oh! sir, it's Christmas eve—don't be hard with us!"

Instead of touching him, this speech irritated him beyond measure. Passing all considerations of her difficult position involved in her piteous statement, his anger flashed at once on her implication that he was unjust and unkind. So violent was his excitement that it whirled away the words that rushed to his lips, and only fanned the fury that sparkled from the whiteness of his face in his eyes.

"Be patient with us, sir," she continued; "we are poor, but we mean to pay you; and we can't move now in this cold weather; please, don't be hard with us, sir."

The fury now burst out on his face in a red and angry glow, and the words came.

"Now, attend to me!" He rose to his feet. "I will not hear any more from you. I know nothing of your poverty, nor of the condition of your family. All I know is that you owe me three months' rent, and that you can't or won't pay me. I say, therefore, leave the premises to people who can and will. You have had your legal notice; quit my house to-morrow; if you don't, your furniture shall be put in the street. Mark me—to-morrow!"

The phantom had rushed into the centre of the room. Standing, face to face with him—dilating—blackening—its whole form shuddering with a fury to which his own was tame—the semblance of a shriek upon its flashing lips, and on its writhing features, and an unearthly anger streaming from its bright and terrible eyes—it seemed to throw down, with its tossing arms, mountains of hate and malediction on the head of him whose words had smitten poverty and suffering, and whose heavy hand was breaking up the barriers of a home.

Dr. Renton sank again into his chair. His tenant—not a woman!—not a sister in humanity!—but only his tenant; she sat crushed and frightened by the wall. He knew it vaguely. Conscience was battling in his heart with the stubborn devils that had entered there. The phantom stood before him, like a dark cloud in the image of a man. But its darkness was lightening slowly, and its ghostly anger had passed away.

The poor woman, paler than before, had sat mute and trembling, with all her hopes ruined. Yet her desperation forbade her to abandon the chances of his mercy, and she now said:

"Dr. Renton, you surely don't mean what you have told me. Won't you bear with me a little longer, and we will yet make it all right with you?"

"I have given you my answer," he returned, coldly; "I have no more to add. I never take back anything I say—never!"

It was true. He never did—never! She half rose from her seat as if to go; but weak and sickened with the bitter result of her visit, she sunk down again with her head bowed. There was a pause. Then, solemnly gliding across the lighted room, the phantom stole to her side with a glory of compassion on its wasted features. Tenderly, as a son to a mother, it bent over her; its spectral hands of light rested upon her in caressing and benediction; its shadowy fall of hair, once blanched by the anguish of living and loving, floated on her throbbing brow; and resignation and comfort not of this world, sank upon her spirit, and consciousness grew dim within her, and care and sorrow seemed to die.

He who had been so cruel and so hard, sat silent in black gloom. The stern and sullen mood from which had dropped but one fierce flash of anger, still hung above the heat of his mind, like a dark rack of thunder-cloud. It would have burst anew into a fury of rebuke, had he but known his daughter was listening at the door, while the colloquy went on. It might have flamed violently, had his tenant made any further attempt to change his purpose. She had not. She had left the room meekly, with the same curt, awkward bow that marked her entrance. He recalled her manner very indistinctly; for a feeling, like a mist, began to gather in his mind, and make the occurrences of moments before uncertain.

Alone, now, he was yet oppressed with a sensation that something was near him. Was it a spiritual instinct? for the phantom stood by his side. It stood silently, with one hand raised above his head, from which a pale flame seemed to flow downward to his brain; its other hand pointed movelessly to the open letter on the table beside him.

He took the sheets from the table, thinking, at the moment, only of George Feval; but the first line on which his eye rested was, "In the name of the Saviour, I charge you, be true and tender to mankind!" and the words touched him like a low voice from the grave. Their penetrant reproach pierced the hardness of his heart. He tossed the letter back on the table. The very manner of the act accused him of an insult to the dead. In a moment he took up the faded sheets more reverently, but only to lay them down again.

He had not been well that day, and he now felt worse than before. The pain in his head had given place to a strange sense of dilation, and there was a silent, confused riot in his fevered brain, which seemed to him like the incipience of insanity. Striving to divert his mind from what had passed, by reflection on other themes, he could not hold his thoughts; they came teeming but dim, and slipped and fell away; and only the one circumstance of his recent cruelty, mixed with remembrance of George Feval, recurred and clung with vivid persistence. This tortured him. Sitting there, with arms tightly interlocked, he resolved to wrench his mind down by sheer will upon other things; and a savage pleasure at what at once seemed success, took possession of him. In this mood, he heard soft footsteps and the rustle of festal garments on the stairs, and had a fierce complacency in being able to clearly apprehend that it was his wife and daughter going out to the party. In a moment, he heard the controlled and even voice of Mrs. Renton—a serene and polished lady with whom he had lived for years in cold and civil alienation, both seeing as little of each other as possible. With a scowl of will upon his brow, he received her image distinctly into his mind, even to the minutia of the dress and ornaments he knew she wore, and felt an absolutely savage exultation in his ability to retain it. Then came the sound of the closing of the hall door and the rattle of receding wheels, and somehow it was Nathalie and not his wife that he was holding so grimly in his thought, and with her, salient and vivid as before, the tormenting remembrance of his tenant, connected with the memory of George Feval. Springing to his feet, he walked the room.

He had thrown himself on a sofa, still striving to be rid of his remorseful visitations, when the library door opened, and the inside man appeared, with his hand held bashfully over his nose. It flashed on him at once, that his tenant's husband was the servant of a family like this fellow; and, irritated that the whole matter should be thus broadly forced upon him in another way, he harshly asked him what he wanted. The man only came in to say that Mrs. Renton and the young lady had gone out for the evening, but that tea was laid for him in the dining-room. He did not want any tea, and if anybody called, he was not at home. With this charge, the man left the room, closing the door behind him.

If he could but sleep a little! Rising from the sofa, he turned the lights of the chandelier low, and screened the fire. The room was still. The ghost stood, faintly radiant, in a remote corner. Dr. Renton lay down again, but not to repose. Things he had forgotten of his dead friend, now started up again in remembrance, fresh from the grave of many years; and not one of them but linked itself by some mysterious bond to something connected with his tenant, and became an accusation.

He had lain thus for more than an hour, feeling more and more unmanned by illness, and his mental excitement fast becoming intolerable, when he heard a low strain of music, from the Swedenborgian chapel, hard by. Its first impression was one of solemnity and rest, and its first sense, in his mind, was of relief. Perhaps it was the music of an evening meeting; or it might be that the organist and choir had met for practice. Whatever its purpose, it breathed through his heated fancy like a cool and fragrant wind. It was vague and sweet and wandering at first, straying on into a strain more mysterious and melancholy, but very shadowy and subdued, and evoking the innocent and tender moods of early youth before worldliness had hardened around his heart. Gradually, as he listened to it, the fires in his brain were allayed, and all yielded to a sense of coolness and repose. He seemed to sink from trance to trance of utter rest, and yet was dimly aware that either something in his own condition, or some supernatural accession of tone, was changing the music from its proper quality to a harmony more infinite and awful. It was still low and indeterminate and sweet, but had unaccountably and strangely swelled into a gentle and sombre dirge, incommunicably mournful, and filled with a dark significance that touched him in his depth of rest with a secret tremor and awe. As he listened, rapt and vaguely wondering, the sense of his tranced sinking seemed to come to an end, and with the feeling of one who had been descending for many hours, and at length lay motionless at the bottom of a deep, dark chasm, he heard the music fail and cease.

A pause, and then it rose again, blended with the solemn voices of the choir, sublimed and dilated now, reaching him as though from weird night gulfs of the upper air, and charged with an overmastering pathos as of the lamentations of angels. In the dimness and silence, in the aroused and exalted condition of his being, the strains seemed unearthly in their immense and desolate grandeur of sorrow, and their mournful and dark significance was now for him. Working within him the impression of vast, innumerable, fleeing shadows, thick-crowding memories of all the ways and deeds of an existence fallen from its early dreams and aims, poured across the midnight of his soul, and under the streaming melancholy of the dirge, his life showed like some monstrous treason. It did not terrify or madden him; he listened to it rapt utterly as in some deadening ether of dream; yet feeling to his inmost core all its powerful grief and accusation, and quietly aghast at the sinister consciousness it gave him. Still it swelled, gathering and sounding on into yet mightier pathos, till all at once it darkened and spread wide in wild despair, and aspiring again into a pealing agony of supplication, quivered and died away in a low and funereal sigh.

The tears streamed suddenly upon his face; his soul lightened and turned dark within him; and as one faints away, so consciousness swooned, and he fell suddenly down a precipice of sleep. The music rose again, a pensive and holy chant, and sounded on to its close, unaffected by the action of his brain, for he slept and heard it no more. He lay tranquilly, hardly seeming to breathe, in motionless repose. The room was dim and silent, and the furniture took uncouth shapes around him. The red glow upon the ceiling, from the screened fire, showed the misty figure of the phantom kneeling by his side. All light had gone from the spectral form. It knelt beside him, mutely, as in prayer. Once it gazed at his quiet face with a mournful tenderness, and its shadowy hands caressed his forehead. Then it resumed its former attitude, and the slow hours crept by.

At last it rose and glided to the table, on which lay the open letter. It seemed to try to lift the sheets with its misty hands—but vainly. Next it essayed the lifting of a pen which lay there—but failed. It was a piteous sight, to see its idle efforts on these shapes of grosser matter, which appeared now to have to it but the existence of illusions. Wandering about the shadowy room, it wrung its phantom hands as in despair.

Presently it grew still. Then it passed quickly to his side, and stood before him. He slept calmly. It placed one ghostly hand above his forehead, and, with the other pointed to the open letter. In this attitude its shape grew momentarily more distinct. It began to kindle into brightness. The pale flame again flowed from its hand, streaming downward to his brain. A look of trouble darkened the sleeping face. Stronger—stronger; brighter—brighter; until, at last, it stood before him, a glorious shape of light, with an awful look of commanding love in its shining features—and the sleeper sprang to his feet with a cry!

The phantom had vanished. He saw nothing. His first impression was, not that he had dreamed, but that, awaking in the familiar room, he had seen the spirit of his dead friend, bright and awful by his side, and that it had gone! In the flash of that quick change, from sleeping to waking, he had detected, he thought, the unearthly being that, he now felt, watched him from behind the air, and it had vanished! The library was the same as in the moment of that supernatural revealing; the open letter lay upon the table still; only *that* was gone which had made these common aspects terrible. Then, all the hard, strong skepticism of his nature, which had been driven backward by the shock of his first conviction, recoiled, and rushed within him, violently struggling for its former vantage ground; till, at length, it achieved the foothold for a doubt. Could he have dreamed? The ghost, invisible, still watched him. Yes—a dream—only a dream; but, how vivid—how strange! With a slow thrill creeping through his veins—the blood curdling at his heart—a cold sweat starting on his forehead, he stared through the dimness of the room. All was vacancy.

With a strong shudder, he strode forward, and turned up the flames of the chandelier. A flood of garish light filled the apartment. In a moment, remembering the letter to which the phantom of his dream had pointed, he turned and took it from the table. The last page lay upward, and every word of the solemn counsel at the end seemed to dilate on the paper, and all its mighty meaning rushed upon his soul. Trembling in his own despite, he laid it down and moved away. A physician, he remembered that he was in a state of violent nervous excitement, and thought that when he grew calmer its effects would pass from him. But the hand that had touched him had gone down deeper than the physician, and reached what God had made.

He strove in vain. The very room, in its light and silence, and the lurking sentiment of something watching him, became terrible. He could not endure it. The devils in his heart, grown pusillanimous, cowered beneath the flashing strokes of his aroused and terrible conscience. He could not endure it. He must go out. He will walk the streets. It is not late—it is but ten o'clock. He will go.

The air of his dream still hung heavily about him. He was in the street—he hardly remembered how he had got there, or when; but there he was, wrapped up from the searching cold, thinking, with a quiet horror in his mind, of the darkened room he had left behind, and haunted by the sense that something was groping about there in the darkness, searching for him. The night was still and cold. The full moon was in the zenith. Its icy splendor lay on the bare streets, and on the walls of the dwellings. The lighted oblong squares of curtained windows, here and there, seemed dim and waxen in the frigid glory. The familiar aspect of the quarter had passed away, leaving behind only a corpse-like neighborhood, whose huge, dead features, staring rigidly through the thin, white shroud of moonlight that covered all, left no breath upon the stainless skies. Through the vast silence of the night he passed along; the very sound of his footfalls was remote to his muffled sense.

Gradually, as he reached the first corner, he had an uneasy feeling that a thing—a formless, unimaginable thing—was dogging him. He had thought of going down to his club-room; but he now shrank from entering, with this thing near him, the lighted rooms where his set were busy with cards and billiards, over their liquors and cigars, and where the heated air was full of their idle faces and careless chatter, lest some one should bawl out that he was pale, and ask him what was the matter, and he should answer, tremblingly, that something was following him, and was near him then! He must get rid of it first; he must walk quickly, and baffle its pursuit by turning sharp corners, and plunging into devious streets and crooked lanes, and so lose it!

It was difficult to reach through memory to the crazy chaos of his mind on that night, and recall the route he took while haunted by this feeling; but he afterward remembered that, without any other purpose than to baffle his imaginary pursuer, he traversed at a rapid pace a large portion of the moonlit city; always (he knew not why) avoiding the more populous thoroughfares, and choosing unfrequented and tortuous byways, but never ridding himself of that horrible confusion of mind in which the faces of his dead friend and the pale woman were strangely blended, nor of the fancy that he was followed. Once, as he passed the hospital where Feval died, a faint hint seemed to flash and vanish from the clouds of his lunacy, and almost identify the dogging goblin with the figure of his dream; but the conception instantly mixed with a disconnected remembrance that this was Christmas eve, and then slipped from him, and was lost. He did not pause there, but strode on. But just there, what had been frightful became hideous. For at once he was possessed with the conviction that the thing that lurked at a distance behind him, was quickening its movement, and coming up to seize him. The dreadful fancy stung him like a goad, and, with a start, he accelerated his flight, horribly conscious that what he feared was slinking along in the shadow, close to the dark bulks of the houses, resolutely pursuing, and bent on overtaking him. Faster! His footfalls rang hollowly and loud on the moonlit pavement, and in contrast with their rapid thuds he felt it as something peculiarly terrible that the furtive thing behind, slunk after him with soundless feet. Faster, faster! Traversing only the most unfrequented streets, and at that late hour of a cold winter night, he met no one, and with a terrifying consciousness that his pursuer was gaining on him, he desperately strode on. He did not dare to look behind, dreading less what he might see, than the momentary loss of speed the action might occasion. Faster, faster, faster! And all at once he knew that the dogging thing had dropped its stealthy pace and was racing up to him. With a bound he broke into a run, seeing, hearing, heeding nothing, aware only that the other was silently louping on his track two steps to his one;

and with that frantic apprehension upon him, he gained the next street, flung himself around the corner with his back to the wall, and his arms convulsively drawn up for a grapple; and felt something rush whirring past his flank, striking him on the shoulder as it went by, with a buffet that made a shock break through his frame. That shock restored him to his senses. His delusion was suddenly shattered. The goblin was gone. He was free.

He stood panting, like one just roused from some terrible dream, wiping the reeking perspiration from his forehead and thinking confusedly and wearily what a fool he had been. He felt he had wandered a long distance from his house, but had no distinct perception of his whereabouts. He only knew he was in some thinly-peopled street, whose familiar aspect seemed lost to him in the magical disguise the superb moonlight had thrown over all. Suddenly a film seemed to drop from his eyes, as they became riveted on a lighted window, on the opposite side of the way. He started, and a secret terror crept over him, vaguely mixed with the memory of the shock he had felt as he turned the last corner, and his distinct, awful feeling that something invisible had passed him. At the same instant he felt, and thrilled to feel, a touch, as of a light finger, on his cheek. He was in Hanover street. Before him was the house—the oyster-room staring at him through the lighted transparencies of its two windows, like two square eyes, below; and his tenant's light in a chamber above! The added shock which this discovery gave to the heaving of his heart, made him gasp for breath. Could it be? Did he still dream? While he stood panting and staring at the building, the city clocks began to strike. Eleven o'clock; it was ten when he came away; how he must have driven! His thoughts caught up the word. Driven—by what? Driven from his house in horror, through street and lane, over half the city—driven—hunted in terror, and smitten by a shock here! Driven—driven! He could not rid his mind of the word, nor of the meaning it suggested. The pavements about him began to ring and echo with the tramp of many feet, and the cold, brittle air was shivered with the noisy voices that had roared and bawled applause and laughter at the National Theatre all the evening, and were now singing and howling homeward. Groups of rude men, and ruder boys, their breaths steaming in the icy air, began to tramp by, jostling him as they passed, till he was forced to draw back to the wall, and give them the sidewalk. Dazed and giddy, in cold fear, and with the returning sense of something near him, he stood and watched the groups that pushed and tumbled in through the entrance of the oyster-room, whistling and chattering as they went, and banging the door behind them. He noticed that some came out presently, banging the door harder, and went, smoking and shouting, down the street. Still they poured in and out, while the street was startled with their stimulated riot, and the bar-room within echoed their trampling feet and hoarse voices. Then, as his glance wandered upward to his tenant's window, he thought of the sick child, mixing this hideous discord in the dreams of fever. The word brought up the name and the thought of his dead friend. "In the name of the Saviour, I charge you be true and tender to mankind!" The memory of these words seemed to ring clearly, as if a voice had spoken them, above the roar that suddenly rose in his mind. In that moment he felt himself a wretched and most guilty man. He felt that his cruel words had entered that humble home, to make desperate poverty more desperate, to sicken sickness, and to sadden sorrow. Before him was the dram-shop, let and licensed to nourish the worst and most brutal appetites and instincts of human natures, at the sacrifice of all their highest and holiest tendencies. The throng of tipplers and drunkards was swarming through its hopeless door, to gulp the fiery liquor whose fumes give all shames, vices, miseries, and crimes, a lawless strength and life, and change the man into the pig or tiger. Murder was done, or nearly done, within those walls last night. Within those walls no good was ever done; but, daily, unmitigated evil, whose results were reaching on to torture unborn generations. He had consented to it all! He could not falter, or equivocate, or evade, or excuse. His dead friend's words rang in his conscience like the trump of the judgment angel. He was conquered.

Slowly, the resolve to instantly go in up-rose within him, and with it a change came upon his spirit, and the natural world, sadder than before, but sweeter, seemed to come back to him. A great feeling of relief flowed upon his mind. Pale and trembling still, he crossed the street with a quick, unsteady step, entered a yard at the side of the house, and, brushing by a host of white, rattling spectres of frozen clothes, which dangled from lines in the inclosure, mounted some wooden steps, and rang the bell. In a minute he heard footsteps within, and saw the gleam of a lamp. His heart palpitated violently as he heard the lock turning, lest the answerer of his summons might be his tenant. The door opened, and, to his relief, he stood before a rather decent-looking Irishman, bending forward in his stocking feet, with one boot and a lamp in his hand. The man stared at him from a wild head of tumbled red hair, with a half smile round his loose open mouth, and said, "Begorra!" This was a second floor tenant.

Dr. Renton was relieved at the sight of him; but he rather failed in an attempt at his rent-day suavity of manner, when he said:

"Good evening, Mr. Flanagan. Do you think I can see Mrs. Miller to-night?"

"She's up *there*, docther, anyway." Mr. Flanagan made a sudden start for the stairs, with the boot and lamp at arm's length before him, and stopped as suddenly. "Yull go up?—or wud she come down to ye?" There was as much anxious indecision in Mr. Flanagan's general aspect, pending the reply, as if he had to answer the question himself.

"I'll go up, Mr. Flanagan," returned Dr. Renton, stepping in, after a pause, and shutting the door. "But I'm afraid she's in bed."

"Naw—she's not, sur." Mr. Flanagan made another feint with the boot and lamp at the stairs, but stopped again in curious bewilderment, and rubbed his head. Then, with another inspiration, and speaking with such velocity that his words ran into each other, pell-mell, he continued: "Th' small girl's sick, sur. Begorra, I wor just pullin' on th' boots tuh gaw for the docther, in th' nixt streth, an' summons him to her relehf, for it's bad she is. A'id betther be goan." Another start, and a movement to put on the boot instantly, baffled by his getting the lamp into the leg of it, and involving himself in difficulties in trying to get it out again without dropping either, and stopped finally by Dr. Renton.

"You needn't go, Mr. Flanagan. I'll see to the child. Don't go."

He stepped slowly up the stairs, followed by the bewildered Flanagan. All this time Dr. Renton was listening to the racket from the bar-room. Clinking of glasses, rattling of dishes, trampling of feet, oaths and laughter, and a confused din of coarse voices, mingling with boisterous calls for oysters and drink, came, hardly deadened by the partition walls, from the haunt below, and echoed through the corridors. Loud enough within—louder in the street without, where the oysters and drink were reeling and roaring off to brutal dreams. People trying to sleep here; a sick child up stairs. Listen! "*Two* stew! *One* roast! *Four* ale! Hurry 'em up! *Three* stew! *In* number six! *One* fancy—*two* roast! *One* sling! Three brandy—*hot*! *Two* stew! *One* whisk' *skin*! Hurry 'em up! *What* yeh *'bout*! *Three* brand' punch—*hot*! *Four* stew! *What*-ye-e-h 'BOUT! *Two* gin-cock-t'il! *One* stew!

Hu-r-r-y 'em up!" Clashing, rattling, cursing, swearing, laughing, shouting, trampling, stumbling, driving, slamming, of doors. "Hu-r-ry 'em UP."

"Flanagan," said Dr. Renton, stopping at the first landing, "do you have this noise every night?"

"Naise? Hoo! Divil a night, docther, but I'm wehked out ov me bed wid 'em, Sundays an' all. Sure didn't they murdher wan of 'em, out an' out, last night!"

"Is the man dead?"

"Dead? Troth he is. An' cowld."

"H'm"—through his compressed lips. "Flanagan, you needn't come up. I know the door. Just hold the light for me here. There, that'll do. Thank you." He whispered the last words from the top of the second flight.

"Are ye there, docther?" Flanagan anxious to the last, and trying to peer up at him with the lamp-light in his eyes.

"Yes. That'll do. Thank you!" in the same whisper. Before he could tap at the door, then darkening in the receding light, it opened suddenly, and a big Irish woman bounced out, and then whisked in again, calling to some one in an inner room: "Here he is, Mrs. Mill'r," and then bounced out again, with a "Walk royt in, if *you* plaze; here's the choild"—and whisked in again, with a "Sure an' Jehms was quick;" never once looking at him, and utterly unconscious of the presence of her landlord. He had hardly stepped into the room and taken off his hat, when Mrs. Miller came from the inner chamber with a lamp in her hand. How she started! With her pale face grown suddenly paler, and her hand on her bosom, she could only exclaim: "Why, it's Dr. Renton!" and stand, still and dumb, gazing with a frightened look at his face, whiter than her own. Whereupon Mrs. Flanagan came bolting out again, with wild eyes and a sort of stupefied horror in her good, coarse, Irish features; and then, with some uncouth ejaculation, ran back, and was heard to tumble over something within, and tumble something else over in her fall, and gather herself up with a subdued howl, and subside.

"Mrs. Miller," began Dr. Renton, in a low, husky voice, glancing at her frightened face, "I hope you'll be composed. I spoke to you very harshly and rudely to-night; but I really was not myself—I was in anger—and I ask your pardon. Please to overlook it all, and—but I will speak of this presently; now—I am a physician; will you let me look now at your sick child?"

He spoke hurriedly, but with evident sincerity. For a moment her lips faltered; then a slow flush came up, with a quick change of expression on her thin, worn face, and, reddening to painful scarlet, died away in a deeper pallor.

"Dr. Renton," she said, hastily, "I have no ill-feeling for you, sir, and I know you were hurt and vexed—and I know you have tried to make it up to me again, sir—secretly. I know who it was, now; but I can't take it, sir. You must take it back. You know it was you sent it, sir?"

"Mrs. Miller," he replied, puzzled beyond measure, "I don't understand you. What do you mean?"

"Don't deny it, sir. Please not to," she said imploringly, the tears starting to her eyes. "I am very grateful—indeed I am. But I can't accept it. Do take it again."

"Mrs. Miller," he replied, in a hasty voice, "what do you mean? I have sent you nothing—nothing at all. I have, therefore, nothing to receive again."

She looked at him fixedly, evidently impressed by the fervor of his denial.

"You sent me nothing to-night, sir?" she asked, doubtfully.

"Nothing at any time—nothing," he answered, firmly.

It would have been folly to have disbelieved the truthful look of his wondering face, and she turned away in amazement and confusion. There was a long pause.

"I hope, Mrs. Miller, you will not refuse any assistance I can render to your child," he said, at length.

She started, and replied, tremblingly and confusedly, "No, sir; we shall be grateful to you, if you can save her"—and went quickly, with a strange abstraction on her white face, into the inner room. He followed her at once, and, hardly glancing at Mrs. Flanagan, who sat there in stupefaction, with her apron over her head and face, he laid his hat on a table, went to the bedside of the little girl, and felt her head and pulse. He soon satisfied himself that the little sufferer was in no danger, under proper remedies, and now dashed down a prescription on a leaf from his pocket-book. Mrs. Flanagan, who had come out from the retirement of her apron, to stare stupidly at him during the examination, suddenly bobbed up on her legs, with enlightened alacrity, when he asked if there was any one that could go out to the apothecary's, and said, "sure I wull!" He had a little trouble to make her understand that the prescription, which she took by the corner, holding it away from her, as if it were going to explode presently, and staring at it upside down—was to be left—"*left*, mind you, Mrs. Flanagan—with the apothecary—Mr. Flint—at the nearest corner—and he will give you some things, which you are to bring here." But she had shuffled off at last with a confident, "yis, sur—aw, I knoo," her head nodding satisfied assent, and her big thumb covering the note on the margin, "charge to Dr. C. Renton, Bowdoin street," (which *I* know, could not keep it from the eyes of the angels!) and he sat down to await her return.

"Mrs. Miller," he said, kindly, "don't be alarmed about your child. She is doing well; and, after you have given her the medicine Mrs. Flanagan will bring, you'll find her much better, to-morrow. She must be kept cool and quiet, you know, and she'll be all right soon."

"Oh! Dr. Renton, I am very grateful," was the tremulous reply; "and we will follow all directions, sir. It is hard to keep her quiet, sir; we keep as still as we can, and the other children are very still; but the street is very noisy all the daytime and evening, sir, and—"

"I know it, Mrs. Miller. And I'm afraid those people down-stairs disturb you somewhat."

"They make some stir in the evening, sir; and it's rather loud in the street sometimes, at night. The folks on the lower floors are troubled a good deal, they say."

Well they may be. Listen to the bawling outside, now, cold as it is. Hark! A hoarse group on the opposite sidewalk beginning a song. "Ro-o-l on, sil-ver mo-o-n"—. The silver moon ceases to roll in a sudden explosion of yells and laughter, sending up broken fragments of curses, ribald jeers, whoopings, and cat-calls, high into the night air. "Ga-l-a-ng! Hi-hi! What ye-e-h *'bout*!"

"This is outrageous, Mrs. Miller. Where's the watchman?"

She smiled faintly. "He takes one of them off occasionally, sir; but he's afraid; they beat him sometimes." A long pause.

"Isn't your room rather cold, Mrs. Miller?" He glanced at the black stove, dimly seen in the outer room. "It is necessary to keep the rooms cool just now, but this air seems to me cold."

Receiving no answer, he looked at her, and saw the sad truth in her averted face.

"I beg your pardon," he said quickly, flushing to the roots of his hair. "I might have known, after what you said to me this evening."

"We had a little fire here to-day, sir," she said, struggling with the pride and shame of poverty; "but we have been out of firing for two or three days, and we owe the wharfman something now. The two boys picked up a few chips; but the poor children find it hard to get them, sir. Times are very hard with us, sir; indeed they are. We'd have got along better, if my husband's money had come, and your rent would have been paid—"

"Never mind the rent!—don't speak of that!" he broke in, with his face all aglow. "Mrs. Miller, I haven't done right by you—I know it. Be frank with me. Are you in want of—have you—need of—food?"

No need of answer to that faintly stammered question. The thin, rigid face was covered from his sight by the worn, wan hands, and all the pride and shame of poverty, and all the frigid truth of cold, hunger, anxiety, and sickened sorrow they had concealed, had given way at last in a rush of tears. He could not speak. With a smitten heart, he knew it all now. Ah! Dr. Renton, you know these people's tricks? you know their lying blazon of poverty, to gather sympathy?

"Mrs. Miller"—she had ceased weeping, and as he spoke, she looked at him, with the tear-stains still on her agitated face, half ashamed that he had seen her—"Mrs. Miller, I am sorry. This shall be remedied. Don't tell me it shan't! Don't! I say it shall! Mrs. Miller, I'm—I'm ashamed of myself. I am, indeed."

"I am very grateful, sir, I'm sure," said she; "but we don't like to take charity though we need help; but we can get along now, sir—for, I suppose I must keep it, as you say you didn't send it, and use it for the children's sake, and thank God for his good mercy—since I don't know, and never shall, where it came from, now."

"Mrs. Miller," he said quickly, "you spoke in this way before; and I don't know what you refer to. What do you mean by—*it*?"

"Oh! I forgot sir: it puzzles me so. You see, sir, I was sitting here after I got home from your house, thinking what I should do, when Mrs. Flanagan came up-stairs with a letter for me, that she said a strange man left at the door for Mrs. Miller; and Mrs. Flanagan couldn't describe him well, or understandingly; and it had no direction at all, only the man inquired who was the landlord, and if Mrs. Miller had a sick child, and then said the letter was for me; and there was no writing inside the letter, but there was fifty dollars. That's all, sir. It gave me a great shock, sir; and I couldn't think who sent it, only when you came to-night, I thought it was you; but you said it wasn't, and I never shall know who it was, now. It seems as if the hand of God was in it, sir, for it came when everything was darkest, and I was in despair."

"Why, Mrs. Miller," he slowly answered, "this is very mysterious. The man inquired if I was the owner of the house—oh! no—he only inquired who was—but then he knew I was the—oh! bother! I'm getting nowhere. Let's see. Why, it must be some one you know, or that knows your circumstances."

"But there's no one knows them but yourself; and I told you," she replied; "no one else but the people in the house. It must have been some rich person, for the letter was a gilt-edge sheet, and there was perfume in it, sir."

"Strange," he murmured. "Well, I give it up. All is, I advise you to keep it, and I'm very glad some one did his duty by you in your hour of need, though I'm sorry it was not myself. Here's Mrs. Flanagan."

There was a good deal done, and a great burden lifted off an humble heart—nay, two! before Dr. Renton thought of going home. There was a patient gained, likely to do Dr. Renton more good than any patient he had lost. There was a kettle singing on the stove, and blowing off a happier steam than any engine ever blew on that railroad, whose unmarketable stock had singed Dr. Renton's fingers. There was a yellow gleam flickering from the blazing fire on the sober binding of a good old Book upon a shelf with others, a rarer medical work than ever slipped at auction from Dr. Renton's hands, since it kept the sacred lore of Him who healed the sick, and fed the hungry, and comforted the poor, and who was also the Physician of souls.

And there were other offices performed, of lesser range than these, before he rose to go. There were cooling mixtures blended for the sick child; medicines arranged; directions given; and all the items of her tendance orderly foreseen, and put in pigeon-holes of When and How, for service.

At last he rose to go. "And now, Mrs. Miller," he said, "I'll come here at ten in the morning, and see to our patient. She'll be nicely by that time. And—(listen to those brutes in the street!—twelve o'clock, too—ah! there's the bell),—as I was saying, my offence to you being occasioned by your debt to me, I feel my receipt for your debt should commence my reparation to you; and I'll bring it to-morrow. Mrs. Miller you don't quite come at me—what I mean is—you owe me, under a notice to quit, three months' rent. Consider that paid in full. I never will take a cent of it from you—not a copper. And I take back the notice. Stay in my house as long as you like; the longer the better. But, up to this date, your rent's paid. There. I hope you'll have as happy a Christmas as circumstances will allow, and I mean you shall."

A flush of astonishment—of indefinable emotion, overspread her face.

"Dr. Renton, stop, sir!" He was moving to the door. "Please, sir, *do* hear me! You are very good—but I can't allow you to—Dr. Renton, we are able to pay you the rent, and we *will*, and we *must*—here—now. Oh! sir, my gratefulness will never fail to you—but here—here—be fair with me, sir, and *do* take it!"

She had hurried to a chest of drawers, and came back with the letter which she had rustled apart with eager, trembling hands, and now, unfolding the single bank-note it had contained, she thrust it into his fingers as they closed.

"Here, Mrs. Miller"—she had drawn back with her arms locked on her bosom, and he stepped forward—"no, no. This shan't be. Come, come, you must take it back. Good heavens!" he spoke low, but his eyes blazed in the red glow which broke out on his face, and the crisp note in his extended hand shook violently at her—"Sooner than take this money from you, I would perish in the street! What! Do you think I will rob you of the gift sent you by some one who had a human heart for the distresses I was aggravating? Sooner than—here, take it! O my God! what's this?"

The red glow on his face went out, with this exclamation, in a pallor like marble, and he jerked back the note to his starting eyes; Globe Bank—Boston—Fifty Dollars. For a minute he gazed at the motionless bill in his hand. Then, with his hueless lips compressed, he seized the blank letter from his astonished tenant, and looked at it, turning it over and over. Grained letter-paper—gilt-edged—with a favorite perfume in it. Where's Mrs. Flanagan? Outside the door, sitting on the top of the stairs, with her apron over her head, crying. Mrs. Flanagan! Here! In she tumbled, her big feet kicking her skirts before her, and her eyes and face as red as a beet.

"Mrs. Flanagan, what kind of a looking man gave you this letter at the door to-night?"

"A-w, Docther Rinton, dawn't ax me!—Bother, an' all, an' sure an' I cudn't see him wud his fur-r hat, an' he a-ll boondled oop wud his co-at oop on his e-ars, an' his big han'kershuf smotherin' thuh mouth uv him, an' sorra a bit uv him tuh be looked at, sehvin' thuh poomple on thuh ind uv his naws."

"The *what* on the end of his nose?"

"Thuh poomple, sur."

"What does she mean, Mrs. Miller?" said the puzzled questioner, turning to his tenant.

"I don't know, sir, indeed," was the reply; "she said that to me, and I couldn't understand her."

"It's thuh poomple, docther. Dawn't ye knoo? Thuh big, flehmin poomple oop there." She indicated the locality, by flattening the rude tip of her own nose with her broad forefinger.

"Oh! the pimple! I have it." So he had. Netty, Netty!

He said nothing, but sat down in a chair, with his bold, white brow knitted, and the warm tears in his dark eyes.

"You know who sent it, sir, don't you?" asked his wondering tenant, catching the meaning of all this.

"Mrs. Miller, I do. But I cannot tell you. Take it, now, and use it. It is doubly yours. There. Thank you."

She had taken it with an emotion in her face that gave a quicker motion to his throbbing heart. He rose to his feet, hat in hand, and turned away. The noise of a passing group of roysterers in the street without, came strangely loud into the silence of that room.

"Good night, Mrs. Miller. I'll be here in the morning. Good night."

"Good night, sir. God bless you, sir!"

He turned around quickly. The warm tears in his dark eyes had flowed on his face, which was pale; and his firm lip quivered.

"I hope He will, Mrs. Miller—I hope He will. It should have been said oftener."

He was on the outer threshold. Mrs. Flanagan had, somehow, got there before him, with a lamp, and he followed her down through the dancing shadows, with blurred eyes. On the lower landing he stopped to hear the jar of some noisy wrangle, thick with oaths, from the bar-room. He listened for a moment, and then turned to the staring stupor of Mrs. Flanagan's rugged visage.

"Sure, they're at ut, docther, wud a wull," she said, smiling.

"Yes. Mrs. Flanagan, you'll stay up with Mrs. Miller to-night, won't you?"

"Dade an' I wull, sur."

"That's right. Do. And make her try and sleep, for she must be tired. Keep up a fire—not too warm, you understand. There'll be wood and coal coming to-morrow, and she'll pay you back."

"A-w, docther, dawn't noo!"

"Well, well. And—look here; have you got anything to eat in the house? Yes; well; take it up-stairs. Wake up those two boys, and give them something to eat. Don't let Mrs. Miller stop you. Make her eat something. Tell her I said she must. And, first of all, get your bonnet, and go to that apothecary's—Flint's—for a bottle of port wine, for Mrs. Miller. Hold on. There's the order." (He had a leaf out of his pocket-book in a minute, and wrote it down.) "Go with this, the first thing. Ring Flint's bell, and he'll wake up. And here's something for your own Christmas dinner, to-morrow." Out of the roll of bills, he drew one of the tens—Globe Bank—Boston—and gave it to Mrs. Flanagan.

"A-w, dawn't noo, docther."

"Bother! It's for yourself, mind. Take it. There. And now unlock the door. That's it. Good night, Mrs. Flanagan."

"An' meh thuh Hawly Vurgin hape blessn's on ye, Docther Rinton, wud a-ll thuh compliments uv thuh sehzin, for yur thuh—"

He lost the end of Mrs. Flanagan's parting benedictions in the moonlit street. He did not pause till he was at the door of the oyster-room. He paused then, to make way for a tipsy company of four, who reeled out—the gaslight from the bar-room on the edges of their sodden, distorted faces—giving three shouts and a yell, as they slammed the door behind them.

He pushed after a party that was just entering. They went at once for drink to the upper end of the room, where a rowdy crew, with cigars in their mouths, and liquor in their hands, stood before the bar, in a knotty wrangle concerning some one who was killed. Where is the keeper? Oh! there he is, mixing hot brandy punch for two. Here, you, sir, go up quietly, and tell Mr. Rollins Dr. Renton wants to see him. The waiter came back presently to say Mr. Rollins would be right along. Twenty-five minutes past twelve. Oyster trade nearly over. Gaudy-curtained booths on the left all empty but two. Oyster-openers and waiters—three of them in all—nearly done for the night, and two of them sparring and scuffling behind a pile of oysters on the trough, with the colored print of the great prize fight between Tom Hyer and Yankee Sullivan, in a veneered frame above them on the wall. Blower up from the fire opposite the bar, and stewpans and griddles empty and idle on the bench beside it, among the unwashed bowls and dishes. Oyster trade nearly over. Bar still busy.

Here comes Rollins in his shirt sleeves, with an apron on. Thick-set, muscular man—frizzled head, low forehead, sharp, black eyes, flabby face, with a false, greasy smile on it now, oiling over a curious, stealthy expression of mingled surprise and inquiry, as he sees his landlord here at this unusual hour.

"Come in here, Mr. Rollins; I want to speak to you."

"Yes, sir. Jim" (to the waiter), "go and tend bar." They sat down in one of the booths, and lowered the curtain. Dr. Renton, at one side of the table within, looking at Rollins, sitting leaning on his folded arms, at the other side.

"Mr. Rollins, I am told the man who was stabbed here last night is dead. Is that so?"

"Well, he is, Dr. Renton. Died this afternoon."

"Mr. Rollins, this is a serious matter; what are you going to do about it?"

"Can't help it, sir. Who's a-goin' to touch *me*? Called in a watchman. Whole mess of 'em had cut. Who knows 'em? Nobody knows 'em. Man that was stuck never see the fellers as stuck him in all his life till then. Didn't know which one of 'em did it. Didn't know nothing. Don't now, an' never will, 'nless he meets 'em in hell. That's all. Feller's dead, an' who's a-goin' to touch *me*? Can't do it. Ca-n-'t do it."

"Mr. Rollins," said Dr. Renton, thoroughly disgusted with this man's brutal indifference, "your lease expires in three days."

"Well, it does. Hope to make a renewal with you, Dr. Renton. Trade's good here. Shouldn't mind more rent on, if you insist—hope you won't—if it's anything in reason. Promise sollum, I shan't have no more fightin' in here. Couldn't help this. Accidents *will* happen, yo' know."

"Mr. Rollins, the case is this: if you didn't sell liquor here, you'd have no murder done in your place—murder, sir. That man was murdered. It's your fault, and it's mine, too. I ought not to have let you the place for your business. It *is* a cursed traffic, and you and I ought to have found it out long ago. *I* have. I hope *you* will. Now, I advise you, as a friend, to give up selling rum for the future: you see what it comes to—don't you? At any rate, I will not be responsible for the outrages that are perpetrated in my building any more—I will not have liquor sold here. I refuse to renew your lease. In three days you must move."

"Dr Renton, you hurt my feelin's. Now, how would you—"

"Mr. Rollins, I have spoken to you as a friend, and you have no cause for pain. You must quit these premises when your lease expires. I'm sorry I can't make you go before that. Make no appeals to me, if you please. I am fixed. Now, sir, good-night."

The curtain was pulled up, and Rollins rolled over to his beloved bar, soothing his lacerated feelings by swearing like a pirate, while Dr. Renton strode to the door, and went into the street, homeward.

He walked fast through the magical moonlight, with a strange feeling of sternness, and tenderness, and weariness, in his mind. In this mood, the sensation of spiritual and physical fatigue gaming on him, but a quiet moonlight in all his reveries, he reached his house. He was just putting his latch-key in the door, when it was opened by James, who stared at him for a second, and then dropped his eyes, and put his hand before his nose. Dr. Renton compressed his lips on an involuntary smile.

"Ah! James, you're up late. It's near one."

"I sat up for Mrs. Renton and the young lady, sir. They're just come, and gone up stairs."

"All right, James. Take your lamp and come in here. I've got something to say to you." The man followed him into the library at once, with some wonder on his sleepy face.

"First, put some coal on that fire, and light the chandelier. I shall not go up stairs to-night." The man obeyed. "Now, James, sit down in that chair." He did so, beginning to look frightened at Dr. Renton's grave manner.

"James"—a long pause—"I want you to tell me the truth. Where did you go to-night? Come, I have found you out. Speak."

The man turned as white as a sheet, and looked wretched with the whites of his bulging eyes, and the great pimple on his nose awfully distinct in the livid hue of his features. He was a rather slavish fellow, and thought he was going to lose his situation. Please not to blame him, for he, too, was one of the poor.

"Oh! Dr. Renton, excuse me, sir; I didn't mean doing any harm."

"James, my daughter gave you an undirected letter this evening; you carried it to one of my houses in Hanover street. Is that true?"

"Ye-yes, sir. I couldn't help it. I only did what she told me, sir."

"James, if my daughter told you to set fire to this house, what would you do?"

"I wouldn't do it, sir," he stammered, after some hesitation.

"You wouldn't? James, if my daughter ever tells you to set fire to this house, do it, sir! Do it. At once. Do whatever she tells you. Promptly. And I'll back you."

The man stared wildly at him, as he received this astonishing command. Dr. Renton was perfectly grave, and had spoken slowly and seriously. The man was at his wits' end.

"You'll do it James—will you?"

"Ye-yes, sir, certainly."

"That's right. James, you're a good fellow. James, you've got a family—a wife and children—hav'n't you?"

"Yes, sir, I have; living in the country, sir. In Chelsea, over the ferry. For cheapness, sir."

"For cheapness, eh? Hard times, James? How is it?"

"Pretty hard, sir. Close, but toler'ble comfortable. Rub and go, sir."

"Rub and go. Ve-r-y well. Rub and go. James, I'm going to raise your wages—to-morrow. Generally, because you're a good servant. Principally, because you carried that letter to-night, when my daughter asked you. I shan't forget it. To-morrow, mind. And if I can do anything for you, James, at any time, just tell me. That's all. Now, you'd better go to bed. And a happy Christmas to you!"

"Much obliged to you, sir. Same to you and many of 'em. Good-night, sir." And with Dr. Renton's "good-night" he stole up to bed, thoroughly happy, and determined to obey Miss Renton's future instructions to the letter. The shower of golden light which had been raining for the last two hours, had fallen, even on him. It would fall all day to-morrow in many places, and the day after, and for long years to come. Would that it could broaden and increase to a general deluge, and submerge the world!

Now the whole house was still, and its master was weary. He sat there, quietly musing, feeling the sweet and tranquil presence near him. Now the fire was screened, the lights were out, save one dim glimmer, and he had lain down on the couch with the letter in his hand, and slept the dreamless sleep of a child.

He slept until the gray dawn of Christmas day stole into the room, and showed him the figure of his friend, a shape of glorious light, standing by his side, and gazing at him with large and tender eyes! He had no fear. All was deep, serene, and happy with the happiness of heaven. Looking up into that beautiful, wan face—so tranquil—so radiant; watching, with a child-like awe, the star-fire in those shadowy eyes; smiling faintly, with a great, unutterable love thrilling slowly through his frame, in answer to the smile of light that shone upon the phantom countenance; so he passed a space of time which seemed a calm eternity, till, at last, the communion of spirit with spirit—of mortal love with love immortal—was perfected, and the shining hands were laid on his forehead, as with a touch of air. Then the phantom smiled, and, as its shining hands were withdrawn, the thought of his daughter mingled in the vision. She was bending over him! The dawn—the room, were the same. But the ghost of Feval had gone out from earth, away to its own land!

"Father, dear father! Your eyes were open, and they did not look at me. There is a light on your face, and your features are changed! What is it—what have you seen?"

"Hush, darling: here—kneel by me, for a little while, and be still. I have seen the dead."

She knelt by him, burying her awe-struck face in his bosom, and clung to him with all the fervor of her soul. He clasped her to his breast, and for minutes all was still.

"Dear child—good and dear child!"

The voice was tremulous and low. She lifted her fair, bright countenance, now convulsed with a secret trouble, and dimmed with streaming tears, to his, and gazed on him. His eyes were shining; but his pallid cheeks, like hers, were wet with tears. How still the room was! How like a thought of solemn tenderness, the pale gray dawn! The world was far away, and his soul still wandered in the peaceful awe of his dream. The world was coming back to him—but oh! how changed!—in the trouble of his daughter's face.

"Darling, what is it? Why are you here? Why are you weeping? Dear child, the friend of my better days—of the boyhood when I had noble aims, and life was beautiful before me—he has been here! I have seen him. He has been with me—oh! for a good I cannot tell!"

"Father, dear father!"—he had risen, and sat upon the couch, but she still knelt before him, weeping, and clasped his hands in hers—"I thought of you and of this letter, all the time. All last night till I slept, and then I dreamed you were tearing it to pieces, and trampling on it. I awoke, and lay thinking of you, and of ——. And I thought I heard you come down-stairs, and I came here to find you. But you were lying here so quietly, with your eyes open, and so strange a light on your face. And I knew—I knew you were dreaming of him, and that you saw him, for the letter lay beside you. O father! forgive me, but do hear me! In the name of this day—it's Christmas day, father—in the name of the time when we must both die—in the name of that time, father, hear me! That poor woman last night—O father! forgive me, but don't tear that letter in pieces and trample it under foot! You know what I mean—you know—you know. Don't tear it, and tread it under foot!"

She clung to him, sobbing violently, her face buried in his hands.

"Hush, hush! It's all well—it's all well. Here, sit by me. So. I have"—his voice failed him, and he paused. But sitting by him—clinging to him—her face hidden in his bosom—she heard the strong beating of his disenchanted heart!

"My child, I know your meaning. I will not tear the letter to pieces and trample it under foot. God forgive me my life's slight to those words. But I learned their value last night, in the house where your blank letter had entered before me."

She started, and looked into his face steadfastly, while a bright scarlet shot into her own.

"I know all, Netty—all. Your secret was well kept, but it is yours and mine now. It was well done, darling—well done. Oh! I have been through strange mysteries of thought and life since that starving woman sat here! Well—thank God!"

"Father, what have you done?" The flush had failed, but a glad color still brightened her face, while the tears stood trembling in her eyes.

"All that you wished yesterday," he answered. "And all that you ever could have wished, henceforth I will do."

"O father!"—She stopped. The bright scarlet shot again into her face, but with an April shower of tears, and the rainbow of a smile.

"Listen to me, Netty, and I will tell you, and only you, what I have done." Then, while she mutely listened, sitting by his side, and the dawn of Christmas broadened into Christmas-day, he told her all.

And when he had told all, and emotion was stilled, they sat together in silence for a time, she with her innocent head drooped upon his shoulder, and her eyes closed, lost in tender and mystic reveries; and he musing with a contrite heart. Till at last, the stir of daily life began to waken in the quiet dwelling, and without, from steeples in the frosty air, there was a sound of bells.

They rose silently, and stood, clinging to each other, side by side.

"Love, we must part," he said, gravely and tenderly. "Read me, before we go, the closing lines of George Feval's letter. In the spirit of this let me strive to live. Let it be for me the lesson of the day. Let it also be the lesson of my life."

Her face was pale and lit with exaltation as she took the letter from his hand. There was a pause—and then upon the thrilling and tender silver of her voice, the words arose like solemn music:

"*Farewell—farewell! But, oh! take my counsel into memory on Christmas Day, and forever. Once again, the ancient prophecy of peace and good-will shines on a world of wars and wrongs and woes. Its soft ray shines into the darkness of a land wherein swarm slaves, poor laborers, social pariahs, weeping women, homeless exiles, hunted fugitives, despised aliens, drunkards, convicts, wicked children, and Magdalens unredeemed. These are but the ghastliest figures in that sad army of humanity which advances, by a dreadful road, to the Golden Age of the poets' dream. These are your sisters and your brothers. Love them all. Beware of wronging one of them by word or deed. O friend! strong in wealth for so much good—take my last counsel. In the name of the Saviour, I charge you, be true and tender to mankind! Come out from Babylon into manhood, and live and labor for the fallen, the neglected, the suffering, and the poor. Lover of arts, customs, laws, institutions, and forms of society, love these things only as they help mankind! With stern love, overturn them, or help to overturn them, when they become cruel to a single—the humblest—human being. In the world's scale, social position, influence, public power, the applause of majorities, heaps of funded gold, services rendered to creeds, codes, sects, parties, or federations—they weigh weight; but in God's scale—remember!—on the day of hope, remember!—your least service to Humanity, outweighs them all!*"

About the Author

Born in Boston, Massachusetts on January 2, 1832, William O'Connor was a son of Peter D. O'Connor and an unknown mother. Little is known about his early childhood other than that he had a disagreement with his father and left the house when he was eight years old. In the 1850s he met Sarah Helen Whitman, a poet and romantic interest of Edgar Allan Poe. Whitman influenced him and O'Connor published several poems similar to Poe's work, and several stories and novels. He was a fierce advocate for the 15 Ammendment (giving blacks the right to vote) and many of his works were published posthumously.

More Anthologies of Horror!

If you enjoyed this creepy collection, you should also check out our other volumes:
https://books2read.com/libraryofmadness
https://books2read.com/tomeoftheterrifying
https://books2read.com/necromoirrium
https://books2read.com/anthologyofthedamned
https://books2read.com/twistedyuletide

www.ingramcontent.com/pod-product-compliance
Ingram Content Group UK Ltd.
Pitfield, Milton Keynes, MK11 3LW, UK
UKHW021947061125
8818UKWH00009B/518

9 798232 616113